# INTIMATE
# DANGER

# INTIMATE DANGER

# AMY J. FETZER

**BRAVA**

KENSINGTON PUBLISHING CORP.

http://www.kensingtonbooks.com

BRAVA BOOKS are published by

Kensington Publishing Corp.
850 Third Avenue
New York, NY 10022

ISBN-13: 978-0-7582-1655-7
ISBN-10: 0-7582-1655-6

First Kensington Trade Paperback Printing: March 2007
10  9  8  7  6  5  4  3  2  1

Printed in the United States of America

*Dedicated with love to my Fetzer nieces*

*Cathy Fetzer*
*Leann Shank*
*Julia Fetzer Schusta*
*Dawn Shank Steffal*
*Laura Winchester Webber*
*Holly Shank*

*Love you all,*
*Auntie Amy*

## Author's Note

Though this novel is a product of my imagination, there is some truth to the plot. There are ruins in the Andes, homes carved into cliffs, and the Loma Negra dig exists. It's the most recent find; and while the Moche flourished in 430 B.C.–600 B.C. before the Inca, they too disappeared from existence after the Spanish invasion. They left behind their homes, art, carvings, wall paintings, and the Quechua language, believed to be their own. Lambayeque and Chimú cultures are the descendants of the Moche.

For more information, try *http://www.go2peru.com/moche_route.htm*
Or my favorite, *www.nationalgeographic.com.*

# One

*0118 hours Zulu*
*Mediterranean Sea*
*Six fathoms below*

*Some people were a waste of human tissue.*

Sixty feet underwater, Cumbiya speeches and tiptoeing around countries harboring terrorists didn't mean a damn thing. No political sanctions, no gray areas.

Just the way Mike Gannon liked it. And if those in the cheap seats yakked outside the *eyes only* perimeter, any investigation usually followed a lot of "I have no recollection of that event, Senator" moments. Like now. Stepping onto Libyan soil was a no-no in the international ball game. Not that he gave a damn.

This time, it was personal.

Mike frowned behind the dive mask when his rebreather suddenly tasted like roadkill, and he checked the filtration gauge for toxicity. Traveling for two miles underwater was pushing it. The last thing he wanted was to suffocate on a bad oxygen mix before reaching the shores near Tripoli.

An ironic epitaph for a Marine.

In the black deep, he watched the glowing green lines of the Global Positioning System, estimating time to target less than five minutes. The propulsion torpedo pulled him through the water and he finned for extra speed, maneuvering beneath the surface like a shark after its prey. Time for some payback.

To the left and right of him, in tight formation were Di-Fazio, Valnik, and Krane. When his fin touched ground, he switched off the propulsion and let it float with him to the shore as well as forty-five pounds of equipment could. He anchored it with his dive weights, then drove a leash spike into the sand. He had just enough fuel to get back to the sub. Maybe.

Removing his fins, he didn't surface till his team was in synch with him, then slowly they rose to eye level above the surface. He switched the goggles from underwater illumination to night vision, then checked the area. The ruins of an ancient village spread over the top of a rock embankment, decaying and uninviting in the dark.

Beyond it lay the target, unlit and about thirty feet above sea level.

Eleven men had escaped from a Yemen prison. Convicted al-Qaeda fighters. Spec Ops had already located and eliminated seven. According to intelligence, the last of them were hiding out here on Farawa Island. A low, flat nothing-but-palm-trees piece of land that was closer to Tunisia than Libya so no one could say al-Qadhafi harbored them. There wasn't a part of the Middle East that wasn't unstable, and no country wanted to send in forces to clean up the mess. Except America. This time, there would be no escape.

His orders were to proceed with extreme deadly force. *When in doubt, take it out.*

The island had few inhabitants, and little tourism since it was under development to be a vacation destination on the other side of the island. *Yeah, sure,* Mike thought. *Come to Libya, dine with suicide bombers. That'll bring them in.*

But the discovery of Roman artifacts put the kibosh on any progress as archaeologists dug furiously before construction vehicles lined the narrow causeway from the Tunisia-Libya border. The advantage for the team was—the place was dead except for a little street traffic. The disadvantage was a boat loaded with sympathizers ready to transport the three targets to their next safe house was four miles behind them and closing fast. They had to be quick and thorough.

At Mike's signal, the team rose out of the sea like serpents, the wet sheen quickly dissolving like a shedding skin, turning invisible in the moonless night. Mike's antiballistic material in his dive vest grew instantly lighter as it drained. Moving low and forward, he pulled back the hood, released the rebreather, and concealed it in the hollows of rocks with his fins. On one knee, Krane took up position to guard. Equipment stashed, they stripped down the wet gear to minimal weapons, then advanced quickly. Valnik remained on the shore, guarding their backs.

The three paused at the foot of the rock jetty. The wind and sand had shaved down the crumbling walls above to no taller than six feet. Mike was forward, his MP5 assault rifle equipped with silencer, scope, and laser track still in the wet pack. He wasn't going for long-distance shots. Close combat was essential for concealment. The 9mm Beretta with suppressor would do the job. Or a knife.

They climbed the rock embankment, soft-soled boots muting their approach. Slipping over the wall, they entered the ruins, clearing each section in a grid. It would be messy if they found lovers hiding in here. None spoke. A whispered voice carried; the erratic noises coming from the target were not enough to cover anything more than muffled footsteps. Twenty yards covered, ten yards, twenty feet. Mike stopped at the southwest corner, beyond the suspicion of light and fusing with the fathomless black of the landscape. They didn't have time to plan this assault; intel confirmation was slow while terrorists moved fast. The analysis was, these guys would be bugging out on the boat tonight. His team was here to stop that little trip.

*I'm getting damn tired of capturing these guys only to do it again a couple months later.*

Krane rushed to disable the vehicles lining the street front, DiFazio watching for stray traffic as Mike slipped around what was left of a wall and kept moving in toward the target, a rectangular building with a glass storefront. The satellite image he'd had only minutes to memorize was accurate: one rear door, and only one side window. From his position, Mike could see the lights of traffic about a quarter mile up the road. He flipped the night-vision visor to thermal and found four heat signatures, all about the same size. Military trained, two of them were the masterminds behind the attack on the USS *Cole*. Mike was alive only because he'd gone topside for some air ten minutes before. The impact had sent him over the side of the ship.

Mike slid around the edge of the ruin wall, and moved in as the rear door opened. A man appeared, a small flame brightening his features as he lit a smoke. He dragged hard, unaware that Mike stood within five feet of him. Carefully, Mike holstered his sidearm and drew his knife. They couldn't afford gunfire this early. Mike slipped up behind him, his hand closing over the man's mouth as he drove the blade into his kidney. The pain was beyond a scream and he held him silent till his muscles went slack. He lowered the body to the ground and continued, Krane falling in behind him.

DiFazio was near the storefront to ensure no one escaped and ready to cut the electricity.

With Krane on the opposite side of the door, Mike opened it. Soft light spilled onto the sandy ground, wind off the sea swirling violently and kicking up fine grains. From inside someone barked to shut the door.

Gannon touched his throat mike and whispered, "Kill the lights."

The area went instantly black. The inhabitants scrambled, falling over furniture in the dark as Mike and Krane slipped inside, heat signatures showing locations. Four shots and the men were on the floor. Four more to ensure that they didn't get back up.

"Clear." Mike advanced, securing the front of the store. Empty.

He inspected boxes from the front to the back, found a wild assortment of snacks and trinkets, keenly searching for—bingo. He located stolen C-4 and detonators that still had the Moroccan Army insignia on it. One was ready to go and he carefully eased the detonator wires from the pliable explosive, then lifted the box, handing it to Krane for transport. He pocketed the detonators, gathered the weapons, cell phones, a laptop, then scooped up paperwork and anything else strewn over the tables. He stuffed it all in a watertight sack. Let intel sort it out later.

"Bug out," he said, moving around bodies to the exit. Within moments, the team was down the jetty to their dive gear, suiting up. As quietly as they'd arrived, his teammates slid into the cold Mediterranean Sea, releasing the anchored propulsion torpedoes. Mike was last, bringing up the rear, strapping on his rebreather as he moved to the water.

He never saw it coming.

Bullets had a strange sound when they impacted flesh. Like a fistful of mud thrown against a stone wall. The *splat* was soft, the pain excruciating as it ripped through his deltoid, just past his Kevlar.

Mike stumbled to one knee, refusing to go face first in the sand.

"Tango One is down," Mike heard in his comms.

"The hell I am. Get your asses underwater," he ordered, and spun with his weapons drawn. Another shot came, missing him, the muzzle flash giving a location as at that moment a car passed, headlights spreading a glow over the area—and silhouetted a child.

Dark-haired and wafer thin, a boy of no more than ten aimed a pistol.

Mike didn't hesitate and fired, hitting the kid's weapon. Ignoring the infantile scream, he hurriedly yanked up his hood, put the regulator into his mouth, and fell into the sea.

He put on his fins and Krane was there, the propulsion launch already churning. He grabbed Mike's wrist and put the handles in his grip.

Salt water stung his wound. It just pissed him off.

Shot by a goddamn kid, and attracting sharks with his blood trail.

As he finned toward the approaching ship to finish the job, he decided if anyone were going to be shark food, it would be the enemy. Ooh-rah.

*Loma Negra Dig*
*North Peru, Same day*

Dr. Eduardo Valez pulled off his straw hat and swiped the back of his wrist across his forehead. The effort was a failure against the cloying heat. He'd grown up here; he should be used to it. Years in the city had apparently softened his mettle. He pushed off the tree stump and moved into the excavation, carefully stepping beyond the string grids and farther into the newly unearthed site.

He looked down at the shards of pottery, the explicit sex scenes depicted in the fine painting still clear after centuries. He didn't see the value on the market or to a museum, but the value to his people. His culture. The world. For years, scholars thought the Incas were the first to build a society here. But the Moche tribe had existed long before.

Slipping out his brush, he wisped at the shard, flushing a little at the position of the lovers. Inventive, he thought, smiling.

"Senor Valez, sections four and five have been cataloged."

"Then package for transport, Gil."

"Me, sir?"

He looked up at the young archaeologist. The man had done everything he could to get on this dig. American born and raised, Gilberto had Peruvian blood and his ancestors, the youth believed, lay in these ruins.

"You are well trained." Eduardo smiled. He'd done the training. "Consider it another trial by fire."

The young man stood a bit straighter and nodded. The gift of confidence was such a little thing to offer, Eduardo thought, turning back to the shard as the young man moved beyond the site to the tents and many crates waiting to be filled. Eduardo inched forward like a duck, accustomed to the position as he reached to brush away more of the land and reveal the history.

His breath caught when he realized he'd found an unbroken urn beneath a stone table. The stone slab was at an angle, half buried from a previous cave-in and before he dug farther, his gaze rose upward to the uneven ceiling of rock as he tried to judge its stability. Removing the slab chiseled by hand was impossible without excavation equipment, and that would destroy the site. If he removed the earth below, perhaps the pot would slide free. He worked slowly, and beneath the bowl of the pot he found bone and a tooth. It galvanized him to keep going. Then he realized the stone slab was not long enough for a table but more of a box. He lost his balance, pain shooting up his kneecap before he braced himself and studied the find.

The ground was usually softer here, and backing up, he brushed at the rock and uncovered sharp edges. A door? As he brushed he wished for some water to rinse the grime as an etching appeared. Almost as if it were freshly chiseled. More warrior drawings. He took measurements of the stone opening holding the urn, then the slab. They were nearly precise in dimensions. A chamber for a single pot perhaps. Unusual. He couldn't be certain and reminded himself that creating what wasn't there wasn't his job. He turned his attention back to the urn.

When he finally unearthed it, the morning had passed, and he thought of his wife's complaints about his obsession. But even Magdalena would appreciate this. A half day's worth of painstaking work later, Eduardo felt the fragile pot shift under his hand. He stopped, simply to control his eagerness that might somehow ruin the find.

"Senor Valez. Professor? It's late."

Eduardo looked up, frowning that the generator lights had come on beyond the entrance, and he could smell the aroma of food. He shook his head, his smile ironic. "This is why my wife threatens to divorce me once a week."

Gil chuckled softly and handed him a canteen. "Must be something good to keep you here for hours."

Gil marveled at the stone tablet carvings but was instantly distracted when Eduardo flicked on a penlight to show the object clearly. He didn't dare tug for fear of cracking it or scraping the delicate artwork.

"Oh, man, it's intact." Gil stooped for a better look.

Groups of ten small offering jars, or *ofrendas,* were found at the foot of the burial site in groups of five, ten, or twenty. Eduardo glanced back at the shallow excavation behind him. Perhaps these were the *ofrendas* of someone important. "A prize for certain, but look at the drawings. It's not the lovers on it as the other shards. But warriors in combat." He'd seen this picture a couple of times before, but only in fragments from a fallen ceiling.

"But none of the drawings show the Moche waging war for conquest or attacking a fortified settlement. No capturing, killing, or mistreating noncombatants."

"Nor did they work as a single coordinated force like a modern army," Eduardo reminded him.

"I think they were guerrillas."

Romanticizing, Eduardo thought, yet the young man had a valid point. This burial was possibly a warrior of some significance. "This drawing depicts ceremonial combat. One-on-one for the purpose of producing a few vanquished prisoners. These unfortunates were needed to fill a central role in the sacrifice ceremony that followed battle. From the drawings on the walls and past finds, we know the warrior prisoners were first stripped of clothing and battle equipment. Then naked and leashed around the neck with a rope, they were brought to a ceremonial center. There the prisoners' throats were cut, their blood consumed by the ceremony participants, and finally their bodies were dismembered."

"Yes, but why? And who fought them? Why not use them as slaves or integrate them into the tribe? If they had, they might not have died out so fast."

"Purity of race, perhaps." Eduardo shrugged. "They needed sacrifices and wouldn't do that to their own if they could avoid it."

"But outsiders didn't believe it was an honor. Poor souls. Professor Calan of UCLA found the burial tomb of a Moche priest and a child, both with a bone deformity. Yet they weren't ritually killed."

"Which proves they honored their own and sacrificed the outsiders."

Gil look disgusted.

"You're glad it's an ancient culture?"

"Let's just say I wouldn't want to meet up with them in the jungle." The young man pointed to the find. "The lid's intact. Can you open it?"

"I want to X-ray it first. Bring me a box please." The jar had a seal rimmed in flecks of gold and a waxlike substance.

Eduardo took photos and measurements, then tied the string grid lines from the rest of the dig to this spot. Until he studied and deciphered the icons on the urn, he wouldn't open it. It had significant weight, and whatever was inside was preserved—and sealed for a reason.

*U.S. Army Medical Facility*
*Virginia*

Clancy's heels clicking on the tile floor were like something out of a slasher movie. Distant and unsuspecting. That she was the only one working after hours magnified her seclusion. She stopped outside the primate lab and swiped her ID access through the security. Quick footsteps from somewhere to her left made her skin tighten.

Sergeant Victors appeared, his sidearm drawn. When he saw her, he pointed it to the ceiling and relaxed.

"Damn." She snapped her fingers. "Lost another chance to fire your gun, huh, Daniel?"

"Oh yeah, I'm trigger-happy tonight. Be careful."

"Next time come at me with more firepower than that. I feel insulted."

He grinned like a new groom as she pushed open the door.

"You'll be okay with that creature?" he asked.

Clancy glanced into the lab at the sedated orangutan in the titanium cage. "That wuss? Oh yeah."

"He's a 250-pound wuss, ma'am."

"Yes, but I think our relationship is in the wooing stage. He tried picking fleas off me this morning."

"Did he find any?"

Her narrow look lost impact when she smiled. "Okay, that does it, you're off my Christmas list."

Waving at him, she stepped into the lab, but didn't turn on the overhead lights. The bluish illumination from inside the glass cold storage locker and the running lights under the tables shone off the black floor and stainless steel with an incandescent glow. Besides, Boris was sleeping and she'd like to keep it that way. Whenever she was near, he shook the cage and dry-humped the bars.

The embarrassment wasn't half as bad as the fact that her only romantic prospect lately was a fat hairy orangutan that was doped up most of the time.

And he had his happy juice three hours ago, she thought, checking his stats for the day. Turning away from the computers, she slipped on latex gloves and prepared a syringe to draw blood. A pinprick was enough to examine under the microscope, but this would just save Dr. Yates from doing it in the morning. Boris had favorites and Francine Yates wasn't one of them. Must be pheromones, Clancy thought, moving to the cage and stroking the sleeping orangutan's forehead.

"You really are an ugly creature," she said softly, swabbing the vein. "But I mean that in the nicest possible way."

She pushed the needle into a protruding vein, then drew back the plunger. Boris didn't even flinch. The syringe full, she drove the needle into the rubber-stoppered vial, then let a single drop fall onto the slide. Bending over a microscope was passé, and she brought the magnified sample up on the larger screen. At two thousand magnification, the blood cells were still working. She sat in a wheeled chair and admired the beauty of a simple cell.

She'd done this a thousand times in the last two months and had completed her third-stage computer synthesized tests just last week. Implanting Boris was only the first stage. They had to let it ride for weeks or perhaps months before they'd know if the pod did any severe damage to the animal's body, mostly the brain.

An injectable bionanotechnology with neuron-synthesized capabilities was not a cold medicine. It altered the brain, the body's ability to function. The reaction to physical antibodies, the breakdown of the technology or white cell damage wasn't conclusive without knowing long-term effects in the test animals.

Yesterday's discussion with the commanding officer and his medical board popped into mind. None of them were pleased with her insistence on a longer test period. Though they were on schedule, it was just not fast enough for the room full of officers. They'd grilled her for three straight hours till she was ready to confess her ex-husband's fetish for wearing women's panties. But then, that would prove the caliber of loser she attracted. Clancy wasn't swayed.

She'd created it. It was her baby, and the only reason Clancy was sitting here in the first place was that her natural ability—found too late in life to make her millions—got her here. Shortchanging herself or the project was simply not an option.

Relaxed in the chair, she stared at the cells on the screen, then turning to the scope, she dropped a pinpoint of a simple flu virus into the blood sample. The blood cells immediately fought it off with amazing speed.

"Yes!"

The implantation was changing his blood, and Boris's behavior, with the exception of his ardent displays of affection for her, was normal. Nonaggressive. Almost no change. A good thing since they were altering his brain and body chemistry. He could, for all they knew, turn into King Kong with a really nasty attitude.

She labeled the vial with time and date, then in the chair, rolled across the slick floor to the cold storage locker and opened the glass door. Frosted air swept around her face as she put the vial in a new rack, then checked the sequential numbers. She frowned, recounting, then realized there was a new set of four samples on the next level at the back. She plucked a tube from the rack and read. No name, only numbers. That wasn't necessary. Boris was the only candidate here this week.

Curious, she jotted down the number, put the pallet of tubes back, then closed the fridge door and pushed off. She glided to the computer, grabbing the desk to stop herself, then opened log files and punched in the new set of numbers. She waited for the search.

Her gaze skipped around the darkened room, flicking to the camera panning in slow, quiet intervals. Colonel Cook's personal eyeball into your life. Did he watch everything around here? Made her almost tempted to flash him. A portion of the massive string of buildings was a hospital, and while it wasn't hidden from sight, what they did here was classified— though there were hundreds at MIT and elsewhere around the world doing similar research in microengineering. Just not this kind.

Down the hall, teams worked on everything from light-weight liquid body armor to global positioning beacons implanted in military personnel before reconnaissance missions. Cool stuff. All to prolong lives in battle.

The ACCESS DENIED icon startled her. *Deny me?* "Oh, I so don't think so," she whispered, spinning in the chair and attacking the keyboard.

*My technology,* my business, she thought and went through the back door of the program. Her fingers flew over the keyboard, syntax and screens of numbers coming up, but Clancy saw through it, saw the program's heartbeat.

"You are completely toasted," she muttered.

Inside within seconds, she opened files, scanned the content, then went into another. She found a report with her name on it, but it was Dr. Yates's documentation procedure for the implantation. Wasn't surprising; they traded information all the time, and she barely glanced at it, about to close the file when she noticed the date. A month old. She didn't get this copy.

Orangutan implantation was two months ago.

Her gaze flicked to Boris snoring inside his cage, then back to the screen. She scrolled and read, checking the vial numbers against the implant document.

A chill slithered over her skin when she realized that Boris wasn't the only test subject. They'd already used it.

On humans.

# Two

"Two minutes to target, sir." *It's like playing a video game,* Sergeant Jason Willager thought as he glanced at the satellite image and maneuvered the Unmanned Aerial Vehicle. They were on loan to DEA, searching for drug traffic and fine-tuning this particular UAV, when analysts saw what they suspected was a Scud missile launcher hidden in the South American jungle. Jason didn't have an opinion. His job was to move it where they told him and let the UAV do the job. UAVs had numerous capabilities. Several were sweeping over Iraq and setting off the insurgent bombs before they could detonate in a crowded mosque or market. Some dropped ordnance without a single soldier getting close to the target. They were safe to personnel, efficient and accurate.

The only problem was, they weren't invisible.

The Predator model, with over a forty-two-foot wingspan and loaded with heat-seeking missiles for battle, was still a target as much as a jet. They didn't make much noise, which gave them better stealth capabilities, but his baby, the Falcon, was smaller and lighter, and while it was armed with Hellfire missiles, more of a deterrent than tactical, its purpose was reconnaissance. She was a shutterbug snooping her way across the Andes along the Peru–Ecuador border. The Falcon could fly higher and faster than the others, and since it was linked to satellites, it had unlimited capability. The Trojan Spirit II Satellite up there was helping Jason along.

He controlled it as if he were sitting in the cockpit. Of course, the Falcon didn't have a cockpit at all. Beside him, four other techs in the thirty-by-eight-foot GCS, Ground Control Station, trailer in the comfort of AC and silence were doing the same thing somewhere else in the world.

"Sixty seconds to target," he said into the comm link to his bosses. They were watching the visual recon on a big screen in some undisclosed location. The information went out to several high-ranking officials. It wasn't a concern. He'd trained two years to get this seat.

"Forty seconds to target." The digital camera detected the darkness of the area and automatically switched to high-resolution infrared. The Falcon was outfitted with night vision, infrared, and thermal. The recording never stopped from the moment it was in the air, but the first hours were nothing but flyover scenery. He maneuvered the craft over the appointed area. More than one flew in South America, just not on this particular part of the border. Ecuador was pretty tight with its border control and neutral about getting into Peru and Colombian drug cartel squabbles. In this area, nothing was safe.

He frowned when something dark colored pierced the green of the jungle.

"Sergeant, what is that?"

"I don't know, sir." Immediately he maneuvered the UAV out of the direct path to the right and made the UAV climb. He turned the UAV so the cameras had a clear visual. *It's gaining speed,* he thought, and in a heartbeat the visual relay went dead. He frantically worked the keyboard trying to bring it back. *Great, the big cheese is watching and I screw up.*

"Sergeant, what happened?"

"I think something shot it down, sir. I have nothing here, nothing."

He turned to another monitor and replayed the data, watching with a bunch of generals as what looked like the nose cone of a small rocket obliterated the UAV. He replayed it in slow motion, magnifying the last few seconds.

*Jesus. Tell me I'm wrong, and I didn't just let a million-dollar aircraft be destroyed.*

"Sorry, sir. We have nothing. Not even beacons are active."

Completely destroyed, Jason thought. Yet that meant the wreckage and the two missiles were just waiting to be scavenged. Along with the evidence that the U.S.A. was snooping in another nation's affairs.

*Subjects didn't arrive at this facility in ambulances; they came in cages.*

The discovery settled inside her with a harsh weight before she realized this was why they were pressuring her to sign off on a completion. They needed to cover their butts because they'd already done it. Oh, jeez. Her tail would be in the fire if anything went wrong too.

Human volunteers. Did they even know the dangers? Her mind filled with all the problems, the risks, and she started to get up to go find Cook or Yates and call them on it, but she stopped. If they kept this from her, what else did they do without her knowledge?

Their betrayal worked under her skin, the wound tearing and burning to anger.

*Damn* them. She stared at the computer. She needed to know more, anything, everything—and she knew where to find it. She drew in a lungful of air, fingers poised over the keyboard. This was a violation of the worst kind, and for a moment she asked herself why she was risking everything for four men she didn't know.

*I created it. I'm responsible.*

She kicked off her shoes and plunged into accessing files, using back doors. She knew computers, especially military computers. She'd worked on them from inside the Pentagon. She pried into Yates's personal files, and read the data about the men. Candidates, Yates called them. Names listed with the vial numbers this time. It made them real to her. Young men. God, who would volunteer for this? It was madness till it was thoroughly tested.

*Get off that horse, girl, it's dead and buried.*

Implantation was a couple of weeks ago, status deemed excellent. No side effects. Like Boris. Maybe she was wrong. Maybe it was fine and she was concerned over nothing. Which would be a real feather in her own cap. *Prove me wrong,* she thought as she read Francine's personal notes, written on an iPod, then downloaded, but it hadn't been turned to type font yet. Her handwriting stank. But the last entry made her breath catch.

*Released for mission status.*

No monitoring? She closed all the files, erased the trace, and then went to level five, into the Pentagon. She was denied twice. That would start a trace to this computer. Her fingers flew over the keyboard so fast her hands hurt. She'd never get inside in time and went into the colonel's file. Only problem was if he was sitting at his desk, he'd know it.

*Come on, give it up, Cook,* she thought. This type of data wasn't recorded, not with any easy access, but Clancy knew where she was going. *I should have done this a long time ago.* She scrolled and read, closing one only to open another.

She found one under an odd title. Crash and burn. Someone had a sick sense of humor. She opened it. Colonel Cook was being kept apprised of the candidate's status, sleep, food, stress, training—mission status. Active.

Oh God, they were on one already. Where? *Where?* she thought, reading frantically, wanting to print it all, yet eager to find where the men were right now. A cluster of words popped out and she zeroed in. Ecuador–Peru border, recon for a downed UAV, and the four men matched the candidates in the other file. Bingo.

She opened their service record files. Young, physically fit, and extremely well trained. A good portion was blacked out. Special Operations, black ops, she suspected, then sent the photos and stat sheets to the printer before she cleared traces, even the echoes. She was reaching for the sheets when the door locks clicked with access. It swung open and she grabbed the papers and stuffed them under the keyboard.

Dr. Francine Yates entered first, followed by two soldiers. Clancy thought about ducking for cover, but nixed that. She had a right to be here, and cleared her throat. The click of pistols and "freeze" came before the lights blinked on. The soldiers relaxed, their expressions unapologetic.

Francine looked over her and the lab. "I will never understand you and this need to work in the dark, Clancy."

"It buffers out distractions and I think better. Why do you need armed guards, Francine?"

"I didn't know you were here."

"Clearly. I was just running another sample." She gestured to the screen. "I wanted to sleep in tomorrow. Blood is drawn."

Francine mulled that over for a second. "Any changes?"

"It's working, if that's what you mean." Her gaze flicked to the soldiers.

"Go ahead," Yates said to the men, and the pair moved to the large orangutan cage.

"Whoa, wait a second. Where are you going with Boris?" Clancy snapped off her latex gloves, but stayed where she was. If she didn't get the computer to reboot, then any geek with some skills could find out what she'd done—and learned.

The men didn't respond, and rolled the cage toward the door.

"You really should stop naming the test animals, Clancy, and he's going to surgery."

Her eyes went wide and her gaze darted to the cage and

the sleeping giant inside. "But there's nothing wrong with him."

"We need to see the progress on his brain while his heart is still beating." She said it as if there were no questioning her decision.

Okay, that was logical, the icky part Clancy didn't want to consider, but why right now? "But we haven't finished the stress and hydration test on him yet. You open up his skull and, provided he lives, you have weeks of recovery." This made no sense.

"Perhaps, but there are other apes and I have orders."

Ah, so that was it. "Colonel Cook ordered this?" Cook was a stickler for regulations, to have all his ducks in a neat row, and though he was pressuring her to change her views on the timelines, he respected her cautions. She reached for the phone.

"Clancy, don't." Francine took a step nearer. "He's not happy. Let him cool off."

Francine's tone warned that if she pushed she could be out of a job, and Clancy heeded it. *If you don't play with the team, they'll trade you. Or kick you out.* Clancy couldn't afford not to be here right now. Not with what she knew now. She was the only one thinking clearly apparently. But she wasn't a doctor with a list of PhDs, and therefore she was expendable. Although Clancy created the microtechnology, she didn't own it. The military research and development did, and that meant the U.S. government held the schematics and the patents. To get this job she'd signed a "fork it over and keep your mouth shut at all times" statement. Fine for her, she had no one to blab to anyway.

Yet she had a feeling that being on the cutting edge of science was about to get her hacked to pieces.

"The colonel made it clear that we can't have anyone on this project who'll refuse orders."

Clancy gave her a look that always got her in trouble as a kid. "You know, Francine, I've served once too, but military personnel also have the right to refuse orders when it's detrimental to life. We need further testing and no, don't give me that *Major* Yates look, this isn't about obeying blindly. Rushing will have setbacks and you know it."

She let out a long breath, knowing she was preaching to the wrong crowd. They couldn't turn back after taking the plunge with human trials.

"What pushed the schedule up to this?" She gestured to the cloaked cage housing Boris as the men pushed it around the equipment. The pod was stable, but the insertion was only a few weeks old.

"Look, Clancy, I agree with you, it needs further testing, and that's where Boris comes in. If you'd just go with the flow . . ."

Clancy blinked, then scowled. Go along when human lives were at stake?

"Fine. Stick to your high moral grounds," Francine said tightly. "But understand that I have a career I love and I got this far because I'm willing to play their games." She touched her shoulder. "I'm sorry you can't."

This wouldn't sting so much if Clancy didn't respect and admire Francine. Aside from being a tall, leggy brunette, Francine Yates was a genius, a doctor, a U.S. Army major, and head of a billion-dollar project. What's not to admire about that? Just staying afloat in a generally man's world was tough enough. Francine excelled. For both of them, it was all about the strides they were making to help troops in the field. But going ahead without monitoring Boris thoroughly first was insane and could bring the whole project down—and kill four decorated Marines.

Clancy felt her stand against this strengthen, and she reminded herself that they'd done this without her, yet put her name on all the reports. Forging her signature wouldn't be difficult. If she tipped her hand now, she'd be fired. Then the Marines would have no one watching their back.

In stocking feet, she took a step away from the desk, her

gaze locked on Francine as she said, "The review board doesn't know this like we do, Francine. You're letting outsiders make decisions and I want to go on record that I'm opposed."

Francine nodded. "Duly noted."

The orangutan stirred in the cage, sitting up, and looking between Clancy and Francine. Seeing Francine, the animal immediately rose and reached a clawlike paw for her, letting out a high-pitched scream and hopping wildly inside the cage. Francine jumped back and quickly ordered the men to remove it.

Clancy went back to the desk and grabbed her shoes from underneath. As she put one on, she pretended to drop it, then hit the OFF/ON button on the computer. From her position the screen blinked and started a reboot.

"I can't understand why he does that to me all the time."

"Change your perfume and see what happens."

Francine's brows shot up. "Maybe he just likes redheads."

Dark auburn, she wanted to correct, but let it go. "Now what? No test subjects? The others aren't up to his timeline yet, nor his level. If he doesn't survive, then you just canned a month's worth of this project." Clancy slipped the service record book pages from under the keyboard and carefully folded them. "Your tax dollars at work, I guess."

"Natasha was implanted at the same time, too," she reminded her.

Discreetly, Clancy stuffed the papers in her shoes. "And a female orangutan is supposed to tell us about the effect on human males?" Testosterone levels alone changed the data. This was a smokescreen and not a very good one.

"It's the progress of the pod first, then the remaining stress tests with the other candidates."

She wasn't telling Clancy something she didn't know. "Better keep a good supply of apes on standby. You'll be running out."

As almost an afterthought, she opened her desk drawer and grabbed the deactivation device, the Terminator, and slipped it into her purse. She stood, removed her lab coat, and grabbed her bag.

"I'm not coming in tomorrow."

Francine sighed and came to the desk, resting her hand on the monitor. It was still rebooting and Clancy hoped Francine didn't notice the flickering screen.

"You won't attend the surgery?"

Clancy shook her head. As far as she was concerned, two years of work was going down the toilet under the scalpel. "A piece of advice."

Francine arched a brow, changing her expression from friend to superior.

"Just be very careful who and where you put your faith, Francine. It'll come back to haunt you, trust me."

Francine's brows kitted, her gaze questioning where that bit of acid advice came from. Clancy didn't share and headed out the door.

Her steps feeling awkward, Clancy tried to leave the building without much notice—-with the Terminator in her purse and classified material padding her shoes.


*Eleven days prior*
*Virginia*


Mike followed orders. Sometimes.

Right now, taking up a hospital bed when there were wounded coming back from the Middle East all the time just didn't wash. He pulled on his shirt and felt only a twinge in his shoulder from the infection he'd contracted in Libyan waters. At least the stitches were out.

"You can't leave yet, Gannon," he heard and kept his back to the nurse as he tucked in his shirt.

"Watch me." He was looking forward to a beer and a night without someone waking him to check his eyeballs or inject him with drugs.

"I have to sign you out."

"Then get to scribbling, Ensign."

"You have to complete the psychological interviews, you know that."

He turned, eyeing the small young woman from head to foot. "My mental health is fine. Not like it's the first time I've been shot."

Her shoulders pushed back as she said, "That's an order."

Christ. Newly commissioned ensigns were a pain in the ass. Especially ones being trained for classified clearance. "Yes, ma'am."

She gestured to the door. Mike grabbed his duffel bag and advanced, but when he was close, she slipped back a quick step. He froze at the door, frowning. *Christ, she's afraid of me.* It put him on edge and he gestured for her to lead the way.

"Don't put that clipboard away, Ensign Durry, I'll be leaving."

Down the next corridor, she ushered him into a conference room, barely able to look him in the eye. Mike recognized the man behind the table and smiled slightly. Dr. Figaroa was a round, dark-haired man with a big Italian nose and easy humor.

"You're a frequent guest, Gannon."

"Let me save you the time, Dr. Figaroa. Read the last entry and we're done here."

The shrink pointed to the chair. Mike dropped the bag and sat.

"What are your plans?"

"A beer, some TV, and if I'm lucky, getting laid. What's yours?"

The little ensign shifted in her chair, but Figaroa just smiled. "I should expect that."

"Then why are we here?" Mike leaned his forearms on the table. "What do you want that I can actually tell you?"

His status was classified, need to know, and these people didn't need to know shit.

She fuddled with papers. "Your rank isn't listed, why is that?"

Figaroa put a hand on her arm and shook his head in warning. Durry was new to dealing with Spec Ops personnel, but even with a class-A clearance, all Figaroa knew about him was his service record; most of it was blacked out. The only smudge on his record was disobeying his senior command orders to watch an al-Qaeda training camp. He went in and blew it to hell. When his commanding officer questioned why he didn't remain outside as ordered, Mike had replied, "Because the enemy was *inside,* sir."

"You think you're special that you don't have to undergo the same requirements as anyone else," the woman said. "There are thousands like you doing the same thing."

He gave her a deadpan stare. "Pretty slim ratio considering there are nearly three hundred million American citizens, huh?"

She flushed pink. "What did you feel when you shot those men?" she asked, reading off a checklist that was as impersonal as her questions.

"Nothing. They'd killed innocent Americans. I'm an expert at an ugly job. I wish I weren't necessary and there was world peace, Miss America, but there isn't. I'd rather not kill anyone."

"Any new women in your life?" Figaroa asked.

Mike hated people asking personal questions. His life was his own, and while his services belonged to the Marines, who occupied his bed didn't. "No."

Next they'd be asking him why he didn't kill the child.

"Look, Figaroa, we all defend America's safety in some form." He glanced at the woman, and she seemed to flinch in her chair. "I go out and find the threats. If there were a reason beyond my countrymen's safety that matters more, I'm all ears. But you lose your freedom once and you'll understand." Mike pushed the memories down and looked between the two.

"This is exactly as you said last time, Gannon."

He looked at Figaroa. "That's because I'm still the same." Eggheads, they just didn't get it. It proved to Mike that military rank didn't mean they understood anything outside their playground. He pushed the chair back. "I'm outta here."

"You can't be listed as ready for active status till physical therapy signs off," the ensign said.

Mike raised his arm above his head, rotated it, then did the same at his side.

"Excellent, but strength training is necessary."

Mike grabbed the extra chair beside him and lifted it above his head. Then he threw. She flinched at the crash. Figaroa chuckled, shaking his head.

"Well, that was helpful," Durry said, indignant. "An amazing recovery."

"For a rat maybe." Mike was a fast healer. Always had been. Probably because he hated sitting still. He'd been working out in his room at night when all the on-duty corpsmen were watching *Law and Order* reruns.

Mike looked pointedly at Dr. Figaroa and inclined his head to the ensign, his look as if to say, "Clue her in, will you?" Figaroa tapped the file and the ensign read. Mike knew what it said. In the last six months he'd won two decathlons. He liked to run and wanted to get the hell out of here and do some of it. The door suddenly flew open and Mike jumped to his feet as his commander entered.

"We aren't finished." Figaroa stood.

"Yes, you are," the colonel said.

Mike didn't let his expression show his amusement.

"At ease, Gannon, and follow me."

Good. He really didn't want to piss off the people that doctored him up. They might leave a sponge inside him next time.

"If he leaves, it's against orders."

The colonel looked at the ensign and she shrank in the chair. *She won't last,* Mike thought.

"Then I guess it is." The colonel quit the room and Mike was right beside him. "Hold your questions."

Mike followed his commander through the hospital, an unmarked building on the outskirts of Manassas, Virginia. Outside, a uniformed Marine held open the car door. Mike ducked in, glad to be out of that antiseptic petri dish. If one more person took his blood pressure, or asked him "how are *we* feeling?" he was going to smash something.

The colonel was in and the car was under way. "Are you ready?"

"Hell yes . . . sir."

"Good." The colonel opened a briefcase on the seat beside him, and handed Mike a dark-printed paper. Satellite photos.

"Ecuador–Peru border?"

Hank Jansen was always impressed that the man could read topography so well, but then he'd spent two years searching the mountains for an American charged with selling weapons to terrorists. It was always the little nuts that caused the big problems, in that case, treason. "Look at the Peru, north Andes."

Mike tipped the pages toward the light.

"Central intel believes those are missile launchers sitting in the mountains."

Tactical ballistic missiles? Mike wanted to contradict, but waited to hear the whole report. "The U.S. is on good terms on both sides of the border. What do they say?"

"Peru says not ours, and Ecuador is neutral, guarding her borders from the Colombian drug smugglers. They say it's not in their territory and won't go in to find out. For fear of a conflict they can't handle. The Peruvian Army dispatched a squad, but it's rough country."

"DEA in the loop?"

"Yes."

"CIA is wrong. They're too small to be Scuds."

"I would agree. But Shining Path is making a resurgence and DEA thinks they are involved with drugs. We sent a UAV to get closer and if confirmed, take it out. Except that the UAV surveying the area was shot out of the sky."

Mike arched a brow. "We know where it came from. Mark the target and take it out."

"Before marking the target with a laser, we had to recover the armed UAV first, so we sent in a team."

"My guys?" Why else would Jansen be here? He had other teams on standby and none of them recently injured.

"Yes, Krane led, with one other, Corporal J.J. Palmer."

Mike's expression tightened. He'd kicked Palmer off his team because the kid was a hothead. Not a hard charger, but a loose cannon. He'd jeopardized two missions, even after a reprimand. Orders and caution meant little to Palmer. He was bucking for a hero's grave. "Pardon me, sir, but you sure that ass bag didn't fuck up the mission?"

If you were on Mike's shit list you didn't get off it, Hank thought. "No, we had a radio link. They were hit." The colonel played the tape.

His elbows on his knees, Mike stared at the spot between his boots. "They survived the crash. But there was no tracer, no warning?"

"No, and the GPS beacon isn't sending, either."

Mike looked up, scowling. "None of them? This was covert?"

"No. The Peruvian government was informed of the recovery mission. They're just as interested in this as we are, but the chopper was technically in Ecuador's airspace. Ecuador insists they didn't fire, didn't crash there, and frankly, they don't have the arsenal to go after it. We had one contact with the team. Under an hour later." Hank played the tape again.

Mike's breathing locked in his lungs. God. It was horrific. Screams, gunfire, a gurgling plea for help from Nathan

Krane. Marines didn't scream like that. Not his men. They'd cut off an arm before showing the enemy a shred of weakness. "When do I leave?"

"Pick a team and—"

"No. Alone."

The colonel shook his head. "Negative."

"Hear me out. A Scud didn't hit that chopper. Not only is that overkill, there would be nothing left and you'd hear it for miles."

Hank nodded. "Agreed."

"And if missiles are in the jungle, why there? For what purpose and, mostly, who the hell would they fire them at? They don't have the range. Five hundred miles at best. South America bombing South America?" Mike shook his head, his forehead tight. "I'd say if anything it's SAMs." Surface-to-air missiles were shoulder-launched and, lately, damn easy to come by. "If it's drug smugglers, they don't come out in the open enough and they're smart." Or they wouldn't be getting drugs into the U.S. "Shooting down an aircraft over *any* territory in that area will bring the Army, so why risk it?"

Drug factories *were* underground so they couldn't be seen from the air. This made no sense. But then, crime rarely did.

"We send in another team and they'll end up like that." He flicked a hand at the recorder. "Or get nothing. A crowd will scare them off. Besides, some people down there owe me some favors." Mike sat back. "Permission to speak freely?"

Jansen chuckled. "When have you not?"

"Scuds? Without DEA or CIA seeing cargo transportation to that area? Nothing stolen? No intel on who's got new hardware or what's in the warheads? Come on, Hank. Cut the bullshit, what's going on? You didn't tell me this because it's my team."

Mike could smell a smokescreen before it hit the breeze, Hank thought, and he knew Mike as well as the man allowed anyone to know him. They'd served together when he was a young, eager Marine and Hank had made certain Gannon came with him. Hank trusted him completely, and was honored that the trust was returned. But Mike's true attributes weren't his special tactics and skills, but that he didn't need anyone to issue orders. He knew what had to be done and how to do it, no matter the risk.

Hank sighed. "Nothing but small arms has flowed through that area. We just don't know what hit the UAV or the chopper."

Mike scowled. Intel knew what the premier of the Soviet Union had for breakfast, but they didn't know this?

"There wasn't a heat signature before the blast."

"There has to be." All weapons radiated heat. A muzzle flash when fired, a warmup to launch.

The colonel handed him sequential satellite photos in closer detail. Mike studied each carefully. The only spot that resonated white on the page was the fire in the chopper's tail. The next photo was a still from the UAV. Same thing. A nose cone, then nothing. The previous photos showed no launch heat. None.

"Jesus. A rocket, small and highly accurate." Mike handed the photos back and looked out the window, thinking of the security risk and the damage just one could do.

A surface-to-air missile without a heat signature would be invisible to radar and thermal tracking. Hell. They'd have no possible means to counterattack before impact.

*And we have no clue who fired it.*

# Three

There were some things about a wild youth that never leave you, Clancy thought. Distrust of authority, of herself, the vigil over your own moral standards—and knowing when someone was following you.

Not close or overtly, but as she left the Starbucks with a double Mocha Latte caffeine fix locked in her grip, her senses lit up. She glanced up and down the street, her gaze flickering past the pale green car before she crossed to her own.

She slid behind the wheel, secured her cup, then pulled into traffic. A moment later, so did the green car. Why follow her? They couldn't know about her snooping. She'd covered her tracks well.

Unless Cook was staring at his computer at the time, she reminded herself. If that was true, why not haul her in?

Just to be sure she wasn't coming up with a paranoid worst-case scenario, she got on the Beltway and drove in the far right lane. Her speed backed up traffic behind her for a couple of hundred yards, and when drivers were ticked enough to blow their horns, she slipped off the exit. A few blocks down, she pulled into a parking lot behind a strip mall, got out, and looked around the edge of the building. The green car appeared on the off-ramp. She couldn't see the driver behind the tinted windows, but when he turned away from her direction Clancy jumped in her car and drove across the lot to the far west side of the mall behind delivery trucks, then took surface roads.

Unless her "tail" had her past laid out in front of him, he wouldn't know her next stop. Ten minutes later, she stepped into the dark shop—through the rear.

The instant Phil Bartley saw her, he went into a series of nervous ticks. He looked bad. His graying hair was gelled straight up, and the nose ring—with a dozen more up both ears—looked as if they were all holding up his drooping skin—and failing. At forty, it wasn't attractive. *And I thought this was cool?*

She'd hung around him to defy her parents. *Well, that's not true,* she thought. She'd done it to outright piss them off.

"How'd you get in here?" He looked beyond her to the back of the shop, for the cops, no doubt. "Get lost."

"You're breaking my heart." He was backing up as she spoke. "Afraid of me? That's a new one."

"What do you want?" Phil grew some courage and leaned back against bookshelves. He tried folding his arms, but his nervousness wouldn't let him. He pinched his nose, coughed, then shoved his hands in his jean pockets. His skin looked papery and she could see the needle marks from here.

She tossed her passport on the counter.

Phil didn't even look at it. "I ain't touchin' that. Get the fuck outta here."

Clancy looked around the dirty smoke shop and sniffed. "Herb? That's a little light for you, isn't it?"

"I'm clean."

"I'm sure." She reached over the counter and flicked the crumbs of marijuana dusting his shirt. "Can't roll a clean joint after all these years?" She tapped the passport. "Duplicate it and change the name."

"To what?"

"Grace Murray."

He snorted, slapped his hand on the passport, and flipped it open. "You in trouble?"

"Not yet." At least she hoped not. Moving to the shop window, she studied the street. She wouldn't be anywhere near a scumbag like Phil if it wasn't for the tail. Or the strange shadows outside her house. Or the crackle on the phone lines. All that meant was she'd get nowhere fast and probably X'd out of the picture before she could do anything to help the Marines.

"Some people think they change." He walked to the rear. "But they don't, not deep inside."

"Shut up." She *had* changed.

She had a career, a mortgage, and had obeyed the law since she was eighteen until today. She closed her eyes and wondered where this madness came from, but she already knew. There were four Marines out there with her technology in them. Time bombs in their heads, changing them physically, mentally. Though she couldn't know the affects for certain—the reason she wanted more testing with Boris, damn it—but she was certain she hadn't perfected it for long lasting capabilities. Foreign objects in the brain?

It would be an ugly death.

She turned and saw Phil stop at a long table, then pull a briefcase from underneath. It was those heavy silver things that carried delicate equipment. When he opened it, she realized it was a forgery setup. Customs stamps, laminates with U.S. holograms, handwriting machine, good grief. *Bet the State Department doesn't have this much in one small case.*

"You've gone state-of-the-art now, I see."

He just sneered and began working.

Clancy didn't take her eyes off him. Phil wasn't trustworthy by any means. But he wouldn't talk, unless he was backed into a corner.

"So whatcha been doing all these years?" he asked.

"Working for the government," she said just to scare him. "Keep going," she added when he stalled. He eyed her for a second, clearly debating calling the police and giving up his stash hidden somewhere in here. The stash won out.

It took over an hour, and when he was finished he handed

it over. The passport was still warm from fresh laminate. In her pocket was the real McCoy from her last cruise with her girlfriends.

She tucked the fake in her purse. "Go to the front."

"Fuck you, it's my shop."

She grabbed the open case and threatened to pull it off the table.

"No! God no. Okay, okay. Be cool. I'm going." He sniffled again and shuffled toward the front.

*What a dweeb.*

While Phil was snorting something illegal behind the counter—the man could never handle pressure—Clancy went to the back door, eased it open, and checked the parking lot before she left. She hurried to the end of the street, crossed, and went to her car parked in a service lot behind a craft store. It was amazing how it all came back so easily.

But one thing she hadn't left behind in her past was thinking like a woman in trouble.

*Guaranguillo, Ecuador*
*Four days later*

*I could live here easy,* Clancy thought. The warmth and lushness of South America didn't hold a candle to Virginia and especially D.C. No concrete for miles. She smiled as the warm breeze slipped through the jeep window, tugging at her hair. Miles behind her in Panama the tour group were boarding the cruise ship to travel up the West Coast. Though going through the locks of the Panama Canal was pretty amazing, she'd left on the pretense of a family emergency and flew to Ecuador. No one checked.

A single piece of luggage, an oversized hobo flight bag, and she was good to go. Though she didn't know exactly where she was going. The reason Fuad, her twenty-five-year-old Quechua Indian guide, was sitting next to her, humming softly.

The intelligence she'd managed to get was vague. Eyes-only files were under heavy encryption, but the Tango team was in south Ecuador on a recovery for a UAV. Simple enough. She'd at least had something to look for aside from men. A crash site. The problem was the terrain, she thought as the jeep whined to struggle up a steep hill. Around her, the forest was like a blanket of rolling green, the air thin and the jungle so dense she could barely see a few feet beyond the road. She'd passed a small village a few miles back, but didn't expect to see another for a while. The jeep bumped along the road ruts so hard that for a second she was airborne, then slammed back into the seat.

Beside her, Fuad chuckled, grinning widely. She didn't think it was amusing, but he seemed fascinated with the ride.

"How much farther?"

"This road, here!" He pointed and she turned slightly.

He wasn't much of a conversationalist. She'd already learned the natives didn't like talking to outsiders, not in the small villages, at least. Even Fuad wasn't much help with communicating. Despite the generous people at her last gas stop in Sumba, her questions were met with silence and stony looks. Apparently, she wasn't as charming as she thought.

"Want some tunes, Fuad?"

"*Sí,* Senorita McRae."

It sounded like mackerel to her. Clancy leaned to tune in a radio station when a lamb darted out in front of her. She swerved left, braked, but the uneven road took the jeep into a gully. She braced for impact and the jeep dropped into it like a penny in a jar, nose down. Her head grazed the windshield, stunning her.

"Well, hell." Clancy rubbed her forehead, waiting for her brain to shift back into place, then tried reverse until she heard the tires spin in the mud. In her mirror, she saw a small boy with a stick herding sheep across the road. She threw her hands up. "Thanks a heap, kid."

The boy just shrugged and laughed, moving on with his flock and disappearing down a narrow dirt path.

"Ya know, I really *love* lamb stew," she griped. All the creatures did was *bahh* as they hurried after their little master. She tried reverse again, the tires spitting mud.

"I think we need to push or get something under the wheels for traction."

When he didn't respond, she looked at him. He aimed a gun at her stomach.

"You little bastard."

Fuad grinned, then motioned with her own pistol.

He looked past her and she turned to the window and found another barrel at her nose. *That's a really big gun,* she thought before the man behind it yanked her from the jeep, then pulled a burlap sack over her head. He bound her hands behind her back and led her around, chuckling when she stumbled. Kicking and screaming didn't do anything but get her smacked around. Besides, by the sound of footsteps, she was outnumbered. Vastly.

From inside the foul-smelling sack, she heard the voice of her guide, the little weasel, and tried to decipher the Spanish mixed with another Quechua.

But she grabbed one word from it. *Rescate.*

Ransom.

Oh, who were they kidding? No one knew she was here, and there sure as hell wasn't anyone who could pay a ransom. She was about to say so, then caught herself. If she was worthless to them, she'd be killed. Heavy hands forced her to a spot under a tree, the relief from the sun instant and welcome. She swore there were bugs flying around inside the sack on her head, yet their voices seemed closer and she realized there were buildings nearby. Then the distinct odor of rotting vegetation, sweat, and booze floated on the air. *I take it back, I don't want to live here.*

In the back of her mind, she chanted, *Don't panic, an opportunity for escape will present itself.* She just hoped her escape didn't include white lights and crossing over to another plane of existence.

An engine rumbled, racing nearer, and she flinched at the skid of pebbles and dirt. A door slammed and a new voice broke past the noise, the command in his tone clear and thundering. Her high school Spanish stank, but he wanted to know who hired him. Him being her guide.

"No one, I swear."

Then she heard a scream and something hit the ground near her. She felt the scatter of dirt and air on her legs. For a moment, she thought Fuad was dead. Then he begged for his life. She tipped her head in an effort to pinpoint voices. The mental picture she had wasn't pretty, and through a thin spot in the hood, she glimpsed Fuad.

About two seconds before his brains exploded out his temple.

Clancy dropped to the ground as people shouted. Gunfire barked through the air and she didn't have time to think of the ugly sound that bullet made leaving his skull, or the dampness on her arm. She rolled to her back and arched, working her bound hands under her butt, behind her knees, then her feet. Men fired toward the mountains as she worked her bound hands over her boots. She yanked the hood off and her gaze filled with Fuad's face, his blank eyes staring back at her. Biting back a scream, she looked away and, using her teeth, loosened the thin nylon rope. Her palm cramped from bending her hand to reach the ties at her wrist, but it slipped slowly. Then she was on her feet and running.

She plowed into the forest, leaving everything she had behind and only thinking of escape. Sticking around would get her dead and she really loved living. She swatted at vines, pushing faster. She was accustomed to the pace, not the heat and thin air. Her breathing strained, her head swam. *I feel tanked.*

Then a figure stepped out in front of her and she stumbled

back, falling on her rear. She looked up. With bushy dark hair and nearly jet-black eyes, he aimed at her head.

"Just why are you in my jungle, senorita?" He pulled back the hammer.

"I'm a tourist, for heaven's sake."

He drew a leather billfold from his shirt pocket and flipped it open. "And I am the police."

Clancy thought, *Saved.*

An hour later, she was wishing she'd stayed on the cruise ship.

*Two days later*
*Near Guaranguillo, Ecuador*
*0500 hours Zulu*

The freezing temperatures of a High Altitude Low Opening jump fell rapidly as he neared the ground. The land came screaming toward him at 120 mph before Mike deployed the chute, abruptly slowing his silent descent into the jungle.

Right into drug dealer heaven.

If anyone saw him, he'd be shot out of the sky.

As he dropped into the deep valley, the wind tore at his black jumpsuit, the fit tight to avoid sound, his body rapidly warming as hot air slowed him further. Through his night-vision visor, he saw lights from Guaranguillo near the mountain slopes. Below him was nothing but a black canvas and coming fast toward his face. It was a personal high. He didn't get excited about many things, but jumping out of a speeding aircraft topped the list.

He aimed for the sweet spot, a small clearing that would be tough to hit without getting snagged in the dense trees. When his boots brushed the treetops, he pulled the suspension lines of the parachute close, bringing him straight down, rapidly.

His feet hit with a jolt that rattled his fillings, and he

tucked and rolled, pulling the black chute with him. He spat out the oxygen mouthpiece, then unhooked his helmet, on one knee, weapon aimed.

He didn't expect company. Switching the visor to thermal, he surveyed his surroundings, sweating inside the suit and layers of clothes. It showed him nothing but dense forest and a couple of monkeys.

Easy in, he thought. Entering the country under radar kept him invisible for now. That wouldn't last long. His passport was stamped, just not in a customs office, but real enough that no one would question it. This was drug and gun-smuggling territory. People didn't ask too many questions.

In the dark, he stripped off the jumpsuit, wrapping his jump gear in the chute, then dug a deep hole. Equipment buried, he positioned rocks and foliage over the pile, dusted his hands, then pulled out his GPS and marked the location. Three miles from the UAV's last location. On a remote part of the border, he didn't expect military checkpoints or patrols.

He shifted items in the pockets of his worn black cargo pants, then pulled a khaki shirt over his black T-shirt. His gear and ammo in an old Army surplus rucksack, he looked more like a digger than a Marine. Letting his hair grow made it itch around his ears, but he wasn't Latin and stood out as it was. Mike didn't want attention.

Though the monkeys were already screaming warnings to each other, he wanted to get in, do the job, find his men, and bring them home.

That they could be dead and buried didn't enter his mind. Defeatist thinking didn't win anything. He'd memorized the topographical terrain before leaving the U.S., but he knew it, two years' worth of looking for a drug dealer and murderer was enough for anyone. Yet in the dark, he had to rely on the glowing GPS. Drawing his machete, he started walking. At over six thousand feet above sea level the air wasn't any thinner than with a HALO jump. Even as dawn broke, the rain forest was wet, hot, and dark.

Mike hacked through undergrowth, listening for anyone else and hearing only the squawk of macaws and seeing white-faced monkeys hovering overhead as he worked his way toward the target.

The sun rose slowly. Giant kapok and rubber trees shadowed the Andean valley, the ground spread with a gray-white mist that wrapped the giant palms and curled toward the sky, where it hovered, hiding in the jungle canopy. The roots smothered the ground so much that his boots rarely touched the soil.

Mike ignored the sounds around him, the movement of creatures, the drop of nuts from trees. A small green iguana skittered, counting coup on him, then vanishing into the thicket. He remembered they tasted good roasted over an open fire. He checked his compass on his watch, advancing to the spot where the UAV was last recorded. As he neared the target, his gaze moved over the land, searching for broken branches, the path of descent.

There wasn't any.

Even as he drew his pistol, Mike got a feeling in his gut, the one that never failed him, and warned that what he thought was out there—was wrong.

He pushed aside giant palm fronds. Should be right . . .

Mike scowled. The land around him was lush and untouched. He climbed over fallen trees to a cropping of granite boulders protruding from the hillside. Red and blue macaws were perched on the jagged rock face like ornaments on a tree, and as he approached, they shrieked at the invasion. A dozen birds flew into the trees and gave away his position.

He was hoping no one was up at this hour.

Mike knelt on the boulders, and through binoculars scanned the area three-sixty.

No sign of the UAV. No crash site. Not even a piece of scrap metal. Bupkes. How could intel be this wrong? If not here, then where the hell did it crash?

And if this intel was this flawed, he'd bet the chopper wasn't anywhere near where it went down. His gaze slid over the land, the Andean mountains in the distance.

So much for being invisible and getting in and out.

The Hellfires were still on the loose.


*Ben Guerdane, Tunisia*
*0200 hours*


The market on the border was empty. All that remained were discarded crates like fragile bones unearthed with the beat of the wind. In the day, traders came in carloads across the border of Libya to sell goods to Tunisian merchants. Now it was nothing but sand and stiff, arid breezes as officers of more than three intelligence agencies spilled out of the van. They didn't pause to check their weapons or to say good luck, but took off in a dead run.

Antone Choufani led them here, his intelligence firsthand. He'd worked for over a year to infiltrate this faction, a bleed-off of the dragon that roared over the Middle East. He believed in Allah, believed in the Quran, but didn't take it to such deep levels as so many others had done. Kill an unbeliever, an infidel, and get seventy-two virgins? He'd had a virgin; it was a tiresome experience. Besides, he loved life too much to strap a bomb to his chest and walk into a mosque. True Islam didn't believe in the murder of their own.

At this storage building, unmarked crates had arrived, yet none left. Unusual because the weapons were always quickly divided, remarked, and sold so fast—by several different means—that they couldn't be tracked once they left. No one spoke about what was in the crates: rifles, grenades, or explosives? He wasn't trusted enough to be told, only to carry them inside.

Approaching the target, the men circumvented the building, one man running forward and setting explosives at the doors. They ignited, popping the hinges and locks. The doors fell and the agents swarmed inside. All Antone could see was the drift of smoke, hear the sound of gunfire and screams claw the night in vulgar spats of death.

Then, for a brief moment, there was complete silence.

The building lurched first. Five thousand square feet of concrete and steel looked as if it would fall in on itself, a giant indrawn breath. Even the lingering smoke from the explosives drew inside. Atone had never seen anything like it. A heartbeat later, the structure erupted like the regurgitation of the earth's core. Flames shot up into the air in broad stabs of orange-red, the base of the explosion already blue hot. Several short explosions followed, driving anyone too close back with a punch to the middle. The fuel or gunpowder, Choufani thought as his fingers worked the grip of his gun. He waited behind the lines for anyone to come out.

The blast took no less than seven Interpol agents.

Someone had seen them coming.

Behind him, hidden before now, the remaining agents were for a moment stunned, then bolted to action. Radios howled with the call for doctors, for the coroner. But they knew the men were dead, that they'd failed.

No one was getting out alive.

Flames ate at the storage house, walls buckled and fell.

Choufani sank to the ground, his arms on his knees, his head in his hands.

*Now we will never know.*


*Guaranguillo, Ecuador*


Mike didn't try verbal communication. While his Spanish was decent, his handle on the local Quechua dialect stank. The villagers forgave him, but communication was a lot of hand signals and half phrases. The villagers were meagerly dressed, but infinitely kind. Dark haired children sat on the ground outside homes and ate passion fruit, offering him a piece as he passed. He took it, knowing they'd share with a stranger when they had little. Women tossed out washwater as a few men headed into the coffee fields to the north, though Mike was pretty sure they weren't growing java.

He paid for a warm soda from a tiny old woman sitting outside her home, beside her a rack of snacks that looked like they'd been around since the eighties. Popping the top, he drank it straight down in one shot and pitched the crushed can in a box near the woman. She offered him another and he smiled, overpaid, and tucked it in his pack. He strolled down the center of the village, an uneven dirt road no more than twenty feet wide. Buildings constructed of wood and corrugated metal sheets were sandwiched up alongside each other so tightly that if one fell, the others would go. His gaze moved back and forth, picking up details like the spent shells near a door, the black stain of blood on the wood frame. There was no shortage of guns. The men wore them openly.

Mike kept his concealed. No use in antagonizing the locals. But with no GPS beacon, and satellite photos murky because of the dense jungle, locating the UAV wouldn't be simple. The chopper had crashed before reaching the last UAV location. A chopper without working avionics could drift for miles for a safe landing or drop out of the sky like a rock. Considering they had tape of the last radio contact, he assumed the former, and that his men were still alive.

He had priority orders. Jansen had done the assessing, and though Mike didn't like it, he knew the colonel was right. UAV and Hellfire missiles, possibly Scuds, then bring the team home. In that order.

At least there wasn't a little black box for anyone to find.

Mike sat on a rough bench near a welding shop and unlaced his boot. He kept his head bent, his gaze slipping over the village. He recognized the sudden tension in the air, most of it from a young boy about ten curled in the doorway of a house, barefoot and dirty. His big eyes watched him as he shook pebbles from his boot. Unlike the child in Farawa Island, this one was unarmed and scared. *But if he were pointing a gun, could you kill him? The enemy has many faces,* he thought, quickly lacing his boot.

Then Mike followed the kid's gaze back the way he'd come. The street was suddenly empty. His gaze flashed to the homes, a couple of people he could see. They peered from behind curtains, taking cover in fragile homes. Then he heard the rowdy voices before he saw a man stumble from behind his shelter and run.

Mike didn't need to be in the middle of a local firefight, and standing, he adjusted the rucksack on his shoulders before he headed out of the village in a casual stroll. The thick jungle closed around him, blocking sunlight, and cooler temperatures created a thick rolling mist over the forest floor. The beauty of it escaped him, his steps slower because he couldn't see the ground well. He'd like to hack through it with his machete, but not enough to give away his position.

He was about thirty yards into the forest when the first shot came.

He went still and let his head drop forward. *You're not the police, you have a job.* Yet Mike was heading back when he heard someone running toward him.

A few yards east of him, the kid shot through the forest like a baby gazelle, jumping over forest debris and shifting left and right. The boy would never outrun whoever was behind him, and Mike caught up with him, snatching the child off the ground and covering his mouth with his hand as he backed into a darkened area off the path. The child squirmed and Mike kept him tight in his arms, smothering a grunt when teeth sank into his palm.

He forced the boy to look him in the eye, and gave him a stare he reserved for terrorists. For a second, he thought the kid would wet his pants. The boy nodded, relaxed, and Mike released his hand. The boy opened his mouth to speak and Mike covered it.

"Not a word," he warned in Spanish.

He released him and the skinny child folded to the ground. Mike motioned him to hide behind him in a burrow of vines, and the kid quickly obeyed. Mike slid forward, his gun drawn as he watched the young men strut through the woods. They were overconfident, laughing about scaring the villagers, and while Mike wanted to teach them a lesson about being bullies, he couldn't afford the attention so early in the game. The trio moved deeper into the valley and he let them pass, then motioned to the boy.

"What's your name?"

"Pablo." He crawled out of his vined hideout.

"Nice to meet you." He didn't offer his name.

"They were looking for you, senor."

Highly unlikely, Mike thought. "Who are they?"

"Smugglers. Drugs, weapons, sometimes just food. We never know. They only come through looking for strangers."

Okay, that he'd buy. Clear out the untrustworthy, threaten the locals, and you've got the bases covered since it was unlikely the police would come this far to the border.

"They go to the river," Pablo said.

"Show me." Mike followed the boy, watching his back, and the kid brought him near a stream. With a finger to his lips, Pablo smiled devilishly, then spied through the underbrush. There were crates stacked in two flat-bottom boats floating in the water. No one else.

The bullies were taking their time getting here.

"They wait till they are alone before coming to the water," the child whispered.

Then Mike heard voices and footsteps and drew the boy back as the trio of young men appeared from the east, and immediately started unloading the large wood boxes, rocking the boats. Hell. The men were only about forty yards away from their positions.

Drug or small arms transport, he figured, but why here? Without checking his GPS, Mike figured he was sitting on the border and there were easier ways to get round here. A jeep for one. Ecuador's military patrolled here because the nearest checkpoint for a border crossing was about forty miles behind him, and while this stream fed into the many tributaries snaking through Ecuador and Peru, it was nearly a hundred miles to the mouth of the Amazon. A boat would run into hazards till deep water. Of course, once they were on that river, it could take them anywhere in South America, but on foot in any direction put them right at the base of Andean mountains. The roughest terrain on the planet, Mike remembered.

For a moment, he considered capturing the three for a little interrogation, but nixed it. His priority was the UAV and the Hellfires, but if the UAV didn't crash in Ecuador, then it drifted into Peru. How far? was the question. He could use a couple of squads of Marines, because the chopper crash was reported at sixty miles farther south in the Andean valley. But so far, his intel sucked canal water.

He focused on the men when one, a hothead, tried telling the others what to do. They weren't having it. A mutiny.

The kid gripped his arm, watching. Mike glanced down at the tiny hand, then shifted and caught bits of the argument. They'd stolen the crates from a local drug lord. Not a smart idea. Cartels were misers and wanted all their profits in their pockets.

Arguing heatedly, they lost their hold on the crate and it hit the ground. The lid cracked, and for a moment they all just stared at the spilled contents, then started accusing the others of stealing whatever they thought was inside. Mike almost laughed.

It was a bunch of blocks. The men stomped around, swearing, kicking at the dirt and the contents. Then Mike heard tourist souvenirs. *Always check the cargo first, pals.* Two were screaming at each other when the tallest man's chest exploded, taking his lungs out his back. Mike pushed Pablo down and aimed in the direction of the shot. He couldn't see a thing. A second later, another shot came, knocking the second guy backward off his feet, a clean hole in his forehead even before the report echoed. Mike was admiring the precision hit as the third jumped into the boat, paddling furiously, and for a second it looked like he'd get away. The jungle hovered over the stream, darkening it in spots, shielding the young man.

The shot cracked, the report a couple of seconds later.

He was about six hundred yards away, Mike thought, in the hills. No noise suppressor, but a scope. That meant the shooter didn't care who saw him.

He felt a hand on his leg and looked down. He'd almost forgotten about the boy. Mike motioned Pablo toward the village as he eased back, careful not to disturb the bushes and give the sniper another reason to shoot.

"Pablo, did you see a small plane crash here?"

The boy frowned. "No, they fly over the fields sometimes, but no, senor. No crash."

How'd it get so off course and why didn't satellite imagery pick it up?

Mike delivered the boy to his worried mother, who grabbed Pablo's ear and berated him for not staying with her. The child looked almost grateful at the ass-chewing.

Turning away, Mike walked south, thinking he wasn't going to trek all over Ecuador and Peru for the UAV. Someone at Langley had dropped the ball. He didn't have squat and he needed accurate intel. If Langley couldn't get it, he'd have to do it himself.

Pablo chased him, grabbing his sleeve. "You leave, senor?" Pablo sounded so young and fragile right then.

"Yes. If anyone like those guys show up, stay with your mother." The kid had seen too much, and if anyone knew, he'd be dead very quickly.

"No, senor, you leave without the American?"

Mike stopped, turned sharply. *Jesus.* "What American?"

# Four

A rat clung to the wall, looking back over his shoulder as if he were running from a predator.

"Go on, it's a nice fat bug, you've worked hard for it, eating your way through . . ." Clancy's gaze flicked to the hole in the wall. "Whatever." She looked at the creature. He was already done and moving on. How rude, she thought, then chuckled to herself.

American jails were so much nicer. At least they gave you food, water, and a cot. Inside here was nothing but a smelly bucket.

"Oh, this is so cool," she said, but just didn't quite make the tone she'd hoped for. That one that gives you the rush of adrenaline that tells you you can achieve it. "Alas, poor Clancy, I knew her well."

*God. I'm getting squirrelly.*

She blamed it on whatever they gave her to put her out. For hours or days, she wasn't sure. All she recalled was the long-haired guy ordering her thrown in the vehicle before everything went black.

She tipped her head back and noticed the rat was gone. "Eat and run, I get it. I'm not good company right now."

The door rattled like dungeon chains and she braced herself for another round of "Hey, *chica*, you wanna do me?" A soldier appeared. At least she thought he was a soldier. Her military training only saw the wrinkled uniform, the abundance of facial hair, and the lack of soap anywhere near him.

"Who are you talking to?" he said, his face against the bars. Was it her that smelled that bad, or him? "Water. Got any?"

"I got something for you." He grabbed his crotch.

*Oh, like that's new?* "Mouth is too big." She pursed her lips tightly.

He looked ready to kill her, then laughed like Boris. But right now, she'd strip for a Diet Coke. Two days in here was enough for anyone.

He tossed her a small plastic bottle and she jumped at it, drinking greedily. He found her so oddly amusing that he started telling the story before he left the cell block.

Cell block. Mom would be just so proud. *Bless her heart, she can't help that she's stupid, but she just shoulda stayed home.* She'd only wanted information. Something to help her find the troops. She'd had to be cagey about it too. The team were Spec Ops guys, and she didn't want to give away whatever they were doing here, but after getting out of the country on a cruise ship and all the way here through Central America, she'd gotten bold.

Bold enough to hire a shitty guide.

The taller policeman had taken her away, tossed her in this cell, and left her here for two days in the sweltering heat. He had her one suitcase and hobo bag, and worse, the Terminator. He could keep the rest, but *that* she needed.

She gripped her head. *I'm so screwed.* No one knew she was here. All that sage advice from her dad, "Clancy, honey, look before your leap and look hard," went right out of her head. She'd walked right into the danger without considering the consequences.

What did she really think she could do? Look for skilled Marines who didn't want to be found? Once she found them, would they be so jazzed on the effects of the pods that they'd ignore her warnings? Would they even believe her? They'd volunteered for this; surely Yates had informed them of the risks.

Suddenly a thought occurred to her. Guinea pigs.

The military were used all the time to test new drugs. It wasn't common knowledge; the government had hid it for years but it had happened. Every time they forced her to have a flu shot, she got sick and not with the flu.

Her head shot up when she heard footsteps, and she pushed off the concrete floor. She adjusted her clothing, brushed off the dirt. She had to get out of here. Calling the embassy or consulate wasn't really an option. These guys didn't have phones. Only radios. Not that anyone from the embassy would come for her when she'd arrived under a slightly false passport. She felt the real one sticking to her skin down the back of her pants where she'd stashed it. The Grace Murray one was out there with her money. The copies of the Marines' files—what little she could get at the time—were folded and in a plastic baggie inside her boots. The packet made her feet sweat.

A man, Richora, appeared from the small hallway and unlocked the cell. He grabbed her hands and slapped on bright silver handcuffs, then motioned her ahead. Clancy moved past him, thinking someone probably just bought her for the whopping sum of fifty pesos. Two men had come to look her over last night. They hadn't said a word, just looked at her in that creepy lip-smacking, "I'm gonna have fun with you" leer.

Richora gripped her arm, pushing her forward.

She yanked free. "I can walk, ya know."

"*Basta ya*," he snapped, keeping hold of her elbow as he ushered her through the police station. It was an old house, really old. Water-stained walls and ceilings, worn desks, and a bulletin board with yellowed wanted posters near a drinking fountain that was stained with rust said just how old. There was so much dirt on the wood floors that it kicked up as she walked. Clancy stretched her neck to see out the windows. It had been nighttime when they dragged her in, but all she saw now was a cracked fountain in the courtyard, overgrown grasses, and great, a stone wall surrounding it. The green land beyond practically made her mouth water.

Richora forced her into a room, and she wasn't prepared when he pulled out a chair, told her to sit, then took out a small pad of paper. They were actually going to ask her for the truth? When they'd left her in jail for two days?

"What are you doing in my country?"

"Sightseeing."

"How did you know those men? The *Sendero Luminoso*." Oh God. The Shining Path? "They're disbanded."

"Is that what they tell you in your America? That we have conquered them?" He shook his head. "No, they merely hide better than before, senorita."

"Not really," she said. "I found them easy enough."

"You are a woman. They wanted your body more than your mind."

"At least I have both."

His scowl darkened, winging his brows low over his dark eyes. "It would be wise to be polite to me."

Perhaps, but she didn't think good behavior meant anything in a place like this. "Are you charging me with something?" Was he a real cop or just pretending, going through the motions? Then she remembered he'd killed Fuad in cold blood.

"We are collecting evidence."

"Like what? I was forced from my jeep and you raided it two minutes later. What do you think I know? Or saw?" Nothing, she thought, all this got her nothing.

"Why do you insist on lying?"

"Why are you being an asshole?"

He laid his hand on the table, and when it came away, Clancy saw the Terminator, a gizmo she'd created to destroy the pods without destroying the brain. She lifted her gaze.

"Explain it."

"It's an MP3 player."

He nudged it toward her. "Prove it."

The cuffs scraped the desk as she picked it up and turned it on its back. The slim pale gray device was shaped like the nanopod, an oval, almost teardrop, yet flatter. It did a lot of things, but it didn't play music.

She turned it on. The miniscreen flashed open and it asked a series of questions. Then the key for the high-frequency pulse radiated at a decimal level no human or animal could hear. It would do nothing to them, only the technology, and she had to be touching the troops to use it.

She handed it back, the figures on the screen in the language of computer science.

Richora glanced, frowned, clearly confused. Clancy was hoping he was too proud to admit he didn't understand.

"Explain this as well."

It was classified. To do so was treason and she'd already pushed her limits to get here. "No."

Suddenly Richora grabbed it and threw it against the wall. Clancy flinched as it hit and shattered. She closed her eyes, unable to look. "You bastard." About a million bucks' worth of hardware was in pieces.

"If it was expensive and worthy, then neither of us has it."

He just killed the Marines. Destroying the pods was the only way to save their lives, and with no Terminator to alter the implants, Clancy was helpless. She couldn't re-create it, and even if she found the men, what could she do now?

Then Richora pulled her purse from the floor and dropped it on the table. "Why do you have a tracking device in your handbag?"

Her head jerked up. "What? No, there isn't."

He turned the bag over, spilling her things, and she grabbed for some before they rolled off the table as he pulled the handbag inside out. There was a slice in the lining, obviously restitched, and Clancy's eyes widened as he pried for a second, then held up a small rectangular chip encased in plastic.

*They've been watching me all this time.*

"You are CIA."

*I wish.* "If I was, I'd be out of here by now."

"Not necessarily."

This man was different from the others, more refined, his accent heavy, but his diction was perfect. "Who are you?"

"That is unimportant."

"You could be a cop on the take with the dealers, for all I know." Though that seemed kind of obvious right now.

"I am not, let me assure you."

"It doesn't." She rose and moved to the room's only window. There were no two-way mirrors, one window, one exit. She peered out the window, judging the distance to the ground, then inspected the sill. Painted shut.

"Sit down."

"I've been sitting for two days. Give me a phone. I'll call the U.S. consulate and get out of your hair." She had to get out of here *now*.

"They will not get involved."

"Guess again."

"They do not know you are in this country."

She looked at him. Why would he say that? The U.S. consulate couldn't keep track of every U.S. citizen on foreign soil.

"You could die and none would find you."

"Is that a threat?"

"Tell me the truth!" He left the chair so quickly it shot back and hit the wall. "What are you doing there? What did you see?"

"Nothing!"

"Why have you come without escort?"

"I did, you killed him!"

His rage gave his eyes a demon glow, and she was thinking up some juicy lie when he backhanded her across the face. Clancy reeled with the impact, hitting the wall, her face exploding in hot pain.

Her eyes watered and she worked her jaw. "That's not going to get you anywhere." She spat blood at his feet.

"You cannot escape." He stepped close and she put her hands up.

"Okay, okay, no punching! Maybe we can work a deal."
She moved to him, her expression giving new meaning to the
words *Come on, honey, I'm yours.* "Just you and me."

He smiled as if she were the stupid kid in the class and
reached for her.

That's all she needed. She grabbed his wrist, dug her thumb
into the apex of his finger and thumb, and twisted hard, forcing his arm and elbow backward. He reached for her, for the
chair, but Clancy threw her weight into it, lowering him toward the floor. Then she slammed her knee into the side of his
head. He dropped like a stone. Clancy stepped back.

"Now, *that's* what I'm talking about," she muttered,
stunned it worked and warmed with her victory.

The pain in her kneecap burned up her thigh and she
rubbed, then quickly searched him for the cuff keys. It took a
second to get them off. She put them on him, hands behind
his back, then stole his gun and a fistful of bullets.

Grabbing her purse, she swept everything off the table and
inside, then dropped the tracking chip to the floor. She
crushed it under her heel. *Screw you, Cook.*

Richora stirred, pushed up, and she kicked him in the
head. He flattened to the floor and Clancy gripped her bag
and looked around. *Now what, smart-ass?*

The window was painted shut, and there was one door
with another ten *policia* on the other side.

Choufani moved through the blackened remains. What
once stood eight wood crates high, now barely covered his
boots. He squatted, pulling a pencil from inside his jacket to
flick at the evidence. The piles of crates had exploded up and
down into the floor. The gulley around him was more than
twenty feet wide. What could have done this? A large bomb,
certainly, but the depth and width of the explosion told him
it was high-magnitude explosives. Yet everything was right
where it had been, except contained. No real scatter, but the
bodies were in pieces and shriveled.

Choufani dug, moving charred wood and burned rifle stocks. That wasn't all that was in here, he knew. But this was all he'd been allowed to see. The group had not trusted him enough, but there had been more than small arms in the crates.

In the black debris soggy from firemen's hoses, from the rain that had graciously fallen since the explosion—he found something angular. He started digging with his hands, the black muck climbing up his arms. He loosened the object, frowning at the long slightly curved piece that was practically untouched by the flames. Black and dense, it was as if it had melted. He tapped it on his watchband. Solid plastic? Not resin, nor steel. So then, what was it?

He lifted his gaze from the sooty block to the warehouse. Jail for arms was a great deal less . . . uncomfortable than for acts of terrorism. Even in Libya, they had strict ruling over crimes. If it were not so, Muammar Abu Minyar al-Qadhafi would not be in power. But was it worth dying for? Your beliefs, your country, yes, but keeping secret a cache of arms? They could be had across the border for a price. In Libya, an AK-47 went hand in hand with the rising of the sun.

In Tunisia, not so, Choufani thought.

But the dead had taken their intended target with them. Destroying their weapons rather than be taken alive. Unfortunately, this was not the first shipment.

He straightened and went to the forensic table, pieces of evidence bagged and logged. Broken jaws of teeth, a charred hand. He knew these men, and others like them. He had prayed four times a day as they did. For Choufani, they had achieved their goal.

To make the world see Islam *their* way.

Clancy had no way out and minutes before someone came in here and saw that she'd beaned the big *jefe*. She struggled to open the window, and sunlight blinked off her diamond ring, a hawking big thing she'd had redesigned after her marriage ended. It was worth too much to be pissy and toss in the Potomac, and she hoped Steven was still paying on it. Quickly, she worked it off, then pressed the edge hard to the glass, running it the circumference of the window a couple of times. It did nothing. *Rats.* She tried once more, harder, then tapped the glass lightly. Her eyes widened as it tipped outward. *Oh my God.* She caught it before it fell and pulled it inside.

Holding her ring in her teeth, she set the glass down, then pulled a chair close. She stuck her head out the window. The area was empty. She didn't trust it. Putting the ring back on, she lowered her bag out the window. The gun made a heavy *thunk* when it hit the ground. Her gaze lit on the entrances to the courtyard. One at a side gate and another at the front. Side, she thought and climbed out, dropped to the ground, then slung the bag over her shoulder and under her arm.

She ducked low, running like a duck toward the gate to avoid being seen through another window. She met the edge and stopped, flattened to the wall. There were two men smoking at the front under the shade, piles of trash and old typewriters in the back. The gate was about forty feet ahead of her. She didn't know if it was locked or not, and studied it for a second. *Man, that's high.*

Then she heard shouts. *Oh, crap. Time's up.* She bolted for the gate. It was locked, and she worked her hand through the bars to the other side and tried opening it. Not locked, but so old it was rusted in place. The pound of footsteps thumped behind her, shouts to surround the area.

*Please, Goddess of the stupid people, don't let me die here.*

She ran back toward the building. Then as fast as she could, she took off, leaped at the scroll ironwork, pulling herself up. They were right behind her, and as she swung her leg over, someone fired.

The bullet hit the stucco wall, chipping away a large chunk near her butt. *Oh, jeez.*

She threw herself off and fell to the ground so fast she didn't have time to get her legs out in front of her. She landed on her side, and for a moment was stunned. The voices were closer, men trying to get over the wall or shoot through the gate. Clancy pushed up, got a knee under herself.

Then a pair of heavy hands slapped on her shoulders, grabbed tight, and dragged her into the jungle.

When the woman came flying over the gate, Mike couldn't have been more surprised—and disappointed. He'd expected to find his men. One, at least. She dropped to the ground, and he thought, *That's gonna leave a mark*. Then he heard the troops, the gunshots, and didn't think about his decision to help. But she fought him, landing a kick to his shin, and all he could do was drag her.

Out of sight, he gritted, "Stop fighting me, damn it."

Clancy turned wide eyes toward the voice. An American. Where did he come from?

He didn't give her the chance to ask, moving on long legs, pulling her with him, then paused long enough to toss her unceremoniously over his shoulder and grab something off the ground. Then he was off again, running hard, each jolt punching the air out of her lungs and making her want to puke down the back of his trousers.

"Stop," she choked. "Stop!"

He didn't.

So she cupped his rear and squeezed. He nearly stumbled. "Stop, damn it, please!" she hissed. "I can run."

Mike set her on her feet.

Clancy pushed hair from her eyes, then reached out when the world tilted. Her hand landed on his hard shoulder. "That was unnecessary. Nice butt, by the way."

"We have to move."

She met his gaze and thought, *He's huge*. "Who are you?"

"Help?"

"Yeah, well, I was doing okay, sorta."

"If you wanted a bullet in your head, sure. Get moving."

Clancy was about to bitch when she glanced back and through the trees, saw troops. She looked at him. All he did was arch a dark brow.

Great, big, handsome, *and* arrogant? "Lead the way."

He didn't wait for her, and Clancy struggled to keep up. For a big thing, he was agile, leaping chunks of ground while she raced over it.

"They took my jeep," she said into the silence.

He glared at her and thumped a finger to his lips. He waded into the water, his machete in his hand as he turned back for her. She held out her hand. He stared at it for a second and she wiggled her fingers, her expression pleading for help. He grabbed her hand, pulled her the last couple of feet to the shore. She smacked into him, her nose to his chest.

She met his gaze. *Thank you,* she mouthed exaggeratedly, and his lips curved. She had a feeling he didn't do that often. He turned away, kept the steady pace, and she thought, *Somewhere at the end of this better be a bed and a hot bath, and lots of room service.*

No such luck. Just more jungle.

Mike listened for her footsteps instead of looking behind himself. She barely made a sound. What the heck she was doing in jail was something he'd learn later. Right now, getting out of here was essential. He didn't want the notice and pissing off the *Federales* wasn't good any way you looked at it.

When he felt they'd lost the troops, he stopped. She slammed into his back. He twisted, grabbing her before she fell. She was winded, sweating, not unusual in this country, but she looked like a drowned cat. Wisely, he didn't say so.

"Okay, chief, you're gonna have to cut the pace a little." She bent over, her hands on her knees as she dragged in air.

"It was only a mile."

"At top speed when it's a hundred ten out here?" She tried to put some force in her words, but it just sounded like whining to Clancy. She hated whiners. "I run five miles, three times a week for years. But you . . . you'd clean up in the Olympics."

"Keep up or I leave you behind," he said coldly, then frowned at the GPS.

Cute and crabby, who knew? "Well, that would just ruin my day," she bit back.

His gaze flashed to hers. "You want to be a fugitive?"

"No, but I'm still wondering why they wouldn't let me contact the consulate."

"Maybe because the nearest one is in the capital."

"You're kidding."

His frown deepened. "Who arrested you?"

"Some *jefe* . . . Richora?" His features smoothed and Clancy said, "What?"

"You pissed off the wrong guy, lady. He's corrupt as hell."

She'd figured that out easy enough. "Abusive, too."

Mike just noticed her swollen lip. "Richora won't let this go. This is his jungle."

Clancy didn't need an explanation. He owned the people, not the land. Richora ruled, and she didn't doubt that the smugglers who took her jeep handed it right over to him.

His gaze moved over her slowly and she felt, well . . . so thoroughly undressed she looked down to see if her clothes had suddenly melted off.

"If they search you, what will they find?"

She cocked her hip. "Tits, ass, and a gun."

Both brows shot up this time.

"What could I be hiding? They killed Fuad, took my jeep, and have my good panties and makeup." She wanted to shout, to really let it loose, but that was just plain stupid. But whispering at him like a madwoman wasn't helping her case either.

Mike grabbed her bag, and since it was still looped around her, the motion pulled her close. He dug in it.

"All you had to do was ask," she said, yet understood this man didn't ask for anything.

Mike fished and found what he was looking for. He opened her passport. "Grace Murray?"

"Here, teacher." She grabbed for it.

He held it away, then found her wallet. It was empty except for some cash and a credit card. "No other ID? Who are you?"

Clancy just tipped her chin up, refusing to answer, and for a moment she thought he'd given up till he pulled her close and ran his hands firmly over her body. A little gasp escaped when his hand smoothed between her legs, then up the back of her thighs.

"Shouldn't we date before you get this familiar?"

Mike ignored the sound of her voice, but this close, her words skipped down his spine. His hand slid over her tight little rear, and his look went as dark as the ocean floor.

"Interesting hiding place."

His big hand dove down the back of her slacks and pulled out the passport. Inside it was her Virginia driver's license. He took a step back, examining it, and then only his gaze shifted. "So, Clancy, Moira McRae, why two passports? CIA?"

"You know, that's the second time someone's asked me that. What is this area, spy central?"

"Other than intel operatives, people who are dealing in illegal contraband need more than one passport."

"I'm neither."

He studied both, then waved one. "This is the fake."

She grabbed them back. "How did you know?" And did Phil screw it up on purpose?

"I just do." He inspected her gun, checking the ammo. "Can you even fire this?"

She took it back. "Yes, I can, and lay the hell off." She cocked the slide and pushed it down behind her back. "I'm not your problem."

"You are right now." He grasped her arm. "We're going to do this the hard way." He forced her ahead, sticking right behind her, then in front, leading her God knew where. She didn't trust him. He was *here,* a little too convenient and the whole passport thing was surreal. A merc, she thought as he walked faster to the right.

She stopped in her tracks when she saw the bodies. One in the water, two on the bank. "Did you do that?"

"A sniper did." Mike stilled, a chill of caution tightening the back of his neck. The crates were gone, not even a piece of the contents left behind.

"And where was he?"

"That's a thing about snipers, if you see them, they've failed." He waded into the water after a flatboat.

Clancy couldn't take her eyes off the young man floating facedown. She'd seen dead bodies, many times, but something chilled over her when he pushed the corpse aside to get to the boat.

"Move it, they're still coming."

She looked back, frowning. She didn't see or hear anything.

"I can smell them."

"Whoa. How's my perfume, then?"

"Like a dirty jail."

"A man with no tact, how novel."

He scoffed. "Clam up and get in."

She obeyed, only because she didn't have any other option, she told herself. She needed to get back on track, and that was far away from whatever he was doing in the jungle around dead bodies.

He let the boat float while he went to a thin tall tree, pulled a knife from behind his back, and chopped. It sliced through the tree in record time, and as he waded to the boat, he cut off the branches. Then he stabbed holes in the second boat, but it didn't sink.

In the craft, his feet wide apart, he pushed them off the bank.

"Who are you?"

"Mike."

"Just Mike?"

"All you need."

He was scaring her. He let the boat slide over the water for a few yards as he worked off the khaki shirt. Muscles rippled inside a black T-shirt as he pushed the pole into the water.

"We'll get to a town first." When she started to question, he cut in. "I'm dropping you in the safest place I can find. End of story." The sooner the better. The longer it took to find the UAV, his men, and the Hellfires, the bigger the chance they were long gone or dead. A long to-do list, he thought, and he couldn't do shit with her along.

"Fine with me." She had places to go, people to find. She looked back and her eyes flew wide. "Troops!"

Before she could draw her weapon, he swung around, aiming his.

Clancy's gaze filled with the sight of him. How fast he moved, how comfortable he looked with that weapon.

"How's your aim?"

"Marksman." But that was when she was young and stupid and really wanted to point a loaded weapon at a homicidal maniac.

His sideways glance said he wasn't expecting that. "Good. Get ready to fire." He pushed his weapon in his waistband.

He was going to make her defend them? "Oh shit." Clancy aimed, the gun heavy as her gaze slipped over the bank. She tried remembering everything about her training as footsteps pounded the ground with orders in Spanish to "kill the woman." Richora was being really pissy about a little bump on the head.

Mike pushed the pole into the water, swiftly sailing them down the stream. The troops appeared, and a hail of bullets hit the water near the boat.

"Fire back, woman!"

Clancy pulled the trigger. Her aim was dead-on.

# five

Colonel Carl Cook laid down the phone and spun in his chair. The view outside the window was anything but interesting. More buildings housing laboratories and a hospital near the street side.

She'd found the tracking chip. It was necessary, though opposed to by many on the medical board. Yet considering the top-secret value of the projects and the high price tag, he felt that monitoring his people was necessary. Especially those with a class-A clearance.

To Carl, proof came when she slipped past the surveillance team tailing her. Why she went to a junky in a paraphernalia shop was inconsequential; by the time they reached the shop, she was gone and the owner was too doped up to be much help.

Yet now McRae would be more difficult to locate. He'd known she was in South America since she'd hopped off the cruise ship. But that she was there now told him she knew far more than her pay grade allowed. How she'd learned it was a mystery and meaningless now. But she did know about the human candidates. For a brief moment, Carl suspected Francine of giving her the information, but he'd no evidence to back that up. Besides, Francine was looking for a promotion from this and the credit for the creation. McRae had given that up. Francine had not.

He never considered informing his superiors. They didn't put him in the position to come crying at the first sign of trouble. All else was going well. The test subjects were in cages, and although someone would retrieve the men, if they were still alive, it was already clear the technology could be accepted into human implantation.

That was all he needed to further the study to help troops in the field.

His concern was Clancy McRae. She was a righteous woman, making her feelings on rushing the testing clear to all who were authorized. Her sudden disappearance, though, gave Carl the opportunity to set things back on track.

Permanently.

Boris was alive and untouched by a scalpel.

Francine had plans for him that Clancy wouldn't consider, or approve; the reason she was kept out of the loop. She felt lousy about lying to her friend, but orders were orders—and Clancy was a bona fide rebel when she had a cause.

The government wanted results, and Francine was ready to oblige.

Francine stared at the orangutan, walking slowly near the habitat. He didn't reach for her, didn't shake the bars, only tilted his head, looking more human than primate.

Clancy was right. It was the perfume.

She held out the steel ball, and through the bars, Boris took it. Gripped in his big hand, he crushed the metal like a soda can. The orangutan let it crash to the floor.

"Good boy." Even if he didn't understand the sign language Francine had used to communicate with the creature, he could tell by her tone that she was pleased. He postured for a bit and she offered him a treat. He ate the fruit whole, reaching for more. She obliged.

"Appetite substantially increased," she said into the Palm Pilot recording her notes. He'd already consumed his daily diet and took his meal up into the trees of the large cage that stretched the length of a warehouse. While titanium bars separated them, with a glass wall that slid over that, he had room to move from one branch to another inside the habitat painstakingly re-created with hydroponically grown fruit trees and bamboo to resemble his Borneo home. Though he'd never seen Southeast Asia. Boris had been bred for research. For neuroscience, he was perfect, his genetic match 90 percent to humans, yet differences in brain size and intellect were in thyroid and steroid hormones. Inject him with enough and his genome was nearly 100 percent. That didn't increase his brain activity; the pod did.

Getting him to do the testing wasn't hard. His mental ability had increased as well as his appetite. The realization that the pod worked this well made her almost giddy with excitement.

"Begin the game, Boris." He just stared at her. "Initiate the game," she said and still he did nothing. How did Clancy phrase it? "Let's play with the toys," she said.

Boris climbed down the tree and went to the puzzle. He looked at the empty chair, and Francine knew that Clancy sat close to him and they competed with putting the puzzle together. She repeated the command. He sat in a chair like a human, and stared at the table. The surface was thick with shapes routered out of the wood, beside it a stack of wooden shapes that fit into the molds. Francine frowned when the orangutan gathered up the shapes to his chest. *He's going to throw them*, she thought, but he studied the molds, then one by one, started putting the pieces into the slots.

He didn't once look at the pieces to see if he had the correct one, and put them in the right cutout without having to adjust. She glanced to be certain the camera was still running. This was spectacular. Despite being bred for research, he was still a wild animal and sedated often, but his increased intelligence overshadowed his calm.

She praised him, offering this time a piece of chocolate. Clancy had rewarded him with it, and she hoped it endeared the orangutan to her. But he didn't touch the chocolate and made a deep hoo-hoo sound, as if asking where Clancy was. She offered the chocolate again, but he just nudged it back out of the cage.

"Fine, fine. I know you miss her." Damn it.

Boris leaped, brachiating from tree to tree and stopping in the tops some thirty feet high. She could barely see him if not for his reddish hair. He let out a long call, a series of sounds followed by a bellow that made her skin chill. Its meaning could be anything from calling to a female, to warning males off his territory, or staking his claim to the territory. He'd done that several times since she'd taken him from the main testing lab.

Francine went to the console and keyed open a portion of the retracting wall inside the cage. The wall slid back like a pocket door, and a computer screen and simple keyboard slid out, the screen coming on. He made a loud noise and slowly descended, curious and hunched, his knuckles scraping the dirt floor. He looked at her, snubbed the air, drawing his lips back and showing large incisor teeth. She remembered those claw hands reaching for her, and quickly she keyed the program, then edged back to watch. If the nanopod was really doing its job, he should be able to do the next test without trouble.

She was bending to pick up the chocolate when she heard the locks click. She turned as the door swooshed open. Colonel Cook strode in and her heart did a little trip. He really was a dashing man, she thought. Tall, erect posture, he had just a touch of silver in his dark brown hair. He was never without his uniform—well, almost never, she thought, smiling.

"Have you found her?"

"You asked me that this morning. Don't you think I would have said something?"

"I never know with you."

"Yes, you do," he said and she moved toward him, tossing the data sheets on the table, then was against him, kissing him wildly. When she pulled back, her hand slid down the front of his trousers, molding his quick erection. All she did was arch a brow and smile as he trembled. She loved power over powerful men.

"The camera is on," he said, exhaling through clenched teeth.

"It's not panning here, only the cage."

He glanced to make certain. "How is he progressing?"

"His skills and strength have increased measurably."

"Then he can break that cage."

"It's titanium, Carl, and he's been calm for days." Almost sad, she thought, annoyed that he was so attached to Clancy.

The computer chimed, and Francine whipped around, looking from the orangutan to her screen. It showed his attempts to complete the matching puzzle. "Oh my God." She hurried across the room.

Cook moved to her side. "What's that?" He gestured to the screen and leaned over. In the corner it said *Trials initiated*. Beside it was the ratio.

"He did it all."

"All what?" Carl asked.

"All of the program, in ten minutes. He completed the whole thing."

"Certainly, he's done the test before."

"No, not this one." She told him about the primate doing the shape test without stopping and was keying up another level. "I tried another, a new one Clancy had just created for him. Look at his score."

In the lower right corner red numbers blinked: 100/100.

"My God. Watch him, Carl, watch."

The animal stared at the screen, watching the instructions, which were simple patterns like the last one, but this was a rudimentary human IQ test. After a moment, the orangutan lifted one finger and started tapping keys.

"Increase his steroid injections," Cook ordered. That test was proof enough.

While Francine was smiling like a parent at a piano recital, Carl was scowling. "This stays with you and me," he said and she looked at him, frowning. "No more interns, no assistants."

"There's Clancy." He shook his head. She recognized the look and what it meant. "Oh no, Carl. You can't cut her out, she created it." When he just stared, her skin went pasty as she understood. "You can't be serious."

"I am and you're either with me or not."

She looked at Boris. "I'm in."

Carl kissed her cheek and thought, this was going to be big. And now McRae was a true liability.

Richora rushed to the other boat, climbing in and grabbing an oar from the bottom. He ordered two men to join him and they were barely inside when he pushed off. His gaze was on the pair moving past the slight curve of the stream, and he hurried to catch up.

"Shoot them!" he ordered and they fired without true aim.

The woman was low in the boat, taking her time and then firing. The bullet hit the side of his boat, passed through, and hit his soldier. The man screamed, sharp and abrupt, and Richora reached to check the wound, and realized his sister's son was dead. *I'll torture the little bitch for this.* And for what she'd seen, if anything. Then she fired again, wounding another, the impact sending a man rolling in pain in the bottom of the boat. Richora looked between the female and his troop, weighing his options. Then he ordered his men to row faster.

Mike pushed the pole into the water, but it was useless. It was like stirring soup and he grasped an oar, digging in hard. "Good shot, McRae."

She just waved a hand over her head.

Mike felt a twinge, something he didn't want to examine,

when she pressed her head to the rim of the boat. Shooting was easy for him, always cut-and-dry. But she'd done the job. He admired that push-comes-to-shove attitude in a woman, though he'd met a few who were far more ruthless. His gaze traveled over her dark reddish hair, choppy and wildly layered. She was a little thing, pixie compact, with beautifully expressive whiskey-brown eyes. His hands almost itched with the memory of her tight, firm shape under his palms. He wouldn't mind exploring it a little more.

He dragged his gaze from her to the terrain, shoring up his guard. No involvement with civilians, ever. *Ditch her and get on with the mission.* "Don't relax your guard."

"Relax? I just shot a man."

"Two, but who's counting?" She looked at him, horrified, and he regretted his bluntness. "Keep your hands out of the water. This is piranha country."

Clancy jerked back from the edge, staring at the water for a second.

His gaze flicked to the shore, into the trees. "We're too out in the open."

The boat suddenly shifted, moving faster and to her right. She looked around and spotted the bow of the other boat.

"Shouldn't he be sinking by now?" she said, aiming.

"He should. Never mind shooting. Get an oar." The water boiled hard beneath the boat as the river widened, and Clancy rowed.

"Right, go right." He was steering backward, watching Richora's approach. They neared a sharp bend. "Time to get the hell outta here, Clancy. Stand up."

She did, rocking the boat.

"Get ready to jump on my back."

"We're in the middle of open water." With *things* in it.

"Not for long." He gave the long oar a hard shove, moving the gondola-like boat into the dark overhang of trees. "Grab on."

Clancy hopped on his back a moment before he reached

and caught a thick branch. Vines choked the gnarled twisted trees and Mike did a chin-up, his feet leaving the craft. The boat sailed down the river without them.

She clung to his big shoulders, her legs around his waist. "I really don't see how this is better."

"Give me a minute. I'm just glad you're a lightweight," he grunted.

They dangled over the water, creatures slithering into the stream and heading toward the offer of fresh meat as Mike inched along the branch. It started to crack.

"Grab the branch, my left!"

Clancy reached, the limb so broad her hands scarcely wrapped it.

"Can you hold on?" Her legs were still wrapping his waist.

"If my choice is being piranha entrée? I think I'll manage."

Beneath her, small broad fish stirred the water as if scenting a meal. Mike swung himself and hooked his legs on the branch. Then hanging by his legs, he reached for her, helping her get a better handhold, then a foothold at the trunk of the tree.

She let out a breath and he grabbed her bag, pushing it into the foliage. He shushed her. They held still as seconds later, Richora's boat slid over the glassy water. Right past them. They waited till he was downstream a bit, then Mike moved painfully slow to avoid shaking the trees. Clancy was closer to the trunk and started inching her way to the center. Then they heard gunshots, panicked voices laced with curses. Richora was sinking.

Mike winked at her. "Timing's a little off, but good enough."

She smiled and gripped the trunk of the tree like a favored doll. Mike worked his way toward her, his size not giving him many options. Then he was in the branches with her.

"Now what?"

"To shore."

She looked at the ground. Several feet below, it was a

soggy, watery mess and several yards to higher ground. She hoped the baggies in her boots were still sealed. "You didn't think of this before now?"

"Nope, and not of him either."

She whipped to the right. A caiman, an Amazon alligator, slid into the water on the other side of the stream.

"I can't shoot it or all this daring will be for nothing."

Give away their position, she realized. "I get it, but if that thing starts chewing on my butt I expect you to wrestle him to the death."

"It would be my honor to save that behind from such a fate."

"And people call me a smart-ass."

He instructed her to the point that she looked up at him with sarcasm written all over her pixie face.

"Ya know, if I look like a complete moron, tell me, because then I probably need to rethink my hairdo."

His brows shot up, a sexy little smile curving his lips. "Message received, ma'am. Have at it."

Clancy concentrated, every muscle tense as she worked toward the ground, her gaze flicking to the gator floating in the water a few yards away. *Stay there,* she thought. *I'll taste really bad.* When her feet touched the ground, she pulled her purse in front of herself and walked carefully across the soggy earth, wading through the knee-deep finger stream. It wasn't easy, thick with algae-covered vines and water plants that clung to her pants and ankles as she passed, snagging her. Her feet sank deeper into the muddy bottom, and she tried pulling free and got tangled worse. Mike was there, slicing at the vines with his big-ass knife, then taking her with him to higher ground.

He didn't let her catch a breath. "Keep going, the gator wants to visit."

They ran, pushing at the underbrush, water flowing from her clothes and feeling like worms on her skin.

"Personally I would have taken a road, but the end justifies the means?"

"Most times." Mike had been forced to live with that. He didn't want to think about the times he'd killed several to get a few. "There should be a village up here."

The terrain rose steeply and Clancy's thighs ached as she tried to keep up with him. "Village? I've been in a village. I want a town with a hotel and some room service." She was whining, hating it, and really missed that cruise ship right now.

"Come on, McRae, no muttering in the ranks."

Definite military, she thought and really wasn't paying attention to where she was going and plowed into his back. He pulled her down to the ground with him and pointed. Ahead, the forest thinned out, sunlight penetrating the trees and showering on a little village. It wasn't even a village, really, just a couple of wood homes that a good rainstorm would wash away.

"Oh God. That's my jeep." It was parked on the edge of the shacks.

"It's a rental?"

"No, I bought it."

He frowned.

"It was actually cheaper." Her brows drew tight. "Fuad, my guide, betrayed me to them. Tried to ransom me or something." She shrugged, still clueless. "That guy in the jeans, he's the one who took the jeep. Before someone shot Fuad in the head. The little weasel."

"I think you stepped into something you shouldn't have," he said, staring at the long-haired man in dirty jeans, then looked at her. "He's probably Richora's man." Which meant he was in on the arms or drugs trafficking. "What happened that he was so hot to jail you?"

"To experience more of my sparkling personality?"

Mike grinned. She was adorable.

"Nothing really, they blindfolded me. Then Richora busted onto the scene." She told him what happened, leaving out the detail of the tracking chip. That still pissed her off, but giving him too much information wouldn't be smart. "In jail he kept asking me what I'd seen. Which was nothing."

Ransom. It happened a lot here, so much that people had kidnapping insurance. The men took her for another reason, Mike decided, but Richora didn't like it. Mike didn't have time or reason to look into Richora's operation, but an officer on the take wasn't going to make the government happy since they'd expended half their treasury to try to stop the drug trade inside their own borders.

Mike's gaze moved rapidly around the village, the jeep, the position of the men in the camp. "You have the keys?"

"They took them, but . . ." She searched her bag. "The spare was under the wheel hub, and I thought with all the mud and debris on the roads I'd lose it." She held it up like a trophy.

"Excellent. Hold on to it. Stay hidden, I'll be a couple minutes."

He started to move away and she caught his arm. "Where are you going?"

He smiled and the excitement in his eyes hit her like a punch to her heart. "Trust me."

Before she could say anything, he was gone, melting into the forest. She strained to see him, but it was impossible and she hunched down lower for the longest five minutes of her life. Getting any information on the troops around here was a bust, and she tried to think of a way to regain the ground she lost. Nothing came to mind. Suddenly her skin rippled with awareness and her head snapped to the right. Mike moved in as quietly as he'd left.

He had a funny smile on his face. "Ready to blow this town?" She nodded. "When I signal, run to the jeep." He held a small disposable phone, and hit a button. A second later, the ground on the other side of the village exploded.

"Jesus, Mike, you could hurt someone."

His glance was bitter. "I checked. Nothing there except piles of garbage."

Even before he finished speaking, the sky rained with rotten food and fish guts. Together, they ran toward the jeep, and climbed in. She slapped the key in his hand and he turned over the engine.

"Crap, hardly any gas."

"Who cares! Drive. We're getting noticed." Two men shouted, aiming machine guns at them as Mike threw the jeep into reverse and hit the gas.

"Mike!" She drew her gun.

"Shoot something!"

Clancy fired at their feet, the noise making her ears ring. The men danced back as Mike swerved the jeep, but the guys recovered and sprayed them with bullets. Clancy heard them hit the back of the vehicle.

"When you said blow this town, I didn't think you meant *blow* this town!" She held on to the roll bar as the jeep jolted over the uneven road.

"Never pass up an opportunity to mystify a woman," he said.

"We're both pissing off the wrong people." She needed to get lost fast and looked behind. "No one's coming, yet."

Mike didn't slow down, and kept checking in the mirrors.

"I don't know whether to thank you or bean you."

He just glanced at her, offering a small smile.

"What were you doing in the jungle anyway?" she asked.

"Archaeology on a recent site."

*What a crock.* "Well, now that we've both established we're liars, what's your sign?"

He scoffed a laugh, but didn't comment, and tried working off the rucksack. Clancy helped him. She was still for a moment, tempted to look inside, but he noticed.

"Don't even."

She made a face and pushed it between the seat to the rear. "They'll be chasing us for a long time."

"We'll be gone."

"I don't think that will matter." Mike glanced to the side and she tossed a thumb to the backseat. "We just became drug smugglers." There were several well-packaged blocks of something in the rear.

Mike looked. "Fuck."

"Fitting, since we're screwed."

"We have to ditch that."

"And you don't think they'll come looking for this jeep, me, and the stash?" She scoffed, then glanced at the kilos of drugs, thinking Phil would have an orgasm over that. "We have to leave the jeep, just as it is."

"That would be possible if they weren't there." He nodded and Clancy saw the line of federal police, Richora in the road. Soaked to the bone and steaming mad.

"This guy is so screwing with my chi."

Dr. Eduardo Valez watched the machine sweep over the urn several times and thought archaeology had progressed a great deal. The scans would give him slivers of the urn and its contents without breaking the seal. While his colleagues wanted to push ahead to open it, Eduardo wasn't as eager to ruin the find just yet. Carbon dating put it pre-Inca, 450 B.C. A group of graduate students had copied the etchings on the urn by photo and hand, and were just beginning the painstaking process of accurately deciphering them. It had become a teaching tool, since Eduardo understood the iconology that depicted the fierce Moche warriors who were equal to the gods.

A complete contradiction to their beliefs.

He looked at the screen as the images blinked up, each one the same, except for the design on the urn itself and the gold and wax seal. It was real gold, of course, and despite its age and purity, it was nearly perfectly intact. The room was kept chilled to preserve the seal, but other than that, the urn was nearly flawless.

The Moche didn't have a written language. Only pictographs on pottery and cave walls. They did have numbers, deduced from the grouped sets of artifacts found in tombs. But these icon etchings were neatly formed and spaced, yet ones he'd never seen before in his thirty years of archaeology. Deciphering them would be a challenge, yet the gold and waxlike seal was highly unusual for a simple jar, and bespoke of something precious. Or something deadly.

Either way, it was a warning he would heed.

The surgeon removed the bandages slowly.

Nuat Salache felt the drugs lace through his bloodstream and soften his body. He didn't fear pain but he suspected the doctor feared him. He felt the wrappings lift off his skin, his eyes closed. He was alone, his preference at this moment. No one saw the results before him. Yet when the cool air-conditioned air spread over his warm skin, he felt the anticipation come alive in him.

The doctor did not speak. He knew the routine by now.

For weeks, he'd worn the silken mask of gauze. It was replaced daily, and between stitches removal and cream treatments, no one, not even himself, would see the final result. This was his sixth surgery in four years. The doctors had warned him that he could take no more, but Salache knew better. Improvement was always to be had somewhere. He simply found a surgeon willing to do the work.

When the last of the cloths were removed and all that remained was the final thin hood, the doctor stepped back.

"I will leave you now."

Salache nodded and waited till he heard the door close. Behind the thin veil of gauze, he opened his eyes, making certain he was alone. Salache pushed the button on the reclining chair, and it brought him upright with a slow hum. He grasped the silver-handled mirror and lifted it, then pulled the remaining fabric from his face. For a moment he recognized nothing of the man in the mirror. Perfect.

He inspected and studied the face in the mirror. The reflection showed a handsome man, a dignified nose instead of the bulbous one birth had given him. A square strong jaw instead of the pointed receding jaw that had made him so horribly ugly that people turned away. No one had listened to the man he was, no one respected his innovations, his ideas.

He smiled slowly, perfectly aligned teeth flashing in the space where crooked and broken ones once mangled his smile.

This was only one portion of his new life. He was a visionary, and had already achieved what others had dismissed as impossible. As madness. The true achievement was that no one knew. No one. And this new face would keep it secret for as long as he needed. To the time of his choosing. To let loose the deadly repercussions on those who treated him as worthless.

# Six

"Give me one of those things."

Clancy offered the kilo, and Mike put it on his lap, then pulled a knife from inside his boot.

She flinched when the blade popped out and said, "Don't cut that!"

He stabbed the kilo. White powder puffed in the air.

"Oh, jeez." She covered her mouth and nose, and he held it out the window, then shook it on the ground. "He's *already* pissed!"

"Hold on." He hit the gas, speeding toward Richora.

*Oh my God.* Clancy braced for impact. Bullets hit the jeep and cracked the windshield. Mike dropped the kilo to punch the glass and Clancy covered her face as the wind blew glass back inside. He was either the most clever man on earth or the craziest.

"Toss it out. The dope, toss it out as we get close, but save me a couple."

She plopped a kilo on his lap, then pitched the others out the window. The men scrambled to retrieve them and Mike headed toward Richora standing in the middle of the road, defiant, aiming a big gun.

Clancy's eyes widened and she thought one of those bullets was going to hit them or the engine. Then one did, the jeep's engine smoking and filling the air around them. She coughed and choked on oily black smoke, and Mike cut the kilo on his lap, this time nearly in half. He never let up on the gas, the damaged engine grinding as he headed right for Richora. The man refused to move, almost daring them to hit him.

"He's insane!"

"That makes it easy." Mike never stopped and leaned long out the window and threw hard. The kilo shot through the air like a football, spilling chalky dust. Around him, men scattered, some getting hit with pure drugs and falling instantly to their knees, but Richora saw it coming and bolted.

"It was a good try."

"Yeah, damn it. Stay low."

He gunned it, the black smoke of burning rubber boiling through any space in the jeep, and Clancy bent over as gunfire plinked on the jeep's metal shell. Flames burst through the dash and he slammed on the brakes.

"Bug out!" He grabbed his pack and bailed.

Clancy leaped, hitting the ground for the second time today. The pain was the same, ripping up her shoulder. Mike rolled into a ditch, then was up, looking for Clancy, and found her on the side of the dirt road. He hurried to her, pulling her from the ground. They ran, veering off the road to another. Mike paused for a moment, listened, then pushed farther. The forest thinned and he moved laterally. They hit a barrier.

Traffic. Everywhere, buses and cars, horns beeping. People walked on the side of the road. It was all at a standstill. Mike urged her along.

"Too fast, slow down, damn it."

He didn't. "We need to keep going."

She didn't look back, but when he pressured her in another direction, she put on the brakes. "Wait a second, why are we going this way? What is this?"

"A random checkpoint."

"Are we crossing the border?"

Mike frowned at her. "Sorry to break it to you, but we're thirty miles from the border. We're in Peru."

Clancy's gaze shot to the kiosk, the line of people passing through. The only reason they weren't spotted was the crowd of people sitting on their cars while they waited in line. Some had radios going, and kicky Latin music filled the air. Kids sat on the ground playing games, still close to wary parents. They kept walking and she glanced back and saw the sign behind and to the left. It hung over the road. Forty kilometers to Ecuador.

They'd manage to slip around the first sentry.

"Oh, hell, we crossed the border without a passport check."

"So you *do* get it." Mike walked briskly along the edge of the road.

"We can't go back." Richora would be looking, and far away from him was a good thing.

"Looks that way." It didn't make a difference to Mike. He'd planned to cross the border, just not right now.

Clancy felt him fidgeting. "Mike?"

"Smile, laugh, just don't look confused and scared."

She plastered on a smile, and Mike used her body to block whatever he was doing as they headed to the final checkpoint.

"The only way we won't get arrested is if we don't pass this checkpoint."

She inhaled when he touched her bare spine.

"Are we dating now? Because I'm really expecting dinner first."

Mike smiled, enjoying her dry sense of humor. "Want to get caught with a weapon?"

"Oh God." Clancy felt the gun slip free, then his body tense against her side as he threw it. It shot like a bullet into the forest and she breathed in relief as they walked straight to the border officer to show their passports. Mike dropped his passport, and when he picked it up Clancy realized he used the moment to look behind them. But his expression didn't give her an answer.

One shout from Richora and it would be over. He kept her close in front of him. "Give them the real one," he said in her ear, "and try to behave like a tourist."

Clancy smiled up at him. "Honey, think we can make a trip to Machu Pichu?" She poured on a twangy southern accent that made him cringe.

"Jesus," he muttered, then glanced back to see Richora pulling up in a four-by-four truck. Damn. He looked a little doped up, but clearly giving orders.

Mike nudged Clancy, and she spotted him. Then to avoid notice, she instantly turned toward the person in front of her and introduced herself. He was German, young and blond, looking like a cast-off from a youth hostel. She kept the conversation going, asking him questions about what he'd done and seen. People liked to talk about themselves, and he was no exception.

They approached the final guard. He studied their faces and passports for a couple of seconds, then handed them back. She sagged against him till they were far enough away, beyond to a grouping of tour buses.

Clancy slowed her breathing as she ran her fingers through her hair, pulling bits of leaves, then did her best to look presentable. There wasn't much to work with. She held out her shaking hands, flexed her fingers, then shoved them into her pockets.

*I was better at this when I was a kid*. Fearless.

She looked at Mike. "It's been real. This is where I'll get out of your hair." As much as hanging around with him was a wild ride, she had to ditch him. She didn't want him asking more questions, and Clancy had a feeling Mike was a bit of a buttinski.

Mike scrubbed his hand over his head, his lips quirking.

He was about to say the same thing and his gaze slid to the busload of tourists. Safer in numbers, he thought. He couldn't be near her. He had a job to do and a short time to do it.

"If luck holds, Richora won't look too hard. It's not a Communist blockade. People pass these borders all the time without seeing a soul."

"Only if he can explain away a body and kidnapping. Of course, there were no witnesses, not any who'd testify, if it ever went that far." Richora killed her guide just for bringing her into his business. Her life would be meaningless. It was a scary thing to know.

Mike listened to her rattle on, talking more to herself than him.

"I guess my one advantage was I was hooded and didn't witness anything."

Mike's look said that wouldn't matter much.

Behind them, people boarded the bus and Clancy stopped the German. "Save me a seat, will you, Gus?"

The young man looked between them, frowning a bit, then nodded and climbed the bus steps.

"Gus?"

She shrugged. "Gustave something or other. He's been traveling for weeks, rather talkative for a guy."

Mike pulled her away from earshot and jotted something on a slip of paper, then slipped it into her bag. "If you're in trouble." Though he shouldn't care, or get involved, this little Irish thing wasn't a woman he could forget easily.

"I'd feel better with the gun. We're both unarmed."

His gaze traveled down her body. "I wouldn't say that."

She laughed, tension sliding from her body. "Oh, Mike, whoever you are, you're something else. Thank you."

"You're welcome." Though he probably just made it worse for her.

She held out her hand for a shake.

Mike's gaze flicked to it, then zeroed in on her pretty eyes.

"We've exchanged gunfire together, I think a kiss is in order."
Her lush mouth looked made for it and was already driving
him crazy for a taste.

She blinked, grinning. "So you *ask?* If you were really
heroic you'd just sweep me—"

He was there, his arms around her, his mouth on hers, and
Clancy felt the hot explosion inside her, her skin tightened on
her bones. His mouth slid wondrously over hers, and she
gripped his big shoulders, felt him bend her slightly back and
mesh his hips to hers. *Oh God, this is a real man kiss,* she
thought. Nothing like her ex or the geeks she'd dated since.
Nothing.

He was huge and muscular, and for a guy who pulled a
trigger easily, she felt almost fragile in his arms, his kiss tender, as if waiting for her to give him more. And she did, deep-
ening it and savoring the hard feel of his—oh, man. Her
fingers swept up his chest and she moaned a plea for more.

And Mike gave it. Like a moment of insanity, he had to
have more, an eating kiss, his mouth trailing her throat, then
back to her lush lips. God, she tasted good, he thought, and
took ferociously with a hunger that shocked him and stole
his strength and half his brain cells. Then the lusty comments
from onlookers sank into his brain.

He drew back a fraction, breathing harder, and murmured
against her lips, "That works for me. Heroic enough for
you?"

"I feel your potential accelerating."

He laughed softly and the broad smile changed his face so
drastically, it made her giddy. "You can do that again." She
was very aware that he hadn't let her go yet.

"If I do, we might need a room and a very big bed." For a
long time, he thought.

That sent a bolt of electricity down her body, settling low
in her belly. "Oh, you wish," she said, shoving out of his
arms, yet it was a lousy protest. A couple of hours alone with

him would sure make up for a disgustingly long time without pure male contact. The naked, hard, and ready kind.

"That's all I got this week." He let her go, but not before he stole another quick bone-melting kiss. Then his expression changed, his brows drawing down. "Whatever you're doing here, don't."

She frowned for a second. "I could say the same to you. Archaeology, my ass."

He showed her a pack of tools in a leather holder.

"Yeah, yeah, they look too new." She didn't believe him. He was nearby, in such an isolated area, already sent up a few flags, then tack on that he wasn't ill equipped and he was a full blown contradiction. How many people carry explosives in their backpack? Other than terrorists, she added, taking a step back from him. She wondered why and how long he watched the police compound—mostly why—but she knew she was lucky to be alive after enraging a drug lord and nearly getting killed. She owed him.

She cupped his jaw, smiling, loving the way his gaze ripped over her face. *Please don't be a mercenary or something awful,* she thought. "Nice meeting you, Mike." She climbed onto the bus, stopping at the first step and hanging out. "Oh yeah—" His gaze flashed to hers. "*Semper fi.*"

The look on his face was priceless with surprise, and she laughed as she boarded the bus.

"I'll be damned," Mike muttered to himself, then thought of all the things he'd said to her. He wasn't accustomed to being near a civilian on a mission, and that she had experience, at least with a weapon, said there was a lot more to Clancy McRae. Mike debated following her for some interrogation, but had easier ways of getting information on her. She was in the wrong place and the wrong time—yet evasive about why. He didn't like cagey females. They always led to lies and broken promises.

He should know. His life was a complete secret. Sometimes, even to him.

Tunisia

Choufani sat back on his rear and stared at the rubble. He'd combed it for two days, trying to find more than melted and charred pieces of rifles. A nagging worked up his spine and he kept wondering why the faction was so secretive within its ranks.

His gaze moved over the warehouse, and the markers left by forensics. The Tunisian government had let several intelligence agencies inside to help. Choufani had a heated discussion with a Saudi intelligence officer who wanted total control.

Antone grabbed the trowel and pushed at the blackened material. All he needed was one small piece, a direction. The end certificate for the shipping on the crates was forged, its destination somewhere in Afghanistan. It never made it and he doubted it ever would have, considering the circumstances. The men were the Most Wanted and their movements tracked. But Choufani had a sneaking suspicion this wasn't so simple.

They had died for the weapons. Not for the cause.

He tapped his fist against his lips, then looked at his single piece. More misshapen in its construction than from the explosion and fire. Under a microscope it showed the carved markings, but again was too disfigured to decipher. He pushed off the floor and crawled on his hands and knees, ignoring comments from the other dozen men in here examining and cataloging body parts and rubbish.

He heard his name and looked up. A man on the far side of the storage house gestured to him. Choufani pocketed the black chunk and stood, carefully crossing the area.

"Since you are searching so hard I thought you would want to examine this first."

Choufani looked down. It was half a human body, the lower half, and missing its feet. He wasn't amused, but noticed the trousers were relatively intact, and he bent to one knee, fishing in the pockets.

His gloved fingers grazed something and it crackled. He

pried open the pocket and with tweezers caught the inside fabric and pulled. A scrap of folded paper, worked and worn, slid out. He unfolded it.

"Do we know who this man is?" he asked, reading the paper, then tipped it toward the light.

"No. There are more parts than people here."

They'd have to wait for DNA testing but Choufani was hoping it was their leader. His gaze whipped over the sheet, nearly untouched by the flames. "Find out. As soon as you do, I need to know."

Clasped between the tweezers was a lading order. It wasn't all that significant, no names, no company of origin or destination, and probably forged. Arms dealers didn't follow international laws, let alone leave a paper trail, yet when Antone shined his penlight over the paper, then under, he recognized a watermark.

Now he had something to track.

Ensign Durry positioned her cover just so on her office sideboard, then removed her jacket, careful to get the shoulders on the hanger so it wouldn't crease before she turned to the stacks of paperwork. This was a waste of her talent, she thought, but the road to the goal. She logged on through the network of security firewalls, then started entering data. She wished people carried an iPod and she didn't have to be a secretary. She had a degree in nursing, a minor in intel, and graduate work for the past three years in intelligence and code ciphering. Yet here she sat, transcribing medical records for Special Operations personnel. She sorted her stack by priority, then broke it down into groups.

She immediately took Gannon's file off the top and set it aside. He was already active and she understood he was more in command than the generals. She remembered that flush of fear near him. Well, not really fear, but that she knew she could never hold her own around him. He'd turned her into a flinching fool when he wasn't trying to be the least bit intimidating.

*I bet he gets the job done,* she thought, then opened the first file of a Marine on an active mission, status unknown. That could mean anything from MIA to top secret. Her clearance wasn't high enough to know. Yet. She glanced at the name, Nathan Krane, then brought up the file. *He's one of Gannon's,* she realized when she added the data from his last physical. It was right next to the previous physical and mental health comparison that kept his mission status active. If it were any less, he'd be taken off the roster. A little spot in her heart ached when she realized that he hadn't reported back yet.

Then she glanced between three-month-old data to the most current.

Her curiosity piqued by the vast differences in the scores made her turn to the short stack, and hunt down any other drastic changes in physical abilities.

At least now, she thought, the task wasn't so boring.

Mike felt a sweet adrenaline rush.

No pack. No M16 or MP5, no team. Alone he worked faster, worried about his back and no one else. He ran hard, his gaze flickering down the alleys.

In the twilight dusk, Mike bolted through the streets, leaping piles of garbage and a kid's rusty tricycle. Two blocks down, he stopped short, his gaze scanning his surroundings; then he made a sharp left between two buildings. At the end of the alley, he flattened to the wall and listened for footsteps. About a minute passed before he heard them, and as they came close to his position he stuck his arm out and clotheslined Hector.

The young man's throat impacted with Mike's arm and Hector hit the ground hard, flat on his back. He didn't move.

Mike squatted beside him. "Why are you running from me, DeNegra?"

Hector gasped for air.

"Get up, that's undignified."

Hector stood slowly, then fell back against the wall heaving for air. He made a dash for escape, but Mike was there, his fingers wrapping his skinny throat and pulling him back.

"I don't need this, you know it."

"*Sí, sí.* You just scared me."

"Like hell."

"I'm not talking, not to you."

"Why's that?"

"People get killed around you."

"Only the really bad ones. Talk."

"What about? My mother, my sister?"

Mike squeezed. The town was barely a village on the border, lots of drug dealers and gunrunners in the mix with some good folk. Hector was slippery and saw everything. "I could give you to Gantz."

Hector's dark eyes flew wide. "No, no."

Mike let go. "What did you see?"

Hector rubbed his throat, cleared it. "Nothing, there is nothing to see here. Look at this place, this town is barely alive."

"That depends on your perspective." While sunbaked and slow moving, there was more to Namballe than the killing heat. It was on the edge of a bird sanctuary, which didn't mean much but attracted visitors to the clean, brightly painted town. A jumping-off point for a lot of tourist excursions up the Amazon. Easy place to get lost, he thought. For Mike, this was the nearest town to the last location of the UAV crash. The folks would have seen something. The chopper had crashed farther in somewhere east, but it would take a couple of days to reach the coordinates. Mike was interested in finding the Hellfires first and they had to be transported.

Mike took a step closer, and Hector's eyes colored with fear. Giving Hector the once-over didn't infringe on his moral standards. Hector was a petty thief and once tried to sell his little sister to him. Mike took his character from there.

"I'm hot, tired, and impatient, Hector." Mike checked the slide of his latest acquisition. "The gun is new, I haven't tested it." He put it in Hector's face.

"*Madre de Dios*." The thin young man swallowed hard. "They sent out a group of men to the east," Hector blurted.

"They?"

"The mayor, his brother, he's the chief of police."

Probably thought it was a chopper full of drugs since it wasn't marked with any military insignia or paint.

"They did not find it."

Good. One up on the locals at least.

"The explosion, we all saw. Big." Hector added sound effects.

"Where's the mayor and his little brother now?" Mike asked.

"They never came back."

Mike frowned. "How long?"

"A couple days maybe."

"No one's gone to look for them?"

"*Sí*. The police, and they too did not come back."

Mike had seen the memorials on the streets. Pictures surrounded by candles and crosses. What did they see to get killed? "The jungle is busy, huh?"

"Always. If not for *la touristas* we'd be bored to death."

"I'm sure." Probably picking pockets or helping sell a pretty European to the local guerrillas.

Hector thought Mike was someone dangerous, unsure if he was a good guy or not. Mike wanted to keep it that way. But he'd been in South America so often with the DEA, for a while he had a sweet little place in Belize. Some wreck diving, a lot of people who didn't know him or weren't pointing a gun in his face. Isolation from the dirty world. He'd bet Clancy would like it.

He sighed. Hell.

Mike slipped his weapon behind his back under his loose shirt, and inclined his head. Hector frowned, leery of leaving, then took a step away. "Get lost."

Hector didn't waste time.

Mike turned toward the village proper in time to see a hammer of a fist come barreling toward his face.

Colonel Jansen was just leaving for home when a knock stopped him. He continued putting on his Alpha blouse. "Enter." He fastened the belt as a man stepped into the office. "Good Lord, don't you ever sleep?"

"Not really."

"Can't this wait?" His wife would give him hell if he missed another family dinner.

"The Libyan prisoner assault?"

Jansen froze for a moment, his arms falling to his sides. "Continue."

"The team confiscated a great deal of information, but one piece has us stumped." The CIA officer pulled something from his pocket and placed it on the table. In the evening light, it seemed to glow with fractures of gold.

Jansen picked it up. It looked almost like a totem pole, crude big-eyed faces carved into the rectangular block no larger than his palm. "Looks like something they sell to tourists."

"Our assessment as well. Finding the seller is next to impossible since most locals sell handmade souvenirs all the time. We've tested the components. It's a very hard plastic. Most statuary like that is made from resin and painted. This is solid color."

"It looks like it's broken." Jansen ran his thumb over the jagged corner.

"Yes, but it's a very precise break."

Intentional? Jansen rolled the piece in his hand, thinking that Gannon needed to see this. "So, the question is, what is something from a South American street vendor doing in the hands of four wannabe suicide bombers?"

# Seven

Mike pushed through the door of the large house, and as a guard came running down the hall he raised his weapon. "Not a good idea."

The guard stopped, looked at his comrade. Mike held him off the floor by the back of his shirt.

"Don't bother telling him I'm here." He aimed again when the guard put the radio to his mouth. "He knows."

Mike walked, dragging the unconscious man across the slick, tiled floor and down the hall. *Business is good,* he thought as he passed large oil paintings and pieces of sculpture he was sure were stolen from a museum. Mike walked through the last doorway.

August Renoux sat behind a desk. Relaxed, his hands across his large stomach, his eyeglasses on the top of his bald head, what little hair the arms dealer had was long and fuzzy gray. It gave him the unkempt look of a professor. Unsuspecting. Pretty clever for a man who marketed Chinese tanks and Russian attack choppers for a living. He should be in jail, but he was slick enough that he'd evaded doing time for over thirty years, running to the nearest country without extradition treaties with the U.S. With his duel citizenship, American and French, he skated the rim of international law, selling arms, and while he had to have the approval of the U.N. National Security Council to do it, someone had their pockets greased. His business was war and conflict, same as Mike's, yet Renoux profited.

Mike's pay would cover the electric bill for a place like Renoux's.

He released the shirt, and the man dropped to the floor with a hard *thunk*. "One of yours, Renoux?"

"I told him to just see what you were up to." Renoux's gaze flicked to Mike's red jaw. *"Pardonnez-moi."*

"Well, since we're sharing, you won't mind talking."

"Business is good. Not great, but good."

Did everyone intentionally miss the point today? "After pissing off the Peruvian military?"

"Our transaction was perfectly legal."

"Legal? A trash drop to a government? You aren't that stupid, Auggie."

Dropping weapons by parachute from a plane practically sent out an invitation for theft. A degree off on the coordinates and a miscalculation of wind speed, and the trash drop of arms meant for the military fell into the Colombian cartels or whoever was hanging around. Mike figured it was a scam to force the Peruvians to order more to arm themselves like the enemy. One reason Mike was surprised to see him here living like a king.

"Why the hell do you want in my business, Renoux? Or have you forgotten?"

Renoux went perfectly still for a moment, a piece of food on its way to his mouth. "Of course not, but where you Americans go, there is often a group who might be interested in my products." He popped the fried pepper into his mouth, grinning. "And that airdrop, I had End Certificates, and the arms arrived where they should. What happens after that is not my concern. Besides, if I wanted to sell to the Colombians, which I do not, small arms are not worth it to me."

Mike didn't believe that for a second. He'd blown up enough munitions that were dropped from choppers or jets flying over a conflict area. Arms dealers were all about the money, taking no sides. Unlike in the U.S., Russia, and China, the biggest arms dealers in the world, very few shipments fell into the wrong hands. It was hard to stop weapons from killing innocents when there were so many out there and people were willing to supply the worst of mankind with it. Terrorists were armed—some better than Mike.

Renoux supplied the demand.

"Tell me about the explosion."

"Ah, that. It was at night and several witnessed it, as you know."

That told Mike that the crash was farther southeast. Intel was looking in the wrong place, but what had the power to throw a half-ton aircraft off course?

"Who's out there, Renoux? Someone killed the mayor and his family." Before Clancy arrived, he thought.

He shrugged. "In those mountains? There are tribes still there that have not progressed in the last thousand years."

"Convenient to blame, huh? And considering they are still there and alive, seems to me it's the way to go." Mike raised his gun and cocked his head. "I'm really not here to discuss anthropology."

"Or you'll what? Call the police?"

Mike pulled the hammer back. "I don't need the police, Auggie."

The fat man swallowed hard. "There are rumors. Sightings."

"What kind of sightings?" Mike's first thought was alien landings or ghosts, both bullshit.

Renoux shrugged plump shoulders. "You know how the locals can be about superstitions. All I know is people are yanked out of the forest, as if they were never there. Vanishing."

"Not what I need to hear."

"They are specific, ah, selective. Men only, the women are left alone."

"Don't make me come over there." Mike didn't have to

take a threatening step closer. Renoux knew there was little to stop him. Mike liked the fast and accurate way to a source, none of this hunting for days. Go to the top and extricate the intel, move to the next resource, then check it against U.S. intel. If that wasn't possible, wing it.

"Would you be interested to know that the last sighting was where your unmanned plane exploded?"

Mike hadn't mentioned the plane, but he wasn't surprised Renoux knew about the UAV. He probably had better intel than half of D.C. Even Mike didn't have a decent location. "Now you're talking. Where?"

"The foothills."

Of the Andes? That stretched through three countries. "Be more specific."

Renoux let out a long-suffering breath and looked around as if the police would jump from hiding. "East. Near San José de Lourdes."

Another sixty miles or so. That was doable for drift. "Who's got my Hellfires? And if you shrug that 'I don't know' shit, I'll make it physically impossible to do it again."

Renoux pushed out of the chair, an effort, but Mike didn't have to track the man. He was a big target. But his guards were another story. Loyal little bastards. The man who had hit him stirred on the floor, and Mike was tempted to put his lights out again, but the blood pooling near his mouth quelled the urge. Mercy.

"So when are you coming to join my operation?"

"Never, and quit asking. The Hellfires?"

"They exploded on impact. Ask anyone in the east, they will tell you the sky lit up. But then I ask myself, where is the debris? There's none to be found. It was by chance I was traveling in the east. My sister's husband, a fool of a man, he—"

Mike sighed, scrubbed his hand over his head, then fired at Renoux.

Mike almost laughed as the fat man danced back a step.

He turned the gun toward the hallway when his men came rushing in. Renoux waved them back, insisting he was fine and, truthfully, he didn't look the least bit ruffled.

Then he glared at Mike. "I told you! Things are being plucked out of the Andean Mountains like vultures to the dead."

"Without being spotted when we were looking for them? Try again."

"No, my friend, not the missiles. But the men."

Something in Mike just froze. "Go on." The chopper crashed too, days later. Near San José de Lourdes.

While Renoux fixed himself a drink, the mention of his men battered Mike with the sounds of their screams. It was constant, the tape recording playing in his head. He tried to block it, but too often it slipped past, and his imagination drew images of what made them scream in such terror. He'd seen enough to have a good comparison, but it made him more determined. Regardless of the outcome, payback was a sure thing.

Renoux peered over his glass. "Recon?"

Mike just stared.

"No matter. One explosion they might ignore, but two within days? People are curious, but no one is talking openly. They are scared."

More likely because a squad of Peruvian soldiers was missing too. People disappearing wasn't uncommon, but it was for a native, and most especially for a Peruvian soldier. To assume an entire squad was murdered by smugglers and do nothing told Mike there was more to the vanishing act than an exchange of gunfire. Leaving them to rot was a slap in the face to all who served.

While the CIA had a satellite watch on the area, they were the same people who told Jansen Scuds were in the mountains. Mike couldn't wrap his brain around that still. Scuds weren't exactly small. He'd seen the satellite photos. It was a slick black spot and could be a chunk of stone for all they knew. Yet there had been no contact, no beacon, no frequency spikes, nothing. Heavy-handed manipulation, but then, he liked a challenge.

"Someone's talking if you're getting all this. Who?"

"My trip, the reason I was there . . . it was a meeting. And might have nothing to do with anything particular."

"Does it?"

"A man wants to purchase space on my transport planes. It was weapons or why come to me, eh?"

"But you said no because that's illegal, isn't it, Auggie?" Mike spoke as if he addressed a ten-year-old who'd eaten too many cookies and complained of a stomachache. Weapons transport not sanctioned by a particular government sent up red flags to the intelligence agencies.

"Of course, but one never turns his back on a potential customer."

"A name, a location, give me something because you know how I feel about a bullet in the chamber and not firing."

Inwardly, Mike rolled his eyes at his own drama. But it kept the "badass to badass" ratio in his favor. He knew he could be scary, remembering Ensign Durry at the hospital, yet an instant later he thought of Clancy. He liked her for more reasons than that she wasn't intimidated by him. Though it was a rare occurrence lately. One reason he stayed alone.

"We never met. Something called him away."

Mike didn't bother to ask a name. Renoux preferred some anonymity with certain customers. Half the reason the ATF was up his ass.

"What I found so odd was anyone who inquires about the explosion, we find in the Amazon. Well, parts of them at least."

Mike remembered the tape Jansen played for him. The screams of his friends. They were alive when they crashed, and if they weren't now, then Mike was hunting a murderer.

\* \* \*

Clancy was methodical, orderly, and was accustomed to testing many theories in computer-generated synthensization before moving on to another step. *Start with the basics and build from there.* The basics always worked. She smiled to herself. Probably why they were called that.

Unlike most geeks who were never far from their computer, Clancy left her job at the lab, refusing to travel with a laptop. A good thing since Richora and his merry men would have her state-of-the-art Alienware laptop if she had.

With a plan in mind, she left her hotel, freshly showered and in a new outfit, her only bag slung across her body as she went on a search for a network connection. If she got a hold of a decent computer, she could do more than the average person because they weren't aware of some accesses available on the Web and the codes for them. But she had to know if the men were here or back in the U.S. already, and she pulled out her cell phone, debating using it. It could be tracked, and so would a credit card, but Cook would have to be pulling a lot of strings while trying to keep the reasons why quiet. She wouldn't put it past him.

The American public would not like the idea of injecting their heroes with anything so dangerous. Especially something untested.

But she had skills and planned on using even the dirty ones to get what she needed, yet her brisk steps faltered when she approached a black iron gate. Flowers were jammed in every curl of iron, and candles crowded the ground below it. Her heart tripped when she saw the picture was of a young man in a uniform. Peruvian Army. He couldn't be more than eighteen. Was he the man she shot? She strode past, pushing that young face from her mind, when she came upon another. Twisting a look around the area, she found another across the street littering the church steps.

Her first thought was earthquake, but there wasn't any destruction in the town. From her position, she counted seven memorials. She thought of Richora, the man with him, and felt a terrible pull of guilt. *He was shooting at me,* she reasoned. She hadn't meant to kill him and turned her blame on Richora.

Traffic slowed and she darted between cars, crossing to the only Net café within a hundred miles. A few minutes later, she was sitting on the edge of a bistro with a laptop connected to the Net.

"Ain't technology grand?" she mumbled. She connected the cell to the computer and worked the keyboard, her magic, jumping off the cable line in Peru to a satellite-linked network in Venezuela. From there it was the freedom of the cyberwaves. She created an onion path, which would bounce from country to country through a wireless network. If Cook were monitoring her mail, then he'd think she was in Tanzania before he realized what she'd done.

She fished in her bag for the files, flipped through the worn, crumpled pages to the unit information, then dialed the phone. On a small window on the screen off to the side, she saw the connection jump. She used Francine's name, figuring they were accustomed to hearing Major Yates, if only once, and one by one she asked for the Marines. And she got the same answer.

"I'm sorry, ma'am. He's not available either."

"This is unsatisfactory." She tried to sound crisp like Francine. "They were scheduled to report for some tests." Francine had to check her results constantly, and that she wasn't said there was more to this implantation than the scientific.

The man hesitated and when he spoke again his voice held the lilt of confusion. "I don't know about that, ma'am. Would you like to speak to the colonel?"

*Oh, jeez.* "No, no, if they're not there, there's nothing to be done now. Thank you, Sergeant."

She hung up and quickly severed the phone connection, then turned off the phone. With her luck, there was a GPS embedded in it. At least she knew they were not in the U.S.

Sorta. It was all she had to go on and was folding the papers to put them back in the baggie when she paused, staring at the stoic military photo. By now she knew all the men by name, where they were born, when they joined. None of them were married, most without much family. She smoothed her finger over the outline of the Marine's face, promising to make this right.

Then swiftly she put it all neatly away and focused on the computer. Yet because of the cable to satellite link, downloading on this end would be a bit slow. In the States, she'd already have downloaded and studied the schematics for the drone, the UAV Falcon. Long and narrow, under its wingspan Hellfire rockets. *Bet that's why they sent the Marines in so quickly.* WMDs on the loose was everyone's worst nightmare, someone with the potential to hit you in your hometown. Be more afraid of the fanatic guy who wants one, she thought, than the country with a thousand. She'd searched Google Earth too, but hadn't found anything substantial. Loads from the site weren't exactly fresh but days, even weeks old. She had to check the date of each one.

It was worth another try and she pulled up the town for a base to start. The picture appeared as if taken from a plane. She peered close, her gaze picking out the main avenue, the church steeples; then she passed the cursor to pinpoint northeast into Ecuador. If the UAV crashed where the mission orders said, there would be something like skid marks on the treetops. It had been only days. Trees wouldn't have healed and she'd see some damage. She scanned for several minutes, certain she was looking in the area where she and Mike had been. She recognized the thick wall surrounding the police station.

But there was nothing to indicate a crash. Of any kind.

She switched directions, and it took time to reload and resize itself to narrow the picture and bring in a clear shot of the jungle. It all looked just . . . green. She sat back and sipped incredibly good coffee and watched the picture download. She was starving, but café rules; she had to give up the computer to order food. For nearly an hour, she studied the terrain near the border, but found nothing that looked like a crash site or even a path from scavengers. The Falcon had a twenty-nine-hour fly time and was seven hundred pounds of lightweight, high-strength composite materials, including its wings. It could fly over forty thousand feet, and there was no evidence of the crash? Satellite imagery didn't show *anything?*

She knew satellites couldn't hover and any pictures were conducive to the timing of the target and the satellite's position. *You'd think we'd have some overlapping up there,* she thought.

Clancy wasn't buying any of this, and with the local soldiers coming up missing, she knew they were somehow connected. She kept surfing, and waited, watching cars speed past, yet in the dusky stillness beyond she saw the German talking to a couple of local girls. He didn't look much different from when he was on the bus, kind of grungy, but whatever he said made the girls giggle. Gustave looked up, saw her, and waved, smiling, then walked on.

Clancy focused on the screen again, moving in increments east from the border. Nothing. The lack of speed made her carefully inspect each part of the jungle and the villages beyond. While she waited for it to finish, she logged onto her e-mail account. There were several from her mother asking where she was, why didn't she call. Lord, teach the woman to use a computer and she was all over it. She answered, giving little information. "Deep in the project" was usually good enough for Mom. She checked the map and saw the high-peaked terrain of the Andes where it sloped to the rain forest valley and the Amazon.

Then she saw something.

Not anything glaring, but there was a definite mark on the valley floor. The only reason it stood out was because the surrounding area was untouched. The spread was wide, yet faint, almost like wind brushing grasses flat. It could very well be, she thought, thinking of crop circles or animals. The shadow on the screen disappeared under the trees, and a closer look showed the ground torn. That could be a couple of things, the shadow of the Andes or the angle of the satellite for Google. U.S. intelligence would have scoured several versions and angles, if they had satellite coverage at the time, but she didn't have anything close to that luxury.

A good and bad thing was the Marines were still unreachable. That meant still on assignment. Maybe. If they were back, the reports on the project would have contained some results. *Talk about by the seat of your pants, McRae,* she thought, yet a small part of her, one she refused to let take hold, reminded her she wasn't skilled enough for this, that it was hopeless to hunt for men trained to be invisible.

Doubt was erased by her gut instinct, her need to correct this. She had to get it out of them before it killed them. She'd created it. She'd developed it to its present state, and while initial trials proved excellent, she blamed herself for giving Cook a deadline, a possible moment of human implantation they could see on a calendar.

Cook had taken it and ran.

She wasn't going to allow Yates, and Cook with his hurry-up attitude, destroy something with the potential to help millions. Clancy had a personal stake in this, in more than her career, yet from the first moment she'd learned of the human implantations, the candidates, she wondered, *why?* They risked their lives for their countrymen, but for experimental nanotechnology that hadn't been fully tested, one that they couldn't even see? The scales were tipped too deeply for her to grasp that.

It made her wonder; did they really volunteer?

Richora waited for a half hour before he was escorted inside. This would not be pleasant, he thought, or he wouldn't be kept waiting. When his escort finally came, the man said nothing, stopping in the foyer and waiting till he noticed him and stood. Then the escort turned, walking briskly through the hacienda that was modern with a shell of the old world.

He passed through a wide courtyard with brightly colored tiles, and an elaborate fountain spilling clear water from basin to basin, then under the portico and through wide French doors.

With his back to him, Salache stood at the grand window, a twelve-foot length of glass separating him from the humidity and heat. The Andean Mountains loomed close, the frosted peaks hidden in the clouds.

Then he turned. Richora tried to school his shocked features and failed.

"Comments? Make them now please."

The voice was the same, his manner the same as he sat carefully and drew a magazine close. But the face matched nothing of Richora's memory.

"You look healthy," he said, knowing Salache wanted a compliment. What was left to do to his face and, mostly, why? Why did he cut up his face and change himself all the time? To avoid capture perhaps, but then, his wife and children were not altered and they would be recognizable. Richora counted four surgeries since he'd met Salache, and that had been less than two years. How many did he have before he met him?

His gaze slid to the far left, to the open door leading to the pool, a private one for his family. The staff used another on the other side of the property. Yet through the opening, he saw Salache's wife and his two children. What strangeness did they see working in the man? A man who kept changing his appearance, always for the better, that was certain. Salache was forty years old, yet looked no more than twenty-five. What did his beautiful wife think? She'd married a man with a different face and Richora accepted his desire for

Marianna, one he would never approach. She was exotic and delicate, yet there was nothing fragile in her dark eyes. He turned his gaze back to Salache and found him scowling.

"You want my wife."

The edge in his voice gripped Richora. "No."

"Then why do you stare?"

"She is beautiful, you're a lucky man."

"Apparently not or my business wouldn't be interrupted with these mishaps."

"I have taken care of it."

"All of it?"

"Don't worry, I'll do my job."

"Then clean it up!" Salache snapped.

"Have I failed you yet? Not my men, but me?"

Richora moved closer, and noticed that Salache was flipping through a gay men's magazine, ripping out pages and circling body parts.

"We are on schedule. Taking the woman wasn't a planned action, simply a greedy one," Richora said. "Fuad was not smart, and an intelligent man would not have hired him."

Salache's gaze flicked up. "A smarter one would not have killed him before we knew for certain."

"I didn't. He was shot from a distance."

Salache frowned, the muscles in his face barely moving. Richora thought, *Does he feel anything after all the operations?* He was barely accustomed to the last face; now a new one? "One of yours?"

"Actually no," Salache said. "But someone could have taken it upon themselves." He seemed to think for a long moment.

Richora frowned. He wasn't concerned? "If not, then we are found out."

"That's my problem. The woman is a witness."

Richora shook his head "Though she was hooded, she didn't—"

"I don't care if she is blind! No witnesses or we fail."

His tone was brittle and absolute, and while Richora believed the woman had witnessed nothing, she'd killed his nephew. *She* he would kill with his bare hands and the man who helped her escape. Yet Richora agreed that the fewer eyes looking in their direction, the smoother the work would go. They'd already had to deal with one interference.

"I have something else for you."

"Anything."

"That's what I like to hear."

"Anything can be had for a price."

"Your cause is not enough?" Salache tore another page out of the magazine and slipped it into a file in the desk drawer.

"A cause is only as great as the money behind it. Are the others going to assist?"

"They are wanted, Richora, you are not."

"So many secrets could spill to the wrong ears."

"If it does, I will carve up that handsome face so your mother wouldn't recognize you."

Richora shrugged, not offended. "My mother never knew me." *And neither did yours,* he wanted to add. Wealth brought a certain power and arrogance Richora never understood. He was Quechua, from the mountain tribes, raised by strangers in a mission, and dirt poor for years. Yet Salache had hidden his native origins from the world, and he wondered if the man's lovely wife knew where he came from, his true roots.

While Richora admired him, his skill, his cunning, and his astonishing intelligence, he was never certain if Salache created the weapons for his own personal cause, or if he wanted to sit back and watch the world terrorize itself into Armageddon.

Choufani's research told him that only one company manufactured that particular vellum. It was not cost effective for most printers or stationers shops to carry the brand. Its particular shade of white lavender and the scent the paper carried marked it for certain as *Trazado en Flores*, scribing with flowers. It was a blend of pulp and lavender, the flowers giving the paper its slight purple cast. It was feminine and not something you'd find in the pocket of a Hezbollah terrorist.

This particular paper was manufactured in small quantities in Peru, a specialty of a small paper mill. The little company prided itself on its environmentalism by not cutting down trees and instead, using the castoffs from road clearings or mining. In a time when greed launched all causes, he found that admirable.

He pushed through the door of the mill, and the noxious odor from outside lessened a bit. Yet he could hear the machines pushing pulp through massive strainers. The mill was well beyond the city for that reason, he suspected. Noise and smell didn't bring tourists.

A door to the left opened and the noise increased as an older gentleman stepped through, smiling. Antone matched his face with the ones over the desk and knew this was the owner.

"May I help you?"

When Antone explained that he sought the exclusive paper, the man was more than a little delighted. It was part of his wife's design collection, but his excitement faded when Antone asked for a list of purchasers.

"No, no, I cannot do that. I must respect privacy even for something so trivial as a purchase of my paper."

Antone tried to convince him. The man did not need to know his paper was somehow linked to a crime, but finally, he showed his badge.

The old man straightened, pursed his lips. "Very well." He turned to his files. Still the owner was reluctant to hand over the list. "These are my patrons. Mostly women."

Antone suspected his wife's friends too. "I promise not to disturb your buyers, senor. This will be conducted electronically, they won't be aware. I'm sure it's nothing, but I must confirm every possible lead." Antone would have a visual, but the man didn't need to know. While his superiors were vocal, deeming the lead not worth following, Antone's instincts said differently. If anything, he would discard it from his list of evidence and move on to another.

The old man made him swear, and amused, Antone tucked the paper in his pocket, purchased some of the lavender paper, and left on a new hunt.

*Primate testing lab*
*U.S. Army Medical Facility, Virginia*

Francine hit the lock on the door, then strode to the exam table. She checked her instruments, then looked at the wireless pod intelligence load and waited for the green flash on the screen. In the 10 cc's of saline, the pod floated, invisible to the naked eye, and even a microscope. She placed the EEG leads on her chest, then snapped on latex gloves, her hair already swept to the side and tied off with a tourniquet. She adjusted the mirrors stacked on seven-inch-thick data files, then lifted the syringe. With her fingers, she probed her throat on the side beyond her ear, judging the connecting nerves. Using mirrors, she palpated to under the base of her skull. The cerebellum. She'd done this before, but never on herself.

She inhaled and let it out, then positioned the thin long needle and pushed. She didn't feel it, the area numb, but the painkiller wasn't deep enough. The EEG registered her elevated heartbeat. Her eyes watered as she felt the needle hit a tendon. She was forced to move it, and while her nerve faltered, she didn't have anyone to turn for help. Mentally, she followed the line into her skull and pushed the plunger.

Done.

Slowly she removed the needle, then turned to the keyboard, the EEG monitoring. It was the simplest way to track implantation at the start. An elevated heart rate followed by elevated white count of the body trying to reject it. Clancy had figured out how to maintain peak optimal status without rejection. She matched the white cell to the nano. Eventually the body accepted it as one cell.

As with all the pods, they had a fluorescent tail that allowed them to follow the path. The fin would dissolve after a few hours and tracking ended. Francine could see that hers was progressing slowly, and while other enhancements would travel in the bloodstream, this was injected into the brain stem to ensure its most useful location and application.

She felt the hum first, and walked to a chair, staggering a bit before she sat and gripped the arms. She dug in her pocket for her iPod, recording the experience.

Prior to this, injection was done under anesthesia and the candidates felt nothing until they were wakened from the induced sleep. Bringing in an outsider wasn't possible. While Francine offered her medical expertise in every aspect, Clancy had created it, then adjusted the minute technology to its precision perfection.

And it was perfect.

She closed her eyes, experiencing what no one else had.

Clancy wouldn't approve, not of this. It stung that she didn't believe in the work as much as Francine did, but Francine understood her concerns. It was new, untested—and dangerous. But unlike Clancy, Francine felt it was ready.

She was betting her life on it.

# Eight

*San José de Lourdes, Peru*

Mike was breathing fire. Not because he believed half of what Renoux said, but the man had no reason to lie and knew Mike would come find him if he did. His men snatched out of the jungle? By what, who?

He needed reliable information. Now. The longer it took, the more likely his men were dead.

Unacceptable.

He slammed the brakes and cut off the engine. Beyond him were narrow streets leading in three directions, a traffic circle with speeders tearing up the road, while a man walked a burro down the side of the street. The contrast was enough to make his temper simmer, and he let out a lungful of air and scrubbed his hands over his head.

He wanted to hit the jungle in a dead run, search, but without decent coordinates, a little gear, it would be a long haul and the jungle would kill him.

He knew. It had been tried before.

Pushing out of the truck, he strode briskly down the street. Approaching the front of a tailor shop, he smelled that funny odor that came with new fabric before he slipped into the alley and overtook the narrow staircase running alongside to the second floor. He knocked. The door swung open on its own.

Mike drew his weapon, nudging the door and sweeping the room. Gantz waved from his spot on the balcony.

"You ass. Are you looking to get caught with your shorts down?" Mike holstered his gun.

"I saw you coming," Gantz said, from his spot in the plantation chair, his bare feet on the balcony rail. He tipped his Panama hat back and held up his glass. "Join me, the view is great."

Mike scowled at the amber liquid in the tall glass.

Howard Gantz had quit drinking four years ago when it nearly ended his career and his life. He was on a rampage then, hunting for the killer and drinking himself to death. He'd wanted to die, to end his grief. Then he'd found the people who killed his family, and Mike took care of the rest, including drying Howard out so he could function.

"It's tea, taste?"

Smiling at the dare, Mike crossed the room to the sunny side and leaned against the balcony door frame. The city, sun washed and peaceful, stretched out before them, beyond that the slope to the mountains topped with clouds, and the river in the valley below. A slice of paradise, Mike thought.

Below, people waved. Gantz called out a greeting.

"They think I'm a writer," he snickered like a teenager with a secret. "Good cover actually, they leave me alone when I want and people chat like crazy if they think you'll put them in a book. Even the bad ones want to be immortalized in fiction."

"That's why they do bad things in a loud and grotesque manner."

"When did you lose your sense of humor?"

"Last week, about five thirty," Mike said, smiling for the first time since leaving Renoux's. He didn't have to ask Gantz why he was here. The CIA didn't need a good reason. He was a snoop of the first water. He watched, listened, chatted, no one paid him much attention. Howard Gantz was as unassuming as air. About fifty, he wasn't tall or striking, just the average Joe. Mike had seen him portray a priest as well as a scholar to get what he needed.

"Any potential characters?"

"Nah, a couple I'm watching with a source north, but pretty quiet."

There had to be movement, but the stone walls Mike hit told him when he unearthed this mess—and he would—it was going to be ugly.

"I know why you're here."

Mike wasn't surprised. "My guys, they're out there somewhere."

Gantz immediately dropped his feet off the rail and stood, moving to the desk. He handed over a sealed package. "Spec Ops sent this for you."

Though it had a DOD address, Mike knew it was from Jansen by the mark on the seal. A pass code he'd used when he was much younger, leaner, and had worked for Jansen. Triple stars. Your eyes only. He tucked it away, then said, "I need all you have."

"You got it. I've been getting satellite photos for an hour or so." He glanced at the clock. "Out of range in about fifteen minutes, should have come for breakfast."

Gantz hovered over a simple desk stacked with equipment that shut into cases. His gear was anything but eye-catching. The laptop looked beat to hell and out of date, a Web cam, a couple of digital cameras, and listening equipment, but that was about it. If he had more stashed, he wasn't showing his cards.

"Don't scowl at my babies, they do the job, just don't look it. I can contact Moscow on this." Gantz worked the keyboard. "The Falcon isn't at the last location, I've been looking."

"It should have caught something on fire."

"Shoulda, coulda . . . not here." Gantz tapped a key and pointed to the screen. "You're in the right country, I think."

The world's greatest superpower and the damn CIA couldn't give him accurate intel. That didn't bode well for the good guys.

Mike studied the terrain. High and low country from mountains to jungles on the Peru side. They were over Peru's airspace when they were shot down, he thought. Not Ecuador.

"Wanna hear my theory?"

Mike straightened. "Yes, surprisingly."

Gantz smiled. "The rocket that shot the UAV out of the sky knocked it farther than we think. The last UAV location was here." He used a pen to point at the computer screen. "I think it was here." He pointed about twenty miles or less to the east. "Now, the chopper, your guys, they were about thirty miles from the target when they were taken down. Took out the tail rudder. Then nothing. A satellite pass got the explosion but not the rocket launch. We were out of range then, but the second pass, eight hours later, showed zip. Not even smoke. There just wasn't shit to see."

But there was, Mike thought, the terrifying screams pealing vividly through his mind. He rubbed his forehead uselessly. "The distance between can't be that far, Howard. Heavy stuff hits the ground fast."

Gantz made a sour face, then drew a paper map from the desk and flattened it to the wall. "Sure, but I figured possible range to targets, speed of the UAV and the chopper at the time, and impact." He slapped up tape to hold it there. "Rockets, even small ones, move at 715 miles an hour."

"We had satellite photos ASAP after the UAV hit to see where debris fell. The second pass didn't show squat."

"Scavengers are good, but that good?" Gantz said, doubtful.

"They're covering a trail and trying to keep anyone out,

that's a given." Mike's gaze slid over the map of colored lines and math equations on the edges. "Busy, were you?"

"I'm not just a pretty face. This is your possible theater." He outlined the small orange triangle. "All the villages *surround* that area," Gantz said. "Sometimes geologists and anthropologists get in this section to study the river tribes." He tapped a spot in the Andes. "But it's damn rough. Well, hell, you know that. You don't live where the mountain, the jungle, and the river meet. Good for the gods, but us?" He shook his head. "Bad juju."

"Oh, Christ."

"Hey, monsoons fill the valley, mud slides off the mountain, and the river is the most dangerous in the world, especially when it overflows, what's not to love?" He stepped back and flicked a hand toward the computer. "There you go. See what I see."

Mike cupped the screen and Gantz rushed to shut the curtains against the glare. "There's a trail."

"Not much."

"I have what I need." The spot of pale land, torn earth showing in discoloration. Satellite imagery wasn't perfect. That would be too easy. He compared it to Gantz's wall map and orange triangle. Dead-on. Outstanding.

While Mike studied, Gantz said, "I didn't get down here till two days ago. I expected you last night."

"Ran into a little trouble."

"Drugs or weapons?"

"Five foot six, auburn haired, and Irish."

"God, introduce me."

"You're old enough to be her father." Sorta.

"And this means what in terms of a piece of ass?"

Only Mike's gaze shifted. The reference to Clancy annoyed him, but he let it slide. "She split. Give me a topographical of this, then thirty miles east."

Gantz nodded, taking the GPS pilot Mike offered.

"Are you the idiot that said there were Scuds in the mountains?"

"Not me, hell no. Tried to tell them. Visual is poor, but the damn things are the size of a school bus. That would sure stick out."

"Unless they were modified."

"Now, there's a thought." On the computer, Gantz drew up the photo. Mike looked, though he didn't need to see it. He'd studied it on the jet over here. It was a slick area that reflected light. A definite even surface on the east mountainside, but nothing that looked like missiles. Launchers, yeah, he could see how they came to the conclusion, but the photos showed only so much. The rest had to be human intelligence.

*That would be me,* he thought.

"The rocket, what I saw on the film, was small and it probably needs a custom launcher." The lack of heat signature still had him stumped. Mike knew weapons. He'd disarmed and destroyed more than his share, even carried several out of hostile territory on his back. It would take a physicist, and design engineer's expertise to create something that would propel into the sky at terrific speeds without detection. Maybe someone in the DOD was looking up possible suspects. Mike didn't have the time to wait and see. His men were out there. If they could have, they'd have left him a trail.

Mike used the computer to do a search on Clancy. But he got stopped by firewalls, locked out to the public. He scowled at the screen for a moment before he dialed his satellite phone. "By the way, your buddy paid me a visit."

Gantz looked up from the GPS. "Renoux? Jesus, the guy's got balls, huh?"

Mike told him about Renoux's messenger and his conversation with the arms dealer. Gantz laughed at the story, yet bagging Renoux was an obsession with him. He'd tracked the man for nearly fifteen years, managed to get a couple of indictments, but Renoux had friends in high places, people who wanted his weapons to sell and put pressure on the U.N.

He received no more than a slap on the wrist and was kicked out of whatever country he'd pissed off at the time. The crappy angle was Renoux was warmly welcomed by the enemies of the U.S. and Britain. Gantz lived for the moment to stop him. Mike understood the need to nab the one that got away.

"The bastard has the devil on his shoulder. I almost had him last year." Gantz finished the load. "You believe his story?"

Renoux's location matched Gantz's triangle, but that was about it. "Some, but he was more than pissed about it and scared."

"What the hell scares a man who's dined with Saddam, a few ayatollahs, and that bloodthirsty ethnic cleansing bastard in the Congo?"

"He mentioned sightings. Strange happenings." Mike gave him a heebie-jeebie look.

"Oh hell. Now I'll never get the bastard, he'll claim insanity."

Mike smiled widely, then held up a finger. The call went through encryption, and Jansen picked up. He gave his report.

"I'm not invisible anymore, least not here. So it will be slower. The package?" Mike turned away from Gantz.

"CIA found a chunk of . . . something in all that you collected in Libya," Jansen said. "You've got just a small piece. Test stats are inside the package, just thought you should have a look-see. The intel on the computers was excellent, but nothing leading to your theater of operation."

"Roger that." Mike felt the package. Whatever it was, it didn't weigh but a few ounces. "I need a favor, sidebar."

"Continue."

"There was an American woman in a border jail. As far as I can tell she wasn't doing anything to get thrown in, but she was near the suspected crash site."

"You didn't interrogate?"

"No time. But I need some information on her, and fire-walls are stopping me. There's a lock on her job." She was in the UAV area and traveling under a false passport; that was enough to tickle his internal alarms. He gave Jansen her name. He ended the call and looked at Gantz. "Any weapons?"

Gantz fished in his pocket, then tossed him the key to the trunk. Mike unlocked it and pilfered.

"That's all you're taking?"

"I can improvise." Mike grabbed his GPS, shook his hand, then left.

"Jarheads," Gantz muttered as the door slammed after him.

Francine smiled brightly as she walked into the lab. It was a good day, she thought. She'd already run with some Army Rangers this morning and loved that she had to slow down so she didn't look so obviously faster. Fortunately, no one saw her slip through the trees and beat them all back to the base. She kicked off her heels and slipped into flats, then pulled on her lab coat, stopping short when she saw Carl already there.

It annoyed her. This was her domain.

"What are you doing in here?"

"Observing your primates." He didn't look at her, his hands behind his back, feet apart. She wondered if he ever really shed those eagles on his shoulders and became human.

The thought made her stop in her tracks. She knew the man under the uniform, the recipient of some very attentive sex, but the real Carl Cook was hidden away. She hadn't cared, she didn't want a relationship to travel that deep, not yet. Not till she was ready, and her career and this nanopod meant more to her than anything right now.

Fran moved to Carl's side and watched the primates going through the mating ritual. Natasha had been introduced to Boris only a day before, and the pair were each just realizing there was another occupant in the giant cage. It was Boris's domain, fitting for primates, and Natasha was still investigating. Francine flipped on the speakers and heard Boris sound a mating call, the high-pitched shriek shaking the trees. The female barely glanced in his direction and continued picking something off her toes.

"Not good."

"It's only been a day and actually it *is* good. This means they are aware of each other and neither sees the other as a threat. Now, if I put a male in there, they'd kill each other for her. She has no idea she's a hot property today." Fran laughed to herself and went to the console to key up the series of intelligence games, some that normal schoolchildren took. When they passed those, she'd increase it for the female. Boris's abilities were already exceeding his baseline potential.

Cook turned his head. "Why are you moving so fast? In a hurry?"

She stilled. "I'm not." At least she didn't notice. She continued typing. "But I'm anxious to get in the gym for a bit before I start more testing."

"Maybe I'll join you."

She didn't look up, and thought of making an excuse since she'd already worked out today, when a strange feeling rushed through her. Anticipation? She'd run with him before and he always outdistanced her. "Then I'll see you in an hour."

He was prepared for exercise. Francine was beginning the tests on herself. Running with the Rangers she'd held herself back. She could hardly wait to see his face when she smoked him.

Marianna Salache noticed the man at the gate again. He stared inside, yet made no move to ring the bell. She shifted away from the window, wondering how often he would come by before he tried to enter. Perhaps he was one of Nuat's people. Another guard.

She glanced up from the magazine when she heard footsteps, and saw Richora stride through the foyer. "Alejo?"

Richora stopped and hesitated before he looked at her. She rose and came to him, smiling. "We have not seen you in a while. How have you been?"

"Fine. Very busy."

His brisk answer put her off and she frowned.

Richora closed his eyes for a moment, then met her gaze. "Marianna, forgive me."

"Nothing to forgive. Is Nuat still in his offices?"

"He is."

"His face startled you, didn't it?"

He nodded. "It is . . . dramatic."

She looked toward the offices. "He is the man I married, inside he is." Even to herself that sounded unconvincing.

"And when he is not?"

Her gaze jerked to his. "He will always be." *He must.*

Richora's shoulders slumped. "Good day, Marianna." He nodded once and left the house.

Marianna rose and kept watching as Richora climbed into his truck. Like her husband was now, he was a pretty man, beautiful warm golden skin and coal-black hair. Yet her husband's face was created, manipulated. He'd not been an ugly man. Not by her standards. He was simply average-looking. She might not have looked his way when she was young, but it was his intelligence that drew her to him. He was a visionary, with the mind of a genius, and she still admired that he could call up vast amounts of knowledge instantly, yet he never once spoke to her like she wasn't at his level.

He always patiently explained things to her, and she felt he took pride in his education. She had been to the university in Brazil, but her education was nothing like Nuat's.

She glanced back into the recesses of the house as if she could see him, working on whatever he had been planning these long months. She didn't ask, almost afraid to know. She had not married a rich man, yet wealth was at her fingertips now. Nuat's patents provided well, and he had no obligations to anyone except himself and his creative dreams.

She turned her attention to the window in time to see Alejo pass through the electric gate. She admired him too. He was comfortable in his skin. Whereas her husband was not.

At least the spying man was gone.

For the better part of a day Clancy refused to accept that if she didn't have a Terminator, this was over and she had to back off. In between this rebellious *my way* streak that was far too familiar, she searched every electronic shop in the small city. She would build it again and considered buying online and having it FedExed to her, but that would mean a credit card and a trace plus customs. Time she didn't have.

The nanopods had been inserted for a month already. The first test of insertion into an orangutan had killed it within three days. They hadn't tried again. Till now.

Yet after nearly two hours of trying to explain to the owner what she was looking for, she realized that she'd just have to buy entire pieces of computer equipment and strip it for parts.

Improvise a little.

Her thoughts went immediately to Mike, and after reliving that kiss for the fifth time today, she thought it was too convenient for him to be in that part of the jungle, alone. Just in time to save her life. Or trail her? If he was following her, then why not take her in? No, she decided, he wasn't after her, but something else. It was a big city. Avoiding him would be easy.

Several hours later, Clancy hovered over the desk with a soldering iron that cost more than half the equipment, and as she touched the silver to the chip she knew it wouldn't work. She set both down and pulled off the safety glasses.

She was fooling herself. Create a million dollars' worth of hardware from parts? Without the electrical engineer beside her like before? She could adjust the components only so far. What she really needed was the equipment to make one, but that was impossible. There wasn't a college for miles, and certainly no static clean labs. Clancy looked at the piles of computer parts and left the chair, pulling off the headband that held her hair back. She'd have to think of something else. Go back to the basics again, she thought. After washing off the black stain from the wires, she bagged her failure and threw it in the trash. Then she did her most favorite thing.

She crawled into bed and ordered room service.

Outside Dr. Figaroa's office, Ensign Durry sat erect as she waited. She tried not to grip the file too tightly and ruin the newness of it. She knew it was anal, but concentrating on her recent discovery just gave her a headache. As much as she knew she was correct, the evidence said she was dead wrong.

When Dr. Figaroa finally came out, she practically rushed into his office.

"Begging your pardon, sir, but I need to speak with you, right now. Sir."

Frowning, he closed the door behind her. "You said you found something strange in the records. Is it administrative?" He moved behind his desk.

"No, sir." She opened the file and laid out four separate sheets in front of him. "The left is the men's physicals and testing from six months ago. The one on the right is a few weeks ago. Look at the fitness testing."

Dr. Figaroa stared at her for a moment, thinking he'd never seen her ruffled and she was fighting it with everything she had. He looked at the data sheets, leaning over and running both fingers down the two columns. Then he stopped.

"That's not possible." Scowling, he pulled a ruler from his desk drawer and realigned the pages. Then following the ruler, he looked again. "Can this be a misprint?"

"No, sir. I verified it on the encrypted disk."

"That's a large increase. One number off and it would be only a few degrees."

"Taken alone, sir, that would be my estimation, but coupled with all four Marines having relatively the same percentage of increase in strength, intelligence, speed, and accuracy . . . no. All toxicology is negative for all substances. All. Yet, these men could win the Olympics by themselves." She lowered herself into the chair.

"Didn't you find one drug that would do this?"

She smiled. Dr. Figaroa was already used to her thoroughness. "Many street forms of speed would, but not at that decimal."

Figaroa said, "I have to agree. It would even take months of steroids to increase strength, but they don't do a thing for the intelligence."

Figaroa sat now, reading again and comparing it to the previous month's testing before the men were given the all-clear for duty status. "Jansen needs to see this." He stood, abruptly, then moved around his desk, laying the files down long enough to strip off his white lab coat and tell his receptionist he'd be gone for a while.

Durry was relieved he believed her. "Thank you, sir."

"You're coming too, Ensign."

He steered her with him, and she snatched her cover off the table. He rushed her so fast she felt like she was running. "Doctor?"

"We're leaving the building."

"Going where?"

"The Pentagon."

Barbara thought, *Oh God, what have I done?*

Clancy woke instantly, her spine feeling tight.

She'd experienced it before. It was as if someone shook her, yet she remained still, opening her eyes in time to see a gloved hand come down over her mouth. She screamed as his heavy weight pushed her into the mattress, his knees pinning her arms. He bent close, his mouth near her ear.

"Go home, McRae."

A chill ripped over her. *Oh God.*

"It will get worse."

She struggled beneath him, pushing against his weight, and for the first time she felt completely helpless. She hated it and bucked, unseating him, and when he struggled to right himself, she drew up her knee, knocking him in the nuts. He grunted in pain, but held tight, and she pushed her knees against his chest.

"Get the hell off me!" she screamed at the top of her lungs. He tried to cover her mouth as she twisted wildly on the bed, shoving and kicking until she planted both feet dead center on his chest and thrust. He went flying backward, hit the desk, then rolled around and darted out the still-open door.

Clancy shot off the bed, looked around for a weapon, then grabbed a thick glass ashtray and followed. "Oh, I'm so going to hurt you."

She rushed down the hall, moving back and forth away from the doors, then flew to the staircase, overtook half, then paused at the window. In the center of the night, the city was awake and brightly lit, and she searched the crowd till she saw a man running against the edge of the buildings. *Gotcha,* she thought. Her rapid steps drummed in the stairwell and she pushed through two doors and out onto the streets. Her bare feet slapped the concrete as she ran after him. It was a block before she faced that she'd lost him and she turned back. She heard a catcall and looked up. Around the outdoor bistros and in front of shops, people stared at her, and a couple of rude remarks blistered the air.

*Oh, this has got to be one of the most embarrassing moments of my life,* she thought, backing into the hotel while holding down her T-shirt. Since that's all she wore.

Inside and moving down the hall, she let her anger simmer, yet when a door opened and a man in his pajamas appeared she snapped, "Oh, so now you come to see what happened?" He retreated into his room.

She hurried past. Inside, she threw the lock, drew the chain, then braced a chair back beneath the knob. Holding the ashtray defensively, she checked the room, then laid it aside and plopped into a chair.

She covered her face. *I'm in way over my head.*

The only person who could possibly know where she was or what she was doing was Colonel Cook, and that was a couple of days ago. He had to keep it quiet or his career was over for authorizing the insertion. If she knuckled under to this warning, he'd win.

The Marines would lose.

She wasn't going anywhere, least of all home. She jumped up and went to the closet, dragging her flight bag to the bed and throwing her few things inside. She'd hide, get far away from this hotel.

But first, she needed a gun.

# Nine

Mike stared at the small black chunk of plastic the size of a walnut.

The diagram and photos were on the seat beside him. They told him little, but like the colonel, he wondered what this was doing in Libya. The solid black material had gold in the grooves. It meant nothing to him but a bunch of squiggles and lines, and they were still trying to make something out of it. It led him nowhere and he slipped it into his pack and left the truck. A few feet away, his satellite phone rang.

Jansen. "I've got the background on the woman. How well do you know her?"

"Very little." He ducked out of sight and explained.

"Clancy Moira McRae, four years in the Navy, then transferred to the Pentagon. Computer Intel Division. Honorably discharged, college, graduate study at Cornell."

"And?"

"She's one of ours, Mike. Military contractor."

That meant she was hired by the Department of Defense to do something. "Is there a reason you're giving me this piecemeal?"

"That's it. I can get more on her, but not on her job. No details. There's a permanent lock on her job."

That could mean anything from NSA to Homeland Security. "Clearance?" Mike asked.

"Class A."

Mike's brows shot up. His was class A.

Jansen said he'd look into it, and Mike was about to sign off when he heard a woman scream, then another panicked shout.

"Later, sir," he said as he hurried toward the sound and rounded a corner overgrown with vines and flowers. He saw the heavy stainless steel cart rolling down the street, the slope of the road sending it barreling toward the low side of the street.

There was nothing to stop it. Except a child—and Clancy.

Mike bolted, but Clancy was fast, grabbed the child, tucked him to her body as she spun out of the path so fast they fell.

The cart shot past and crashed into a parked car. Plastic taillights went flying and people converged, yelling as a woman pushed her way between the people to the boy. She yanked him into her arms, then helped Clancy up in almost an afterthought.

The boy thanked her, shaking her hand, but when his mother scrubbed her hands over his face and shoulders, he clung to her.

Clancy leaned against the nearest wall, shaken.

The owner of the cart rushed to apologize, claiming the rope broke, then had to deal with the man's wrecked car. Mike's gaze shifted to Clancy as she walked to the vendor cart, took a slushy drink tottering on the edge, then rubbed it over her forehead before she drank.

Mike remained hidden and walked on the opposite side of the street, out of the sun and away from her; then he stopped in the spot where the vendor cart had been. Covertly, his gaze followed the path, the bumps in the road from the iron loops in the stone walls for securing cars or animals. Necessary in the steep area; even the sidewalks tilted. Accident, he decided, then bent to grab the rope and let it slide through his fingers to the end. He started at the tip.

Okay, maybe not.

\* \* \*

Fifteen minutes later, Mike stood outside her hotel room door. She was gone. The maid was in the room, her cart blocking the door. Mike pushed it aside and entered, and scared the maid in the middle of stripping sheets off the bed.

He asked anyway.

"*Sí*, in the middle of the night, senor."

"Do you know where she went?"

The maid shook her head, and Mike moved in and looked around. The young girl remained perfectly still, only her eyes following him. He thanked her and headed to the door, then stopped and went to the trash can. It was filled with boxes. Then he noticed more boxes in the maid's cart. He expected to find a receipt, or something to lead him to her. But electronics? he questioned, pulling out tangles of wires and chips. There were parts he recognized and most he didn't, but a DVD player, a cell phone, and a soldering iron? *Christ, Clancy, what are you doing?* Traveling under a false passport, a lock on her job, tearing apart the insides of computers. She was building something.

He thought the worst and tried not to. He pushed down his instinctive response of defense and attack. There had to be a reasonable explanation and he hoped she had one. More than he wanted, or should, he liked her, she was . . . scrappy, a fighter, and turning him on was easy for her. If she knew, he'd be cannon fodder.

He threw the electronics back in the trash and left. Everything wasn't as it seemed, he knew from experience, and until he had information, for all he knew, the lock on her job meant she was CIA.

In the early morning, Salache stood from an apartment three stories up. With a perfect view of the park below, he watched his wife and children romp on the grass as he sipped a soft drink. Marianna tickled them, the giggles making him smile as he waited to learn something that revealed why she'd been so distant lately. Briefly, he suspected a love affair, but dismissed it. Not out of arrogance, but because he knew Marianna. She would never betray her beliefs, and "thou shall not" was etched in her soul.

He glanced back into the apartment, his gaze moving slowly over the couple sitting on the sofa. Bound, gagged, and still in their pajamas. He didn't want to hurt them, but finding the perfect, completely unsuspecting way to observe was valuable. Advantages, each set in motion with the belief that at least one would fail. Always have a backup. There was no perfection. He rubbed his smooth chin, smiling. Not yet.

Watching his wife, he stiffened when she called out to the children to join her as she started for the parking lot. Marianna didn't drive. His pulse pounded as he waited for his fantasy to be shattered, and then he felt instant relief shudder through him when her chauffeured car slid to the curb. Her guards were not close today. She despised that they trailed her, but he refused to bend to her wishes, yet he saw them now, leaving their hiding spots in doorways and cafés. When his family was a couple of blocks up the street, he called her.

"We just left the park, we're going home. Are you there now?"

"No," he said. "I'm in my lab but I'll see you in a half hour or so." They hung up, and he pocketed the phone and crossed to the couple.

They flinched when he sliced through the bonds, then yanked off the tape.

"I apologize for scaring you. Know that this has been for love." He didn't warn them, didn't threaten. It was pointless, they knew. He headed to the door, stepping over the dead dog, then pausing to wipe its blood off his shoe.

He left, smiling.

If he was wrong about Marianna, she would never know he'd distrusted her. If he was right, well . . . she'd feel the wound she'd inflicted on him.

\* \* \*

Mike wanted proof the Hellfires were destroyed. Evidence. A chunk of the fuselage would be nice, he thought, and knew he couldn't close the book on the UAV till he had the verification in his hands. There were roads on the edge of the rain forest. After that, it was by foot or the river, and the UAV crash wasn't anywhere near the water. He hoped Gantz's math equations of the trajectory were accurate or close to. Walking around a mountainside for days was nothing compared to live-fire combat and evasion. A stroll.

He'd rather be having a deep discussion with Clancy, and was still bothered by the electronics in the room, but questioning her wasn't an option. He had to respect her clearance. She'd obviously earned it. It was the lockout on her job that gave him the willies. He just couldn't picture her as CIA.

In the early morning, the air hung thickly, though cooler, almost dense to the touch. He listened carefully as he moved, deciphering his own breathing and footsteps from the little creatures moving in the distance. They were aware of him and watching. He was keenly aware that this part of the world was dangerous and it had nothing to do with predators. The plants could kill, sticky and poisonous, and his gloves saved him from having to look where he touched.

Mike gripped a tree root and pulled himself up the incline. Then in the clearing under the sun, he drew his palm-sized binoculars, a Cyclops version. He tested the movement of the autofocus, then scanned the area once, and started from nearest to him, systematically clearing the area of predators before moving outward. Mike swung to the right, lower in the valley. Movement was sporadic, the flutter of birds moving from branch to branch, monkeys doing the same, and he could see only the tremble of bushes and trees, like short, quick bursts of air. He followed it, and where the trees thinned he hurried to focus. He jerked back, squinted, then focused again.

Now why would she be out alone?

Mike swung farther right, and saw something behind her, about two hundred yards and coming fast. She was walking slowly, unsuspecting of the predator. Immediately, he slid down the hillside on the side of his boot, then hit the ground running, hoping to intercept before they reached her. He pushed himself, batting at obstructions, jumping debris. He grabbed a vine and leaped over a creek, then stopped.

He listened, closing his eyes for a moment, separating his breathing and heartbeat from other details—the scent of disturbed earth, the buzz of insects stirred from hiding, monkeys swinging above him. He tipped his head, his gaze sliding over the ground, and he could feel it before he saw the snake wiggle out and shimmy across the ground. The soft thump of footsteps hummed under the thick heat, and he turned in the direction.

Clancy swiped her face and the back of her neck as she walked. No breeze and the sun barely skipped the forest floor. She held a Palm Pilot, minus a few processors since she'd used and destroyed them to re-create the Terminator. She checked the map to make certain she was still aligned with the river, then threw her leg over a fallen log. Her bootlace caught on a broken branch and she twisted to look, then went perfectly still.

She wasn't alone.

Her gaze moved across the ground, then up from the bare muddy feet. She saw bare skin, painted to look like the jungle, yet when she still saw skin at the thighs, she was afraid to look farther. Her gaze shot up. Indian. Quechua? His clothing barely covered the essentials, his painted body ropy with muscle and whipcord slim.

Then he started toward her.

She rushed to unhook her boot and was building up to one hell of a scream when he reached for her and covered her mouth. Then with a strength that belied his size, he backed away, carrying her into the forest. They didn't go far. He stopped, faced her in another direction, then pointed over her shoulder. His hand remained on her mouth, the pressure clutching her back against his chest. She barely heard the footsteps over the wild beat of her heart. A rapid trot, she thought, then saw a man between the trees run right past their position.

Carrying a high-powered rifle.

With a scope.

Mike raced to intercept. It was like calculating the trajectory of a bullet, leading his target. He heard the whip of leaves against flesh and quickened his pace. Then he ducked in behind a tree, using the mass as a shield. Mike didn't have time for the rules of engagement and remained hidden, listening to the approaching footsteps. Louder, closer . . . he rolled around and punched the man in the throat. He dropped on his back, choking. Mike grabbed him by the shirt and delivered a blow to his nose. The man never saw it coming. It was less painless that way.

Mike pulled the rifle aside; then his gaze ripped over the man's face. His first thought: *A hitter, the man's an assassin.* Clancy? Till he learned about Clancy, no one knew Mike was here, yet the evidence at his feet, one Ryce P. Denner, he read in his passport, said he'd been close and following her for a long time. Then he found Clancy's picture in his shirt pocket. Mike wanted to pound him all over again and quickly bound and gagged Denner, then lashed him to a tree. Satisfied he couldn't move without strangling himself, he looked into the forest.

Clancy should have been this far by now.

When the man was gone, the Indian released her, but Clancy still frowned at the jungle. She'd never heard him. Nor the Indian. Then she groaned, just remembering she was armed. Hesitantly, she looked at the Indian, forcing a smile. Which wasn't easy. He was scary looking, his body painted black and green and blending in where he stood. He held a sharpened spear and a small black shield inlaid with gold on his forearm. Why did he warn her? Then suddenly he grabbed her hand and said something. She shook her head and tried to draw back. His grip tightened and fractures of fear riddled up her spine.

*Nobody's kidnapping me again.* She shook her head. He frowned, confused, looking so young under all that paint. He really believed she'd leave with him. For what, a mate? *My prospects are improving over an orangutan and my ex.*

An instant later, she flinched when Mike appeared, blocking her with his body, breaking the contact and aiming at the Indian's head.

"Don't." *Where did he come from?*

"Did he hurt you?"

"No." She pushed his arm down and stepped between them.

"Jesus, woman!" Quickly, Mike aimed over her shoulder.

The Indian looked between the two for a moment, his hand on his knife, then immediately turned away, melting into the forest. They were both quiet, just staring at the empty spot in the jungle.

"You feel like you were just in another century?" Mike said into the silence.

"Yeah, how cool was that?" she said, then turned her head. "He looked so deadly." But couldn't be more than twenty.

"You had a tail."

"Yeah. Tarzan warned me, then wanted to date me, I think." She was a little flattered, a thought probably deserving of some serious therapy. "You have the guy with the rifle." His presence here said he'd done something about him. "Who was it?"

"The German."

"Probably not German at all, huh?"

The sun blistered down on the open market, a maze of street vendors filling the park, locals in colorful clothing milling with the tourists, the poor with the wealthy. Music and singing came from somewhere to his far left, and Antone decided he liked Peru. The people, they were always so happy with what they had. It had been a long time since he'd seen his own people like this. Yet his attention was on the woman, and Choufani watched her stroll through the crowded market. She hadn't done it much, at least not alone, he thought. She kept glancing back at the two men trailing her at a distance. As if she wanted to escape.

She was beautiful, and reminded him of a Polynesian woman he'd met once. Her skin the color of creamed coffee, her ink-black hair straight, falling down her back and tucked in a sparkling clasp. Effortlessly, she moved between the busy vendors and customers, as if she were air. They didn't seem to notice her or respond to her presence until she stopped to inspect a scarf. The vendor rushed to her side, smiling and bobbing as the delicate fabric slipped over her fingertips. She smiled, saying something that made the vendor look bashful. She went to pay for it and one of the two men rushed forward.

She waved her hand, her tone sharp and decisive, then continued to dole out money for the goods. The vendor glanced at the bodyguards, then went back to changing money. She was Marianna de la Rosa Salache, the wife of a local businessman, an entrepreneur. A man who hadn't been seen in over a year.

But his mark was everywhere; he'd learned from the locals. Their family name was on a plaque inside nearly half the buildings in the city. Salache had designed the most amazing fountain he'd ever seen, yet he didn't come to admire his work.

Marianna tucked her purchase in her handbag, then looked up and met his gaze directly. He felt struck by her light eyes, and he nodded ever so slightly. She stared at him with unquestionable interest and confusion. He'd made no effort to disguise his presence, and this would not be the first time they would meet. He would make certain of it.

The lavender paper had come from her home. Found in

the pocket of a terrorist who'd bombed a wedding, killing nearly a hundred, including the new bride.

His sister.

As far as Choufani was concerned, she was his prime suspect.

Clancy trailed Mike, his strides long, and she occupied herself with trying to put her feet in his prints. It was better than thinking about what he'd just told her.

"Did you hear me? He's a hitter," Mike said quietly.

"Assassin, I get it." This was unbelievable.

"He's after you."

"How do you figure?"

"That we've seen him before says he's been following you," he said. "And I just arrived." He didn't say how, but till Pablo told him about her, no one had really seen him.

"And then this was on him."

He paused long enough to hand her the photo. Clancy took it, more than a little shocked to see herself shopping in Panama. Oh man. She'd seen the German or whoever he was a couple of times, at the café and before she went back to her hotel after the cart cut loose. Then there was last night and now this? Changing towns and hotels hadn't done much good, obviously. Cook knew where she was by the tracking chip, but she'd crushed it two days ago. Then how did the German know enough to be at the Peru border when they were? Or was that just chance? Did Cook really have the guts to send someone to keep her quiet?

Someone paid to take her life. A killer.

"The cart that almost hit you," Mike said and she looked at him. "The rope was cut, not old." She didn't say anything, but Mike could tell this was crushing her. Reality bites sometimes.

"You saw that? Then *you've* been everywhere I have too." What was she thinking? It wasn't Mike last night. She'd have known just by the raw sexy pheromones the guy radiated.

Suddenly Mike stopped and cursed. Clancy moved around him. He stared at the tree as if it would grow new limbs any second.

"That's impossible."

"Where is he?" She looked around for a trail and found only her own. "It's been cleared, they cleaned up." She pointed to the brushstrokes on the dirt floor.

"Not quite," he said from the opposite side of the tree.

Clancy came to his side. Black slip ties were cut in pieces on the ground, but what shocked her was the blood. Everywhere. It scraped up the sides of the tree. She leaned close. "Is that skin?" Bits of bloody pink clung to the trunk. "Oh God, that's disgusting." She turned away from the gore. "I guess you didn't tie him up all that well."

Mike turned his head and gave her a hard stare.

"Okay, Boy Scout, then where is he and what could do that?" She pointed to the blood and tissue.

"Nothing. He had help."

"It looks almost as if they dragged him up the tree."

Mike lifted his gaze to the treetops and thought of Renoux's words: *plucked out of the Andean Mountains like vultures to the dead.* He looked at her. "We need to move."

His tone grabbed her, and then he did, pulling her with him. They weren't alone, she realized, and with him ran through the forest, relieved when she saw it thin. But it was just a path. Mike took it, then turned off, ducking behind some brush and pulling her down beside him.

"You think whoever did that to the German is out there?"

"Yes, and he wasn't a German," he whispered. "His name is Denner." He fished in his shirt pocket and handed her a stack of passports. He kept watch on the area, waiting for something to tell him whoever was out there.

"Bolivia, Hungary, Hong Kong, French, U.S.?"

"That's the real one." He tapped the U.S. passport.

"You'll have to teach me that."

"Notice the countries?"

She frowned at each.

"They're strategic jumping-off points, all over the world."

"This guy could have a Bolivian passport and travel freely in South America," she said. "A Hong Kong one and the Far East was open to him."

"He's CIA or a hired asset."

"I feel so important." She sagged beside him. "How do you know?"

"I've seen him before. Or his file. I didn't notice it at the bus, but clean him up and cut his hair? Yeah, he's company." He looked at her. "If he's here, then it's sanctioned."

She shook her heard. "Colonel Cook would never let this out." She clamped her lips shut. "Crap." Why was she confessing to *him*?

"Let what out, and you don't mean Carl Davis Cook?"

She frowned hard.

"He's a former deputy chief, Clancy."

"Of what?"

He aimed his gun. "DIA."

Defense Intelligence Agency. Could she dig her own hole any deeper?

"And he's got some nasty people who owe him," Mike said, his gaze on their surroundings.

"We've met, thank you," she said. "A man broke into my room last night."

He looked at her sharply and she told him what happened, minus the part about running into the street half naked. She turned her arms out and showed him the purple bruises. "Think it works as an accessory?"

"Christ." The marks were dark and brutal, stirring something in him. No wonder she left in the middle of the night.

"What do you want? Oh, woe is me, protect me? I'm not a kid."

"What are you?"

She jerked back, brows high. "Excuse me?"

"What are you doing here that people want to kill you?"

"I can be a real bitch sometimes." He wasn't amused. "And I could ask you the same thing. I bet there are a handful of people who can spot a fake passport and handle explosives so easily."

He met her gaze, and she felt it tear over her, in that intense way he did everything. She wasn't telling him anything, for more reasons than security, but because he wouldn't understand. There was no gray area for Mike, she thought. Only right and wrong, black and white, fast or slow.

"We both have a class-A clearance and we're going to stop this dance today," he said, and Clancy felt a chill from his determined tone.

"You had me checked out? What gives you the damn right to nose into my business?"

The next sound spoke volumes. The shot tore through the leaves and underbrush, and Clancy heard it shoot past her head. She'd never forget that sound and dropped to the ground, drawing her weapon.

"That?" Mike said dryly, then glanced at her. "What do you expect to hit with that peashooter?"

She looked at the .22. "Hey, it was cheap and available. Got something better?"

Mike slipped a pistol from a holster under his pant leg and handed it over. Then he just pulled off the holster and gave it over too. "They're after you."

"My assassin is dead and gone. They're following us, I agree. After me? Not so much. But I plan to find out." She stood in a trapezoid stance and aimed. "I'll wing him and you can beat a confession out of him."

She was something else, he thought, yet knew she was serious. "No, we make them come to us."

Her gaze flicked to his. "Agreed."

He was off in a shot. Clancy was behind him, struggling to keep up. *Now we see the difference of a treadmill and the road,* she thought. Impact to her legs exhausted her, and she was a big drenched mess when she grabbed his shirt and jerked him to a stop. She collapsed on the ground, then waved him on.

"Dying here, leave me, save yourself."

"Oh, Christ." He smiled.

"Who is it?"

"One guy, not too good at hiding."

"Okay, take him out, I'll just rest."

"Come on, McRae, we've got less than a half mile to the town." He pulled her up and pushed her along. "My truck is on the other side of the valley. We have to hoof it."

"Hoof. Do I look like a pack mule?" She was whining again, but inside her boots, there were blisters screaming at her to stop.

It wasn't until Mike pushed her into an alley that she realized they were already near a town. Whether it was the one she left or not didn't enter her brain. She slid to the ground on a path under some trees.

"No, no resting yet." He pulled her up. "Take cover."

There was nothing behind her expect trash cans and the back of an adobe building. She used the tree and checked the load of her pistol. "What do you want me to do?" He issued crisp, clear orders. She grinned at him.

"What?"

"Hi, Marine."

He didn't say anything.

"Give it up, Mike. You aren't fooling anyone, least of all me."

Not a word. But then, she didn't think he would. He'd probably fall on his sword before giving up information. "I was a medic in the Navy, I practically lived with you guys for two years."

"I wouldn't broadcast that if you want to keep a good girl reputation."

She snickered to herself. Boy, was he in for a shock.

"Combat?" he asked. Jansen had told him only the minimal.

"Desert Storm. First land assault."

He frowned hard, his gaze skipping over her and ending on her face. He hadn't noticed her age on her passport. "You don't look old enough."

She smiled. "Oh, be still, my heart. Wanna card me?"

"Just stay back, jailbird."

"Wow, a sense of humor." She smiled to herself as he moved farther to the edge of the path. She heard the footsteps. This guy wasn't hiding a thing about his approach. Either he knew no one was around, or he didn't care if he was heard. Not a good sign.

Then Mike moved deeper into the forest again.

He'd gone farther than she thought when she saw him to her left and come up behind the man. She spotted the guy's legs through the brush, and then he wasn't on them, lifted off the ground. No gunshot, no punch, and then a moment later, Mike held the man in a headlock and forced him out into the sun.

Clancy stepped out, aiming. "He won't roast on the spit well, Klugg, throw him back. I wanted mastodon."

Mike tried not to smile as he twisted his captive toward her. "Meet Howard Gantz, CIA. Now you believe me?"

Clancy replied with a punch to the agent's face.

Eduardo felt the rushing heat in his blood, the feeling that drove him into archaeology: the chance to see something that hadn't been viewed in a thousand years. Wearing gloves and in a clean room, he stood before a long steel table, lights beneath it under a frosted-glass top to show any fractures and breakage. He almost didn't want to open it. The iconology warned him not to break the seal.

The figures depicted warriors with no weapons. Highly unusual. Joined hands and crossed spears as if guarding this urn alone. The swirls etched alongside the warriors he'd never seen before, yet common etchings showed the gods of the mountain and water.

Oddly there was no moon and sun god depicted, another unusual find. Eduardo knew it meant the breath of the gods and possibly coming from the warriors' mouths or through them. As if at some point the warriors had the power of the gods. A poison perhaps, or some drink giving great strength? Or a hallucinogenic. Peru was filled with wild coco fields, and cultivated ones unfortunately. He didn't know since little was known about their alchemy.

With a razor, he made a small slice in the wax seal. It was surprisingly soft. He'd never have expected anything but chips, yet the stone sarcophagus that held this would have been sealed airtight. Only a recent cave-in near the dwellings had unearthed it. It was the wonderful thing about exploring Peru, there was still so much to find, so much hidden in the Andes.

The wax flecked off in spots, showing boldly on the lighted surface. He carefully made a small enough hole to insert a syringe, the urn bracketed with mechanical arms and easy to maneuver. Beyond him were three undergraduate students.

"You may ask questions," he said, picking up the syringe. He inserted it in the small hole, frowning when he heard a slight hiss. *My God, it's airtight.* He drew the plunger. The needle was wide enough to draw any loose substance, but if the container were filled with anything else, nothing would happen. Then he would have to lift the seal.

Eduardo felt as if he were prying into something sacred. The process was slow, taking several attempts over days because keeping the layers of wax intact would tell them where the wax came from, if it was indeed wax, and possibly where the Moche had been before this spot.

Archaeologists knew they had formed bands and lived on the coast. There were several sights, Lord of Sipan, and Trujillo. They had been opened and displayed, yet the Loma Negra dig was the most recent, and he and his team had sole possession of the find thanks to a benefactor who remained anonymous.

He drew the needle farther back, disappointed when there was nothing in the tube. He hadn't expected there to be. The X-rays told them whatever was inside moved slowly, the consistency of honey, and something solid, perhaps the possibility of rock or bone inside. He tried again, and withdrew the plunger, and went still, careful not to break the seal. He had to stop. Any more movement and he could destroy the contents. He withdrew the syringe, excitement coursing through him as a pale substance swirled inside the tube, as fine as ash.

One assistant held open a bag. Before he put it inside, he turned back to the table, took out a dish, and tapped the tip on the petri dish, before bagging it. There was only a few spatters of ash. Nothing more than a speck for a microscope. Odd. The X-ray showed much more inside. Why wouldn't it draw in the syringe?

"The urn is two thousand years old at least," an onlooker said. "There is already proof that Moche predates the Inca, but what if this find is an offshoot of the same society?"

"Entirely possible. It is a theory coined by several scholars. I don't believe in that theory as well. From what we've unearthed I believe this is the central hub of the society, and the coastal tribes were a part of natural migration."

"Or running in fear?"

He looked up, frowning.

"It wasn't a society for longevity, Professor," the young woman said. "Ritual death, drinking blood of the slain. That would scare anyone to moving away."

"If you knew otherwise, and had experienced another lifestyle perhaps, but they were born and raised into this strict society. They knew nothing else."

"Wouldn't you, no matter what," a somber student said, "want to leave a place that offered up humans to the gods of the sun and moon?"

"Yes, *I* would. That is the mystery of the Moche. They remained and flourished."

"None of them exist."

"Perhaps you should review your studies. The Lambayeque are direct descendants, and we cannot discount that the Quechua Indians have many similarities."

Some of the tedious work was taken away by modern science, and technology. He'd photographed it all, yet was recording on video so he didn't have to pause to take notes and make the painstaking re-creations he did as a student. But this was what he enjoyed most, clearing away the depth of time to see the mark of mankind beneath.

With tweezers and a gentle touch, he started to pull off the first fragment. He saw the imprint of a thumb, and excitement bubbled through him and his patience waned. The door opened sharply.

"Gil, please."

"Professor, you should read this report."

Eduardo looked at the young man and thought, *He's been up all night doing a chemical analysis on the wax.* He held a sheaf of papers. But it was his expression that made him lay down the tweezers and step back from the table.

"What's wrong?"

Gil glanced at the other students, then the professor. "All the iconology was common, what we've seen in every dig except this one." He pointed to the sketch on the wall. "The warrior is defending with no weapon, and yet unlike the other pictographs we've discovered, in this urn"—he gestured—"the gods are depicted right beside them."

He understood now. "They didn't consider themselves equals to the gods in any form. They worshipped and feared them."

Gil stared at the urn. "Enough to believe they trapped one in there?"

"Why would you say that?"

"Because that's not a wax seal, it's human skin."

# Ten

"Apparently the lady is pissed, Howard."

"Christ, let go so I can defend myself, then."

Clancy looked at Mike, confused. "Gantz? But that's the name you put on the paper."

"You shot at us?"

"No, not me. I heard it."

Mike released Gantz and checked the man's gun. He shook his head. It hadn't been fired. "So why are you following me?" Mike asked.

"Not you, her." Gantz strained to look up. "There's a flag on her, Gannon."

Gannon, she thought, realizing that's about all she knew about him, really.

"Confirmed?"

"No, no yet, but it's on the loop." The man straightened his clothing.

Yet Clancy's attention was on Mike. He was too quiet, and when he looked at her she knew everything had changed. The air practically frosted between them.

Then he came toward her. "Let's go."

She backed up, more than a little stunned. God, he looked ready to choke her. "Whoa, stay right there." She backed up another step. "What's the matter? I get that a flag is serious stuff, but what is it?"

"It's a watch list, Clancy. Homeland Security, FBI, Interpol, CIA, the works." He pulled her close, holding her nearly against him as he searched her and quickly relieved her of her weapons.

"You have no right!" She tried to take the gun back.

He held it out of her reach. "Don't, and I do." Over her head, he said to Gantz, "My truck. That way, two miles. Take a cab." He tossed him the keys.

Gantz obeyed and Clancy glared at Mike, wondering who the hell he was that CIA officers jumped through hoops for him. "I'm not saying anything to you, Gannon, and if you think you can bully me, you're mistaken." She yanked her arms free and folded them over her middle. "But kind soul that I am, I'm ready to listen while your chauffeur brings your truck around."

"Flag means if you're spotted, capture. If not possible, eliminate."

"Oh, for heaven's sake. He could be lying, you know?"

"Yes, and until I confirm, you're mine."

"I'm all aflutter."

Mike slid her a thin glance, yet said nothing. Nothing was his motto, she thought. She still had choices: the press for one, the Senate another. Provided she got out of Peru alive. But that he went ice cold on her, like she was some package to be picked up and delivered, stung. A lot. "And here I thought I might mean something to you."

Mike stared into the whiskey-dark eyes and almost folded. She was the first woman who didn't back down, who gave as good as she got. She wasn't all tears and complaints, but getting it done, and he was saved from saying anything when Gantz barreled down the road, a flock of chickens skipping out of the truck's path.

He stopped, threw the truck in neutral, and left it running. "I'll be waiting for your call."

Gantz looked at Clancy, rubbing his mouth. She snarled at him like an angry cat. Mike arched a brow at her, then gave

Gantz Denner's passports. "Find out what you can on him. He's a hitter, after her."

"Figures." Gantz flipped through them. "You leave him alive or not?"

He told Gantz about what they'd found, and Gantz looked pointedly at Clancy. "She doesn't look capable."

"She was with me."

"All the time?"

Mike delivered a look that said *don't question* and Gantz shrugged and left them. At the side of the truck, Mike stared at Clancy, deadpan. "Get in."

*This is the ugly part,* she thought, and having no choice, she climbed inside.

Richora backed away from the street, turned, and walked in the other direction. He holstered his gun, disappointed he'd missed her. "But what have you done to anger your rescuer?"

Even from the distance, he could see the man's fury. But Richora wasn't concerned about killing the couple. It would be a pleasure he'd stretch out till he could avenge his sister's son. Yet that they were still together warned him they weren't without some skills. Salache wanted no witnesses, and Richora considered that when this transaction was over—he too would be a last witness. One who knew Salache's real face, though the memory of it was fading in his mind.

He'd have to find a photograph to remind himself of exactly who he was dealing with. While the face changed, the man inside did not. Salache wasn't flicking his nose at governments; he planned to bring them to their knees.

The car door was standing open when Richora slid into the rear of the sedan and patted the side. It rolled away, his men hopping into cars. Behind them, the streets started to fill with people again, some watching the car drive away. They wouldn't ask; it was better to be ignorant of these matters. Then a thought filled his mind.

Ignorance is the single greatest tool of oppression. He knew of that firsthand. His people, the first inhabitants of Peru, were pushed farther into the jungle by the Spaniards and the Dutch. They had survived centuries and still lived the same culture as their ancestors. Primitive, yes, but happy. Untouched by greed. Richora had been touched by greed or he wouldn't be in this deal with Salache. He didn't want what Salache had, nothing except his wife, yet she was out of his reach and money was a greater comfort.

His phone rang and he slipped the earpiece in before answering.

"Back off, he might see you."

"I'm well aware of that," Richora said.

"He doesn't know a thing and he's not here for you. Let it go."

"But I am here for them." Richora was amused with himself. He was sounding like Salache.

"Not if you want to sell this product. He's hunting. Retreat or you'll regret it."

The threat made him stiffen. "What do you plan to do?" Alejo said.

"Not me, *him*."

The phone went dead and Richora looked at it. He snapped it closed, pocketing it, then smiled. An adversary. A healthy battle before the final victory. He looked forward to it. The man was clever and resourceful, Richora recalled, still fuming over the holes in the boat. But that he destroyed his cargo was unforgivable. Before he would die, this man wouldn't know why, only that he had wronged him. He could go to his death haunted already, he thought, smiling as he checked where they were, then ordered to stop. He rolled down the window.

"Marianna, what are you doing out here alone?"

"I am not." She gestured behind herself to the guards yards back and kept walking.

He left the car and came to her. "You're crying."

She looked away as she discreetly wiped her tears. "You are mistaken, I forgot my sunglasses, and the sun is too bright."

He stepped in front of her. "Who has hurt you?" he said, crowding her when he wanted to touch her. He waved her guards back when they approached. "Marianna?"

"I can't share this with you, Alejo."

"He has done this to you." She knew who he meant.

She looked up. "No. No," she said more firmly. "I have done it to myself." She moved around him and Richora watched her go. The bodyguards passed him and he grabbed one, then simply inclined his head.

"She will not say. Not to Salache either."

Richora dismissed them, yet continued to watch her hurry away—and his heart broke for her.

The room was shut up tight, and despite the hundred-degree temperature outside, it was cold. There were no restraints, no threats. No touching. But he was interrogating her just the same.

Clancy shifted in the chair, drawing her legs in. Mike didn't pace like a caged animal, nor raise his voice. He was more subtle, occasionally moving behind her back on the pretense of getting water, or a bag of stale chips, his hand coming so close several times to stir her hair, let her feel the breeze on her neck. It was starting to make her flinch. Exactly as he wanted. Now he was several feet away, his back against the wall.

"This is what I know, Clancy Moira McRae." He dug into the chip bag. "Arrested for grand theft auto, and drug possession, you were looking at four, five years in jail, hard time." He crunched a chip.

Clancy stared, oddly curious about this side of him. "That was over fifteen years ago."

"So the judge said, four years in jail or four in the Navy, am I right?" He waved with a chip, then ate it.

Clancy inhaled. "How did you find that out? My records were sealed." She'd just turned eighteen then, old enough to go straight to jail without passing Go, and it wasn't her first offense. But the judge tried her as underage. It was the only thing that kept her butt out of prison. That and the Navy.

He slid her a look that revealed little, munching away like a Saturday picnic. "Your Desert Storm record is impressive, then to the Pentagon, computer counterintelligence, and artificial intel. Hum? College on the GI, bioengineering graduate study at Cornell, and now you work for the Department of Defense. What section?"

Clancy looked at the floor. He was pissed, and while she didn't think he'd hurt her, she knew he wouldn't give up.

"There isn't just a flag on you, it's a red one. Priority. Bin Laden's on it." Her eyes got the doe-in-the-headlights look and Mike wanted to stop. Throwing dirty laundry at her like this would make her hate him. "Yeah, that asshole and you, same boat. You're in deep kimchee, and I'm apt to believe them."

"For what reason?"

"A forged passport, in the company of known criminals, building something electronic in your hotel room." Her eyes kept getting rounder. "And you're here, in Peru alone with an assassin after you. And then there is this whisper of conspiracy."

"Conspiracy is a crock." But it would work, she thought. Even the subtle word of it here and there. Smear her first and Cook looks good. Colonel Cook knew that even if she was proven innocent, and that was debatable considering she stole classified material—she'd never live it down. Her career was over. But then, so was his. The truth would come out. Suddenly, she doubted it was Cook. He had as much to lose as she did. "From who?"

"Doesn't matter."

"Perhaps you should check."

"Maybe later."

"No, now. Find out who put that flag up, find out who's waving it under your nose like a matador."

"No." He popped a chip in his mouth and crunched.

*Clearly, he's not giving an inch,* she thought, and looked at her hands on her lap. She needed him on her side. If she didn't get his attention, he would send her packing back to the States under heavy guard. She didn't want to go back in handcuffs. Not without the Marines.

She tipped her head back and looked at him. "Someone's leading you around, Gannon. That red flag is unnecessary and let me tell you what I know. You're Spec Ops, team commander probably, and you're here to recover some hardware, right?"

Mike didn't move a muscle.

"The UAV that crashed."

There was recognition, not anything one would see, but she did. Just below the surface, he tensed, right along his ribs. The man had incredible control, she thought, and she left the chair and went to her bag, digging her hand inside. "This what you're looking for?" She tossed him a chunk of something.

He caught it, and stared at the thick piece of gray material. He studied the depth of it, pulling out his knife to scrape the edge. It bent, flexible, a polymer fiber and aluminum compound, probably. Then he realized it was the tail of the UAV. *Jesus.*

"Where did you get this?"

"I'd been in the jungle since dawn and was on my way *back* when the German—Denner showed up." She pulled out the Palm Pilot. "I found it here."

She pointed to the east, and Mike thought, it was possible. It was inside the area Gantz had calculated. "We met here, with the Indian."

It was nearly four miles. Nearer to the mountains. "You're certain?"

She nudged him. "Yes, I can read a map. A couple hundred feet up are the ruins, some ancient Inca dwellings." She shrugged. "Just holes in the side of the mountain. They weren't on a tour map."

"Moche," he said and looked up. "The Moche, not Inca. They're older than dirt."

"Wow, we *are* a font of knowledge."

"I minored in marine archaeology. It was a chapter, nothing up close and personal." Yet he hoped the UAV didn't crash into something that could never be recovered. He ran his thumb over the piece and the small numbers still printed in black on the edge. "Was there more?"

She shook her head. "Pieces? No, and I looked. Not long or far, I'm only so adventurous with a peashooter." He slid her a glance that hid a smile. "There was an impact mark on the ground. Not really noticeable either."

"The thing weights seven hundred pounds. It should have made a dent the size of a car."

"Makes you wonder who's going through all this trouble to erase it and why, huh?"

He lifted his gaze to hers, and Mike experienced an unfamiliar feeling, as if he was looking into the face of his ideal match. Just as a piece of contentment he hadn't known in years settled in him, he mentally shook himself, reminding himself she was under some heavy charges. Conspiracy to commit treason, betraying your country were grounds for execution.

"But that"—she waved at the fragment—"was as if that was just dropped there."

"Well, we know that's not possible."

"What do *we* know, Mike Gannon?"

As he held the fragment, only his gaze shifted to her.

"You're looking for that and the men the U.S. sent to recover it."

His dark eyes narrowed dangerously, so intense it cut off her breath for a second. "Fine, then don't expect more from me."

Then his voice went soft and she felt it roll down her spine and leave a warm trail over her. "You can tell me, Clancy."

"That's really smooth, Marine. That tone get you laid a lot?" He choked, but she didn't stop as she said, "I'm curious, is the Spec Ops Marine asking, or the guy who kissed me at the bus stop?"

His gaze lowered over her, a powerful stroke over her skin. "Both."

"I don't know you well enough to trust you with classified material." He wasn't happy about that. "If I tell you anything I want your word that it won't go further."

"No."

"Say again?"

"No, I won't give my word because if you have intel on my men, then I want it now."

She stepped back. "*Your* men?" No wonder he was hellbent on information. "If they are your team, then why weren't you with them?"

He pulled up his T-shirt sleeve to show the red scar on his shoulder. "Recovering."

Clancy came to him. "How old is this?"

"A month or so."

"You heal quickly." For a moment Clancy thought, if they injected four, then why not five? But she dismissed the thought after she discreetly looked for the insertion mark. Mike was fast and strong from years of training. If he had a biopod in him, he'd be dangerously out of control by now.

"What have you got to do with my team?"

She lifted her gaze. "DiFazio, Valnik, Palmer, and Krane."

His dark brows pinched, and he loomed over her.

Time to get his attention, she thought. "They were volunteers to use a new technology, field enhancement."

Mike thought of the lock on her job. "It's not gear or a new GPS, is it?"

She shook her head and began explaining and with each word, watched his fury build.

*Special Operations*
*The Pentagon*

"Dr. Figaroa is here, sir."

Jansen didn't look at the speaker and blindly tapped the button. "Please tell him I don't have a spare—"

The door opened and Figaroa strode in. "You need to find one, Hank."

Jansen sat back. "Can't this wait? I have an appointment at NMCC in fifteen minutes and with traffic . . ."

"No, sir, you need to see this."

Ensign Durry stood beside him at attention. "At ease, Ensign, please have a seat."

Figaroa did and she followed suit. Jansen listened as Dr. Figaroa explained what she'd found, then took a moment to study the findings. It was amazing. "You're certain this is not a typographical error."

"Yes, sir, I triple checked it," Durry said.

"Ensign," he said, looking at the papers. "You have a comment before we go further?"

Her brows knit for a moment. "No, sir."

"Good, what you find in these files is classified."

"Yes, sir, of course, sir."

"Which means if I hear about it, I'll know where it came from, correct?" Her brows drew a little and he knew he'd just insulted her, but better to have her on guard than not.

"Absolutely, sir."

There was a little snap to her reply and Jansen met her gaze. "Is this everything you have?"

"Yes, sir." She sat up straighter.

"Then I'll take it from here. You're dismissed."

"Sir?"

Her expression pinched, then smoothed out, and when he simply stared at her she stood and executed a perfect salute. But the colonel was already ignoring her.

As Ensign Durry walked into the outer offices, leaving the

two men alone, she thought, *I'm being shoved out and it will be buried.*

Why else would he ask for all her paperwork so far?

Mike heard the words, but it took a moment for them to sink in. Nanotechnology. Biosynthesized neuron-enhanced something or other. He let it stew, his mind ticking off reasons this was a bad idea. Putting anything into the body that didn't belong there never was. "What's it do?"

"Increased strength and resistance to antibodies, increased lung capacity. Intelligence quotient increases, forcing the brain to use more than three percent. Smell, taste, touch, sight, all heightened and reaching beyond normal levels. It maintains from the body's own electromagnetic field. Can you imagine the things we can do? We could develop it for the deaf, the paralyzed—"

"Permanent?" he cut in, crushing her excitement.

"Yes, until it can be destroyed. It's designed to dissolve, then be swept out through the bloodstream."

"And you invented this?" He admitted it. He was impressed.

"The actual pod, yes, with the help of a medical doctor, Dr. Yates."

"You know how this sounds to me? Like science fiction. You've created a human weapon, judgment-enhanced by this pod. We shoot weapons, we don't *become* them. We solve the problems. And this just creates more. Christ, next you'll be taking away our conscience and memory so we're no better than those fuckers who strap on a bomb!"

She reared back, not expecting this reaction from him. "That's not true and you're really going over the top, Mike."

He rounded on her and she half expected him to paw the ground. "You created this science project to *control.*"

"Yes, your control, I'm damn proud of it!"

"That you turned people into machines?"

"There is nothing mechanical about it. It's a *bio*-pod that helps them survive! They do everything they can do now, only faster and more efficient. It doesn't give them superpowers, for pity's sake, not something they don't already have. It enhances what's already there."

Mike rubbed his skull with both hands. "You expect miracles and they're people, just *people,* and we're doing the best we can."

"Mike." She gripped his arms, forcing him to look her in the eye. "I know that. I've patched the wounds. I've held them when they died." Her throat burned as battle memories filled her mind. "If this technology keeps them alive just a little longer, long enough to get them out safely, or more help than a medic and some morphine, wouldn't you want it?"

"Yes, of course." He sighed hard, and knew that if his men were alive, this pod might be the reason. "I'm trying to understand your point, believe me, it's the purpose of all my gear, but did you ever think about what would happen if the enemy gets this technology? They have everything else already." His gaze rose to meet hers. "DOD thinks you're giving it over."

"You don't know how laughable that really is. It's not a file I can hand over. I don't have it. I can't create it again without the right facilities and equipment, and lots of time. It's locked up in an Army medical facility under layers of security."

He frowned, curious. "Then how'd you find my guys?"

"I have skills. I hacked."

"Christ, you're a national security risk all by yourself."

"Aren't you glad I'm one of the good guys?"

He smiled for the first time since dragging her back here. "I should probably tell you that when they sent my team in after the UAV, the chopper was shot out of the sky."

Her smile fell. "Oh no, Mike. Any trace?"

"Not a one."

She frowned, thinking about the Google earth photos she'd seen, the smooth path in the jungle. "That's impossible. A fire, the explosion, a heat signature at—"

He shook his head. "No heat signature at all. Satellite picked up the hit, but not the launch. The wreckage isn't showing. It knocked it so far off course that I was looking in Ecuador. There's no way to locate where it came from." Except for Gantz's calculated theories.

"They're wrong. There's nothing that can do that. Thrust for launch takes compressed propulsion. It explodes and that's what gives it thrust. The explosion *has* to generate heat."

She wasn't telling him something he didn't already know and had speculated over since leaving the U.S. "Not this time."

Clancy couldn't imagine how that could happen. Even alternative fuels generated heat for propulsion.

She was still shaking her head when he said, "If what you say is true, then my men, my friends, are out there, and if they are alive—"

"They could very well be."

"—if they are alive, then where are they? Why haven't they used this enhanced intellect to get out of there? And if the enemy is some damn cartel and has them? Jesus, this was too dangerous to start!" They'd be dead, executed for trespassing into cartel territory. DEA agents had vanished in the fight against drug lords, some horribly.

"Sorry you feel that way, Mike, but it doesn't change the fact that it exists. It's here, now, in use in primates, and it works." She was very curious about how Boris was handling it, but not enough to call Francine.

"And the results?"

"We weren't done. Haven't you been listening or are you always this pigheaded?"

He smiled. "There's a reason they call us jarheads."

"I learned they inserted it into your friends without my knowledge and without full long-term testing. If I hadn't been drawing blood from the ape, I would never have known. Last year we injected the nanopod for the first time in an ape and it destroyed his central nervous system and killed him within hours. It's been refined quite a bit since then, but not enough." She shook her head. "Not nearly enough for humans. They don't want anyone to know it, and with good reason."

His gaze thinned.

"Refined or not, it could kill them, Mike. Reaction is different for any candidate because no two people are alike. Different weight, muscle mass, brain function."

"How bad?"

"We don't know."

"Guess."

"Insanity."

"Christ."

"The pod is injected into the cerebellum, and then it attaches itself to the wall. Neurosynaptic sensors implant and boot the cerebral cortex." Her voice trailed off when she noticed he wasn't interested, but furious.

"How could they do this to them?" He rubbed his head, turning away.

"Don't go there, your men volunteered." He whipped around, his dark eyes savage. "Volunteered," she said more softly. "I wasn't in the loop. They superseded me in secret."

He was quiet for a long moment, his gaze intense. "Bet that fried your ass."

"Enough for me to come down here."

"To do what?"

"Find the men, destroy the pods."

He scoffed, almost amused. "Honey, you wouldn't know if they were two feet from you, and if this pod is in their brains, how the hell can you destroy it?"

"Ah, now you see my problem. I had a device, but Richora smashed it."

The electronics in the trash, Mike thought, stiffening. She tried to make another. "Is there another way?"

The glass window exploded behind him, fragments rocketing across the room. Mike hit the floor. Clancy was already there next to the bed, staring at the bullet embedded in the opposite wall.

"That was meant for you." He was in the line of fire.

"Oh yeah." Mike crawled across the floor, pulling gear to him and grabbing his Cyclops. He shifted to the window, peering over the edge. Night Vision illuminated the area. "The shot had to come from another building. It was suppressed or people would be running for cover." He lowered and looked at her. "The streets are packed."

"Probably didn't hear it over the music. You're on someone's mean and nasty side too."

"Pretty much." But most didn't know who he was. This wasn't the first time he was out in the open. Going in silent and getting out made covering your ass a lot easier. "I think it's time to leave this town."

Crouched on the floor, she grabbed her bag and adjusted the straps, slung it across her body. "They'd follow."

Mike was almost hoping they would so he could put an end to this. "Sure, but we're fish in a barrel here."

She was on the floor, flat on her stomach, and she wiggled beside him. "So, let's talk, Gannon."

"Now?"

The single word was punctuated by another shot blasting into the room and shattering the mirror over the dresser.

Clancy flinched, yet didn't miss a beat. "Probably not the best timing, but that's been stinking all the way around since I got off the cruise ship." She reached in his pack and took back her pistol. "You want to come with me, that's fine. I'll show you where I found the piece of the aircraft." She rolled to her back to load the gun. "And as much as I'd like to hike all over the Peruvian jungle and mountains, I'd like some backup. Preferably yours." She cocked the slide and looked at him. "But I will find them."

He held her gaze, his lips twitching. "No wonder you got tossed in jail."

"I have been known to cause some trouble, yes."

Training said *don't trust her, keep her gagged and cuffed.* Instinct said there was too much truth to this. His team had been unreachable since he was in the hospital with the shoulder wound, and none of them told him of this, which sort of swung both ways in her defense. Believing her was a stretch, but then if it wasn't true, why go through so much to make this right and help his buddies? And what good did it do to put her on a watch list?

High priority for certain, but it brought questions. Dangerous ones, and while her nanopod wasn't easily reproducible, it was remarkable even in its concept. Downside was it was worth billions. That kind of potential had big protection. It wouldn't be long before they sent someone else after her. If they hadn't already. They weren't taking any chances with her surviving, and it pissed him the hell off.

Alone, she'd be dead in a day.

"What do you say, Marine?"

"Deal." He leaned in to kiss her just as something lobbed in through the window. "Shit!"

Mike grabbed Clancy and rolled, throwing her on her back. He fell on top of her, covering her eyes and ears just as the flash grenade popped, brightening the room and making his ears ring and burn.

He rose up and rolled off her. "You okay?" He cupped her face, making her look at him. He checked her eyes.

"Yeah, yeah." She wiggled her finger in her ear.

He pulled her hand away. "It will stop in a few minutes. Come on."

"Was that a flash grenade? Where do they get these things?" she said, following him on her hands and knees and feeling the wobbly effects of the grenade.

"Put your gear in this." He shoved a backpack at her, then rolled toward his gear. Ditching the old rucksack, he filled a large pack, one with braces.

Clancy stuffed her flight bag inside the backpack. Reaching the door, he cut the lights, then stood carefully. "They're trying to make us leave and we're leaving?" she said when he opened the door a crack to check the corridor.

"Don't try to find the logic." Out in the hall, he gripped her hand and pulled her with him down a service stairwell.

Clancy held her gun clasped and low, following behind him, watching their backs. Then he stopped, peering through the glass of the service door.

"My truck is still there."

"The upside of that is . . . ?"

"We split up."

"You're leaving me?"

At the doubt in her voice, his brows thickened with a frown. "Oh, hell no, we don't go forward with that sorry attitude."

"Yes, sir," she said sourly.

His features smoothed, tenderness in his voice. "I'm not leaving you, Irish."

Relief swept through her and she searched his face, liking the man beneath the gung-ho, do-or-die barrier. He trusted her, for right now he was laying it on the line for her. "Me either."

"You're going to the truck. I'll cover you till you get inside it."

"They shot with a rifle. Who's to say they aren't waiting for us sniper style?"

"It's possible, so move fast. There are four entrances to this hotel. I'm going out one of them and will cover you from another direction." He gave her the keys. "You drive it two blocks north, then three west."

She was shaking her head. He cupped the back of it, and kissed her forehead. He knew she was scared. There was no doubt she was hunted.

And he was in the way.

"Alive. That's the prime objective. Stay *alive*. We're in enemy territory now."

# Eleven

Mike grabbed her wrist, looked at her watch, then his. "Wait two minutes, then you go."

"I got it." He was still standing there. "Go, go, then." She shooed him. "I'll be fine." Or dead.

He smiled, took a step, then cupped the back of her head and kissed her, hard and fast, and when he released her she fell back against the wall.

"Whoa. Screw the bad guys. Let's find a room, Boy Scout."

He chuckled as he hurried around the staircase and headed to the front of the hotel. She breathed deep, checked the time. It dragged, and she rocked from side to side as seconds ticked off, then she gripped the knob. Opening the door, she kept the gun at her left side, hidden by her thigh as she left the safety of the building and moved out in the open. She walked swiftly to the truck and slid behind the wheel. She looked up and saw Mike, sandwiched in an alley, nod to her, then head north.

Letting out a nervous breath, she started the engine. It clicked. "Oh no, no, no." She pumped the gas, tried again, and failed. There was no charge at all. Her gaze slid to the area around her, up to the rooftops and open windows before she climbed out, impatience and fear riding her. *Someone's out there with grenades and rifles,* she thought, and Mike was blocks away by now. Running like a bat out of hell would raise suspicion, and while a moving target wasn't easy to hit, there were people in the streets partying who could be.

*Maybe it's just the battery cable,* she thought, slinging on the pack. She went to the front of the truck, running her fingers under the metal lip for the latch. Her fingers brushed it and she bent to look. Two black wires were curled under the hood.

"They are so screwing with my karma." She drew her hand back slowly and straightened, turning away. She took a few steps before she bolted, shouting at people to run. They just watched her, drunk and happy, and then she screamed, *"Bomb!"* and they scattered.

But Clancy wasn't looking, arms and legs pumping. Five blocks, five blocks, she could do it. *Mike will be there.* She overtook two and turned west when it hit. The explosion roared through the streets, shaking the ground, and shattering glass and wood. She felt the burst of hot air on the back of her head and turned to look, stumbling. Orange fire blazed into the night sky, white smoke turning black and sooty before another explosion broke windows. She ran west at top speed.

Almost there, almost. A man stepped into the street, blocking her path, and even at this distance she knew it wasn't Mike. He was just a few yards away and coming closer. She veered left and he did too. Clancy turned back and ran into a side street, the man's footsteps echoing behind her. She spun around and fired without aiming and missing by a mile. The man returned it, clipping close to her feet, and she ducked out of range.

"You are trapped now," he shouted

*You think?* The only things close to her were more walls and an open area with nothing for cover. If she ran, he'd shoot her in the back. She peered, and he stood in the center of the street, unafraid, showing off straight white teeth and a .357. Clancy closed her eyes briefly, knowing it was him or her. Before she could adjust her aim, he shot three times, one bullet passing through the trash can and chipping the wall behind her head.

She called out and stood. *Think of something. Don't die in an alley.*

He raised his weapon. "Hand ups," he said, then with the gun motioned her closer. "Throw the gun down."

She obeyed and, alone in the damp street, she started toward him.

"This won't hurt much."

Clancy moved slowly, staying out of arm's reach. "Who sent you?"

"I never know." He shrugged indifferently. "It works better that way." He kept his aim tight on her, circling and forcing her where he wanted her to go. "Where is your big friend, *chica?*"

"Behind you."

The man spun and Mike punched hard. The guy went down like a sack and didn't move.

"That was amazing. Excellent KO," she said, skipping past the fallen man, snatching up her gun.

Mike reached for her, and she fell against him. He squeezed her hard, then cupped her face. "Are you okay?" She nodded and they hurried away. "I take it I don't have a truck anymore."

"Yeah, I meant to tell you that." Clancy stalled when she ran past a body in the street. *He's been busy.*

"Then we need another ride." Mike scanned the parked cars, spied one, then hurriedly jimmied the door and climbed in to hot-wire it.

"Why am I not surprised?" She hurried to the passenger side.

"Shouldn't you be doing this, bad girl?"

"Not one of my skills." She laughed as she slid into the seat. Mike kicked over the engine, threw it into gear, and gunned it, flying down the street. Lights flashed behind them and he glanced in the rearview.

"Shit! Incoming!" He pushed her head down and ducked. A shot shattered the rear glass. Mike drove with one hand and turned once to fire.

"God, they didn't waste time. Can I sit up?"

"Yeah, but stay low. Don't give them a target."

She shook glass out of her hair and shimmied down into the seat, holding her gun to her chest like a puppy. "Gotta plan?"

"Evasion. Resistance." Mike checked the rearview and made a sharp turn. "Oh, hell. He's got relatives."

Another car pulled up behind them, tapping the bumper and trying to run them off the road. Mike turned into a narrow side street, bouncing along, and then there was no place to go except into buildings and homes. Headlights brightened in the broken window.

She cocked her weapon, smirking up at him before she faced the rear between the seats and fired. "Step on it!"

"This thing doesn't go any faster."

"Pull ahead some."

"Get it over with. Double-tap them."

She looked at him, horrified.

"They'll do it to you. Enemy territory," he reminded her.

*Us or them,* Clancy thought as she fired, hitting the right side of the car. The guy jerked the wheel, clipped the curb, and the vehicle hopped and rolled over.

"Outstanding! But he'll be back."

She rolled her eyes and watched behind. "Do something creative, the inbred brothers are still coming."

"I see that."

She twisted. Another car was in front, coming straight at them. "Man, I really need a bigger gun." The car came closer and wasn't stopping.

Neither was Mike.

What was with men and playing chicken? "Don't, Mike, please don't!"

He didn't listen. "Hold on, Irish, it's gonna get a little wild."

\* \* \*

Hank Jansen flipped a hamburger on the grill and inhaled the aroma. Behind him on the patio, his children were laughing and he glanced to see his first grandchild wave her chubby little arms. His mind was barely on the grilling, still turning over the files Ensign Durry had given him.

He hadn't discussed it with anyone, and made the decision to investigate on his own. He'd have to handle this with some delicacy. But the minute Durry brought this to his attention, he knew where to start. The military medical community had tried enhancements before, with steroids, full-spectrum drugs, and biomarkers. But they needed full approval and Hank would have been in the loop. He wasn't on this, and whoever was behind it, they damn well better outrank him.

He wondered if Gannon had any idea, but the man made contact only once. Not unusual, Gannon rarely did until the mission was done. But just the implication that a U.S. government facility could have used troops as guinea pigs for some science experiment had his back up.

*Don't fuck with my troops,* he thought, then noticed his wife as she came toward him, that pinched look on her face a warning.

She held out the phone. "I thought for one day I'd get you *really* here with us," she said.

"I am here." He flipped a burger, then reached for the phone and tucked it against his chest.

"It's Groden," she said and spun on her heel.

DEA. This won't be good. "Colonel Jansen."

"So sorry to bother you on a Sunday afternoon."

"But you will, won't you, Tom?"

A light chuckle came through the phone. "Well, I thought you should know this before it went out over the waves to NMCC tomorrow."

"Give it to me fast, my burgers are flaming."

"The UAV recording."

Hank perked up.

"It covered a lot of area before it went down."

Yes, about the size of Illinois, Hank thought. It was the DEA operation, but when it crashed it became his. A few million in hardware lost to the war on drugs.

"We've noticed something remarkable."

"Like the location of the aircraft?"

"No, sir, but there should be something there, even if scavengers took the wreckage. But there's *no* traffic in the area."

Hank turned his back on his family and handed over the grilling job to his oldest son. "None? It's the Amazon, for chrissake." Hank didn't have to look to know his wife was glaring at his back.

"Yeah, I got that too. But there's no pirates, no drug traffic, boats, only the tourist ones, and they stick to the same route away from the smaller tributaries, since, well, kidnapping is a national pastime down there."

"So your job should be easier."

"Yup, you'd think. Street price for coke is sky-high too. That tells us a lot and I know I'm dragging this out but, sir, what would stop all drug traffic in that triangle?"

Hank was silent for a moment as his brain rolled over some facts and what-ifs. No severe weather, no earthquakes lately. A drug war wouldn't stop production and export, just leave bodies.

Then he straightened, feeling a cold chill pour down his spine. "They have a new commodity for sale."

"Kind of scary, huh?"

Clancy braced against the seat as if it would help. It didn't. The car rumbled down the street, the speed of it tossing up trash.

"He wants to play chicken."

"Jesus, Mike! There are people here!"

Mike gunned the little car, and Clancy prepared for a head-on collision. Closer. Closer. The headlights were blinding, but

Mike kept it steady, laying on the horn. Closer. People scattered, jumping a low stone wall, some flying into buildings. The engine screamed and they were within yards.

Mike didn't flinch.

The other car veered off sharply, its speed sending it into a stone wall. As Mike shot past, the car careened off it and spun. Behind them the car collided with the one on its side.

"All right!"

Mike grinned.

"Don't do that again!" She shoved him.

"No guts, no glory."

"Stupid ass."

He chuckled lowly and reached for her. "Take a breath. We're okay for now."

She collapsed in a heap, gripping his warm hand.

"You did good, Irish. Really well." He pulled free to drive.

Clancy wanted to grab him back. "Not to be repetitive, but now what?"

"We eliminate the problems. We hunt them."

"Food? Water? Sleep?"

"Whining?"

"Personal observation. I've been awake for nearly forty hours."

"We need to get out of sight and ditch this car."

"I'd like more preparation."

"Like you had one going into this?" He slipped his satellite phone free and glanced at the keypad. "What were you thinking?"

"Keep them alive."

He stilled, meeting her gaze. He didn't know what he expected to see, but the pure honesty in her eyes wasn't it. Without any help, she'd managed to get this far, into trouble, sure, but Navy medic training didn't entail search and destroy alone. But she was ready to take the badasses on alone. He admired that.

"I don't suppose asking you to hide out while I take care of this will do any good?"

"Not a bit."

He nodded slowly, exhaling. "Just checking."

She jutted her chin at the phone. "Who are you calling at this hour?"

"Gantz."

"I don't like him."

"He's an acquired taste, but a good guy." He speed-dialed, his gaze flicking around for more idiots in cars. "Oh, quit bitching, you didn't need sleep anyway," he said to Gantz. "I want intel on some scientists."

Clancy frowned.

"That's a big pile, be more specific," Gantz said sleepily.

"Design engineers. Anyone who's crossed the line, or has a flag." He glanced at her and she made a sour "get over it" face. "Try rocket scientists. Someone had to have created that rocket. Someone smarter than us."

"Now, there's a stretch," Clancy muttered, keeping watch for anything suspicious. Mike was still driving at top speed and the ride was anything but smooth and made her feel punch-drunk.

"What about Denner?"

"You were right, he's a hired asset."

Non-CIA hired muscle? Mike scowled. "Whose?"

"You don't want much, do ya? And if they don't want us to know, we won't."

"Use those tricks, Gantz, I need this. Is that flag confirmed?"

"Funny thing, my sources say it's not on their data alerts, and it's not turning up as an across-the-board watch. Makes me think it's personal. You have her, ask her."

He did and knew, but Gantz didn't need to know about the nanopod. "Keep digging."

"What do you want me to do with this, Gannon? I have my channels but—"

"Send it to Jansen." He cut the call.

"I heard," she said. "There is hope for Gantz yet."

He loved it when she grinned like that. All sappy and feminine, like she had a secret you were dying to know and knew you never would. "Whoever sent Denner after you," he said. "Could be anyone. A sanctioned hit on a noncombatant civilian is rare. Very rare. Officially, it doesn't exist. Unofficially, it takes a lot of confirmations and it's a last resort. The absolute last. Capture alive first."

"That's been waved obviously."

"Gantz thinks it's personal."

"I was convinced it was Colonel Cook, but he has as much to lose as I do." It was lost already, Clancy thought, but she refused to let an ass like Cook send her career completely down the tubes.

"Not if he sweeps all the blame on you."

"He could. I'm the chief designer. I have access to all data. He could say I was party to it and that he knew nothing. The most he'd be accused of was failure to watch his own people. The only person who could say otherwise is Major Yates, and she's in the sack with Cook."

Mike didn't see beyond that Clancy was the one getting screwed. "A regular family affair."

She shrugged, indifferent. "It kept the money flowing into the project. She's a good person, just follows orders better than I do." She told him about Boris and the autopsy. "Boris is alive. Even she wasn't dumb enough to cut open the ape without waiting for more reactive testing. They were going to push me out before I ever learned about the guys."

"Because they were going into places you wouldn't."

She nodded.

*Don't trust what you see the first time,* Mike thought. *Everything is different with a closer look.* She'd gone from prisoner to partner in record time, and he liked where she was coming from, liked what he was seeing. He smiled.

She met his gaze. "Don't give me that movie star smile,

Gannon. I've told you considerable classified information, and could go to jail for it. Yet you've told me nothing."

"Catch that too, did you?" She didn't smile, waiting, and if she were standing, Mike imagined she'd be tapping her foot. "You're so cute when you're trying to be intimidating."

She blinked. "Some other time and place, that might get you somewhere, but not today." She laughed when he looked crestfallen. "You were sent to recover the UAV. Was it loaded? Hellfires?"

Mike felt her stare as if she were nudging him along. "My sources say they blew up on impact."

"Trust the source?"

"Hell no. Renoux was as conniving as they come." He told her about the arms dealer.

"You have some dangerous friends." Her gaze caught on the sideview mirror. "Gun it! We have company and he's got better wheels than we do!"

Mike hit the gas and looked in the rearview. One big black all-terrain truck. *Crap.*

"He's going to fire!" Clancy ducked low in the seat as the man leaned out the window to shoot.

Mike swerved and for a moment Clancy thought, *He's going to play chicken with that monster truck?*

Then the tire exploded.

Richora closed his cell phone and tried not to throw it. The Americans were fast becoming a thorn in his side.

Salache looked at him, arching a brow. "They escaped?"

"Not for long."

"Now they're in my territory." Salache picked up the gun lying on the desk and pointed it.

Richora wasn't afraid. "You need me."

"Do not think that you aren't expendable."

"And who will cover your borders, your shipments? They are my men and follow my orders."

"There are enough of the others."

"But you don't speak the language."

Salache was thoughtful and tipped the weapon to the ceiling.

"What are you doing?" Marianna stood in the doorway, and from the look on her face she'd witnessed the exchange. "Answer me!"

"My sweet, it's not your concern, just men posturing." He stood and walked nearer.

"With a gun? Why do you have that in my house? You know how I feel about weapons near my children."

"Your house?"

She stiffened, her gaze shooting to Richora, then back to Nuat's. "Do not, husband. You will regret it."

Salache's gaze narrowed, and for a moment Alejo thought he would strike her. He'd have to kill him then, he thought, yet watched as the man crossed to his wife and pulled her into his arms. She was reluctant to go.

"I swear to you, I will have the weapon removed now." He glanced at Alejo and inclined his head.

Richora took the gun and slipped it behind his back. She really didn't know anything, he thought. She has no suspicion of what would soon transpire. Of course she didn't. Salache sheltered her inside his kingdom of money and power, and all of this dance with people and cargo was a skilled manipulation to avoid detection. Especially by his wife.

Salache kissed her gently and she melted into his embrace. Richora looked away from the tender sight.

"I am going to town for the day with the children."

He nodded and she backed away, glancing once at Richora. In the single moment, he saw her private agony. "Get rid of it." She left.

"Give it to me."

Alejo frowned and dragged his gaze to Salache. He held out his hand. "You swore to her."

"I have done so many times, and will, I suspect, again. She is a woman and needs her world to be protected. She understands that. But I have enemies and this is necessary to protect my family." He put the gun in the desk drawer, then met his gaze.

He didn't need the gun, Richora thought. Not unless a predator could get past the electrified wall and gate, or the guards placed where few could see.

"Is the first shipment ready to leave?"

"Two days." Salache knew this and Richora wondered if he asked just to hear the sound of his own voice.

Salache smiled and settled in the leather chair. "Did you find the bodies?"

"You know we have not."

Salache smiled. "If I am lucky, they have been dismembered and fed to the caimans."

Lightly swinging in the leather chair, Salache stared at a glass-front cabinet and Richora turned to leave.

"Take care of this American problem yourself, Alejo."

He looked back over his shoulder, and just realized Salache was admiring his face in the glass.

"Prove that your people are better than the primitives they are."

Richora stiffened with outrage. It seemed that Salache's new face had wiped the slate clean of more than his past.

Dr. Valez was exhausted by the time he reached the dig site. He could have taken a helicopter but the privilege had too high a price. *My age should make it a requirement,* he thought wryly, trying to slow his breathing in the thin air. Gil pushed on ahead of him, but Eduardo's head felt light and he fell back against a tree and swiped off his hat. He ran the back of his wrist across his forehead.

He was anxious to reach the site. He hoped the urn's home and surroundings would reveal more about the urn's contents. It was being tested. The miniscule amount of sandy gray material in the dish was the consistency of talc, and he suspected it was ashes. But if it was, the icons made no sense.

Breath of the gods, a warrior's battle? Yet the warrior's face bore the huge fangs and big eyes; a Moche version of a scare tactic, but the human skin on the seal troubled him more than the gruesomeness of the fact.

It had been layered with the waxlike substance experts were having trouble defining. He was not a chemist and could do nothing until they did. The human skin was shrunk tight around it, obviously never to be opened. Why, was a question he couldn't answer.

A shriek startled him, and he shook his fist at the monkey dangling in the tree and hissing. Pests, he thought, pushing off and walking up the slope to the excavation site. Gil was already several yards ahead of him when he entered the center of the encampment filled with tents erected to the right and left of the site. A small Bobcat earthmover sat a few yards back, its engine silent.

Gil came out of a tent, scowling. "They must be at the site."

Eduardo strode to his tent, batting back the folds. The papers scattered on the British campaign desk told him everything was as he'd left it, and empty. He left the tent and called out for his people, then noticed a man coming up the ridge.

The young man rushed to him. "Oh, Dr. Valez. I'm glad you're back."

Valez grabbed his tools and with Gil, they followed the man to the dig. "Did you find something?"

"No, but we were cleaning up the site and had to stop yesterday to shore up the ceiling. It has caved in in small areas, but not the chamber."

Cave-ins weren't uncommon and Eduardo insisted on bracings each step of the way. He heard voices, the scrape of stone and wood, and found the team working efficiently to brace wood on the cave entrance. Though it wasn't truly a cave, but a portion of a city, now underground. Over time, the mountain had swallowed it.

Farther down the mountain were more dwellings and digs excavated and searched decades ago. This one had only recently been unearthed. He passed the undergrads and workers, the students trying to get in fieldwork for college credit. He hated to tell them that archaeology didn't pay much at all, yet knew only the dedicated would remain in the field. He loved the energy and excitement of young people, yet today he needed some he could depend on and glanced at Gil. The young man was so excited to join him this time, and Eduardo had assumed he'd found his calling boring. Sometimes it was, but then, a find like the urn changed that.

"Why do you think they used human skin?" Gil asked.

"A protection of some sort. They would not have worked gold into it without some significance. Perhaps it wasn't meant for us to know."

Gil looked at him, a studious scowl on his face. "I've a feeling we shouldn't open it at all."

Valez glanced. "Superstitious?"

"I'm Latin. Of course I am." He smiled. "At least we have something to test."

"There could be anything inside there with it." It wasn't showing well on the scans, just a mass that was loose and dense.

People greeted them at the entrance and he smiled, sending several off on a break. No one entered the cave without people on the outside ready to help, or call for help.

"How safe?" he said to the site manager.

"As well as it can be, senor. Have a care near the walls. It has caved in a bit since you left with the urn."

Eduardo nodded and stopped at the entrance to put on his gloves and mask against the dust. His glasses would help deflect it, and when he looked at Gil, he smiled. The man had his head wrapped like a turban, a sash of muslin across his mouth.

"I choked on that stuff last time," he said through the rag.

"Dust and dirt is the way of this life," Eduardo said, ducking inside the long narrow tunnel. It was excavated in stages that often turned into levels. Then it opened and he straightened, the ceiling high in the chamber, the gas-powered lights bright inside.

The interior wasn't shored by the workers, but by the Moche. On the far end was a doorway, small and no more than a molded frame. Long, narrow stone beams held back the earth, above it a stone crossbeam. Each five-foot-long rod of granite was notched and tightly fitted, yet beyond it was the remnants of the chamber that had held the urn. Inside, it was smaller, the ceiling lower. A temple, he decided. He crossed to it, kneeling with Gil to get inside.

"We need another rubbing of this." He pointed to the stone slabs that had fallen when he'd pulled the urn free.

"There isn't anything on it. It's cut stone."

"I want to be certain." He ran his hand over it, his fingers as sensitive as the blind. "There are markings, below the cuts, small ones."

"How did you know?"

He looked up, his glasses already dusty, and he brushed at the lenses. "I don't. I am assuming there's some warning, because there was one on the urn itself."

Gil nodded understanding, then pulled a pack of rice tissue from his satchel and unfolded it. He placed it over the edge, and with charcoal he rubbed it while Eduardo rubbed the frame and right side. After a few moments, they had several pieces, each marked sequentially. Aboveground, they could lay the tissue out and have a replica of the urn's final resting place.

Gil was bent over the find, carefully slipping the rubbings into a plastic sleeve. "I'll send this back with the next group."

Valez shook his head. "No, I need them here because you're as skilled at deciphering the hieroglyphics as I am."

The young man scoffed. "Get real."

"You see the details that have, I'm afraid, escaped me lately." His wife wanted him to retire and travel with her. Perhaps he should, if he was not a good enough teacher.

"That's because I look with a fresh eye and not that of a seasoned scholar."

"Are we done with compliments? Let's see what we have."

The pair gathered their tools and sacks. Gil left the chamber first. He was so tall he had to squat to get out the framed door. Beyond it, he waited for Eduardo.

"Doctor?"

"I wanted a last look. I have missed it."

Gil shook his head, smiling. Dirt sprinkled his shoulder and when he looked up, a few stones rolled down the angle of the dirt walls. Then he saw a crack in the heavily packed earth. "Professor, come now. It's starting to cave!"

Eduardo crossed the large open room, careful not to step on the cut granite that portioned off the urn's chamber.

The ground shifted again, this time harder, and Eduardo fell, his hand catching on a sharp edge. He winced and cradled his hand to his chest, climbing to his feet, dirt rolling down the walls like rainwater. *No, please no,* he thought, and ran to the exit.

Gil was still on the other side of the framed door, waving him on. "Come quickly. It's falling!"

Eduardo darted through and backed away with Gil, both moving to the tunnel entrance, yet too fascinated not to look. Chunks of earth fell, the dust cloud filling the first chamber, and they turned into the tunnel leading to the surface. Then it abruptly stopped. They exchanged a look that spoke of prayers and wishes.

"That was close."

Gil only nodded, his gaze on the stones. Black and polished, they'd held the dirt in the shape of a door again. Crude, but efficient, and as he approached he studied the oblong columns. Then the stone pylons started to slip. Gil stumbled back. The left fell first, the impact felt through the ground. Flat across the entrance and creating a stone threshold. And without support the top crossbeam's left side slid downward, looking for a moment as if it would tumble out. Dirt fell.

"It's caving in on the other side," Eduardo said, backing up into the tunnel again. The two sides leaned slowly inward, the earth above spilling between the two pieces, filling the gap before the ends hit. It stopped moving. The cave-in halted. Then as if a hand packed it, the loose earth jammed against the pieces by the weight above.

Gil rushed forward, running his hand over the pieces. "They're locked in place. This is amazing."

Eduardo held his brush, and started sweeping away the dirt. The shine of the rock showed, and as he cleaned he realized it was painstakingly polished and carved. He went to the other joints and found the same.

"It's a puzzle piece, carved to fit into place." Eduardo's gaze toured the stone quickly, then once more slowly. "It was supposed to fall. Yet it makes little sense. You can still pass through, so it does nothing." The dirt level was only halfway, and a look inside said it hadn't caved in but a little.

"If it was a barricade, then inside should be caving in completely."

"Yes, but why hide this with traps and levels? We are nearly fifty feet below the structure that is already yards below the last avalanche."

"Doctor. Step back by me."

The older man turned to the voice. Gil was a couple of yards back, nearer to the tunnel. Eduardo followed the direction of his gaze as he slowly back-stepped.

"It's a triangle."

"Yes, and mechanized to fall like that. The Moche were far smarter than we think."

"They could smelt gold, they were whizzes, except the ritual blood thing," Gil said, sounding so young to Eduardo just then.

"There's no triangle in anything we have seen." Eduardo slid his fingers over the edges. "The symbol has several meanings in different cultures. The Egyptian pyramids, holy trinity of Christianity, the pagan Celts, the symbol for fire." Eduardo glanced at Gil. "We need a rubbing of this shape now. Quickly."

After a few moments, Eduardo sat back and said, "It's a warning. Passage into here is certain death." He pointed to the icons showing the dead littered on the ground. "But no bloodletting, no cups catching it." He admitted he was more confused and shone a light into the second smaller chamber where they'd found the urn. The slabs of stone once housing the urn had tumbled, revealing a small low tunnel behind the stone box. He felt air pushing through the chamber, and Eduardo moved to investigate it when dirt sprinkled on them.

The two men exchanged a glance. "Let's wait till the crew can shore this up again. I'd feel better," Gil said. Eduardo agreed and they walked up the low-ceilinged tunnel back to the surface. "Professor, did you notice the color in the etching?"

"Yes, I did." Eduardo paused, and said softly, "Keep it to yourself, please. I have seen men die for a discovery like this." Gold.

When Gil nodded, they continued up the narrow passage. All around them was black granite. Not surprising in the area, but that it was polished to a glossy sheen after thousands of years said the Moche were more progressive. Yet the purpose of the urn chamber still eluded him. Why lock it away and set traps to guard it? And the hole behind it? He must return.

The long narrow slabs had fallen inward, revealing the outside edge once buried under tons of earth. The three lengths of black stone now faced each other in a perfect triangle locked in place, its inner band etched in gold. It wasn't the precious metal that fascinated him, or that the gold lining the carving was still as vivid as the day they created it.

What concerned him wasn't the deadly message, but the air whispering through the chambers. What else was beyond the wall?

# Twelve

The car jolted and rode on the rim.

"What? There are no *good* police in this town?" she said through her teeth as Mike fought with the wheel.

"Some long arms of the law, huh?"

A loud *thwap* said the tire just ripped off the rim and Clancy twisted to see sparks flying from the wheels. The loud, shrieking grind made light come on in homes as they headed out of the town.

Then he headed into the jungle. "Well, we were going here anyway," he said, and she knew they couldn't stop. "We have to get to where you found the UAV piece, a-sap. It will put us near the crash site. That's if Gantz's trajectory is right."

They turned onto a narrow road, the surface decently smooth, and she breathed relief till Mike shut off the headlights and kept driving.

"You like living this dangerously? Jeez, Gannon." She pushed back in the seat, just waiting for him to hit something. Yet he was calm, steering as if he could see. Then the car jerked to a halt as the rim stuck in the ground.

Clancy put her hands out to keep from hitting the windshield, then scowled at him.

"Sorry," he muttered, then gave it gas and the car spun sideways. "Bug out, Irish," he said, leaving the car and pulling on the pack.

Clancy climbed out, adjusting her pack, and quickly they headed off the road, the car blocking travel.

He thrust black gloves at her. "The plants are as mean as the animals."

She slipped them on, hurrying behind him. "Oh yeah, like we don't have enough trouble." Thankfully, they had a Velcro tab because these things wouldn't fit anything less than a gorilla. She saw the flash of light. "They're here." With him, she ran several yards, her only point of reference in the dark the glow of his GPS.

"You locked and loaded?"

*Oh, shit.* "Yes."

"Watch your six."

"You're trusting my aim more than me."

"I'm trusting a lot more than that." His voice came softly and Clancy squeezed his hand. He squeezed back and some little spot in her coiled right up.

He made a turn, and she knew he was getting them to a spot that wasn't visible from the road. They pushed between the trees, the ground vegetation dense and dripping with twilight dew.

"This is good enough." For a brief moment, he shone the light toward the road, then cut it off. Mike felt for his satellite phone and shut it off. They sat, and he rolled down his sleeves and told her to take off the pack. He stashed them under forest debris, then swept the ground around them, hiding tracks.

"They aren't giving up." Her voice was soft in his ear, her breath sending a shiver down Mike's throat.

He tipped his head, his lips brushing her ear. "I wouldn't."

Clancy smoothed a moan and thought, *Oh, please keep doing that.* "This is well over the top. Why so persistent?"

Mike was thoughtful for a moment. "Hell if I know. We can't identify anyone but Richora. What did you see?"

"Nothing, except where they stopped me." As succinctly as she could, she told him about the lambs and going off the road. "Richora asked me what I saw and said the men who tried to take me were Shining Path."

"Oh, hell." Jansen had mentioned them. Shining Path was alive and kicking, just under a couple of different names. Like Nazis. They wanted the same thing—oppression. Communists, Islamic Jihad, Congo rebels, Tigers, whatever they called themselves, a maniac with a WMD was a high-priority problem. Unfortunately, most of the intel community thought they were put down. They'd just risen under a new flag.

Clancy could feel Mike's concentration. "Richora knew my guide. I got that someone hired Fuad to kidnap me, or at least make it possible so he could." She paused, a chill gripping her. "That's what I thought before Richora shot him. But I was hooded."

She didn't see it. "The guy in your room, Denner?"

"That's saying they are one and the same. But it would explain why he was at the bus stop. He'd been there already trying to kidnap me. Which is pointless."

"Not if he wanted to let the rebels take care of the job for him. It's been done. Hire someone to do a job and he gets more out of it by using other people to do it for him with threats."

"I don't really know the criminal mind anymore."

Mike held back a chuckle, suddenly frowning at the road, and they moved back a little farther.

In a moment, she heard the footsteps and the brush of leaves. *How does he do that?* A bright light swept back and forth over the jungle. It wasn't dense where they walked; land developers were trying to put in a highway through the Amazon. The men neared and Clancy held her breath.

Mike pushed her head down, leaning over her like a shield. The crack of dry, dead branches snapped crisply in the dark. Without a choice, the men moved slowly into the jungle. A couple of charges to knock them off their feet would have done nicely, he thought, but hadn't had the time. They were less than twenty yards away, the light faint till it speared near them. Flesh would glare in the dark, the reason he'd rolled down his sleeves. Clancy didn't have any.

He closed his eyes, and smelled the musty earth tossed up with each careful step, just as he could feel Clancy's heart pounding where his hand rested on her back, his arms curled around her to hide her skin from the hunters. In his hand, he held his pistol, cocked and locked.

The men shone the light at their feet, took a step, then swept the area high and low. They couldn't do both. On the jungle floor, there wasn't a shred of moonlight and it was uneven and combing with exposed roots. It was their one advantage. Mike could see boots now, hear the shift of the dirt and pebbles beneath them. They shuffled, the movement of unsure steps.

Mike slipped his finger over the trigger. Five against two wasn't good odds. A firefight would bring more of Richora's personal brigade.

Then a radio crackled and he heard a man respond quickly in Spanish. "*No, we haven't found them. We're forty kilometers in.*" There was disgust in the caller's voice, but with the distortion, recognition was impossible. "*Come back. We will go at first light.*"

Mike didn't expect them to give up. They wanted them both dead. There was something big in this area, in the jungle. Something worth killing all the witnesses to protect. He could think of no other reason for the vanishing act of his men, the crash, the Peruvian troops. But it was clear they weren't taking any chances.

The men paused to discuss the orders and seemed glad of it. Except one man, his face bloody. Mike figured he was one of the drivers who'd crashed. The man turned and aimed into the forest. The bastard cracked off five shots.

The final bullet hit.

Choufani had seen her from a distance and intentionally kept in her path. In either her line of sight or physically being near her, he wanted her to know he existed and that he was watching her. He kept back so she'd have no reason to summon the police. He'd have considerable explaining to do and no means to do it. He truly didn't want to sit in a jail till his agency came for him. They were slow at that sometimes.

But she noticed him. Each time she saw him it was a longer look, a little softer smile. He'd merely nodded and kept walking. In the park, he walked to a small frozen treat vendor, and bought a frosty ice cream. He was dragging his tongue over the chocolate when he backed away for another customer and found Marianna three feet away. He went still for a second, thinking it was too soon to approach her, then backed farther away.

She paid for ice cream for her two children. None for herself. And after the children had theirs, she took their hands and turned toward him. She looked him dead in the eye, then walked toward the stone path.

As she passed, he heard her say, "Stop this, please. For your own sake."

Choufani schooled his features. She didn't miss a step as she strolled with her children down the park lane, smiling down at them, taking a lick of the sweet ice cream. Guards followed her at a distance. Then she looked back over her shoulder.

Antone was struck again by her beauty, and then by the venom in her eyes.

Mike felt her flinch hard and held her still. It tore at him not to check her, to hold her and be unable to move. As the man stepped away, he leaned close to her ear.

"Are you okay?"

"That was right by my knee!"

He felt her trembling, and still shielding her, he watched the men retreat. He didn't let her up or speak till the men were far enough away. "They're leaving. Definitely Richora's troops."

"He's really taking this too far, ya know."

He let her up, yet spoke softly. "He'll take it to the end. Remember the sniper near the border river?" She nodded. "Those shots were from an elevated range."

Clancy looked toward the mountaintop in the far distance, its highest peak topped with snow and mist, and glowing in the crescent moonlight. "So now we have to watch out for a sniper? At least he can't see us in the dark."

"Unless he has thermals," Mike said.

"You are just such a bag of optimism, aren't you?"

He chuckled as he stood and helped her up. "We need to keep moving." He turned on the GPS. "We're a half mile in." He met her gaze. "You were three miles in last time."

"Seemed a lot farther." She swiped at her hair and Mike noticed her hands were shaking. He reached for her, tugging just a bit, and she went into his arms. She gripped him tightly. "I needed that," she muttered into his chest, and Mike rubbed her spine.

"I know you're not used to this."

"I'm not scared."

Over her head, he smiled. She sounded like a kid who didn't want to go to bed. "I am."

She leaned back and searched his gaze. "You big fat liar."

Mike's smile was slow and she joined him. "I'm not fat."

She laughed and pushed out of his arms to grab her pack and pull it on. They walked for another half hour before Mike shone the light long enough to see his surroundings. "We need to climb."

"Oh yes, let's," she said dryly.

They did. Her legs burned from strain, and when he stopped, she leaned on a tree.

"We'll rest here till sunup." With his back to the twisted roots of a tree, Mike settled down to the ground and patted the space beside him.

"Oh, thank God." She dropped the pack, then sank to the

ground, snuggling up to him and using his chest for a pillow. "Wake me if the bad guys show."

She exhaled long and low, and in moments she was asleep. Her hand on his chest, Mike disengaged her pistol from her grip as it went lax. He stretched his legs out and laid his own weapon at his side, and kept his gaze on the nearest path several yards ahead. He snuggled her more comfortable. It felt good, her compact body wrapped around his. It had been a while. Mike didn't cultivate relationships very well, and after a few disasters he stayed celibate till opportunity knocked. It was as much his fault as his job's. Most couldn't handle it, nor understand his real purpose. He didn't bother to explain, and secrecy kept women back.

Clancy's hand shifted to his stomach and Mike felt his muscles instantly flex. He moved her hand away from the danger zone and tried not to think about her touching him with nothing between them. He wondered how long he'd last without tasting her again. There was almost an innocence in her kiss, yet from the dossier Jansen had first given him over the phone, he knew she'd been married. He smiled to himself when he thought of her past, such a little bad girl. She snuggled closer and he thought, two hours to sunrise. He'd be lucky if he made it.

At least the hard-on she gave him would keep him alert. He had to trust her, but not completely. People did weird things when they were threatened. Yet he had every reason to believe her and even more not to take her word that the nanotechnology was real.

He hated the thought of his men volunteering for such an experiment. Yet it could be the very thing that saved their lives. A nice little double-edged sword, he thought.

"What are you thinking?" she said, and it startled him.

He tipped his head to look at her. She never opened her eyes. Why did women always ask that? "Honestly?"

"Of course."

"I don't know whether to be grateful or angry with you."

"That happens a lot to me."

Mike smiled. "Sleep, jailbird."

"Choice is yours," she mumbled sleepily.

Mike couldn't seem to make it. That double-edged sword again.

The sun peaked over the horizon in pink, but to Clancy it was crashing through the trees like a spotlight in the darkness. Clancy lay perfectly still, enjoying the feel of a man— no, this man beside her. It was like sleeping in a rock, though, every inch of him ripped and hard.

"Playing possum?"

She tipped her head, smiling. "This is a good-to-be-alive smile, in case you didn't notice." She pointed to it.

"Optimists," he said, rolling his eyes.

She laughed, her hand on his chest moving upward to the back of his neck, her fingers pushing into his hair as she pulled him down.

"Are you always this straightforward?" he said, leaning.

"Yup."

Mike went willingly, and when his mouth touched hers, it was all he could do not to devour her whole. She was warm, her mouth soft and playful, teasingly taking her time, refusing to let him rush it. He loved it; patient when she was so impatient before. It was strange, he could have sent her stateside in handcuffs and leg irons just hours ago.

*You're a sap,* he thought, and while internal warnings were going off inside his brain, the sudden dark need for her smothered them as he kissed her back. Her response knocked him sideways, and when he ran his hand down her spine and pulled her tighter, he knew he had to stop this before he lost control. With Clancy, that was getting easier by the hour.

Mike drew back, running his fingers across her lips, and heard her breath rushing in her lungs.

"Damn those bad guys," she said, then grasped his hand,

drawing it back and looking pointedly at the gun in his hands. "There is something just so not sexy about that."

Mike rolled back, wondering what kind of man that made him when he could have a beautiful woman in his arms and still be aware of the hunter. Good, or just isolated more than he was willing to admit? He figured it was the latter as he stood.

She sat up, brushing off dirt, then reached for the pack. Instead of changing out her things, she just stuffed it inside, then checked her weapon. He held his hand out to her and she accepted it and stood. He gave her a small machete in a sheath that had four straps hanging from it.

"Tie it upside down on your arm or maybe your thigh. Just make sure it's the easiest to grab."

Clancy strapped it on her left arm and drew the knife a few times, freeing it easily.

The defensive stance gave him pause. "It's to cut the underbrush."

She sheathed it. "Scary, aren't I?"

"Just aim for the black hats." He took out the GPS and she leaned over to look.

"Where are we now?" He hit a button and a dot lit up under the screen. "That's two miles." Her hands on her hips, Clancy's look scolded. "Do we have to discuss that pace thing again?"

He grinned, and it transformed his face, giving her breath a little trouble leaving her lungs.

"Just keep up, swabby." Mike led the way.

At least the view was a highlight, she thought, smiling to herself.

It had taken a lot of calls and searching through files to get information on his own team members. That alone made him suspicious and angry enough to throw his weight around and call a favor to the deputy secretary of defense. It was a program, they called it. Experimental technology. Like the bio-markers. Well, they'd taken it a lot further, and he gained the information as if he'd heard a rumor and wanted to crush it. No one knew that he might have proof it was implanted or injected in human beings. It was in the experimental testing stage. They never would have done this, not without Gannon.

Now it was time to confront the source.

Moving through the offices in the medical facility, Hank was unimpressed with the three stages of secretaries that were like a garrison protecting Colonel Cook. He was escorted in by a petite female soldier who'd already done combat time and was full of smiles and accommodation. Better than a fox-hole of sand, he thought and with his cover tucked in his waist belt, he entered the office.

Cook stood and smiled, greeting him. "Nice to see you, Hank. What can I do for you?"

Cook was tall and narrow and he stood behind his desk at parade rest. It told Hank several things; one was that he was far too uptight for his age. Most of his fellow full birds were relaxed, old school, and ready to retire. It meant that they pushed the envelope, not really caring who didn't like their opinion. Cook pushed the envelope in a different direction.

"I've got some troubling stats and I was hoping you could shed some light."

Hank closed the door and went to the desk, setting his briefcase down before he opened it. He took out the stack of files and dropped them on the desk.

"Tell me about this, Carl. What have you been doing here?"

Carl frowned and picked up the top folder, glanced at it, then closed it. "I don't know what you mean. It's a medical record. This is a hospital."

"Look at the stats for physical training." Carl did, humoring him, Hank felt.

"This means what?"

"Well, I'm thinking about a time when you came to us. I

have a report on this project. It was so long ago that I'd forgotten about it."

Carl offered nothing. He wasn't going to play his hand. It sent up smoke signals, and Hank was determined to get past the fire. "This"—he tapped the folders—"was brought to my attention or I wouldn't have noticed."

"Brought by who?"

"That's unimportant. What is, though, is that I recall you coming to the Joint Chiefs with this, and the Security Council. You got the funding, but testing was years off, and a majority of us thought it was a waste of taxpayers' money."

"You included," Carl said snidely.

"Indeed, yet you convinced the committee. Commendable. They don't usually go for the high price tag with such a low yield on the investment."

"It isn't low."

"I'll say, if this is real." He gestured to the files.

"We're doing testing on orangutans. Several. Not men. Are you mad?"

Hank stared at him, letting him stew, but he knew Cook had balls of steel and wouldn't flinch. "I think you overstepped, Carl, again. You're stuck here in the hospital for a reason, and we both know it."

Cook's gaze narrowed and his pinched lips told Hank he'd hit a sore spot. Intentional. Cook was former Spec Ops, DIA division. Yet the man was suspected of waging his own little war with the wrong kind of human assets. There wasn't anything concrete. He *did* have orders to clean up the area near Dafur. He did it too well. An entire town was wiped off the map. He'd been regulated to overseeing this hospital, though there was a civilian and military medical board that ran the show. He was a figurehead and nothing more.

"You couldn't just ride out your career till retirement, could you? You had to push the envelope. What bullshit story did you give my troops?"

"I don't know what you're talking about. We have a military and a civilian contractor in charge of the facility and the program. I just sign the checks."

"You're so full of shit."

Cook's brows shot up and his hands lowered to his sides.

"You're lucky you're not in Leavenworth."

"I have nothing to say, Colonel."

"Fine, keep those, I have the originals." He closed his briefcase and dragged it off the desk. "I didn't think you'd cooperate."

"Do you have a warrant or a summons, at least?" Carl said and knew Hank didn't. "Do you know how ridiculous you sound? Nano in humans? It would be like a death sentence at this stage."

"You better hope not." Hank met his gaze, his outrage scorching. "Fuck with my troops and I'll have your ass on the wire, Carl."

Cook stared, unaffected. "Are you done?"

Jansen stepped back, turned, and left.

Carl sank into his chair. Jansen was the wrong man to anger, he thought, a fucking Boy Scout and wouldn't let go of this bone. He picked up the phone, dialed, then put it to his ear. "It's in the open."

"It was when she left."

"No, someone else knows."

"That's your problem, not mine."

"We agreed—"

She cut him off. "No, Carl, you did. I told you, you can't stop her when she wants something. How do you think we got the project this far in so short a time? She obviously went for help. Deal with it or we're both sunk." Francine hung up.

Carl reared back, stunned by her sharpness, then looked at the files. Just how did the Spec Ops commander get a hold of this information? His men were in the field, under a ten-ton chopper, last he heard.

A damage to the project, of course, but they could simply

start over. He was convincing enough, and funds for this kind of research were under the "save lives" category and Cook knew, he could get anyone to be a bleeding heart for the military right now.

Hank didn't leave and walked through the hospital, his Joint Chief's badge getting him looks. He didn't remove it, though normally he only wore it in the Pentagon. It was a piece of intimidation he needed right now. He found the wing he was looking for, yet there were security locks all over the place. To keep in or keep out?

He strode to the desk. "I need to see Major Yates."

The sergeant jumped to his feet, saluted. "Yes sir, your clearance?"

Hank lifted his badge, the shield of the Joint Chiefs. His ID was beneath it.

"Yes, sir, of course, sir. Step this way." The kid followed procedure and scanned him with a wand for weapons, then keyed him through.

"Down the hall and to your right, sir. The wall color changes to light green."

Hank walked briskly, knowing Cook probably warned the major and they were fabricating a nice little story. Busting the man's chops would make him feel a little better. Hank found another soldier standing post.

"The major should be in the primate lab, fifth door down at the rear. It's the biggest lab, sir."

The hall was long, several doors on either side, and Hank realized this was part of the hospital that from the outside looked like a warehouse. People assumed it was the massive supply and repair area, the industrial operation to keep the hospital online and running. Clever, he thought.

He stopped at the door, peering in through the glass. He could see Dr. Yates at a computer. Hank raised his hand to knock, then saw the name right below Dr. Yates, MAJOR U.S. ARMY.

Clancy M. McRae, Chief AI engineer.

Gannon's jailbird.

Mike taught her how to hide their trail. "Peru has some of the best trackers in the world, and I'm betting one is behind us somewhere."

"There you go with the pessimism again."

"A caution," he corrected.

"And debatable. Think positive, or it screws with your karma."

Mike shook his head, his smile rueful. "I make my karma," he said in almost a snarl. "New Age shit."

Clancy smiled at his back and expected that kind of answer from him.

They'd gone a half mile when Clancy excused herself, not saying anything, but just pointing. He got the message. Head call, the Marine slang for using the bathroom. She moved into the forest and with the machete cut herself a private spot. She was in the middle of relieving herself when she thought, *This is why I hate camping.* She wondered how long the stack of facial tissues was going to do the trick when she struggled not to pee on her boots.

She fastened her clothes and grabbed her pack, walking as she swung it onto her back. It unbalanced her and she fell before she could stop herself. She'd need a chiropractor before she left this country, she thought, pushing to her elbows. For a moment, she stared, and then her skin pulled tight when she realized what she was seeing.

A gray decaying hand sticking out of the ground as if reaching for God.

"Mike. Quickly." Then the foul odor hit her. She lurched back, her wrist under her nose.

"Christ."

She turned her face away. The hand was charcoal gray and curled, horrible not for the decaying sight but because a human being was left like this. Clancy climbed to her feet as Mike knelt.

"Who would do such a thing? Never mind," she added when he looked at her. "I've seen the dead, just not the . . . old dead."

Mike brushed at the ground and leaves, sweeping debris off the body, and Clancy was sadistically entranced. But as he exposed the face, her stomach rolled and she turned away. "Oh God."

He reached back for her. "Sit down, head down."

As she did, he uncovered the body, searched the pockets. "He's a Peruvian soldier."

"The ones that had all the memorials? A local said they never came back."

"They won't talk about it. But they found two, and looking worse than this." He met her gaze. "They didn't have their eyes."

*Gross.* "It's a warning not to come looking for them, you think?"

Mike instantly thought of Renoux's comments about strange occurrences, and Denner's disappearance added to his confusion. Yet this body looked as if it were tattooed without ink, too bloody to define a shape.

"That's the consensus, and remember the sniper? We're on the river." He gestured off handily to the tributary yards below their position. "From the other side of the valley, a sniper could pick off anyone along the bank. And he did." The three with the crates were a threat. To territory or an operation?

Mike looked at her and used his body to block the view. "His weapon is still in his hand, but his throat is cut and he's too white." There was little blood on the body, but he tipped the head, seeing only a small amount settling in his neck. Did he bleed out from a back wound? he wondered and pushed the corpse over. "Son of a bitch, they're here, under each other!"

Clancy saw a mass grave and felt ill. "How many were in the company?"

He looked at her, bleak. "Thirty troops. Only two returned, dead when people found them."

She looked into the jungle to the top of the trees. "What did they see?" She met his gaze. "Like Richora, what did *I* see?"

"Wish the hell I knew."

"Good God, Mike, look at the body. He's decayed a lot more than he should be for a couple days."

Mike frowned. She was right. "Ya know, he looks almost mummified." Mummification took years, yet the soldier's skin was already papery and he seemed—dried up. Mike reburied the bodies and with his GPS marked the location.

Clancy had already turned away. Mike didn't blame her.

"This is where I found the piece." Armed, Clancy moved back to the path. "Up this way. I remember this," she said, slapping a tree broken off at least five feet above her head, then walked around it.

Mike came to her, dusting off his gloves as she led him up an incline. He paused long enough to make certain they were parallel to the river.

"Mike," she said, trying not to shout. She pointed at the ground. "I found it here. See, this is where I knelt to tie my boot." She squatted, her knee impression in the ground still.

"Excellent." Mike switched the screen, showing her Gantz's trajectory points. "Stay here, be my point of reference."

"Roger that."

The comment, one he heard from his Marines often, struck him odd coming from her, and Mike turned back as she sat on the ground. She wasn't a Marine, he reminded himself, she was a scientist. A damn smart one, and while she'd proven herself more than resourceful, she was still untrained.

Clancy gathered her hair off her neck and fanned herself, then twisted, frowning at him. "What are you waiting for?"

"You have ammo?" It was lame, but he wanted to be certain of something.

Clancy didn't have to check. "Three bullets. Got any more?"

He shook his head. "That's my toss-away gun." Cheap and not sighted in.

"Then if I see anyone, I'll just scream *really* loud."

His smile was crooked. "Girls. Just fire off a round. Preferably into the bad guy."

"God," she said in a falsetto whine. "You ask so much of me."

Mike chuckled. "You crack me up, Irish."

She blinked. "Clearly your life is not as exciting as I imagined."

He arched a brow. "Ditto."

"As soon as this is over I'm going back to boring as hell. You just watch me."

But she couldn't. If Cook had his way, she'd be in jail the minute she stepped on U.S. soil. Handcuffs and prison food didn't stack up against lives. Valnik, Krane, Palmer, and Di-Fazio, she repeated in her mind. Men she'd studied so much she'd recognize them on the spot. Inside her boots, her toes curled over the plastic that held their files. She didn't need them anymore, but it was like keeping them close. Her gaze moved over the land, the ancient ruins behind her, the river streaming on the edge of the valley below.

*Where are you guys?*

Mike started to leave, then noticed her rocking, her arms wrapped around her knees. He knelt. "What's the matter, Irish?"

She lifted her gaze. "We have to find them, and *soon.*" The glossy sheen in her eyes left Mike feeling cut open and bleeding.

"We will." He stroked his hand over her hair.

She gripped his hand. "No, you don't understand. Your men—" She drew a breath and blurted, "It could send Di-

Fazio over the edge and do nothing to Valnik except what it should, increasing his present capabilities."

His brows drew down. "Over the edge as in insane?"

"As in murderous."

"Jesus Christ." Mike rubbed his mouth. "How long do they have?"

"I don't know, the pods were inserted weeks ago. Without data, I can't tell." Damn Francine for doing this, she thought and hoped the woman was suffering with her overblown ego.

"Clancy, *we're* hunted: Guess."

Mentally, she calculated from the date of implantation and admitted, "Four days, a week at the most." If she could observe Boris, she might be able to predict, and then she'd know what the men would experience soon.

They'd already been here for two days, Mike thought, shooting to his feet, and with the GPS, started to walk. "I'm not leaving this country till I can bring them home."

Alive or in a body bag. He didn't have to say it. She understood. Clancy followed him.

When he heard her, Mike turned and scowled. "No."

"Find something else for your point of reference, I'm searching. I need to."

He held her gaze, understanding more than he thought. She created it, she had to end it. He nodded.

"And I wasn't asking for your permission," she muttered as she moved past him and gave him a light shove.

Mike just smiled, and watched her six.

# Thirteen

If Antone Choufani hadn't been chasing after his money taken away on the wind, he wouldn't have seen him. He caught the bill, crushing it in his fist, when his gaze landed on a small man walking happily toward a coffee shop. Despite the shaved head, he'd recognize him anywhere.

Rashid ibn al-Dehnwar.

He should be dead.

*We thought he was dead.* Antone felt that glorious moment when they believed they'd killed a commander of the Hezbollah dry up and blow away. Choufani was positive his eyes weren't deceiving him. He'd tracked the man for a year, had seen him go into the warehouse in Tunisia, then watched it blow up. Interpol had identified his brother, in pieces. It could only mean that Dehnwar had known Interpol was coming and allowed his kin to die in his place. The will of Allah was first, he thought, remembering Dehnwar's preaching. *Like you know what God says and thinks,* Choufani thought bitterly, moving swiftly to catch up. When Dehnwar climbed into a sedan and drove north, Antone glanced around for a cab and saw only a motorcycle tour rental. He tossed money at the cashier and hopped on the small dirt bike.

He didn't wonder what Dehnwar was doing here. The

lavender paper was the key, and while he'd like to draw his weapon and end his life now, that wouldn't stop whatever cell was operating here. He kept his distance, even stopping the bike to light a cigarette, and he let Dehnwar get farther down the highway.

Traffic passed in front of him, the heat of the morning already pressing on the small town. People walked with dainty umbrellas, most with hats against the blistering sun. The sweet smell of flowers filled the air, and a breeze blew loose blossoms like the rain of pink snow as the sedan turned. Antone drove the bike toward the cross street, weaving in and out of the traffic that inched along like ants in a farm. He swept the turn and picked him up quickly, then made a left and rode parallel to him to get just a little ahead.

Dehnwar was overconfident, living another life. He'd lead Antone to his people and perhaps he could kill them all. Again.

Francine felt a sting of panic when she walked into the hold. It was a roomful of cages, each occupied by various animals. Several were primates, a few chimps. But her interest was the orangutans. Six had been injected, and the veterinarians overseeing this section called her in.

"I don't see what's wrong. You say they tried to escape?"

"They bent the cages." He tossed back a pale blue sheet that covered all the ape cages. The bars looked slightly damaged, but nothing too substantial. She leaned in to study the animals.

The vet pulled her back. "I wouldn't."

"Don't touch me," she said, grabbing his fingers. He winced, and she let go. He backed up, giving her a dirty look. Through the bars, she examined the animal. "He's drugged, what's the problem?" The ape was useless in this condition.

"No, he's not drugged."

She looked at him sharply.

"That's what happened to that one too. They go wild,

then this. Almost catatonic. If you want to see it in action, be my guest, I can give him something to wake him up."

"Do it." She watched him inject. Minutes later the ape was awake and moving.

The orangutan saw her as he climbed to his feet, and Francine had to look up at the large animal. His fingers swept the floor of the cage, and he started sniffing and coming closer to the bars. Then he gripped them and rocked the cage, but it was harnessed to the wall with straps. When it wouldn't move, the ape pulled.

Francine's eyes widened when the metal bent, the rivets pulling out. "Dope him up!" The vet was already coming forward with a needle. Suddenly, the ape reached between the bent bars and latched on to her lab coat. He yanked her close, his hot breath in her face.

"Quickly!"

His grip trapped her inside the coat and she pried at the ape's hands, but like her, he was stronger than normal, and until the drugs kicked in, she couldn't get free. He roared loudly in her face, and afraid he'd try to bite her, she looked away. He kept screaming. *He's trying to scare me, or warn me that he could kill me?* Orangutans weren't aggressive except toward other males in their territorial home range.

"He should start to fade," the vet said, drawing back with the syringe. There were two guards with weapons flanking them.

"You idiot, get the stick! Now!" she ordered and the vet stuck the electrical rod on the red ape's arm. The charge bolted briefly, yet his fingers only loosened.

Francine pried them off, then back-stepped.

Good God. She'd stopped wearing perfume; it had enraged them. But then, why was he so angry? Could the pod actually give off a pheromone or something? But the others weren't aggressive. When they were wild, they drugged them and then suddenly they were catatonic? It didn't make sense. The nanopod was keeping her awake. Why not them?

She glanced at the vet. "Keep him that way."

"I can't, not for long."

A veterinarian who worked for the government keeping animals caged for experiments didn't have many morals. "Until I understand this change, yes, you can."

Mike squatted, working the GPS, Gantz's mathematical triangle superimposed over a map of the area. They were in the highlands. San José de Lourdes was north of his position, the valley and the Marañón River stretching between.

He looked upward to the ruins of ancient dwellings, the crude windows like eyes in the side of the mountain. Good location for the night, he thought. It was already getting dark under the canopy of trees. He traced back toward Clancy's position, sliding down the hill on the side of his boots. The ground dipped deeply and Mike lost his footing, the GPS flying out of his hand as weeds and plants fell with him into the pit. He winced at the impact of rocks against his shin, and grappled for purchase, sliding deeper, then abruptly stopped. Flat on the inside of the gulley, his feet braced, he climbed out, grabbing exposed roots to hoist himself the last few feet. He searched for the GPS, and frowned when he found it cracked. He tested it, tapping the side. The screen blinked and appeared clear. He looked where he fell.

Suddenly he jumped into the gulley and started digging with his hands. Fresh, damp earth clawed between his fingers and an odor wafted up. Mike brought a handful to his nose. An electrical burn, some metal, some rubber, he thought. The UAV was powered by battery, not fuel. Yet the odor of seared leaves and the lack of burned earth told him Gantz was right, it crashed here. The impact was deep and wide, and he knew the Hellfires didn't explode. At least not both. The damage was minimal and if the rocket had been armed when they were surveying, then the hole would be a hell of a lot bigger. There wouldn't be any trees for a few hundred yards too.

He dug greedily, hoping to find something that proved him right. It was clean and empty. The only remains of the crash was the piece Clancy had found. Pushing out of the hole, he dusted off, marked the location, then combed the area for a trail. It was intentionally cleared. Not even a gouge left from dragging. The Hellfires weren't large and could be dismantled, but as far as he was concerned, they were still on the loose.

Through binoculars, Mike surveyed the mountainside. There was a cliff face above the ruins. Probably why the ancient Indians chose it for their homes. Attacking from above was next to impossible, the cliff shielding them and making it difficult to get to the dwellings below. He imagined the view from up there. They could see anyone approaching, and while the mountain stretched on either side of the plateau, they could protect it from the stronghold. Strategic. Planned. A one-eighty view of the valley, he supposed, an endless ripple of green mountains stretching through the country to Chile.

He thought of the sniper that picked off the guys at the flatboats. Mike could see for miles, and with the right equipment he'd be accurate at long distance. Timing and leading the target were all it took. He scanned, backing out of visual range.

He needed to find Clancy.

Alejo Richora moved swiftly, climbing the mountain without a struggle. The Americans were slower, unaccustomed to the thin air. He'd run these hills as a boy; he knew them. He could find the Americans in the dark, but this was easier. He needed them out of his way, and while he could leave this matter to a few of his men, he wanted to eliminate them himself. It was a matter of pride, he thought as he moved faster, his spiked boots giving him traction. Family vengeance drove him. He would force them to run.

A frightened prey made mistakes.

\* \* \*

Francine couldn't sleep. Her mind wanted to rest, but she couldn't. Her brain was in overload as if she'd put in long hours at the lab, her mind tripping over facts and then doing it again and again like a spinning wheel. Her body felt keen, tight, and packed with new energy. The proof was that at three in the morning, she was running on her treadmill. In the dark. She could see clearly, the room almost glowing with sharp edges. She'd lost weight, despite her increased appetite, and she kept careful notes, testing her blood pressure, her heart rate that surprisingly maintained a normal even rate, and yet she'd already run ten miles.

She wasn't winded, or perspiring, and she made a note of that. The pod could shut down adrenal glands. She hit the remote for the TV, watching channel after channel, and yet it only suited to tear her mind in several directions. Bored, she stopped the machine and hopped off, stretched, then moved to her hand weights. She ran her finger down the series of black dumbbells, then picked up the last, slinging it to do curls.

It flew out of her hand and hit the wall, crashing through the drywall to the studs. She looked at her hand, flexing her arm. It didn't look different or feel different. She crossed to the dumbbell lodged in the wall and thought, *How do I explain that to the super?*

She removed and replaced it on the rack, then tested her strength with a bench-press. She knew better than to take it to the limit. She might have added strength, but her muscles would scream at her for it tomorrow. And she'd still be awake.

Awake for three days, she thought. She wasn't exhausted or stressed. Insomnia was the only side effect beyond her increased appetite. She'd eaten a half dozen eggs and a rasher of bacon this morning and was suddenly thankful for those open twenty-four-hour diners. She'd already cleaned out her own kitchen and hadn't had time to restock it. She grabbed a bottle of water from the fridge, and drained it before she reached the other side of the room.

In her town house, she dropped into a chair and felt her blood racing through her veins. She squirmed in the seat and wondered if a good round of sex would settle her down. She didn't want to drug herself, and she was so horny she'd already used some toys. It wasn't enough and not thinking of anything else, she reached for the phone.

Clancy waited for Mike to find her. He had the big electronic compass, she reasoned. She heard him coming only because he wanted her to and she turned, aiming. Just in case.

He winked, a bit of pride in his smile. "I found the UAV site."

"I did one better." She gestured up the mountain and he looked.

The mass was huge, and covered with deep green camo netting. "No wonder we couldn't see it."

Clancy stared at the treetops and pointed. "Look there, you can see the damage where it fell." The sides of the trees were scraped, exposing the wood and weeping with sap. They could see where it dropped out of the sky, the part in the dense scalp of the treetops open nearly a hundred feet above them. "From here it doesn't look that large."

"It's not. Maybe thirty feet. Pure luck that it didn't take down some trees. This was clever as hell." Then he reached for the edge and pulled, but it wouldn't budge. "It's caught on all the metal," he said and drew his knife. He cut, the blade slicing open holes and exposing the side of the craft.

Clancy inhaled and back-stepped.

The pilot was in the seat, his helmet still on and a scream on his lips. "Look at him, he's like the Peru soldiers." Dried up, she thought, then noticed the tortured look on Mike's face as he stared at the pilot. "Oh God, Mike, I'm sorry, you knew him?"

"Mad Dog Carson. He'd been our pilot for a couple years." Mike had been in the copilot seat enough to know that if Carson had seen the rocket coming, he was the one man who could have flown well enough to avoid it. At least his wife would have some peace, he thought, and leaned in to remove his dog tags.

He looked at Clancy and wasn't surprised to see tears, yet beneath it was a diabolical gleam. She suddenly drew her machete and hacked at the netting. Mike helped her pull at the heavy mesh enough to see inside.

"They're not here." She stumbled back, shocked and grateful. "They're not here."

"Then where?" Mike looked over the terrain. Villages were clustered, yet there were miles of densely wooded forest between them. Hundreds of people perished in this wilderness. Eight years ago, it had almost taken him.

"Someone put this net here. There has to be a trail."

Mike wasn't listening, already looking for one as he passed around the wreckage. "The rotor blades are sheered off, but it's barely scorched."

She searched the ground, bending to follow footprints.

"Those are your footprints," he said and she looked up, chagrined as he leaned inside the wreckage and yanked something free. He tossed a box at her feet. "Food."

Clancy leaped on it.

"Equipment is still here. The guys would never have left it behind."

"Not willingly."

He shook his head. "They'd have destroyed it first." Heck, Krane didn't need a weapon, the man was lethal with just his hands. Mike moved to the outer edge of the site and kept making a circle, wider with each pass. Then he found it.

Clancy was at his side, eating an energy bar. "Leaves stripped off plants?"

"It's Krane. Marking a trail. His hands were in front of him at least." Mike touched the bare stalks, then moved on and found another. He paused when he saw an overturned rock and the toe print in front of it. For a small moment, he let himself hope.

"They left here alive."

"But with no gear," she said, pointing to a vest.

He moved closer, looking around for a second, then grabbed a dead stick and shot it at the vest like a javelin. Booby traps, she thought, and he kicked it over. "No blood. It's standard issue, no markings."

"You had the permission of the Peruvian government, right?"

"Yes, but that's not who rules this part of the jungle." If they didn't run into members of a drug cartel, he'd be surprised.

Clancy's chewing slowed as she looked around. "I don't think anyone rules here but the jungle."

After stripping the chopper of food and water supplies, Mike motioned her to join him, and when she caught up, he touched her shoulder.

Clancy looked at him. His gaze flicked to his right and she let hers drift past him. The Indian. She tried not to notice, glancing quickly away. "Ya know, I thought we were being followed." She kept walking.

"It's your friend."

"Come to see if the competition is up to snuff?"

"I hope that's all." Mike caught up, then pulled her close. Her hands flattened to his chest. "What are you doing now?"

"Proving I'm up to snuff."

"You assume a lot, Gannon."

"No. I don't."

He leaned down and she leaned back. He frowned. "This kiss had better be for me, not him," she said.

His grin was slow, challenging. Then he proved it was for her.

*Oh. My. There is a God.*

Clancy had kissed him before, but nothing like this. She swore her toes curled in her boots, and as his mouth slid over hers, her hands crawled around his waist. She held on. He was ferociously warm and tight against her. Not an inch of him soft, and all of it getting harder. Excitement coursed through her blood and chiseled at her composure. His mouth molded with a fragile pressure that was such a contrast to the man, and made her body tingle with expectation. He toyed, coaxed her to play, and she smiled against his mouth. Who knew? Yet when his hand slid down her spine and pushed her into him, she would gladly have stripped for him right there.

Then his tongue came into play, sweeping and bold, and her mind had somewhere else to live. She could tear into him right now and never look back. His hand slid upward, over her waist, molded her ribs, fluttered across her breast to her throat, gathering her fraying nerves as it went and making her unbearably greedy for more. Then his fingertips spanned her jaw, holding her as if she'd vanish. It was so damn sexy, and she wanted to get closer, unconsciously pushing her hips into his. He drew back a fraction.

"Jesus," he whispered against her mouth. "He needs to go the hell away."

She breathed hard and not because of the thin air. "Well," she said shakily. "If that didn't do it, you'll get a spear in the back."

"Your concern is touching."

She rubbed her thumb across his lower lip. "I don't see him."

"I don't give a shit."

He kissed her again, fast and hot, and she thought, it was a little hard to run from anything when her knees were mushy. "That was so . . . amazing."

It was incredible, but he didn't need to say it. "You're vocal," he groaned.

She laughed softly; that just plain dared her. "I keep nothing inside, Mike. That's what got me in trouble."

"I could get you there again," he said darkly, and the sly look in his eyes said it had nothing to do with the Indian or the corrupt police—and everything to do with misbehaving somewhere in the dark.

"Oh, don't say stuff like that, I've got a weakness for bad boys in white hats."

He groaned, half smiling, in the best agony he'd been in for too damn long. She was such a turn-on, he thought, and finally let her go.

If he didn't they'd have been giving the Indian one hell of a show in short order.

She blew out her breath, looking him over with a sexy promise in her eyes that drove blood to his groin. Again. *She's killing me,* he thought, and ushered her along.

"Don't look around for him. He has to think we didn't see him. Takes away the threat. Confrontation is out of the question unless forced. No interaction with the local populous, and if so, the absolute minimum."

That sounded straight from the regulations. "What fun is there in that?" She hacked through the foliage.

"That's the job."

"Not all the time."

"I don't have much else going on."

"You expect me to feel sorry for that?"

He scowled at her back. "Hell no."

"Good, because I won't."

He shook his head, smiling. "Have you always been such a hard-ass?"

She was quiet for several steps. "No. I had a normal life with friends and family and I ignored it all, thinking I deserved more attention than I was getting." She glanced and met his gaze. "I'm sure you know the rest."

"I'm curious about one thing, how did someone so intelligent, get into so much trouble?"

She paused and looked back. "I wasn't always smart, Mike." She wiped sweat from her eyes with her sleeve, then raised the machete. Mike touched her arm and moved past her, making a corridor in one pass with his blade.

"Show-off," she said, and they walked for a while before she said quietly, "How well do you know them?"

Her voice sounded so frail just then. "We've been a team for four years. They're my brothers."

She understood the kinship. She'd made a lot of friends in the military. "Have any blood ones?"

"Yes."

Clancy opened another energy bar, and tapped him with another. He took it, stuffing it in his pocket. "Not Marines?"

He scoffed. "Oh, hell no."

"Cowboys?" He glanced over his shoulder and made a face. "Ah, bikers."

"They're geeks like you."

"So you're the black sheep?"

"Sorta, yeah."

"Me too. Sorta."

Suddenly, Mike shot forward and scooped something off the ground. He turned to her and held it out. A rifle. More specifically, an MP5.

She nearly choked on the energy bar, swallowing to talk. "Are you kidding? Who in this part of the world would leave that behind?"

Mike checked it. "It's loaded." He pulled the clip. "Never fired." They'd been positioned to repel from the chopper, Mike remembered from the radio transcript. Maybe they were thrown clear. Mike slung the rifle and walked farther out from the wreckage and found a load-bearing vest, then the flack jacket with Kevlar. It was as if they were stripped of their gear as they were pushed along.

Clancy met up with him. "More prizes." She held a pistol holster, and a Camelbak water system. "Who wouldn't want this?"

"Locals. They wouldn't know what to do with it, and no one packs heavy in the jungle."

"Except us."

"Maybe they had enough to carry."

"Like a teammate?" she said.

He nodded. "They'd strip down to weapons, comms, and water." He dropped the vest, then removed anything useful from the gear, and she crouched, helping. "Stay here, I'm going to make a circle for more." But he came up empty. No Indian either. He held the GPS and compared the crash site and this one, to the GPS of the *guestimated* launch site possibilities opposite the impact areas. Mike turned sharply. "Gantz's calculations put the rocket launching from there," he said, pointing.

"That's the other direction." South.

"Yeah, and it isn't any more logical than leaving the gear behind."

They widened the search again, each turning in the opposite direction, and made a circle to the original point. No prints, no stripped leaves. Plucked out of the jungle, he thought, like Denner. But they were here, he thought, and that's more than he'd had.

Mike looked at the woods, expecting to see Clancy any moment.

But she didn't come back.

# Fourteen

Mike felt an unfamiliar sliver of fear just before Clancy came trotting down the slope, holding out a piece of cloth. It was covered in blood and it wasn't fresh.

"It's a T-shirt, one of those under-armor wicking things." The material stretched to fit skintight and draw the sweat away from the body so it would dry faster. Only recently developed for the military, it was used in tropical and desert warfare. "It's been cut, too."

He reached for it.

It was a split-second moment. He didn't have time to shout, or shield her. The bullet splattered through the piece of cloth and Clancy jerked, then dropped to the ground with him.

"Goddamnit," he muttered. He'd let his guard down, and they almost bought it. Stupid, he thought, damn stupid.

Another shot came, a couple of feet from his boot, and Mike fired back.

Clancy aimed, squinting.

"Don't waste your ammo." Mike held the assault rifle.

"You get all the fun," she said, and was already crawling higher.

"Good thinking, get out of range." He couldn't see shit in the jungle, and when the shooter fired again Mike rolled and laid down suppression fire, cutting a line through the jungle.

"Not exactly my first thought, but yeah."

He crawled with her for a couple of feet, motioning her on, and he faced the shooter, almost daring him. Mike needed to see the muzzle flash. Then she slapped her hand on his shoulder, gripped a handful of shirt, and jerked hard. "If it's Richora, he's got men. Today *they're* ruling the jungle."

Mike rolled around. She was right, damn it. "Ya know, I'm supposed to be the expert."

"That's okay, you're stupid from my fabulous kisses."

"Got that right," he muttered under his breath, low-crawling away from their last position. Mike pulled into a crouch and watched behind them.

Nothing moved. Maybe he hit the bastard.

"Mike," she whispered and he inched up near her. She pointed to footprints.

Mike pushed aside vegetation to see the detail. "They're combat jump boots." He followed them, and after a few feet realized they went toward the ruins. "It's too out in the open. They wouldn't have gone there, not with all this left behind." He meant the discarded equipment, and weapons.

"Where else? I don't see a door. We can at least see someone coming."

He shook his head. "It's strategically ideal as a fortress, but escape? There's nowhere to go."

"There has to be." She shifted to the tree line, her weapon down. "They wouldn't be that stupid to lock themselves in their homes."

"Two thousand years ago, they weren't that slick."

"Stop being a cynic. Have you ever seen the Inca and Aztec stone mechanisms? They were brilliant."

Mike watched behind them, his back to a tree. "I'm not convinced." It was still a good half mile away.

Then automatic weapons fire blistered through the trees and they took cover. There wasn't much of it, the terrain rocky, and thinned of trees. But Mike saw the muzzle flash. It wasn't wide. *He's got a suppressor.*

He fired and heard the yelp of pain, hoping there was only one out there, then urged her on. Neither stood until they were at the west-side base of the ruins. He could barely make them out, the sun long past behind it. They skirted the forest edge, the ruins to the right, sun-bleached orange shapes in the mountain, below it a deep gulley, a moat that had protected the inhabitants. The footing narrowed, the rise of stone wall forcing them to move like rock climbers.

Mike glanced down. The excavated dig site below was nothing but a stone framework of corridors that looked like they might have been tunnels, and he thought, *She could be right.* Those corridors could lead into the homes cut into the sides of the mountains.

Clancy moved with Mike, her fingers gripping the stone and shifting sideways. They had to move fast. They were too exposed despite the low light. She could see where he was headed, and with the angle of the sun they were visible more by shadow than themselves. Just a few feet, she thought, and he slung himself inside the small doorway. Then he turned and reached for her. Clancy moved her feet carefully and lifted her hand to him. The ground crumbled under her right foot, sending her forward.

Mike grabbed her shirt and held on. Then it started to rip.

Alejo limped through the forest, pausing to snap off his bandanna and tie it over his leg, slamming his eyes shut as pain vibrated up to his hip.

He took several deep breaths, angry now, and kept them in sight, then brought his weapon forward. He could see them higher up on the mountainside and he shouldered the rifle, then peered into the scope. They'd already found the crash site. It was unfortunate and he suspected they were sent to find it. Not much left to find, eh? The men who were on the helicopter were dead, tossed out of it when it was going down, he didn't know. When they found it, the fire was out and the men were gone, as if they were never inside it. He'd sent his own soldiers to cover it, and it worked well till these two arrived. He'd called for some help, yet wouldn't wait and took careful aim, the pair close enough now that he could get them both.

He put them between the crosshairs, smiling.

The bitch needed to die.

Bullets chipped the stone, fragments peppering his face. Mike pulled. "Grab my arm!"

She reached. It was too far, her balance leaning on one foot. She stretched, her right foot searching for purchase. Shots came close, and Mike knew he didn't have much time before the bastard got a clean bead on them.

"I've got a foothold," she said, but he didn't care. He heaved her up into the narrow doorway, then rolled with her deeper inside.

"You okay?" He kissed her forehead, held her face in his hands. "All right?"

"Yeah, yes." She nodded. "Shoot him, will you?"

Mike moved to the edge with his weapon, sighting through the Cyclops binoculars. He turned on the night vision. The area was black and he switched to thermal. "We've got someone out there, but he's not moving."

"I hope he has a hole in his ass."

Mike smiled slightly, keeping watch. *He's wounded,* he thought. He heard it.

Clancy scooted back on her rear and felt for the ground, the inside too dark to see beyond her face. Mike eased back from the window, then pulled a Chem-lite from his pack and cracked it. Green light shone as he highlighted the walls and floor, ancient paintings faded and barely visible on the walls.

"We're in some fix, huh?"

"Maybe not." He moved toward another opening in the wall. "It's another room and I can see one beyond that. It looks communal," he said softly.

There was an open hole near the floor and a dug-out section in the center of the floor. "They shared the fire." He flicked between the two spots. An open hearth was in the next wall and he could see into another section. One family fire warmed inside and offered light to the next. Ingenious, he thought and eased into the next room, the expanse smaller than his shoulders and he had to turn sideways. He stood, careful of his steps. Trusting thousand-year-old floors just wasn't wise.

"I bet they connect." Clancy moved up behind him.

"They go off in different directions like a maze," he said, shifting the Chem-lite to the right, and the glow flared off more openings in the earth.

Clancy looked up, an uneasy feeling spinning through her. "We're under the mountain?"

"Inside it." Yet something in her voice made him turn back and he shone the light. "You okay?"

"I'm beat, hungry, and people are shooting at us in the dark." She was whining, but she could barely stand without support.

"It's as good a place as any to hold up till sunrise."

She dropped to the ground, shouldered off her pack as Mike looked over the exits and defense. Clancy just wanted to sleep.

"This place wasn't on the tours?"

"It was, but there are more near the coast, in Trujillo. It's gorgeous over there and I guess the appeal is greater." She yawned widely. "This site doesn't have easy access."

His back to her, Mike blocked the doorway. "I think I know who's out there." He flicked on a penlight and shone it on the back of a room.

Clancy leaned up to look. "Oh, man." There were stacks of wrapped kilos against the wall.

"Yeah, we've crossed over into someone's territory all right." He moved in closer. "There are footprints here."

"Combat boots?"

"Yes." He looked back at her. "They go deeper into the mountain."

Her gaze flicked around. "To where? It's solid rock. We can't follow, we have no light, and morning sunshine isn't going to light that any better."

"It will some. The holes in each dwelling line up and must shine light into here till evening."

"See, I told you they were smart."

"Yeah, yeah, but we need to find the way out."

"Go for it."

He looked back and she squinted against the light as she unstrapped the machete.

"Stick a fork in me, I'm done." She shoved her pack into a corner and used it for a pillow.

His lips quirked. "Well, I guess there's no discussion."

"It's not a democracy, Gannon, but feel free to investigate."

Mike knelt and gently kissed her forehead.

"You'll protect me, I know." She patted his knee.

He really had pushed her hard, he thought, and admired her resilience. It's not every day someone gets shot at and springs back. He scanned beyond the opening that served as a door. The forest was nearly soundless except for the whisper of a breeze coming through the holes in the ruins. Not even a monkey moved out there. Come to think of it, he hadn't heard any birds and this would be a prime place for them and bats.

With his penlight in his teeth, he checked his gear. Enough food and water to keep them alive for a day but no more. Mike set a trap near the door, then settled down, feeling the warmth of the adobe walls against the chilly air coming into the ruins.

He held the satellite phone near the opening, and didn't want to risk speaking and having the sound echo out. He sent a text message to Colonel Jansen, informing him of his findings and that Clancy was with him. Jansen wouldn't be expecting it. Mike rarely made contact till he was bugging out. Done, he flashed a light toward the kilos, wanting to destroy it all right now.

While the boot prints led inside here, that didn't mean they belonged to his guys. With jump boots the exception, combat boots were pretty generic. But that the kilos were stored in the ruins meant they were sitting with some cartel's stash.

It wouldn't be long before someone else knew they were here—and came hunting.

Years of practice sprang the lock easily, and Antone slowly pulled the heavy chain free. Opening the door a foot, he slipped inside the factory. It was a long low building with several windows and a back veranda for employees. He'd seen it in daylight, the soothing colors of it, the accommodations made for the staff. The factory created items for the tourist trade, anything from statues to straw hats. There were two locations on either end of the town. He chose this one to start because it was nearest her house.

Marianna Salache was the owner. She owned the lavender paper he'd found, and the deliveries from the paper mill were split between the two factories and her home. Inside he flicked on a penlight and passed it over the office. His search would take a while and he truly didn't know his target, but even a cursory look didn't bring up anything peculiar.

He moved to the factory floor. Presses and machines sat like ghosts. They created a lot of small items, all sold at a low price to local vendors for resale. He knew enough that Marianna was generous and not a good businesswoman. It cost her nearly as much to make the items as to sell them at a discount as a wholesaler. Near the machine press were barrels of dark pellets, and Choufani removed his gloves and passed his fingers through the pellets. *It's not plastic,* he thought, shining the light on his hand. It was stained as if he'd had his hands in ash. He scooped up a handful, weighing it. Not all of it, at least. Too much weight and density.

Something familiar slipped through him and he started searching boxes, moving directly to the die-cut press. He found molds, small ones, some no larger than the width of his hand. He glanced at the windows, aware that the light could be seen from the street. Shielding the bulb, he flipped on the machine's light. It spotlighted the operational board of the press. He moved to the left, pulling it through one revolution, and smelled the scent of scorched plastic.

He used his penlight to closely examine the press. Molded pieces that didn't connect to anything and some that were like the little statues sold all over South America. He took a piece, and gripping it in his hand, he headed to the door. It felt familiar, the weight of it, and the realization hit him.

*Marianna,* he thought, *what have you done?*

Mike felt the warmth of her body curled around him as he woke. Her hand was on his chest, her head tucked against his shoulder. He enjoyed the moment and couldn't remember the last time he woke with a woman in his arms. One he wanted around later. He lay still, listening to her breathing, and heard the scuffle of stones. Carefully he disengaged from her and went to the opening. He scanned through the binoculars on thermals.

It was still dark, but the land was alive with red and orange. Christ. He could make out the four figures closing in, trying hard to be silent and deadly. He turned to Clancy, his hand over her mouth as he woke her. She grabbed at his hand, her eyes wide for a second; then she softened.

"We have company again," he whispered.

"Uninvited, how rude. Shoot them."

He shook his head. "They don't know where we are in here exactly, and shooting will give us away. We can't be exposed."

"They want their drugs."

"Then we let them have it."

Her brows knit as she met his gaze. "What do you mean? How can we?" she whispered. Then it dawned on her. "Oh, you've got to be kidding!"

Francine watched the screens show four images of the primate home. For days now, Boris and Natasha were going through the mating rituals, picking fleas off each other, bringing food, chasing each other through the forest that was completely man-made. She typed in her findings, smiling at her speed, but she frowned when she made a few mistakes. Her skills hadn't improved. She had the primate habitat speakers off or she would have noticed sooner. When she did, she wasn't shocked. Boris and Natasha were mating, vigorously.

Then she looked closer. She was out of the chair and flying down the hall to the lab, frantically hitting locks and codes to get inside. She rushed to the glass wall and hit the intercom speaker. "Boris, Boris! Stop!"

She hit the emergency pad and the blare of it inside the compound jungle shook the windows separating her from the apes. But Boris kept mating. Faster and harder, and Natasha was grabbing for anything to pull herself away, and screaming horribly.

*Oh God.*

Forced mating wasn't uncommon but Boris was violent, out of control. *It's rape,* she thought, but didn't dare enter the habitat or he might turn on her. Francine loaded a tranquilizer dart into the handgun and hit the compound locks. The glass shifted slowly back and she took aim between the bars.

From behind, Boris pounded into the orangutan wildly, caught her shoulders, then pulled her back against his hairy body. The orangutan climaxed, and let out a harsh roaring bellow that sent the few birds in there to the sky-blue ceiling, and a shiver down Francine's spine.

She fired, but it wasn't soon enough. Boris gripped Natasha's head and in one hard motion, snapped the ape's neck.

Francine lowered the tranq gun as the drugs kicked in and Boris slid to the ground, unconscious. She laid the gun aside and rubbed her face.

"Dr. Yates."

She flinched around, and stared into blue eyes blistering with rage.

Colonel Jansen.

"I think you'd better tell me exactly what you did to my men. Now."

Gantz bit into the fleshy cherimoya, slurping sweet juice and reaching for a napkin as he listened to Renoux's phone call.

He'd been doing it for a couple of days. Since Mike mentioned that Renoux had a client who wanted space on his ships. To keep his nose clean, Renoux had to abide customs and international laws. He wasn't. His ships were sitting in a port on the coast of Peru. That was a damn long way to transport illegal contraband—right through the drug cartels. Passing through territory was costly, and the price would increase with each leg. Someone was cutting him a deal, or he was airlifting it out.

Since Renoux had pissed off the Peruvian government with a trash drop of weapons that ended up in the hands of the cartels, the inspections were thorough. He wasn't getting anything out of Peru without the Navy or Army down his throat.

Howard didn't hear anything about the Hellfires. Renoux coded his conversations. He'd been tracking the little bastard for years. He understood them. He was waiting for his money before he'd agree to transport.

That could be done electronically and be over in a matter of minutes. Damn difficult to trace too; Gantz had a transaction alert on Renoux's accounts. So far, nothing. *Bet that's pissing him off,* he thought.

But one thing that really bothered Howard was the sound of Renoux's voice, as if defying the buyer for up-front money was not something he did often. *He's scared of his customer.* He replayed the conversation, listening to the tone again, how Renoux hurried to explain between the stretches of cold silence. He tried a trace, but the phone number was routed through several countries. It wouldn't matter; the caller kept his tone even, almost droning. It kept him from getting a voice analysis ID. *This guy is smart,* he thought.

As he listened, his second computer ran a search for Mike on watch list scientists. So far there were a lot of names to go through, and as Renoux ended the call Gantz changed Mike's search to add last known locations. He didn't think he'd get much and kept the program running as he pulled off the headphones and stood. He started packing his cases, and his personal gear.

Renoux was leaving the country.

It was time to get up close and personal with his favorite adversary—again.

Then the search pinged and Gantz knew, change of plans.

They went deeper into the ruins.

Clancy rushed ahead of Mike, feeling her way in the dark.

"Come on, Irish, they're climbing." He could hear them out there.

"I'm trying, I can't see with this thing. Gimme the big light."

He slapped it in her hand and she turned to shine it on the ground and made the mistake of taking a step.

There was nothing below her. Clancy let out a scream as she fell hard and fast, nothing stopping her for several feet. When she hit, her teeth cut into her tongue and the air punched out of her lungs as dirt and rocks fell on her. In some surreal place, she heard Mike fall somewhere nearby. She gasped for air and inhaled dirt, tried to push up, but more dirt fell, and she collapsed under the weight of it.

Mike rolled from the downpour and kept backing away. On his knees, he threw off the pack, tearing over the ground for the flashlight he could see under the dirt, then swept it over the cavern. Dirt spilled from the gaping hole in the ceiling onto a pile of stones and dirt.

Clancy was beneath it, only her hand and legs visible.

"Oh, Jesus." He rushed to her, frantically digging and his fingers grazing sharp rock and no woman. "Clancy, honey, come on, move." He swept dirt from her face and mouth, shoving stones off her. "Clancy!" Dirt crumbled from above, pelting his shoulders.

He freed her, dragging her limp body from the dirt. She wasn't moving. His heart thundered as Mike laid her flat, clearing her mouth, then breathed for her.

She coughed, turned her head, and moaned. "Well, that sucked."

Mike grabbed her close, sweeping his hand over her head, nearly crushing her in his arms.

She patted his back. "Great timing, Boy Scout. The white light was really big. At least I think it was white."

Over her head, he closed his eyes, pressing his lips to her head, her temple. "Are you hurt?" That was a long way down and the only thing that saved her was the mossy landing.

"My shoulder's taken a beating this week, but I don't think anything's broken." She looked at him, then up. "Did you fall or jump?"

"Fell. You broke my fall." He glanced around. "Look for a way out of here. They'll be coming."

"No, let's turn off the lights and watch them fall into the hole in the ozone." She pushed herself out of his arms and stood. Her balance folded and Mike caught her.

"Take it easy." He looked into her eyes with the light. She

flinched away and he forced her back. "No concussion." She was bleeding from small cuts, but nothing too serious.

"I've looked better, just so you know." She brushed dirt from his hair, really glad to be alive and aching all over. Then she looked around. "Oh, wow, it's a cave." It wasn't big, but the walls were concave and uneven, sparkling with crystal flecks. It was beautiful, the only light coming from his flashlight. He shined it to the ceiling. Over forty feet up was a gaping hole.

"Got any rope in your bag of tricks?" she said, and he heard the fear in her voice.

He walked the perimeter, already searching for a way out. He hooked his pack on one shoulder. "Wouldn't matter, there's nothing up there to secure it."

"Fortunate for me," a voice said, the sound echoing.

Mike instantly dove to the left, pulling Clancy with him, then pushed her behind him.

Richora stood on the edge, his thigh crudely bandaged and bloodstained. Three men stood near him, lost in the shadows, but the automatic weapons aimed at them were unmistakable. Then he sprayed the area with bullets, half of them ricocheting off rocks.

Mike went for his gun lost in the fall.

Before he reached it, Richora cocked his pistol. "Don't tempt me again, I owe you," he said, tapping his thigh.

Mike eased his hand back. "Come down here, and we'll go for it."

Richora chuckled to himself. "You should have left it alone."

"You covered the wreckage," Mike said without question. "Where are my men?"

Richora shrugged. "There are many dangers in Peru. You see now how the mountain can kill." His tone was philosophical and it just pissed Mike off more.

"What do you want?" Mike snarled, and out of the corner of his eye he could see the MP5 rifle a few feet away. But Richora would shoot Clancy before he could reach it.

"For you to die."

Mike's scowl darkened. This couldn't be all about drugs. Half the reason the DEA, and Peru's version of the agency couldn't nab these guys was that they moved the goods too quickly. Yet stacks of kilos were still there.

"Or better, just vanish." Richora snapped his fingers to the man beside him and he put something in his palm. "Join my ancestors." Richora held his hand over the opening, smiling.

Then he pulled the pin and dropped the live grenade.

As it fell like a single raindrop, Mike snapped his arms around her waist and hurried her into the curve of the stone walls, shielding her against the blast seconds before it went off. The explosions ripped, the sound loud and echoing, and she screamed, flattened to the wall with him. Mike grunted as rocks and dirt smashed into his back with the force, the heat of the blast searing through his clothes. Overhead, stone and dirt broke away in chunks, the ground and walls vibrating as they hit.

Clancy gripped his hand, breathing hard, and he heard her whimper of fear. He held her tighter as the ruins disintegrated. Mike chanced a look, his gaze flickering over the immediate area, and he saw a dark shadow in the stone, then pulled her into it with him. Together they fell into the hollow and onto the ground.

Clancy moaned, and Mike held her, the rumble of earth and stone pouring into the cave behind them. Dirt and rocks shot like knives, pelting them, and it went on for a minute and felt like a lifetime.

"Clancy?" he said close to her ear. "Talk to me, honey, are you hurt?"

"No, no, oh God, Mike." She clung to him, her fingers digging as she choked on dust and tried not to cry.

"Take it easy. Breathe with me." He rubbed her arms and back, trying to calm her when he could feel her quaking against him. After a moment, he eased back, grateful there was still space over their heads and air to breathe. But for how long?

Mike swiped his sleeve across his face, then helped her sit up.

"This really isn't a good week for me." With the back of her hand, she smudged muddy tears, then searched for the flashlight. Mike found it first, and shined it on the entrance. "We are so screwed," Clancy said, sagging.

The cave was gone. A wall of dirt in its place.

Mike stood, half hunched, and touched the dirt. "Maybe we can climb over it, if it's not—" It crumbled, started filling the small space. "Guess not." Mike turned to the area behind them, sweeping the light over the walls, then stepped around her. "It's open, another tunnel, I think. Maybe it leads out."

"Or maybe it just leads deeper into this mountain."

He looked back at her, and the tears sliding down dirty cheeks cut into his soul. "We don't have a choice." The air wouldn't last and he'd no intention of dying here.

They had to go deeper before they could find a way out.

*There has to be a way out.*

# Fifteen

Richora was gone before the explosion hit, the men cursing him as they rushed to get out of the ruins. The ceiling showered crumbs of dirt as men quickly passed the kilos out the openings to be stored again. "We take this out now," he said. There was no need to hide it any longer. Taking possession of it would move this great dance along.

He moved past the men, then struggled to climb down, his thigh throbbing. He felt blood soaking his trousers and seeping into his boots. He cursed the American.

If the man wasn't already dead, he'd kill him again. If he was alive, he was trapped. Permanently. Richora was certain. He had three of his own men still wandering around down there in the maze of tunnels and caves—for months.

He dropped to the ground, regretting it as a pain drove up his thigh in sharp spikes. The men continued to unload the kilos with the efficiency of water carriers to a fire.

Richora stepped carefully around the ruins, his respect for the place extending only so far. He bent to resecure the bandage on his leg. A rifle shot cracked in the morning light. Stone broke away near his head. He looked, the long bullet barely penetrating the rock. He grabbed at it, but another shot nearly took off his hand.

Men dropped kilos and ducked for cover, but Richora

fired several shots at their feet. "Do as you're ordered!" he shouted, moving low and into the cover of trees.

Another shot followed, chunking the ground near enough to him that he knew he was the target. Instantly, he suspected Salache. The man wasn't worthy of trust. Eliminating him would lose too much for Salache. He needed him. Richora had the manpower and knew these mountains. He'd grown up on them.

*Where are you, little killer?* he thought, using binoculars to search the tree line. He knew he'd find nothing, yet swept to the lowlands. The question wasn't who was out there, but who was he working for? He remembered Fuad, his head exploding and decorating his clothes, and the three bodies of the thieves they'd found near the river.

Was the shooter amusing himself with killing from a distance?

Or did he have a purpose?

People cleared a path for him.

The security guards jumped to their feet as he strode briskly past. It was easy, his muscles loose from running with Fran. She'd beat him for the first time and it amused her. He was perfectly content with a strong woman. She wouldn't get into his business and he didn't want to be in hers. She had her life.

But for now, they crossed and he was still annoyed with her call at three in the morning. He went to sleep with a hard-on because he wouldn't come to her.

It was ridiculous, aside from the fact that he didn't allow women to manipulate him.

Francine rarely did.

Which made this odd, Carl thought, keying himself into the lab and looking around for her. The door to her offices was open and empty, the computers running a program.

He studied the screen, smiling at the stats he could decipher. Excellent progress, he thought, his hands behind his back. He stopped at a console showing four screens, each with four divisions showing the camera angles of the habitat. Boris moved around more like an old man than an ape, his arms swinging almost childishly. Then the ape dropped sullenly to the rock.

"Oh. Hello."

He turned as Francine came toward him. She was tucking in her blouse in the waist of her skirt, her iPod in her hand. She was rarely without it. She carried it like most carried a cell phone. She pulled the earphones out and clipped it to her skirt.

"What's the matter with him?" He gestured to the ape.

"Natasha passed away."

"He's mourning?"

"Of course."

"She wasn't with him that long."

She shrugged. "She was the only one he knew."

"What did you learn from the autopsy?"

"I haven't done it." She smoothed her hair that was already perfect.

"When will you know what killed her?"

She turned slowly and lifted her gaze. "I already know."

He simply stared.

"Boris. He killed her. Her, ah . . . neck, he broke it."

Very quietly, he said, "Excellent."

"What?" Again, her hand went to her hair, and then she plucked at her waistband.

"It means that it's giving him some aggression."

"But they can't control it. Look at him, he's regretful. He knows what he did."

Carl scoffed. "No, he doesn't." It was an ape. Its entire life was finding food. He looked her over. "Why are you twitching so much? And you're talking fast again."

"You're just slow," she snapped.

Carl dismissed that.

"This isn't good, Carl."

She had a strange look on her face as she stared at Boris. "Fran?" he said.

She met his gaze. "Sorry about the other night."

The complete shift took him off guard. She'd done her level best to get him to come over, including every detail of what she wanted to do with him. "Were you drinking?"

"No. I wanted you. You have a problem with me wanting you at odd hours?"

"No, but out of the blue like that was a shock."

"How about now?" She advanced and Carl back-stepped, recognizing the message in her eyes. She kept moving, forcing him backward, and he went willingly. She was a beautiful, strong woman and he was still holding on to the desire she'd kindled with her late-night phone call. Inside she kicked the door closed, then grabbed his tie and pulled him close. She was already unzipping him.

"You can't be serious, this is the workplace."

"We're locked in and aside from us, the only other person with the codes is lost in Peru somewhere."

"That doesn't concern you?"

"I've got a one-track mind today." She opened his trousers and shoved her hand inside, and stroked him heatedly, quickly. She knew what he liked, and within minutes he was on the desk with her spread on top of him, thrusting away. He held her ass tight, keeping the fast motion, and when she leaned down, her hands on his chest, he was about to climax.

She thrust on him, his dick like a knife inside her. Her hands slipped to his throat. She jerked back for a moment and he smiled, and she let her hands slide to his throat again.

Then she squeezed.

It heightened the sensation, letting him feel the fuck from the inside out.

She pressed hard, and harder still, and his eyes flew open. She pumped mindlessly, her head thrown back, and he felt the strain on his lungs. In an instant, he threw her off, choking.

"What the fuck is the matter with you?" He drew in a lungful, rubbing his throat.

She pushed off the floor, shoving her skirt down. "I don't know." She started looking for her shoes. "I don't." She covered her face, shaking almost violently.

Carl grabbed her arms and jerked her to look at him. His gaze searched her face, her eyes. "Oh, Fran, tell me you didn't use it on yourself."

Her eyes teared and he knew the truth. "It doesn't matter, we're all done," she said.

His scowl deepened.

"Jansen knows."

"No, he doesn't." He thrust her away from him, righting his clothing. No wonder her behavior was so erratic.

"He was here when Boris killed, he knows! He's going to the Joint Chiefs with it."

"You didn't think to tell me! Jesus, Fran."

"He made me swear not to."

"Well, it's clear you can't be trusted."

She blinked. "You bastard."

"What did you tell him?"

"As little as possible. He knows it worked and it's dangerous, but Boris killing the female, that was unexpected. Carl? Are you even listening?"

He wasn't. Carl's mind was going over ways to save this. Witnessing the ape kill would take some skill to work around, but Jansen didn't have any data, just a few stats that could be wrong, and Fran's word. The ape's murder could be attributed to many factors, and he could find a few anthropologists who'd say so.

Carl smoothed his uniform, then checked his appearance in her private bathroom, and muttered a foul curse over the marks on his throat. He went to the door.

"What are you going to do?"

"Does it matter?"

"Of course, this is mine and I want to keep this job."

He looked at her. She'd be court-martialed. "This wasn't the way to go about it." He shook his head sadly. "This testing cycle is over. But you'd better hope those men died in that jungle." They were the real evidence, and they had McRae on their side. Unless she was already dead.

"They volunteered."

He said nothing, opening the door.

"Didn't they?"

The elevator door opened softly and Marianna glanced left and right, then walked down the long corridor. The laboratory loomed at the end, a magnificent space of steel and glass, and machinery. Her husband owned it and occupied this entire top floor, yet he wouldn't be in here. His time was occupied for months in this lab, and now he rarely went here. Always off meeting with someone he insisted she *not trouble herself over.* Her spine tightened. Comments like that had gone beyond irritating. As if she weren't educated enough to understand. She could no longer dismiss them as the arrogance of a genius after he brought a gun into their home.

Her hand touched her handbag, hiding the package delivered without a return address. She'd opened it, though it wasn't something she'd normally do. In fact, she'd kept far away from her husband's business transactions. But she'd recognized the components and she knew her own silence and a blind eye made her an idiot.

*His past is coming back.* He hadn't spoken of his life beyond his childhood and she'd allowed him his privacy because she'd loved him. That man was gone, and now his only feature that remained untouched by a surgeon was his eyes, and in them, she saw an obsession with excelling.

With what, she planned to find out now.

Confronting him wasn't a consideration. His distrust was too volatile after she'd seen him from the apartment across from the park. Just as she'd noticed the man who lurked outside her home trailing her. She'd done nothing wrong, so she assumed it was because of Nuat's projects. The only moment she'd have without eyes watching her was when he was on the mountain. He'd funded an archaeological dig for Dr. Valez. He'd done it for her, because Eduardo's wife was one of Marianna's friends, a professor from college. He had always been generous, but what he was doing on the mountain was a subject he wouldn't approach.

She inserted the code card into the slot and punched in the numbers. The lock sprang, her nose wrinkling at the smell of alcohol and disinfectant. She never understood his need for sterility and it had affected his relationship with the children. He'd never play in the dirt with them. They were young and that cut him out of most of their lives.

She moved quickly to the steel table, the large black shapes littering the surface, and she picked up a piece, then another, confused as she turned them over in her hand. She had an engineering degree, and understood the precise cuts, and she glanced at the machinery for shaping metal into precise figures. She tried fitting them and nothing matched. *Remain true to the simplicity of a design,* she thought, chanting a professor's phrase. Complication breeds hazards.

She went to the computers, sitting, then immediately accessed the files, using the password she'd seen him type hundreds of times. She opened his last file and read.

Her heart pounded with disappointment when she keyed up a schematic drawing. It rolled into 3-D model, spinning slowly on its axis. Instantly, she recognized the configuration.

A fool would.

Howard Gantz scowled at the satellite phone, unable to reach Gannon. The call went through but wouldn't connect. He wanted to have a look-see in Renoux's warehouses, but he owed Gannon more than he could repay so he stuck around. He tried the call again while staring at the computer screen as it showed the top fifteen suspects. All scientists. Fucking *rocket* scientists, he thought, and gave a closer look at their pedigrees. He narrowed the search for people with confirmed terrorists' ties since they all had the skill to create something horrible. It narrowed the results to five. He sat back down and read. Three of the five had been captured or were dead. The two remaining, whereabouts unknown, suspected deceased. Fine with him, but there was no confirmation. No DNA, prints, skulls on a spike.

He read the intelligence reports, easily understanding why they were on it, but not how the two men, scholars, could vanish. Both of them had to get paid somehow, and they owned patents on considerable inventions, most of them weapons.

He brought up an interrogation report. Oddly, they said the same thing. The men were forced out of government contracts for Germany, Britain, and one for a U.S. contractor. They were in research and development and the reason cited gave him chills. Creating weapons that destroyed the targets was their job.

Creating weapons that mutilated and maimed—wasn't.

He grabbed his satellite phone and dialed Colonel Jansen.

Dirt spilled from the sealed cave and kicked up dust.

"This isn't stable," Mike said, helping her off the ground. He snapped out a camouflage-printed handkerchief and blotted at the blood on her forehead.

"I look that bad, huh?"

He smiled. "You look dusted in cinnamon."

"If it's edible, I want it. I'm still starving." She frowned at him. "You haven't eaten in a while, have you?"

He grew thoughtful as he fished in his pockets, handing her a granola bar she'd given him. "Not hungry, and I can pack away the chow." His gear was usually full of food.

She unwrapped the bar and ate, saving half for later. She looked for a clean place to stash it and gave up, shoving it in her pants pocket.

Mike noticed her hands shaking, and he gripped them, rubbing. "We'll get out of this, I swear."

She was against him instantly, gripping. "I really don't want to whine but it's not looking so great, huh?" As if she could take some of his strength through their skin, squeezing him.

"Me trapped alone with you. What could be better?"

"Trapped in a hotel with a soft bed and room service?"

He chuckled and Clancy felt it vibrate into her, warm her, and she admitted she was a sap; it didn't take much more than his strong arms around her to make her feel better. She squeezed him and stepped back, her hand grazing his satellite phone.

"We can call for reinforcements." She pulled the phone from its holder. "Oh, man." It was destroyed, a tangle of chips and wires.

"It won't work through stone, and where's that optimism?" he said.

"Back there under piles of rock."

He tipped her chin, leaning down to kiss her delicately, and a world of feelings opened for him. Not because she was a hundred feet below the ground and he was the best chance she had to survive, but because with each moment he showed her what was underneath that rock-hard ooh-rah shield. A side of himself he probably didn't show many. Not and be who he was, do what he did.

He drew back. Something in his dark eyes sent a fresh pulse of awareness through her. This man made her feel so much at once she couldn't pinpoint anything when he was kissing her.

She tipped her head for more, then drew back, frowning. "Did you feel that?"

"Yes, in very specific places."

She put her hand out. "No, the air. I felt air!" She started to move past.

He jerked her back. "Jeez, the smarts get knocked out of you back there? Go slow." Mike turned to the only tunnel and felt the breeze. "It's cold and damp."

"Smells earthy." When he cocked a look at her, she added, "This deep it would be either dry or musty, like mold. There was moss on the ground back there." She tossed a thumb toward the sealed cave. "That means water gets in here from somewhere."

"There are waterfalls all over the mountains. Maybe there's an underground stream. Stick close."

"Oh, no worry on that." She started to toss the satellite phone, then shoved it in her pack. They moved in small increments and Mike broke off an exposed root and used it to test the path, neither willing to risk another cave-in.

"I hope Richora dies from gangrene."

"I'm sure I can help him along with that."

Clancy smiled at his back. He was certain they were getting out of here, and his confidence boosted her as they shifted through the narrow passageway.

The walls were a chunky mix of black stone and tawny red earth, a web of roots dangling overhead and grazing her hair. Clancy tried not to give in to the claustrophobic sensations and hoped the light kept working. After that, they'd have nothing. She kept close behind him, running her hands over the walls, and felt distinct shapes, but couldn't see more than a vague outline of the sun and moon and some really big eyes.

Mike noticed them too and swept the beam over the sculptures. It showed a remarkably preserved mask with large eyes. "This might be a hideout from the enemy."

Clancy frowned, tipping her head. "Do you hear that? It sounds like thunder."

Mike looked back the way they'd come, scowling with concentration. Then his eyes flew wide. "Oh, holy shit!" He pulled her nearly off her feet, and Clancy dared a look back.

Like a house of cards, the ceiling fell, sealing the narrow tunnel with tons of dirt. They ran, desperate to outdistance the collapse in the narrow tunnel. The ground suddenly slanted sharply downward, and without traction, they slid.

Clancy shot like a rocket to the bottom, Mike slamming into her back and rolling over her. He groaned and pushed up as Clancy crawled toward him, rock piling up behind her. Mike lurched forward, grabbed her under the arms, and pulled, rolling, throwing her on her back, then covered her with his body.

Clancy coughed and buried her face in his chest, holding tight to him as dirt hit them. "I'm so over this adventure," she said, and Mike squeezed her and chanced a look.

"It's slowing down, come on." He rolled and climbed to his feet, and Clancy stood. She brushed herself off, sending a cloud of powdery dust into the air, then just gave up.

Mike's gaze moved over the interior. "This is actually a good thing," he said and when he looked at her, she was wide eyed. Mike crawled over rocks and dirt, pushing hurriedly at the debris.

Clancy joined him. "You can't really think to move all this back to the surface."

"Not hardly."

"Then why are we doing this?"

"This is why," he said and brushed at the steep hill of dirt. Clancy leaned closer as he swept away more, and then she took the flashlight from him.

Dark stone—perfectly flat and smooth.

"This is man-made." He cleared a wider area. "It's granite."

Clancy looked around, then searched for an edge. "A wall? A fallen floor? It has to be more ruins." She couldn't find an edge and realized it was a really huge slab. "But why so rudimentary out there and then this?"

"The Moche had a social caste. Only the rich and noble were allowed in all areas and to participate in ceremonies." Mike asked for the flashlight, shining it around, then maneuvered across the rocks. "Back there, topside, are the simple folk. Here, the aristocracy." He put his hand out. "Air." He sanded his fingers. "And humidity."

"Down here? We have to be at least a hundred feet below the ruins."

"Waterfalls, it's got to be from there." He kept his hand out, taking small steps over the rocks. "It's probably why the ruins are so intact. Moisture kept it from drying out and cracking."

"Till we came along," she said as he came back for her.

"I think I found something."

Mike helping her, they crossed to the far south, the ground leveling out. He lit the wall. There was a door made of stacked stones. Mike gave the center of it a hard shove. It didn't budge. Then he ran his fingers around the edge, and frowned when he felt something. He held the light closer.

"There's a carving, some kind of lever." He blew off some dirt and brushed at the edges. He pressed it.

The walls groaned, sprinkling them with dirt a moment before the door started to fall apart block by block.

"Michael," she said as if he was a kid who'd made mud pies in his Sunday best. "Did you have to push it!"

"Oops." He drew her back with him, shining the light over the interior, then on the door. Stone tumbled inward.

Clancy held tight, and couldn't take her eyes off the stones. "If the ceiling falls again, I'm going to be so pissed at you."

But it didn't, the shaking coming to a sharp halt. The crude door was half gone, and as more fell, a gust of cool air and dampness stroked her face. Without the flashlight there was a bluish glow radiating from the gaping hole.

Mike looked at her, arched a brow, then ducked inside, stepping over the block stones.

Clancy peered from behind him. "Oh my God."

An underground city. Sorta. At least that's what it looked like at first glance. Steps spanning twenty feet wide and at least a yard deep were chiseled in a half moon, and as they climbed over the fallen stones she realized the glow came from a pool of water, light magnifying and illuminating the cave.

"Can you believe this?" She turned full circle, the ceiling fifty feet high, the walls carved with the same bug-eyed faces they saw in the passageway. Some carved, some painted, but in almost perfect condition. Rough crystals glowed from inside big eyes and mouths with fang teeth.

It was creepy.

"The Moche were a strict society. There wasn't any signs of them forming an army and going after another tribe." Mike inspected the walls. "But they worshipped the mountains as their gods, one of many, and sacrificed to them."

"Sacrificed? You mean *people?*"

"Yeah." He found a small clay jar with double handles still brightly painted in cream, red, and black. She came to him and when he shined the light she saw the iconology on the jar and walls. It was a caravan of stretchers carried by two male figures, each bearing a single man, and the procession led to a wide altar. Three male figures were at the altar, but the terror in the victims' faces was eerily clear.

Mike pointed out the warriors with sickle knives. "Human sacrifices began with ceremonies performed in a public square, then concluded in a private enclosure with only the priest and some members of the upper echelon."

"Are we standing in one of the ritual altar thingies?" Only her gaze moved around the cave.

"Possibly."

"Nasty."

"Oh, it gets better. They drank the sacrificial blood. Those cups probably held it," he said, nodding toward the cracked pottery near a stone bench. "In the Moche's universe, human sacrifices weren't just murder for show but part of their religious beliefs. They depended on nature to survive, all of it, sun, moon, water, mountains, and made offerings and sacrifices to those gods." Carefully, he set the jar back in its spot. "They've found entire skeletons of people sacrificed to the gods."

"I think you had a little more than a chapter on them."

"There was a test," he said and gave her a wink that flipped her nerves on and made them dance. At the base, she looked around.

"It's clearly a hall of some sort." She could make out benches of stone and a wall long since tumbled to the ground. "But how did they get in and out?" She moved around the outer edge where the avalanche hadn't touched. There were no more exits, and then she saw a hole. Clancy rushed to it, pushing at the dirt and rocks, reaching over a pile and feeling the wall. "Damn. This was the way out."

"Yeah, *was*." Mike shone the light over the walls as he touched them. She came to him. "The supports fell." The stone columns lay on the ground, broken in huge chunks where they fell. "But this isn't cut stone." It wasn't jagged, but smooth in folded layers of black rock. Like lava.

Mike squatted near the pool of water, dipped his hand in, sniffed, then tasted it. "Fresh, with a little granite on the side. Like you're sucking a rock."

"Ah, yes, *that* food group." She knelt to wash her face and hands.

"This is our way out." He pointed to the pool.

"It's another cave, just filled with water," she said, shaking off her khaki overshirt and using the tails as a washcloth.

"Yes, sure, but look at the water, it ripples, it's moving." He circled an area, pointing the light down inside.

Beneath the glassy surface, it was crystal clear, a blue-white radiance to the uneven walls, but the cornucopia shape did not look promising. "It narrows too much," she said.

"But it also goes deeper." Mike shook off his pack, then stripped off his shirt, then his boots.

Clancy watched him, and when he peeled off his dark blue T-shirt, she hummed a burlesque stripper tune.

Mike went still, his hand at his belt, and only his gaze shifted. He never knew what wisecrack she'd deliver. "It's not looking so bad," he said, gesturing to the pool.

"Looks good from where I'm sitting." She made no mistake about liking what she saw.

It made his muscles tighten, and pull in all the right places. "If this works, you have to go too." He sat to take off his boots.

"We leave everything behind?"

"I'll come back for it. If I can fit through, then the gear can."

Clancy looked down into the pool, trying to judge the distance. "How long can you hold your breath?"

"About two minutes."

She met his gaze. "That's comforting. Unless it's a lot deeper than you think."

"I'll come right back."

"You better," she said. He was lucky she wasn't latching on to his ankle right now, because the last thing she wanted to do was sit and wait for him to return.

"As much as I wish I'd be here to see it, be ready, get out of those clothes."

"You just want to see me naked." She unlaced her boots.

"Got that right."

He stood, opened his trousers, and let them drop. In dark marine-green boxers, Mike set his clothes neatly aside and Clancy leaned back as if on a sofa and whistled.

In the dark, he felt his face warm. "Can it, Irish."

She laughed to herself, her gaze gliding over him, and enjoyed every inch of the ride. Tanned and broad, he was ripped, his muscles long and toned, and her gaze slid to his flat stomach and soft dark hair disappearing beneath the band of shorts.

But it was the scars that dissolved her smile.

"My goodness, Mike." She ran her fingers over the gouge in his thigh, then to the thin scar on his incredibly delicious biceps. "Just who do you work for besides the Marines?"

"The A-Teams."

"Excuse me?" she said, frowning.

"CIA, NSA, DEA, DIA." He shrugged. "Spec Ops, your multiagency help line."

She gave him a deadpan look. "You're being cute. Don't be cute. That's my job."

"I stand corrected." He slid his feet into the pool, then leaned, cupping the back of her head. "I want some more of this when I come back." He laid his mouth on hers.

Clancy's hands rested on his bare shoulders, and she never really knew why she'd waited so long to indulge in him. Somewhere between his rage at his hotel and little tastes of each other something had changed, ignited a blaze they'd suppressed. When it ruptured, she fell back and relinquished herself to it, taking him with her.

He slid his hand heavily down her spine, cupped her rear, and meshed her hips to his. She felt his broad erection through the thin cloth, the warmth and pressure, and she hooked her leg around his, sliding it up his thigh to his hip. Then she arched into him, urging, her hands sweeping wildly over the contours, her fingertips molding to curved muscle and man.

Then her touch slid lower. His stomach muscles contracted instantly as she neared his groin, and his moan of pleasure thrummed through her.

"I'm a mess," she whispered in his ear, his big hands on her ribs and driving anticipation through her like a monsoon.

"So am I."

"Oh, good, we match."

"More than you think," he growled.

"Mike," she said, almost choking on his name. "I need to—" Her fingertips dipped beneath his waistband, her breath hot in his ear. "I need to touch you."

Mike fell apart. Like the stones in the door, his feelings tumbled over each other with the feel of her warm silky palm sliding over his erection.

He curled her tighter to him, kissing her madly, then drew back long enough to murmur, "The cave dive can wait."

# Sixteen

Mike dove into her.

She was an experience—something from the tightly guarded places he rarely visited. Her kiss alone twisted a rope around him, tying him tight. In knots. He didn't know if he wanted to keep her as close as possible or turn in the other direction.

He pushed up her shirt and kissed her ribs, crushing back the need to bury himself inside her quickly and appease this wild hunger for her. But it wouldn't matter. She was more than under his skin. She was inside it. And when her hand closed around him, she took him with her—away from danger and isolation, from ignoring everything for the mission.

Since they'd met, she made him indulge in feelings and sensations. Trapped with her, he gave them freedom. She stroked him heavily, her little hand working him into a frenzy that threatened his control.

Mike gritted his teeth, then grasped her wrist. "Nu-uh."

"You can't be the only one going mad here, ya know," she said.

"I gotta be, this once." He pulled her hand free.

"There you go, assuming again."

"We're finally alone with *absolutely* no interruptions. Baby, I'm having my way with you."

"Oo, prisoner again," she said and they laughed.

She crossed her arms over her chest, pulling off her shirt,

but Mike wasn't waiting, bending to taste the smooth texture of her skin, the simple pleasure of pushing down her bra strap and exposing her so damn sexy. The urge to hurry battered at him.

His gaze slipped over her plump breasts, smoothing the roundness, and then he leaned down. His lips closed warmly over her nipple and he drew her into the warmth of his mouth, watching her expression of pleasure. Her head fell back, her body bending into his. The motion ground her warm center to his erection and she thrust back as he licked and scored his teeth over the soft underside. He held her gaze as he ran his finger inside the edge of her bra cup, then pulled down. Her nipple spilled into his mouth. She smiled, watched him taste her, and it drove her sensations over the top. Mike wished they were in a soft bed with hours of time.

"You're wearing too much," he murmured, destroying her composure with nibbling on her neck as he worked her slacks open, his hand dipping inside to cup and rub. She wouldn't be still, squirming to get the rest of her garments off. She practically tore at his shorts and, naked, he stuffed them beneath her, their clothes a cushion as he licked slow heavy circles around her nipple.

"Oh, Michael. You're good at a lot of things." Clancy was breathless, her body awakened from a long sleep and her hands roaming over his broad shoulders, his sculpted chest. She wrapped her hand around him, slid her fingers over the moist tip, and laughed softly when he groaned, drew in air through clenched teeth.

"Jesus," he said and clasped her hands above her head. "No wonder they locked you up."

Her smile was bone-melting and he swept his palm from throat to hip, molding her flesh, his gaze lingering over her, naked and shameless for him. Her eyes held the awareness of her power, her shape like an hourglass, plush and ripe, and wrapping him in her scent and sensation. Mike felt privileged, the moments of denying himself any bond in his duty for his country magnified as she touched his face, slid her thumb over his lips. It was a simple thing, and he wanted more of it, to connect deeply with her and seal this connection tighter.

His hand rested on her belly, then slid softly to between her thighs. He nudged them apart, leaving a damp trail of kisses down her throat as he parted her, loving her quick breaths, yet he taunted, slowly drawing a line up her center, circling the tiny bead of her sex. Then he found her, slick and hot, and he slid a finger inside without stopping, and loved that she lost her breath. She chanted his name, telling him how she felt, what he did to her, and Mike felt like a king about to conquer a willing captive.

He withdrew and plunged, and her hips caught the motion, and on his side, Mike devoured every degree of her pleasure. He wanted her mindless like him.

"Michael, come here," she demanded, spreading beneath him. "I need something bigger."

But he wouldn't go, watching her twist as he dipped and stroked. Then he introduced another finger and she cupped his face, devouring his mouth with a lush erotic heat and thrusting into his palm. Then she enfolded him and his muscles locked.

She threw her leg over his hip. "There is a better solution," she said, stroking the tip of him against her center.

"Jesus, I'm trying to go slow and you are not helping."

"Then show me some of that Gannon speed."

His gaze snapped to hers. She thrust her hips enough to put him inside her a bit, and he grunted and cursed, then nudged her thighs wider, and slid between. He held himself poised, and a million thoughts ran through his mind, nothing sticking long enough to make sense. He felt privileged and freed, his need beyond passion, beyond control.

Clancy stared up at him as she thought she'd never expected to see this man humbled to anything. Yet he was, in his eyes, his expression as if he was undeserving, and her throat strained. For the world, the enemy, they saw strength and deadly skill. Clancy saw need and unguarded man. She guided him, loving the exquisite pressure, his gaze trapped with hers, and they prolonged it, her hips rising to his. He sank into her, helpless and trembling.

She kissed his neck, then whispered, "Now, that's what I'm talking about, Boy Scout."

He chuckled and lifted his head. "You have no idea what this is doing to me, do you?"

His breath shuddered, almost gasping, and Clancy was so moved she felt her eyes burn. "How can I not?" she said, brushing her fingers across his hair, dribbling down the side of his face. Gently she laid her mouth over his, licking the line of his lips, slowly, before sliding her tongue between and making him crazy.

"You're evil," he moaned against her mouth.

"I prefer wicked." She sat up, forcing him deeper and forcing him back as she climbed onto his lap, never breaking contact.

She straddled his broad thighs, her mouth rolled over his, down his throat, and her tongue snaked to lick his nipple. His grip on her hips tightened as she suckled and he let his head drop back and savored it till he needed that mouth on his again. He took it, cradling her face and savaging her soft lips till she was gasping and wild on him.

"I take it you liked that."

She thrust back, riding the motion. "I like every damn thing."

He gripped her hips, his body nail hard and sliding deeply. Her delicate flesh clasped him in a tight fist, her willowy rocking like a cord pulling him quickly to a climax.

"There's that speed," she said, and the knots in him tightened. Her muscles locked and clawed, and yet she smiled, met him, and thrust harder. Her whispers echoed in the cave, the secrets of the past watching them as she made love with him. He enfolded her breasts, thumbing her nipples, and the sight of him disappearing into her tormented her. She spared him nothing.

Her body rippled like a river, battering him in sleek waves of pleasure, and she quickened, thrusting longer and harder. She was untamed, the wild child breaking free, her kiss more erotic, her fingertips digging into his shoulders as her body spoke to him, urging him with her. He reached between and circled the bead of her sex.

"Oh, Michael," she said softly, drawing it out. She couldn't breathe, her body beyond her control and in his. Her blood hummed, rushing to between her thighs, and she wanted more, only more of his thick arousal sliding into her, her body tightening with each moment closer to the peak. He pushed long and slow, then quickened, and Clancy fought the tension, wanting this to go on, but her body wouldn't allow it.

Then she came.

Mike consumed it. Her soft flesh tensed and clawed him, the grip of tender muscle trapping his erection. He leaned, lowering her to the cushion of clothes, and he pumped, his control slipping. Scarred and seasoned melted with feminine luxury, wet and hot. Primal. Captive sensations ripped free, roaring through his blood, and blinding him.

Yet Clancy matched him, her hips rising to prove her greed. She was quicksilver sleek, pulling him along with her, and he plunged into her with a frantic, erotic pulse. He met her gaze, her smoky eyes intense as her body swallowed him in the ancient ritual.

"Michael, yes," she gasped and he felt it, her climax squeeze him, the flex and pull of delicate flesh. Sitting back on his calves, he crushed her to him as if to bring her into his very core. He pushed on her lower spine and thrust upward, deeply, elongating, and the untamed monster inside him broke free. His groan rose in the chamber, melting with her gasps of ecstasy, and they shivered through the unending rapture.

He held her tightly, his kiss strong and softening as the pleasure ebbed to a humming in his blood. He slid his hand up her spine to the base of her skull, his fingers sinking into her hair, and she tipped her head back. She met his gaze, and Mike swiped his hand over her hair and kissed her softly.

Then Mike understood.

In the isolated cave of ancient gods, trapped with no prospect of survival, he found destiny.

Clancy found part of her soul.

Colonel Hank Jansen grabbed his phone, spoke his name, yet his attention was on the documents in front of him.

"Hank, what are you getting into?"

He recognized General Craig Runold's voice.

"I'm trying to find out what happened to my men, General."

He didn't have to explain. If Craig was calling him, he knew exactly what he was doing. Investigating Clancy McRae, Yates, and Cook. But more specifically, this research project.

"Back off."

"Excuse me, sir?"

"You need to stay out of this, Hank. It's not your business."

"These are my troops under my command. Not Cook's."

"He has the authority to run that hospital."

He looked at the testing and transcripts. Clancy McRae had created something astonishing, and while personally he wouldn't volunteer to have it inserted, he didn't know the mind of another man. "That may be so, but not for human testing." Never.

The general was quiet for a moment, then said, "*What?*"

"They used it on my team."

"That's ridiculous."

"Is it? I have substantial proof in physical test results from Dr. Figaroa." He didn't mention the ensign, knowing full well when the shit rolled downhill it would hit the innocent.

"And my Tango team leader has seen Clancy McRae. In Peru." Runold was well aware that the team was sent in to recover the UAV and never returned. "I think she went looking for the men."

"That's madness."

"Perhaps, but it doesn't change the fact that Cook used my Marines for this. And frankly, sir, putting Cook in charge of anything but the watercooler was the most asinine move the chiefs could have made. His past gives me plenty of suspicion that he authorized this. He's way out of the UCMJ and into federal crimes." The uniformed military code of justice was the law in the armed services.

The general hesitated. "There is more to this."

"I'm not backing down." Not when his men could be dead because of it.

"Hank," he said softly. "I'm getting pressure."

"You're not the one facing their families and having to tell them we used them like lab rats."

"We don't want a full-blown investigation in this or for the press to get wind."

"We can keep it in-house." He already had, and wondered if Major Yates had said something to Cook to bring this on. Cook might be an ass, but he still had influential friends.

"No, you don't understand," Craig stalled, and Hank could hear him sigh. "Clancy McRae is the one we don't want investigated."

"Why?" Hank looked down at the woman's records. "Aside from some trouble when she was a kid, she has a clean record and an amazing mind."

"If anything defaming comes from this it will reflect in a bad light and we can't afford a scandal."

We? As in the U.S. government. "Reflect on whom? Cook? I don't give a damn."

"No, she's Daniel McRae's daughter."

"The Sec Nav?" The secretary of the Navy. This was growing bigger by the moment.

"You see my point, then."

"No, I don't. McRae didn't know about this testing, Craig. Her signature is on some documents, but I'm betting it's forged because the woman has stated clearly in other quarterly reports and documentation that going forward too soon would be detrimental to the entire project. And with the evidence taken as a whole, this says she wasn't in the loop and Major Yates admitted as much to me. It's the reason I think she went south. To look for the men, to help them." What did she know that Yates and Cook had ignored? It was a brave and foolish thing to do. There was a lot more trouble in that little section of the world this week and she was in the middle of it.

"The men are MIA, but if the enemy . . . whoever shot down that UAV and chopper without a heat signature," the general said, "gets a hold of these men? Uses them? Their enhanced strength, intelligence?"

Hank went perfectly still, an icy chill racing under his skin. "You're not suggesting we eliminate the problem, are you?"

"Of course not!" Craig said, insulted. "But they'd have an advantage. They have to be found or confirmed KIA."

"Gannon will bring them home, but you can't have it both ways, Craig. Hidden, I can understand. Swept away, no. Cook is going to pay for this."

"You'll bring Miss McRae down and the Sec Nav."

"Wanna bet?"

Jansen ended the land call, then turned to the computer, tapping to the satellite link. He grabbed his encrypted phone and dialed. He needed to reach Gannon. A-sap.

Circle the wagons, he thought. Then he saw the text message from Gantz.

A new can of worms, he thought.

The buzz of passion lingered, his long drugging kisses melting her insides as he pulled her legs around his waist. It meshed him deeper inside her, stirring her desire.

"Swim?" he said, then fell back into the water with her, kissing her and sharing air as they bobbed to the surface.

"It does taste like a rock," she said, water dribbling over them, and he pushed her hair off her face.

"You taste better." Better than anything, he thought and kissed her again, wanting to remind himself of moments ago, to keep it trapped in her mind like it was in his. He leaned against the edge of the pool, his arms hooking him and his body floating.

Clancy looked her fill. His skin was tanned and tight, his only paleness on his rock-hard rear. She took a single stroke and floated over to him. "You have a decadent smile on your face right now."

His gaze slid over her round breasts underwater and pushing on his chest. "Not nearly as it should be."

She looped her arms around his neck. "Oh, Boy Scout, we've just scratched the surface." She lay fully on him and felt him harden.

*She's got me roped,* he thought. *And worse, she knows it.*

"We really don't have time to play, do we?"

The statement shattered the moment, and his expression darkened. "No, if Richora has the Hellfires, he's moving them somewhere fast." Richora had to have it, he knew too much not to know where they were.

"It's huge."

"Dismantling it wouldn't be hard. It's a rocket, not a nuclear bomb."

"But just as much damage in the right place. He's Shining Path?"

"It doesn't matter. Not to me."

Mike kissed her once, then hoisted himself out of the water. Clancy floated, watching the spectacular twist of muscle as he pulled on his boxers.

Then he reached for her, and with one yank pulled her out of the water and into his arms. Slick and naked, she tempted him to play, but that wouldn't get them out of here.

She went for her things. "This is the only way, I know, but I don't like it," she said, pulling on a clean shirt, but nothing else. She wrung and fluffed her wet hair.

He sat, strapping a knife to his calf, then checked his gun. He took back the calf case he'd given her and holstered it. Then he noticed her boots, and frowned at the plastic packet sliding out of them. He took it, turning it over in his hands, and knew what he held. "This is classified material, Clancy."

She glanced, still. "I told you I hacked."

He opened the plastic and unfolded the papers. The faces of his team stared back at him, the creases telling him she'd looked at them more than a few times. It touched him and Mike realized the magnitude of her quest to find them.

"I know them, Mike." He met her gaze. "Not like you, but I know the kind of men they are."

"Good ones, damn good ones."

They'd have to be, to have a spot on his team, she thought.

"Can you help them? If they've gone ballistic, can you stop it without that Terminator thing?"

The question startled her. "I'm still working that out. I've got to be able to replicate the Terminator's chief components."

"You tried that."

"No, I tried to remake the machine. But if I can replicate one factor of its operation, it might stall it."

"Stall what?"

She met his gaze head-on. "It's implanted, Mike. It will be permanently embedded in a day or so."

"Jesus."

"If I can stop it, they should be okay. If I can't and it embeds, I can't do anything unless we're in the lab. It could leave irreparable damage."

His expression darkened, and she knew that although he had accepted it, he still hated the idea in its basest forms.

She handed him the flashlight, sullen. "I created it to help."

"I know, but . . ." He clamped his lips tight. She didn't inject it. He was pushing his anger on the wrong person.

"No, you don't. Know why I was in jail? Why I got the *choice* of the Navy? Because of special circumstances. I climbed behind the wheel of a car, very stoned, and had an accident."

"Was anyone hurt?"

"My brother. He lost his legs."

"Oh God. Clancy."

She put her hand up to stave off the sympathy she didn't deserve. "He doesn't blame me. He was just as high, and not belted in. I was. But I was driving. *I* blame me."

Mike was quiet for a long moment, trying to imagine her life since then. "I have nothing to say that would comfort you. I can't convince you not to blame yourself, so I won't try."

She looked up. "Thank you."

"Don't thank me. There are some things you carry around with you, always. It makes up who we are now. If it didn't have an effect we'd be zombies. If it was drugs, booze, gunfire, or nothing at all, you either get past it or not."

"I did that." She drew in a breath and let it out as if telling herself enough would do it. "All I wanted to do was help him."

"That why you went into this?"

She stared at her hands and didn't answer at first. "I had a skill and this was the opportunity."

"So you changed your life to prove something to him? Do you think it ever mattered? Not really. He's your brother and he loves you. Shit happens." Mike leaned in. "You did it for you."

"Sure I did."

"To appease guilt?"

"To make a damn difference. Jeez, this side of you is a bit harsh."

He met her gaze and he folded, rubbing his face. "Sorry. I'm used to making a point to my troops—jeez, Clancy, I'm sorry. God, you make me want to run in the other direction." She made him think outside the box, made him dig into places he thought he'd closed.

"Not like you have much choice."

His expression soured. "Not here." He made walking fingers in the air and she smiled. "Here." He put his hand over his heart.

Clancy's lips curved, an almost euphoric feeling spinning through her. This was a big deal. A really big deal. Mike didn't say so much with so few words. Not because of this adventure, but because of his feelings. *How can you not love this guy?*

He shook his head in that way he did. As if he was missing the logic and he had to understand it.

"I don't get it either," she said.

He looked up. "Oh, for the love of Pete," he said and started to turn away.

"Annoying, aren't I?"

"Yes, damn it." He exhaled. "No." Then softer, "No."

"Oh, Michael," she said.

Mike looked at her, *really* looked. He'd never waited for something like this. He didn't think it was in the cards for him, but he wasn't letting her get away. *Don't screw it up.*

She cradled his jaw. "Don't try to figure it out." She squeezed his face with every word.

He grinned.

"You don't have to find the best tactical assault. Don't plan. It's not a mission. Just relax. Well . . . no relaxing on this job. I do want to see where the story goes." She gestured between them in case he didn't get it. "But we need that reactionary, analyzing, highly trained, sometimes-a-jackass brain."

"Sometimes?"

"Less often than not. But we're only just beyond the flea-picking stage." His chuckle rumbled and she kissed him between it.

"We're trapped, you know."

"Hmm, die happy after lots of sex, or die bitching about it. Now, there's a stretch."

"God, you are such a smart-ass."

"I'm playing all week." She glanced away briefly. "I can hide it well in pubic."

"Don't. Jesus, you earned it."

"I'll have to mention that to my mother sometime." She rolled her eyes, handing him the flashlight.

"You mentioned sex?"

"You didn't think there weren't extra treats at this party, did you?"

He grabbed her, his kiss luxuriously powerful, engulfing her, and Clancy knew she'd been right before; her toes really did curl.

Antone refused to let Dehnwar out of his sight. Because the man knew the world thought him dead, he wasn't as cautious. Who would look in a small town on the edge of the Amazon? Especially in a country aligned with America and England. He'd reported it to his superiors, sending them a digital photo. Though he sat in a car watching the man, he expected more Interpol agents to arrive soon. But allowing Dehnwar to slip through his fingers was never an option. Not for his job or his family. His sister deserved justice. He tailed him since he'd first spotted him, using every tactic he knew to keep his presence unobtrusive. A few days' growth of beard and wearing local clothing, he blended in, his features dark enough to be mistaken for Spanish descent.

Yet Dehnwar stood out, his shaved head bearing healing wounds from the blast. He wasn't a tall or large man, and it was difficult to distinguish him from the small Quechua people.

But Antone could.

He was a mass murderer. Antone had seen the work of Hezbollah, the tortured bodies, the twisted and burned from a suicide bomber. But one image stayed with him, of his brother-in-law holding his sister in her last moments, her last breath as she lifted her arm to touch her new husband's face and finding no hand to do it.

Dehnwar had boasted of selecting the perfect spot, the timing, yet no one in the cells knew the exact locations beforehand. Only the bomber knew, and then merely moments before he would detonate the blast. It was how they'd eluded them. His sister's wedding hadn't been the target, but the hotel itself filled with international dignitaries at the time. Choufani had infiltrated and was deep in the ranks when the warehouse in Tunisia was destroyed. They'd made the entire building a suicide bomb, without their leader.

From inside the small car, Antone watched the factory. Trucks were at the rear loading bays, three men filling them as they talked and laughed. But it was predawn, and while Dehnwar entered the building, he knew where he'd been. At the house Marianna occupied with her husband. He was a scientist, a bit reclusive. Yet Antone hadn't waited for the official version. Nuat Salache was a doctor of chemistry and physics. He held several patents that gave him a comfortable life, but it was his swift exit from his corporate life that concerned Antone. He was on and off the scene within six years' time. There was no record on Nuat Salache up until eight years ago, and the photo didn't match the man. It either wasn't him or he'd changed his appearance.

Dehnwar walked from the building out into the loading bay. He helped lift a box, loaded it, then went back for the last. Dehnwar was a Hezbollah leader; why was he loading boxes? Better yet, Antone thought, who had him over a barrel that he would?

The men closed the truck and Dehnwar climbed behind the wheel. *This just gets better,* Antone thought, as Dehnwar eased down the ramp, driving away. A second truck pulled up in its place. Antone put the car into gear, and followed Dehnwar.

Her toes weren't the only thing that curled.

A deep, heavy heat coiled through her body and she wanted him inside her again, pushing into her with the power and drive that excited her with just thinking about it. The muscles between her thighs were already warm and pulsing, the awareness of him making her beg softly. But he wouldn't allow it, in command of everything including her.

His mouth rolled over hers, drawing her into him, and Clancy fell back as he left a moist, hot trail down her body, nibbling on her nipples, the slow slide of his tongue dragging lower and leaving a steaming path. Her stomach muscles jumped.

"Mike, inside me, now, please."

"I love hearing you beg."

"Then show some mercy."

"Nu-uh."

He moved between her thighs, holding her still for his assault, and Clancy loved it, the way he kissed, the way his mouth moved over her skin as if savoring each inch of her like a warm dessert, his grip on her hips as if she'd run from him. Prisoner again, she thought, and then he lifted her hips and she met his gaze as he peeled her wider and tasted her.

She let out a soft shriek, the sound echoing in the chamber and sliding down the walls as his tongue pushed deep. He stroked in circles; then his fingers followed, two pushing between her slippery folds.

"Oh God, that's good." She arched.

Then he wrapped his lips around the bead of her sex and tugged. She came apart, breathing hard, but couldn't take her eyes off him. It was erotic and he made certain she felt every sensation there was, heat and tingling, the slick slide and pull of desire.

Mike watched her come apart like a slow-shattering glass. She cupped her breasts, twisted under his attention, and he pushed her thighs over his shoulders and imprisoned her. Devoured her.

"Michael, please," she demanded, yet he kept stroking her, feeling her climax flex around his fingers.

Then he was there, between her thighs and pushing himself inside her, filling her in one stroke.

She groaned harshly. "You bastard."

"Yeah, I know." He withdrew fully and plunged, but she wanted more and harder, told him so, and he pumped, his own climax rushing to greet hers. She pulled him down on her, wanting to feel his weight, his hips knocking hard with hers.

"I want that speed," she whispered, and he obeyed the command, his heart in her fist and his body trapped with hers.

She chanted his name and Mike cradled her face in his hands, watching her climax in her golden eyes as it clawed through his body. He shoved and shoved and she never broke eye contact as he erupted with a bone-shaking climax.

"Oh, Jesus," he groaned, thrusting deep and fast, slick feminine muscles gripping him, her nails digging into his back. Her legs clamped his waist, and she arched hard, grinding to him, and rode the wild tremors.

"Oh, Michael." She said his name on a rich, gasping breath.

"I know, Irish, hard to ignore, huh?"

"If you can ignore that I'm slacking somewhere."

He chuckled and they sank to the pile of clothing, lungs laboring and a tangle of arms and legs. She curled herself around him, her leg over his hip as his hand smoothed the length of her damp flushed skin. She lifted her gaze to his, and staring into her whiskey-brown eyes, Mike wondered how he'd gone this long without her. He felt liberated from some dark, isolated place, and in the grotto he found a part of himself he'd lost.

Shining brilliantly—in her.

Mike sat on the edge of the pool, his legs dangling. If she touched him again they'd never get out of here. But his mood took a nosedive when she handed him the flashlight, sullen. His chest tightened. She was scared and trying not to show it.

"The light source is coming from somewhere, a steady refraction. It has to be close to be that bright."

She made a face at him. "I took physics too, you know." She drew up her knees and wrapped her arms around her legs. Clancy admitted she was quietly terrified, and the moments in his arms made it more poignant. She didn't want to lose him. She'd rather die with him than die without him. The feeling closed around her, smothering her. Why now? she wanted to say, but a twist of fate put them together and she'd be damned if fate would take him away.

Mike breathed deep and slow, pulling oxygen into his blood, then slid into the water. He looked back at her and she leaned, reaching for him, and kissed him feverishly.

"I'll be right back." He cupped her face, staring into her eyes. "I swear I'll be right back."

Her teary eyes cut into him with a power he didn't think possible. Through this entire mess, she hadn't balked, not one tear, and now she looked ready to crumble. He kissed her again, then drifted back.

"Five minutes. Two there and two back and a minute, if I find something. If not, I'll be back under two minutes."

She nodded, swiped at her tears. "I'll have your slippers and dinner ready." He chuckled shortly. "Be careful please," she said before he submerged.

He gripped her hand. "I will. This isn't about being brave."

*It's about staying alive,* she thought. She'd be dead if not for him. She didn't want to think about the men who might die because of her. She had to stop it.

He kissed her once more, then dove underwater, his kick splashing her. She watched him swim lower, his strong arms pulling him deep, and then he was gone.

The water rippled with bubbles, and alone, she glanced around the hollow chamber and spoke to the ancient gods.

"I am *not* sacrificing him to you. You got that?"

Mike felt the pressure in his ears and suspected he was at least twenty feet below the surface. The underwater cave darkened and he swam hard, thinking of Clancy back there, trapped. Then the pressure lightened and a soft current, barely felt, pushed at him. He went with it, and the light brightened. He drew his gun before he broke the surface. Aiming, he held the penlight against the barrel, shining it over the cave. He didn't need it. Light spilled with water into the large pool and Mike instantly saw the source of both.

A waterfall. Steady but not strong. Runoff, he thought, then focused on the light source. Above the waterfall was a fissure, at its top a two-foot-wide gap. Sunlight hit the pool and reflected like a mirror inside the cave, its brilliance from the crystal quartz in the walls. Climbing up there would be a real bitch, he thought. Especially without pitons and crampons. He didn't know if Clancy could do it and Mike knew the fissure was too narrow for him. He glanced around.

There were dark gaps in the walls. He swam into the center of the pool and saw another fork of tunnels above his level. *At least we have options.* The only way they could go was farther into the mountain. He filled his lungs again, then dove underwater and headed back to Clancy.

When he saw the flickering light shining down into the pool, he propelled toward it and shot up.

"Oh God, oh, thank God! Mike!"

He climbed to the edge and she was there, grabbing and pulling him. He kneed the edge, swiping water from his face. She was in tears, in shambles, shaking violently.

"Jesus, what's the matter?" He went for his weapon, but she was against him, gripping him tightly and sobbing.

"I thought you drowned! I thought you drowned. Oh, Mike." She clung to him in a death grip.

Mike smoothed his hand over her hair. "It's all right, baby."

"No, it's not! You said you'd come right back!"

"I did."

She looked up at him, stricken. "Mike, you were underwater for over twelve minutes!" To prove her point, she showed him her watch.

"Your glass is cracked, look!" He showed her. "It's cracked. It's got to be wrong. That's impossible." He was on the other side for no more than thirty seconds and he couldn't hold his breath for more than two minutes. "No, listen to me, it's *wrong*," he said when she shook her head wildly.

She lifted her gaze, her quivering lip destroying him. "I thought you *died*."

"Aw, Irish," he groaned, pulling her onto his lap. She curled herself around him, sobbing hopelessly, and Mike pressed his lips to her temple and rubbed her spine. "I'm sorry."

She punched his ribs. "Don't scare me like that!"

His lips quirked. He didn't think the panic would last long. But her grip was punishing and he held her tightly, then told her what he found. "I didn't go into the tunnels, but it's better than no choice at all."

"Anything man-made like that granite slab?"

"Not that I could tell. Are you ready?"

"Now?" Clancy wasn't comfortable with swimming in an underground cave, but she kept that to herself.

He studied her. "I won't let you die."

"I'm holding you to that." She sniffled, swiped her tears, then wiggled out of his arms and stuffed everything she had into her bag, with her boots. She wore only a T-shirt over her panties. "I should warn you, I don't swim fast."

"You won't have to."

She frowned, confused.

"It's too narrow for us to pass side by side, and I have to lead the way. I'll pull you." Mike slid his belt from his trousers and slipped it on his ankle, wrapping it twice, the rest loose. "When we're under, you grab on to this, slip your wrist in, and twist it so you're secure. I'll pull you along."

She looked skeptical.

"Trust me."

"I do." She cocked her head. "Or didn't you get that already?"

He kissed her forehead, feeling gifted. "Kick your feet too. I'm towing a lot."

She elbowed him, then jumped into the pool, and Mike glanced back, making certain everything left behind was ready to grab, on the next trip, then slid into the water.

"So you don't use up air trying to grab on, I'll dive and hold. When you're confident, give the strap a good yank."

She nodded, thinking she'd get kicked in the face if she wasn't careful.

Mike went under, executing a dive that shot his feet into the air. Clancy quickly grabbed the strap, slipped it around her wrist twice, then yanked.

He took her under so fast she felt the pressure instantly, the rush of water around her as he towed her like in some *Free Willie* movie.

Mike dug his arms in, taking as wide a swipe as he could through the passage. The underwater cavern expanded, the blue-white illumination growing white and crisp as he neared. He looked up at the jagged edge of the pool, and swam hard, breaking the surface, then instantly bending for Clancy's hand. He grabbed her wrist, freeing the strap, and pulled her above water.

"That wasn't so bad, was it?"

She sank beneath the water. Mike grabbed her back.

Then he realized—Clancy was dead.

# Seventeen

"Oh, Jesus." He held her head above water as he swam to the edge.

Without leverage, Mike put his weight under and kicked hard, pushing, and rolled her onto the bank. Then he was out of the water and laying her flat. He began CPR.

*Don't do this, don't do this,* he thought, breathing for her. His heart pounded like a sledgehammer and he'd never felt so helpless.

He counted, pressing on her chest. He breathed for her and kept it up when he wanted to shout, "Don't leave me." He put his ear to her chest, then pumped her chest and breathed for her again.

"Clancy, baby, stay away from the damn light. You've seen it. Old news."

She coughed, her body convulsing hard, and he pushed her on her side as water dribbled out of her mouth. She started to shake and he gathered her in his arms, rubbing her skin. It was several minutes before she did anything more than breathe, and Mike closed his eyes, thanking God. He didn't even try to excuse away his feelings. He didn't need this threat to make him see the truth, damn it.

He looked down at her, pushed wet clumps of hair off her face. Her lids lifted, smoky brown eyes penetrating his soul and making him hurt. "Don't scare me like that," he said, nudging her.

Her laugh brought on a fit of coughing, and when it subsided she cleaned her throat. Her voice was a little raspy. "See, told you so."

"Yes, you did." What it meant, he didn't know. But he wasn't going to ignore it again. "Forgive me?"

"Yes."

His shoulders sank with relief.

"But I'm going to use this to get my way for a very long time."

His smile was slow, lighting his eyes. "Fire away." Mike leaned down slowly, as if waiting for her to take back her forgiveness. His mouth settled over hers, drugging her with soft moves and a sweep of his tongue.

She hummed against his mouth, touched his jaw delicately. "Thanks for my life," she whispered, and he squeezed her close, the tightness in the back of his throat strangling him.

She curled comfortably in his arms, then said, "Are we leaving this place any time soon?"

"No, baby." Mike looked up at the crack in the mountain. "Not yet."

Maybe not ever.


Francine couldn't handle it. The rush of adrenaline swept her body every hour, increasing every moment, and she couldn't keep still or work. She wanted to hit something, do anything to stop it. She was probably going to jail, and locked in a cell would drive her insane. *This has to end,* she thought and kept searching the lab for the Terminator. It wasn't in its case and she knew Clancy had taken it, but there was more than one. Wasn't there? She shook her head as if her careening thoughts would break free and fall into place, but they didn't, wouldn't.

She went back to the computer, trying to open Clancy's

notes for the operations specification. But Clancy had locked her out of her files.

Francine shoved at the keyboard and pushed back, pacing when she wanted to run. She gripped the back of her neck, massaging the insertion location and wishing she could pull it out. She had time to stop it, she thought. But the only person who could help her operate the sonic machine was lost in South America.

She filled a cup of water, and drained it, drinking four more before the dryness in her mouth felt quenched. She made notes in her iPod. If this was going to permanently damage her brain, she wanted all the information so they wouldn't do it again. It was laughable to think this project would continue, and she regretted her actions. But maybe a private company would see the potential that she and Carl had destroyed. Clancy had created the technology that would someday enable the handicapped to function. *It can't be wasted, no matter what.*

She moved to the bank of screens, watching Boris.

She adjusted the joystick, moving the camera closer. The ape was on the ground, writhing, clawing himself. When he rolled toward the camera, Francine lurched back, horrified as Boris clawed at his face to the point of bleeding.

She rushed to the habitat, pushing past people and sending a soldier into the wall.

"Sorry, sorry," she said without looking back, keyed herself in, and went immediately to the tranq gun. She loaded it, cocking the gun, and then keyed open the wide glass doors. She fired, but Boris didn't move. Francine realized the orangutan was already dead, his torn face lying in a pile beside him, blood dripping from his stubby fingers.

For a long moment, she stared at the gruesome mess. *That could be me,* she thought, then closed the doors. Sullenly, she turned away, grabbing a new cartridge and preparing it for herself.

\* \* \*

Clancy slept and didn't think she'd moved till she tried to sit up. Her body screamed with aches and scrapes, and she inspected her elbows. She really hoped there weren't any more underground streams to swim. She lay back down, the moments when her lungs filled with water playing in her mind. She knew she was dying then. There wasn't much question in that, yet she could also see they were still far off. Signaling Mike would have drowned him too and then neither of them would have survived. He had to live. He had a job to do. It sounded so damn noble, but the reality was, she was *really* glad he'd revived her.

Yet the moment took away her fear and she wondered if this was what he felt when he was on a mission. Kissing death wasn't something she wanted to experience again, but she wasn't afraid. You outgrew the thrill junkie crap, she reminded herself, then heard movement behind her. She rolled and found a little camp behind her, and pushed up as Mike came out a tunnel with an armload of sticks.

When he saw her, he stopped short. *Boy, is* that *a sappy grin!* she thought, feeling suddenly warmed.

"Move around, it will help."

"Says you." She tried to stand and he tossed down the stack and helped her. "I think you bruised me." She rubbed her chest.

"Want me to check?"

She looked at him, emotionless. "I hope you have better lines than that, Gannon. It's almost prehistoric." He just kept smiling, and walked with her around a bit. "How's it looking?" She settled to the ground, and noticed her clothes were almost dry.

"Tunnels go in two directions." Mike built a small fire. "One is blocked with fresh dirt. Richora's grenade did that, I think. The others are narrow, but passable." And they led down, not lateral.

"Then where did you find wood?"

"It's just dead roots from the tunnels, and that's about it

for the stockpile." He laid pieces of torn cloth on the twigs, then struck two rocks for a spark.

"That's good, Boy Scout, but I have a lighter. Oh, it's back . . . there." Her words trailed off when he gestured to the pack off to the side. "You went back? Michael!"

He met her gaze and made no excuses. "You're right, it was twelve minutes. Nobody can hold their breath for half that *and* swim."

"But you did?"

He nodded, scowling as he struck the rocks. The spark shot and the cloth fibers caught.

"Mike, look at me."

He didn't and blew on the fire, adjusting till it caught more. "I know what you're going to say, I thought it too. I was in the hospital, right near your lab."

She shook her head. "You have no marks and you've shown none of the preliminary reactions."

He looked up sharply. "Like what?"

"Dizziness at first."

He shrugged. "I was doped in the hospital, so that's nothing." He built up the fire, then grasped his pack and started loading it.

"Do you feel any different?"

"Yeah."

"Explain."

He held her gaze, laying a positively wicked smile on her, and Clancy experienced it as if he'd held her heart in his palm. "Orgasms don't count."

He burst out laughing, and she launched at him, wanting to get better acquainted with that sound. He held her, kissing her slowly.

"Don't fight it," he mimicked, squeezing her.

"Give me a break. I'm so out of practice, I'm retro."

"Weren't you married?"

"Not really. His sudden proclivity for women's underclothes was a real clue it wasn't going to work." She shrugged.

"He did it to please his family. I was just part of the role he was playing."

"Christ." What a creep.

"Were you ever married?" Her expression melted. "Oh, hell, are you?"

"No, and hell no. You wouldn't be in my arms if I was."

She relaxed, more than delighted with his honesty. "I'm sure you have women stripping on your doorstep, so why not?" Cradled on his lap, she ran her finger over his collarbone, brushing the healed wound in his shoulder.

"No time and no one willing to deal with all the it's on a need-to-know basis."

"And you don't need to know," she finished and he nodded. "I understand. Even my mom doesn't know what I really do."

"Mine either. But she's not uninformed." And she'd love Clancy, he thought, surprising himself. He was suddenly glad his brothers were married with children. "They just don't ask for details."

Her hands smoothed over his bare chest, her mouth on his throat and trailing lower. "We're talking too much," she said, sliding her tongue over his nipple, and heard air hiss through his teeth. She liked that he tried to restrain himself and nipped at his rib cage. His muscles jumped and when she backed off his lap and bent lower, Mike gripped her shoulders, then set her back from him.

She blinked, disappointed.

"Keep that up and we'll never get out of here." He'd never want to, Mike thought, but had men waiting for him to find them.

"Killjoy." She taunted him with another heart-pounding kiss, then eased back. He handed her a granola bar, and she made a sour face, yet ate it in under a minute as she tried to recall the discussion. "Okay, so far we'd learned some of the symptoms are aggression, fearlessness, heightened sex drive."

"Check that one off." He chuckled to himself and she nudged him to hush.

"Increases strength and intelligence, and the five senses sharpen exponentially."

"Senses are acute, but they've always been fairly good. Fearless? No. That's stupid, fear keeps you sharp. The rest, no difference that I noticed."

It could all be explained away with a man like him, Clancy thought. All he did was train for the next mission. "Your speed?"

"I run decathlons to stay in shape."

"Jeez, I bet you're tons of fun on a date. And when we make it out of this, you'll just have to cut back on some of that stuff." His features went soft, then tight with understanding. "A twenty-mile run or sex with me?"

"Now, there's a tough choice," he muttered and she laughed.

"There's sleep deprivation." She frowned, realizing neither of them had time for much rest in the past few days. "When was the last time you slept?"

He was quiet for a moment. "When I got to San José de Lourdes."

"That's two days, Mike."

"I hadn't noticed. But I've gone for days without sleep before." He rubbed the back of his neck.

"I looked before, you don't have a mark." He met her gaze. "When you said they were your men, I checked. I thought perhaps they'd done it to you without knowing. But you have no mark. None. It would have left an injection point." It was a big needle and a deep plunge.

"I heal quickly."

"Maybe so, but holding your breath that long?" She shook her head, sitting back on her calves.

"I know, but if it's in me"—the words stuck in his throat—"then we're alive because of it."

She was right before. His attributes, finely honed from years of training, could be explained away. But what if they weren't? Clancy couldn't consider it. Nano in Mike was just plain unacceptable. Because it would kill him too.

"Let's get out of here."

He frowned. "You should probably rest."

"I'm fine." She reached for her bag. It was empty and she noticed her clothes strung over the boulders. She went to them, snatching them up like retrieving from a panty raid. She turned sharply, giving Mike an amused *did you have fun?* smile. He actually reddened a little. Such a man, she thought.

"Perhaps you should put some clothes on."

She smiled, aware of what she looked like in a T-shirt and pink panties.

Mike glanced up. She hadn't moved and was a damn invitation for sex standing there like that. "Have mercy on me, Irish."

"Not a chance, Marine." With her back to him, she stripped to her skin, then dressed, aware he was watching her. She gave him a show. Then she realized he'd rinsed out her other clothes. She cocked a look over her shoulder. He was gawking.

"That wasn't mercy," he rasped, then cleared his throat. "That was torture."

"I know. Wanna make something of it?"

"Yeah, I will, damn it. When we get out of this place, I want a week alone for some payback."

"Just a week?"

"Christ. Keep talking like that and I won't be able to walk."

She laughed, the sound bouncing off the walls as she grabbed her boots and socks, then sat on the ground. Mike watched as she reverently put the classified data into her boots, then slipped them on.

"So how do we get out of here?" She looked up at the

crack in the ceiling above the waterfall. It was long and narrow, yet aligned with the sun so the place was lit for a good
portion of the day. On purpose or a fluke? "I bet I could
climb that. I've rock-climbed before."

That didn't surprise him. "I considered it, you're small
enough, but not enough rope." It had to be forty feet up and
they needed at least twice that. "I can't get through that
crack, and besides, where would you go for help? We were in
drug territory before. I'm betting up there, it's no different."

"Do we even know where we are in this mountain?"

"South of the ruins, I figure. But the GPS won't go through
this much stone. I can draw up the last map. But there's
enough iron in these walls that my compass isn't working."

He held up his wrist and she could see it quiver. Magne-
tized. "I knew I should have kept that one from the Cracker
Jacks." He smiled to himself, shaking his head. "So what's in
those?" She tossed a thumb at the holes in the wall.

"They go in the wrong direction, down. We head toward
the light." He opened an energy bar that looked a bit
smashed, then pushed a stack of brown packages toward her.

She studied the selection. "Oo, peanut butter and crack-
ers!" She snatched it up.

He made a face. "It's MRE." Meals Ready to Eat.

"They're much better tasting than they were in Desert
Storm."

His head jerked up and his gaze shot over her like a
buzzing bee. "I keep forgetting." He stuffed the pack without
paying much attention to it. "I hate the desert."

"I like my sand on a beach with a mimosa," she agreed.
"You were here before?"

He nodded, chewing and swallowing. "It was a DEA
sweep with Peru's drug officers. I spent five days trying to get
off that mountain."

"Lost? That's not promising."

He looked at her, deadpan. "Lost? No. It was the terrain.

This area is easy, dense, and close to the river. Follow the water and it's a way out. The higher you go, the tougher it is to breathe. I was carrying wounded, too."

"Nathan Krane."

His brows drew tight.

"He's the only one besides you who's ever been wounded."

"Nathan's my closest friend. We were assigned to DEA working a sweep in Colombia and Peru for Shining Path drug factories. Proceeds from the cocaine trade were—are channeled to terrorists in Afghanistan." He clenched his fist. "Man, I really don't want to bring back just his dog tags." He was quiet for a moment, thinking if anyone were alive, it would be Krane. Unless the nano shit went haywire in him. "The source of the water is that way." He left out a breath, shedding his worry, and pointed to the spill of the waterfall. "Somewhere behind it." He closed his pack and reached for a plain black T-shirt, pulling it on.

"Behind? Is it deep enough to get behind?"

"No, we have to find a way around." He stood, tucking in his shirt and dressing in more weapons. He held out a loaded gun and thought, he really did trust her. She put it in the cargo pocket of her pants, the weight making her slacks droop on her hips, and then she shouldered on the pack. Mike put out the fire, then went to the waterfall.

Clancy climbed after him, balanced on the jumble of rocks. The fall looked more like the mountain had sprung a leak. Water fought its ways around the boulders, most of it streaming straight down and flowing into the pool. She put her hand in it and the force of it stung, surprising her.

"It's like a cork." She balanced as she moved the few yards to the fissure, a crooked passageway into complete darkness. "You sure about this?"

"Look." He aimed the flashlight and showed the hollow beyond the fissure.

"Another cavern? It's a wonder it hasn't caved in on itself." A steady breeze pushed through the crack, and she heard whistling wind above the splashing water.

Mike kissed her, then led the way. He'd gone twenty feet before he was forced to take off the pack and move laterally, foot by foot. Clancy followed right behind him, but she kept her pack on.

"Suck it in, Gannon," she teased when the rock pressed against his chest. She held his pack when his steps became increments as he forced his big body between the slabs of stone. "The air is coming harder." Strong enough to push at her hair.

Mike struggled to pass, barely able to bend his knees to lift his foot, yet Clancy was leaning, waiting to inch along with him. Behind her was over thirty feet of stone and rock, and she suspected this had been part of the last room, a sacrificial chamber perhaps. "Can you see the end?"

"Yeah, another forty feet or so." Mike ran his hands over the slick wall to find something to grasp for leverage. "This wall's not a solid slab. I feel grids, stacked stones."

"Man-made is good. They had to get it in here somehow."

"Unless they built it in here."

"No negative vibes, Marine. You're just asking for a bad karma."

He smiled to himself and was about fifteen feet from the edge, the wind pushing hard, but the space was too narrow to draw his arm to shine the light. "Get behind me, take this, and shine it down past my feet."

She did and Mike looked, his body nearly crushed between the walls. "There is nothing there."

She adjusted the light to hold it as high as she could and still point down. "Nothing?"

"If there is, I can't see it."

"Mike?" Clancy straightened, and frowned at the ground. "Am I nuts or—"

"No, I felt it too." Under his feet, against his back. The

ground trembled, rocks sprinkling. It felt as if he were standing on golf balls.

"Go back!"

Clancy shifted quickly, but the vibrations grew stronger, the ground rolling beneath her feet. Then she stopped.

Mike was behind her. "Keep moving."

"We can't!" She twisted and met his gaze. "Look. The waterfall!"

Over her shoulder, Mike saw a blast of white water shooting straight out from the fall, and filling the cave. The twigs were already floating. Rocks tumbled into the opening and took away the choice.

"Oh, Jesus, Mike!" Water bubbled around the rocks in the crevasse, flowing closer. The tremors made the stone shift and bobble, and sandwiched between, he felt the pressure on his chest. His breathing labored as he braced his hands on the wall, barely enough room to bend his arms, and he pushed as if he could move five hundred tons of stone.

Then it did—and brought more water. Mike jerked his hands back, stunned.

"There are round stones under it!" Clancy said, and Mike only heard the terror in her voice.

He pushed again, yet the wall refused to move as white foam rushed around them, soaking them to the knees. *It's filling the cave.* Mike inched to the edge, then reached back for her hand. He squeezed, then let go as he forced his body through the opening, feeling the vise on his rib cage and chest. His fingers curled around the edge of the rock and water streamed down on his head. The fall was above them, he thought, and the quaking earth collapsed the stones. Mike knew if he didn't get out, Clancy would be crushed to death, and he strained, squeezing his body through the opening, then shoved hard against the stone.

He popped out of the crack like a stopper from a bottle and stumbled, then reached for Clancy. For a moment their eyes met, his fingertips grazing hers before he fell backward into the dark unknown—without her.

Jansen listened to the CIA agent, and knew it was time to blow the hinge off this ugly door. Gannon couldn't be reached. The reality of an entire team vanishing made him accept information from any resource, including Howard Gantz.

"I'm getting the pictures." Hank watched the screen download and frowned.

"I can find lots on this guy, but not who sent him."

Jansen recognized the face.

There was no reason to send someone like Denner after her, either. On another computer, he sent the picture into his database, and received instant information. Cook had signed off on the last two neutralizations while in Spec Ops, the bastard.

"I've got his cell phone."

Hank's brows shot up. "The last call was to the medical facility, Army. Right?"

"Yeah," Gantz said carefully.

Cook didn't route his calls? *You're smarter than this, Carl. What do you have up your sleeve to save yourself with?* Hank knew Cook would have someone in his back pocket to ensure that he'd come out with, at the least, his retirement and an order of silence. Hank preferred hard labor in Leavenworth.

"Where was the call to? To which office?"

"Primate lab. Francine Yates, major, U.S. Army."

Mike sailed through the air, then hit the ground, tumbling down an embankment like a kid rolling down a grassy hill. He grappled for anything to stop the rush, but there was nothing but loose dirt and rocks. Then he hit something solid, and before the pain registered, Clancy's body slammed into him. He grunted at the impact, then instantly grabbed her to him, rolling, and protecting her from the rush of water and mud.

Water splashed around them, covering them, and then Mike struggled to keep her head above the surface, their bodies sliding with the force. Clancy grappled in panic, clinging to him, and Mike braced his feet against the flow and held her tightly. Their bodies a dam, water rushed past.

"I have you, I have you." The tremor ceased, but rocks still tumbled.

"I'm really tired of this down-the-rabbit-hole crap," she muttered into his chest. "I just got clean!" She pushed out of his arms, the water flow draining off, and Mike looked around for the flashlight. He spotted a faint beam several yards away under layers of mud and crawled to it, digging it out. It still worked but was fading fast. He moved to her.

"I lost your pack. Sorry."

"It's okay," he said, staggering in the mud. "I lost the rifle."

She gave him her weapon. Mike shined the light over the cavern. Water spilled from the fissure they'd passed through, the pour constant and high. Yet the water wasn't rising around them. Mike stood and with the flashlight, followed the flow. It hit the barrier and coursed left and right, and while it was still coming, it wasn't knee deep anymore. With the light, he chased a stream farther and saw it spill in tiers. He nudged her and shone the light on them.

"Stairs." He moved nearer. "It flows into an aqueduct." He pointed into the darkness below, and Clancy crawled on muddy hands and knees to see a narrow canal of cut stone that went off somewhere into the dark. Mike followed the path with the flashlight, its beam draining the last of the power as he leaned over the barrier.

Suddenly he ducked low, shut off the light, and crawled back to her. "Don't get excited, but we're not alone." The noise of the water and the sloshing mud drowned out any sound but its own.

Clancy gave him a wide-eyed stare. He motioned over the stone barrier. "Stay low," he whispered and Clancy carefully peered over the wall of stone—and saw people. More expressly, Indians. Holding torches, several men rushed into a courtyard in a little panic over the tremors, all shouting the same phrase.

"They seem darn pleased by all that seismic activity."

"Guess they didn't get that the mountain could fall on them."

"They're painted like that Indian who protected me." Green, brown, and black sweeping strokes resembled the fronds and leaves of the forest.

"The best cammo paint job I've seen," Mike said. "If you're into that whole naked dick-swinging thing."

She snickered to herself, then looked up to the ceiling. "These chambers would have been side by side." She gestured to the crack they'd come through that was now smaller than ever. "It's a pyramid." The slab they'd slid down before, it must be the top of the mountain. "Those were doors once, look."

Mike glanced behind, more interested in getting them out than the architecture. But she was right. Over the centuries, it had collapsed in on itself. The section he'd moved wasn't as big as he'd thought. Though over twenty feet tall, it was only a few inches thick, and from here he could see the long tube-shaped stones under it. Most were crushed or broken, but like with the Incas, it was a balance of stone with weighted levers. There was nothing left of it now, but the fat counter-weight that was still wrapped in animal-hide rope. He inched to look over the curling wedge of lava stone.

They had a ringside seat. The immense chamber was like the other cavern, only larger, and looked untouched by time. Crudely carved columns posted like guards in each corner, the aqueduct surrounding the right side and disappearing under more rock. There were two levels, a dais, and below it the wide uneven red stone floor.

"Amazing. You think it's new real estate or a fixer-upper?"

"Fixer-upper," Mike said. "There's a Moche dig nearby, I read it in the papers."

Then she latched on to one thing. "They know a way out."

"We can't ask."

"I don't speak the language, but I'm sure we can get across—"

He was already shaking his head, then urged her to look again.

Clancy did and swallowed her tongue. "Denner?" The fair-skinned, light-haired man looked like a Yankee in Florida on spring break.

"He's not a prisoner, he's a participant." He was dressed like some of the Indians in a dirt-colored tunic and headdress that was a helmet with a thin hammer shape on the top. It looked heavy and he was armed and carrying a torch.

She scowled deeply. "Inducted. How? Why?"

"Your options are no choice or willing."

"He'd have to earn it. A white guy in this tribe? Not hardly."

"He was a sweeper, Clancy. He could probably do the job and be on a plane and in the air before you're dropped."

She wasn't sure if she liked that he knew those things, but she believed him. "His word or reputation means nothing here, so he'd have to prove it. Look at all those tunnels." No less than three were spread out and leading into darkness.

"See the one on the far left? Notice the stone carvings outside it?"

Clancy looked, then scowled at him. "I can't see that far. I don't think anyone without binoculars could either."

It hit him like a slap. The nano, and it worked.

He met her gaze and she pursed her lips. "Coming in handy, isn't it?"

He didn't respond to that, but said, "Those wall carvings are like the ruins on the cliff."

"So we have a tribe following the traditions of a society that perished two thousand years ago."

"Looks that way."

The oblong doorway wasn't large, and his gaze narrowed as more men filed into the courtyard.

"They were ready to come into this place, Mike. Did they expect the earthquake? Praying it would? Or did they think that was an answer from their god?"

Mike didn't like the sound of that. It meant the tribe was pumped, and that would be the equivalent of Medal of Honor–type bravery. There were two of them, and the only way out was past the tribe.

"If they worshipped the mountain, isn't it safe to say they protected it too?"

"Yeah." He saw where she was going with this.

"I bet this is why those soldiers died. They trespassed."

"So did we."

"But I had a boyfriend who protected me. We're in drug territory. How could Richora not know about this?"

"It's a damn big mountain, honey."

She remembered Richora grilling her over what she *saw*. "He didn't want me seeing *anything,* so what could we have missed?"

Mike thought for a moment, then told her about the crates the three men died over. "And then there were the kilos. No self-respecting drug lord wants proof that close to him. But, Irish, I think he's on a revenge high with you."

The man she shot on the river, Clancy thought. "True, but the processed kilos mean there's a drug factory here, and with that amount of cargo, it's a big lab." *That's got to be a year's worth of product,* she thought, tugging her chin for a second, quiet.

Mike simply waited, enjoying her analytical mind.

"You said water was a way out? What's beyond here?"

"The Rio Marñón. It becomes the Amazon."

"That's how they are getting the kilos out, by the river, hiding it in here."

"Too simple and too visible. Peru Navy patrols the rivers. Their DEA watches the drug trade everywhere."

"They killed those troops, Mike. The crashes, we're in their territory too. We got a free pass because of boyfriend, but if Richora put his transports *near* tribal boundaries, he's got autoprotect." She tossed her thumb toward the hall below.

"His own private little army," Mike said. Richora could move anything.

The sound of drums drew them back, and Mike knew that with the torches lighting the areas, the tribe couldn't see much beyond, so for the moment, they were still undetected. He started to rise when he heard Clancy moving and glanced, tried to reach for her, but she was crawling toward the tiered stairs. "Clancy!"

She put up her hand as if to say "just a second," then lay flat, reaching, and nearly tumbling down the stairs. She came back with his pack.

"Good recon. Don't do that again," he said. Everything was there, soaked, but aside from his knives, and some explosives, he had one pistol and little ammo. Shooting his way out of this wasn't his first choice. They were outnumbered and the Indians knew how to get out of here. A quick stampede, he thought, then tried the GPS for some accurate direction, but the screen staggered. He shut it off.

The drums grew louder, more steady, and they focused over the edge. Suddenly, Mike dropped down. He stared blankly, then rubbed his face.

Clancy searched the faces, her heart breaking. "It's Nathan and Sal!"

Nathan Krane and Salvatore DiFazio were tethered like animals, stripped to their boxers and barefoot. The Indians yanked them toward the center of the courtyard with several other prisoners. "Where are Valnik and Palmer?"

Mike joined her. Then suddenly he grabbed her and covered her mouth.

She shrieked behind his hand, and they huddled on the stone, helpless as the ritual massacre began.

# Eighteen

The screams were chilling.

Clancy sank to the ground and cringed at each shriek of agony. Then she heard a gunshot and saw Mike sliding back down to the ground.

"That ought to confuse them."

"And it will signal Nathan and Sal," she said.

But the shot only startled the battle, the horrible sounds dying down for a breath, then increasing with bone-racking horror. The chance that he could have just killed them with a ricochet tore at Mike as he stood. Clancy was breathing hard as she joined him, a death grip on his arm.

Mike aimed and fired. A man about to cut Sal's throat dropped to the ground. Nathan and Sal grabbed the curved knifes from their tormentors, and Mike watched helplessly as Nathan Krane cut his own bonds and unleashed on his attackers.

His speed was astounding. He spun, his leg shooting out to connect with an Indian's throat and knock him back. Then he went in for the kill. Within a moment, his immediate area was cleared. Mike glanced at Clancy, and her horrified look made him pull her down behind the boulder.

She swallowed repeatedly, her eyes wide yet staring at nothing. He knew what she was doing. Reliving it. "Clancy, baby, look at me."

She did and he kissed her, squeezed her.

"Enemy territory," she said. Clancy had seen this before, been in it, but oh God, it was still unbelievable. Then Mike was gone, moving down the tier. She scrambled after him. "No, no, Mike. Please don't." All she could hear was the clash of weapons, the tortured screams, and wanted him nowhere near it.

But she knew. He couldn't leave them to die.

He eased carefully down the tiers slippery with moss and steep. Half the stairs were shielded by broken slabs of stone, but for several yards to the doorway they'd be exposed. He took careful aim and fired, then moved his arms to the left and fired again. Then he hurried out of her line of vision. Clancy slid down a couple of steps, grappling to stop herself, then looked. She shouldn't have. Mike was fast and lethal, and she jerked back, closing her eyes and washing the image from her mind. Guns were one thing, but hand-to-hand was ruthless and brutal.

She couldn't help. Without a weapon, she was defenseless.

Then someone touched her shoulder and she flinched, batting them away.

"Clancy?"

Her head jerked up and she sighed with relief and launched into his arms. "Stop scaring me," she said softly.

"I'm trying." He helped her over the aqueduct.

"Nathan," Mike called, and Krane spun, defending with two curved knives. It took a moment to register. "Krane. It's me. At ease."

Nathan lowered his arms, then glanced at Sal standing at his back. "Fazio," he said. "Look who showed up."

Mike grinned and crossed to them, gripping Nathan by the arms, then giving him a bear hug and the same to Sal.

"Thanks for looking," Krane said.

He was about to thank Clancy when he turned for her. She kept her gaze locked on Mike as she crossed over bodies to him.

"Where are Valnik and Palmer?"

Krane frowned at her, then Mike.

"Clancy McRae. Long story, you can trust her."

"Valnik is dead and Palmer, we haven't seen him since the crash," Nathan said. "He didn't get captured with us."

Clancy would think of the young man alive until she had to, and her gaze bounced all over the men. She was more than curious. She'd spent years of her life working on a technology that would keep military alive in battle. Now she got to witness it.

"Don't mind her," Mike said, turning toward the doorway. "She's—"

"Damn glad you're alive." She pumped their hands, smiling brightly.

Mike tapped her and inclined his head. "That's going to alert some more," he said, and she came to him, grabbing a knife off the ground and swiping the blood on a dead man. She stopped short, looking around at the dead.

"Clancy, don't look at them, look at me."

She waved that off. "What's that?"

Mike came to her and stared not at the dead man, but the small shield he had over his wrist. Mike slid it off and held it up. The outside had the distinct black numbers of registration.

"The dismantled Hellfire," Krane said.

"All of it?" Mike said.

Krane moved quickly around and Clancy made herself look at the weapons and not the bodies, but one person stood out. Denner lay dead at her feet. She reached for a wire braided around his throat as Krane came back with earrings and adornments.

"They used the guidance, chips, wires, all of it." He held them out for a look, then tossed them aside. "Probably left the good parts on the mountain." Fuel and explosives. Clancy knew if it was whole, Mike didn't have enough explosives to follow orders and blow it up.

"You know how to get out?" Mike said to Nathan.

He shook his head. "It's a maze of tunnels and rooms. They scattered that way." He flicked his hand toward gaping doorways edged in stone carvings.

"How many?"

He looked around. "Sixty maybe. Less now."

"Women, children?"

His brows drew down. "We heard them, but never saw any, so they must be kept elsewhere. They eat vegetables so they have to leave this place somehow."

Mike opened his pack and handed over food. They devoured the protein bars and water in short order. All he had left was a bit of explosives and a single detonator.

Clancy was still staring at them. "How are you feeling?"

Mike glanced at her, frowning. "You can put us all under a microscope later, babe," he said. He'd personally strip for her.

"You have to admit, it hasn't had any adverse effect on you, and it could be the same for them."

"What's she talking about?"

Mike gave Clancy a *let's get out of here first* look, then grabbed a torch off the wall and eased into the gap in the wall stretching up more than forty feet. Behind her Krane and DiFazio did the same.

Mike looked at the compass on his watch, and though it was jumping, it was a general direction. South. Near the river. They moved swiftly, all but Clancy's head grazing the ceiling, and when they met a fork Mike kept walking.

She touched him, stopping him.

"I hear water," he said.

Clancy didn't hear a damn thing.

A few more steps and she heard the chime, the copper coin medallions on their costumes making a soft clink. Krane and DiFazio moved past her just as the Indians rushed them. Mike used his ammo to clear a path, and then Krane and Di-

Fazio instinctively sandwiched her between them and guided her past the dead.

"There's a chamber, I think, but I see light."

Clancy moved up beside Mike. "They've opened the wall somehow." She pointed to the far right, the dirt on the ground swept left near a low wall that separated a meeting area. "Did they leave that way, the rest?"

"Possibly, but light is that way."

"Wait a sec." Krane came near and picked up a large rock. Mike frowned at him, confused. "I've seen some interesting things here." He threw it hard at the tiled floor.

It shifted the ground, breaking away and leaving a path of square stone on top of some sort of pylon and nothing around it. Dirt still fell.

"I didn't hear it hit bottom," Krane said behind her.

"Okay." Clancy peered over the edge. "Next option?"

"We walk across."

She made a face at them. "How about edging it?" she said. There was a small space of stone near the wall to get started and she went to it. Clancy clipped the pack's waist belt and went left to the wall of rock.

"Clancy, honey."

She looked back. "I'm not going over that. It's a puzzle, Mike. We have time to figure out a puzzle?" She knew they didn't. "End of story." She gripped the rocks, moving slow and sure like a spider on the wall.

Mike just shook his head, then followed.

"Boy, does *she* sound familiar!" Nathan muttered softly, and Mike glanced, smiling.

Clancy rock-climbed to the entrance, then pushed off and hopped into the tunnel, pulling her knee up, grappling on the edge till she gained leverage. She sat back, waving them on.

Then the six feet of floor surrounding her—crumbled.

Hank Jansen didn't go directly to the lab. In civilian clothes, he went to Major Yates's home. She hadn't reported to work since the animals had died, though he didn't think she was mourning the orangutan. He rang the bell. He glanced around at the Tudor town house. The grounds were unkempt, nothing personal outside, and with the shades drawn, the house look empty. He heard scuffling, and waited for the Gothic door to open, but only the small eye-level spy door did.

"Please leave, sir."

"Open the door, Major."

"This is my home, you have no authority here."

Hank scowled darkly. "You cannot turn off your rank when it pleases, Major. You are, until your enlistment is over, still in the Army. Are you refusing a direct order?"

"I can bring the police."

"I have no problem with that, but neither of us wants this made public."

With a huff, she shut the little door and Hank heard the locks slip. She opened the door and wrapped her arms around her middle. She looked tired, her hair mussed, but even in sweatpants and a T-shirt, she was a beautiful woman.

"May I come in now?"

She waved him through and Hank followed her into the living room. Then he realized she wasn't just tired, but haggard. Her eyes were swollen yet with dark purple circles beneath. She shot him a nasty look before she dropped into the corner of the sofa.

Hank remained standing. He'd learned early the first defense was intimidation.

"What do you want, Colonel? Aside from ruining my career."

"You did that all by yourself. My concern is my troops. I want to know how to stop it."

She hesitated, rubbing her forehead, trying to hold back more tears, he thought. Her hands trembled violently. "I can't," she said. "I wish I could. Believe me."

She said it with such feeling, Hank frowned, noticing his

surroundings. Broken dishes littered the wood floor, bric-a-brac piled at the far side of the dining table. She swiped it off, he realized. Then he saw the kitchen cabinets, ripped out of their frames, and the handles looked as if they'd been blasted out with a shotgun.

"What happened here? Were you robbed?"

She shook her head and reached for a water glass. Before she brought it to her lips, the glass popped, and shattered in her hand. She stared at the blood on her palm, unmoved. "I don't even feel it," she said.

Hank rushed to the kitchen for a towel, then returned and wrapped it. She took it from him, holding pressure, and Hank heard bones snap. "Good God."

She held up her uncut hand; her index finger was broken. "It's blocking a pain receptor."

"You implanted it in *yourself?*"

She nodded, then lifted her gaze. "I wanted to experience what they did. It's amazing, really. A day ago, I could run a two-minute mile. Today, I can't function. You don't know what it takes just to sit here. I'm having a rush of adrenaline that's killing me."

He couldn't care less right now. "Explain."

"It's one of the effects we suspected. The glands produce more adrenaline. It was *supposed* to produce more. We designed it for highly trained commandos. It's a . . . fearless rush, and I'm so pumped right now I could take over Iran."

"Jesus."

Gripping the bloody towel, she left the sofa so fast he barely saw her move. "Boris tried to tear off his own face last night. Tried?" She scoffed. "He did it. He's dead. The primate, Natasha, she was implanted at the same time and it had no effect on her. None. She had a teachable intelligence that's been recorded in any other study, but the pod didn't do anything to her. Boris, on the other hand, became extremely aggressive. To his mate, sexually, and then to himself."

"Is this going to happen to my men?"

"I don't know. It's clear with two specimens that different reactions occur in different candidates."

"I want the testing files on my troops, all of them."

"I don't have them anymore."

When she refused to meet his gaze, Hank had his doubts.

"They're with Colonel Cook."

And Cook was running to the nearest senator to spill, he thought. God, the ramifications of this would echo through the military. "Can this pod be removed?"

"No. It wasn't designed for removal. It's too small, sir. Nano," she stressed. "We made a device to, in a sense, shatter it, and let it be absorbed into the bloodstream." She snickered to herself, the sound bitter and tired. "It took two years to create, and it was easy to destroy. Clancy McRae, the chief designer, called it the Terminator."

"Then why haven't you—" He stopped midsentence. "She took it."

Francine nodded. "I looked. I practically destroyed the lab looking. I even tried breaking into Clancy's house, but the gate guards wouldn't let me in since they knew she wasn't there. I almost hit the guy. I was so hyped up that I could have easily killed him. So I came home and locked myself in."

And did damage to her home. Her thoughts were rational, yet the nano overrode them.

"I knew this was wrong." She waved at the mess in her home. "I wouldn't find anything, but I kept going. I couldn't stop." She looked at him.

"You lost control."

"Yes, sir, I did, and that means they will too."

His shoulders fell. "They're alive, they survived the crash. Does Colonel Cook know you put it in yourself?"

"Oh yes."

For a moment, he wandered over her dark blush, then dismissed it.

"If you want to start an investigation you're too late, Cook just left here."

Hank tensed. "To where?"

"Either to destroy every piece of evidence, though that's several millions in government funding he'll have to answer for, or take it all to the Senate Oversight, or the Joint Chiefs, probably to dump the blame for this on Clancy McRae."

"He didn't just dump the blame, Major."

She looked up.

"He sent someone to kill her."

"Oh God." She shot out of the chair, and staggered, but waved him off when he tried to help. "We have to stop him. She doesn't deserve this. She was right, she was right," Francine said over a sob. "I knew all this time she was, but he gave me direct orders to push ahead."

"Commendable. But authorization for implantation came from Cook, and you went along with it. Cry in your beer all you want," he said, unsympathetic. "He set *you* up."

She frowned, panicked.

"You made a call from your laboratory phone to a hitter. To kill Clancy. You're in this deeper than you think."

"I didn't! I would never do that!"

Hank would let NCIS sort it out. "And implanting my men and yourself, were you thinking of lives or your own career?"

She looked up, bleak. "Both. I still believe in this technology, Colonel." Her chin lifted a bit, the truth finally spilling. "Your men did volunteer, just not for the implantation." At his look, she hurried to say, "I swear to you, I only learned they hadn't a couple days ago. They thought they were agreeing to a stress test for comparisons for the future. Cook told me they'd volunteered for the insertion. I saw the paperwork, and I wanted to believe him. It was a blind test, no knowledge. We told them the injection was the latest biomarker to monitor them when they were out of touch. It was a lie, all of it. But you know that, don't you?"

"What I know is if my men die, you'll go to Leavenworth. With Cook."

She swallowed and confessed, "It's in Gannon too."

He felt his skin grow hot with outrage. "Prison is too good for you." He spun on his heel and headed to the door.

"They won't do anything. He knows too many secrets, Colonel. You'll have to jail him or silence him."

At this point, Hank didn't have a problem with that.

Clancy smothered a shriek as she grabbed for the wall, but she couldn't grip, sliding down into the dark pit below. Suddenly, she stuck her foot out, hitting the pylon, and she stopped short. The pylon tottered.

"Oh, Jesus," she heard Mike say, then strained to look at him.

"Oops. My bad."

Mike tried to reach out for her.

"No, don't, don't!" she said. "Go back. Walk it. It must be a pressure-sensitive combination. You can't cheat it."

Clancy couldn't move a fraction or she'd fall. Her grip was stretched to the limits of her reach. The dirt beneath her foot was too soft to hold for long, and she forced herself to be rational. If she pushed off, it could possibly destroy the last pedestal step. The guys had to cross first. She was balanced out in the open, her body as if ready for a jackknife into the endless cavern. And, jeez, there were spears down there. *Who did I hurt in a past life to get all this bad karma?*

DiFazio hadn't started to rock-climb and he overtook each step quickly, wobbling on the last. "I'm jumping past you."

Pushing the torches into the holder, Mike shouldered off the pack, dug in it for the nylon rope. Yet with her precarious position, there was no way to reach her from here. He had nothing to rope except her neck. Sal aimed somewhere past her.

A twenty-foot jump? "That's too far!"

He ignored her and leaped. He landed hard, then immediately braced himself to reach for Clancy. She met his gaze. "I can't move."

"When I have a good hold, push off toward me," he said, then grasped her wrist, his left hand gripping the rock for anchor. He nodded. She pushed off, swinging her left arm around. Her fingers grazed Sal's as her footing started to crumble. Sal lurched, gripping her with both hands, and pulled, nearly throwing her over his head.

Clancy hit with a teeth-clicking impact, wincing, and then she scrambled back from the edge. Mike was halfway across and moving fast. She had confidence in him and not the technology. He jumped and Sal grabbed him, then swung him deeper into the tunnel. They turned for Nathan. Long-legged, he landed easily.

Krane glanced back and said, "Better than a land mine."

Immediately, Mike went to Clancy, grabbing her up and hugging her tightly. "I hate watching stuff like that," he said before he kissed her, devouring and heavy, his hands pushing her into him, and his pent-up emotions flowed through her like pure energy. She hung on, savoring the power he wanted her to feel in a kiss that was less about desire and more about everlasting.

When they broke apart, she rubbed her thumb over his lower lip, then flicked her eyes toward their audience. DiFazio and Krane just stared, highly amused. Mike shot them a no-trespassing look. Clancy winked at Nathan, then behind Mike, walked into the dark. The flashlight was dead, and without torches the darkness forced them to go slow. The corridor turned slightly and light suddenly silhouetted Mike. He lurched back.

Clancy curled up behind him and peered past his shoulder. "We find the most interesting things on this trip."

It wasn't sunlight.

Incandescent bulbs whitened the entire chamber, shining down on rows of wood crates like the ones he'd spotted with the trio back at the river. They were in the process of being sealed and loaded, he realized. Hammers and bags of nails were left near the crates. He eased along the wall, aiming his gun. Krane and DiFazio split up and circled the chamber from both sides, then met in the middle. Mike waved Clancy over.

"This is what they're protecting," she said softly.

DiFazio covered the single exit and Nathan came to them.

Mike reached inside and held up a rock. "Unless there's diamonds inside these, I don't think so."

Clancy hurriedly searched the crates. "Rock. Just freaking rocks?"

"And kilos." Nathan held up a block neatly sealed in plastic. "The freshness is locked in."

Clancy's lips barely curved, her attention on the crates. There were wheeled handcarts to pull them out.

"The trio that were on the river," Mike said, and she looked at him. "They were stealing a crate of rocks. It was further north."

Clancy inhaled sharply. "That's what we saw, at the river, when they kidnapped me. The crates." With the flat of her hand, she patted the top of the wood box. "*These* crates."

"They are sending rocks up the river masquerading them as drugs? That's just asking for it."

"But you said intel wasn't getting anything here. No movement. If they were caught, the police wouldn't find any evidence for charges. And Richora's the big banana, so police weren't getting close unless it was some outside agency, DEA, Peru Intelligence?"

"It's a shell game," Nathan said quietly, and DiFazio glanced back once, frowning. "It's a diversion. Watch the left so hard, you don't see what the right is doing. There's hundreds of eyes on this area to stop drugs. Ship this down the river like a drug cargo while the real cargo is transported in plain sight."

"But the kilos are here, and we're near the river."

"This shipment must leave when that one does," Clancy said. "Somewhere close by."

Then Mike laid the bomb. "Gantz's trajectory of the rocket put it somewhere around here." If he could get outside and turn on the GPS, he'd know exactly where.

"We have movement," DiFazio said, and Krane moved up behind him. "They probably evacuated at the earthquake and are coming back."

"These are harmless right now." Mike inclined his head to the crates. "We get out first." Blowing it was out of the question. Mike didn't know how deep they were in the mountain, and that would bring it down on them. They moved along the wheel tracks and Mike felt the change in grade, the lower pressure on his ears. As he looked at his compass watch, the needle jumping lessened. Toward the river, he thought as the air changed, the dry earthen mustiness of the inner cavern freshened, damp now. The sound of water strengthened and he saw a crack in the cavern wall, water fountaining. Clancy was the first to stick her face under it and drink. Mike leaned over for a sip, then moved carefully around a turn. True sunlight spilled. He jerked back and held up his fingers, all of them. There was over ten men out there. That he could see.

Clancy's eye flew wide and she grabbed his arm, shook her head. He mouthed, *Trust me,* and Krane and DiFazio took up position opposite Mike with an angled view outside.

"One operation," Mike said. "All in the same area. This is secret, the rest in the open."

Clancy signaled Sal, scowling. "Don't leave me out."

He inclined his head and she darted to him. Clancy inhaled the fresh warm air and saw a warehouse. From her angle it was low, maybe fifteen feet tall, and completely hidden under vines and trees. The outside was painted brown and green, its wide doors open. With more pallets and crates inside.

"We need a look in there."

Clancy wanted to say, *No, we need to go to the hospital,*

but it would take time to convince these guys to stop now and get a checkup. "That's right across the middle of them."

"We go around again," Mike said.

"I just hope there's no more water," she muttered, still dripping from the last dousing.

Mike looked at Sal and Nathan. "I'd say use extreme prejudice."

"With knives and how many bullets?"

Mike didn't have to pat his pockets. He knew exactly how much ammo he had left. "Four."

Clancy dug in the pack, then inside her flight bag and tossed him the magazine. Fifteen more shots. "Sorry, I forgot about it. You gave it to me in the jungle."

"Clearly you two have had a long and fulfilling relationship." Nathan glanced between them.

Fulfilling? Oh, heck yeah, she thought, meeting Mike's gaze. Neither said a word, but Clancy felt a blush rise up her face. Nathan chuckled as Mike motioned her between him and Sal.

"Far right, then straight. We'll figure out how to cross the road later."

Morning sun spilled through the trees, casting the ground almost yellow, but Mike's attention was on the ten or so men out there. They weren't waiting for them, just milling near flatboats and some heading to the river. Mike realized Clancy was right. Richora was using the tribe to protect his operation, but the man wasn't smart enough to create the rockets, so who did?

He brought Clancy's hand to his lips for a quick kiss, and met her gaze. "Get ready to run."

Eduardo's heart pounded violently, as he waited for his death. He was underground in a narrow hole behind the urn's chamber, and after a brief moment the tremors stopped. He could hear the panicked shouts of his workers and Gil. He tugged on the rope tied to his ankle and shone his flashlight into the area that had collapsed, behind the urn's chamber. The tremors had opened it wider.

Someone tugged at the lead rope around his ankle. "I'm fine, I'm fine," he said and had to shout.

He heard the faint reply. "Professor, please come out. We could have another tremor."

"A moment or two, nothing more. Tug if you get nervous."

Eduardo elbowed his way deeper. It would be much easier if the ceiling wasn't so low. The icons on the stone triangle warned of passing through the tunnel. The depiction was of opening the urn and releasing a death, a plague of sorts. The chemist couldn't understand what it was, and he chose not to open the urn or break the seal. He wasn't superstitious, but so many traps and warnings were wise to heed. Other scholars were balking at his decision, but because the excavation was privately funded, he had the choice. Breaking a seal of human skin kept intact for two thousand years to learn the contents was simply selfish.

The breath of man stolen by the gods still held no logic.

Working forward slowly, he passed between the narrow corridor of stone and knew his wife would chastise him for doing this at his age, but he couldn't ask his students to risk their lives. The rope was taut on his ankle and he was reassured, but cave-diving wasn't his talent. Yet as he pulled himself into the chamber, he understood the path that led him here when he heard voices.

*Voices.*

The realization that he might be in something other than a cave made him cautious. Drug lords were all over the mountains. He shimmied through the opening like a worm, and for only a moment looked up. On his hands and knees, he scrambled into the darkened corner by some boulders under the shadows of a torch. His view was only slightly obstructed, but the scene before him left him breathless.

A village. Alive with movement. Women adorned in gold stirred pots in a communal area, children playing around them, laughing happily. Men converged in conversation, armed with spears and knives, yet beyond them lay a great cavernous mouth, yawing into the sunlight. *It faces west, into the next valley.* The area wasn't inhabited by more than animals. More people vanished in the mountains than the Amazon. Yet here was a society on the edge, surviving. The cavern stretched wider than a football field, the ceiling over a hundred feet high. A maze of staircases led to the homes carved into the wall like a honeycomb.

*Like the ruins in the north.*

They were empty, the people living their daily life in the center of the village. His gaze swept high and left, at the urns secured in holes in the wall, straps anchoring them in. *Like mine,* he thought; then his gaze caught on an old woman, wrapped in a grass mat. With a bone instrument, she adorned an urn much like the one he'd found. How? he wondered. How could this entire society exist under the mountain with no one discovering them all these years? He didn't for a moment believe this was a Moche tribe, but possibly the ancestors who *chose* to live this life. He would find no documented truth here. He didn't wonder if what he'd found initially was false. Carbon dating had ensured against that. But behind it, in the belly of the mountains, they were surviving here, in private peace. It was more than remarkable.

At first, Eduardo thought of the find, what it would do for the culture locked in time, and wanted to study them. Live with them for a time perhaps. But interference would destroy this, and while Moche were barbaric, he didn't think they did many sacrifices since there weren't many people who ventured into this area without a skilled guide. But they could be the reason many vanished. He studied, absorbing as much as he could from the shadows. The modern touches blared back at him.

The metal tools of steel and aluminum, pieces of colored wire. Discards from those who ventured too far into the Andes?

Then he noticed the gray material one man was hammering into a bowl or a shield. The constant hammering would thin the material and allow it to be shaped. The metal technique was a modern one. Then he noticed the number on the underside of it. The crash of some plane, he realized, the one the Peru troops were sent to find and died trying. To protect their way of life, he realized, and they used what came to them.

He felt a tug on his ankle and he instantly made a decision. He turned back, slipping through the opening and working his way to the dig. He would not open the urn.

*Remain undisturbed, my friends.* He would keep the secret. Even from his beloved wife.

Mike bolted for thirty yards, then dropped to the ground. Clancy knelt beside him as a truck pulled up in front of the building, then backed in, a sailcloth canopy hiding it from the road. He pointed, then to his eyes. She saw the machine guns steepled near the building's doors. There was no one near them now, but the warehouse was occupied. Another truck did the same, side by side. The building doors spread wide, men opened the rear of the truck before the engine died. With a forklift, they loaded a pallet onto the first truck, but didn't touch the second.

A bald man hopped out of the second truck and walked to her left toward the river. From behind, Nathan grabbed Mike's shoulder, and he glanced, but only nodded. Clancy saw it in his face. The change was instant, a look of pure hatred. Her gaze followed the short bald man. She didn't recognize him, but that didn't mean anything. All she knew was what was on the news. Mike went into the belly of the beast.

She reached, grabbing his arm and squeezing. He snapped

a look at her and his hard expression instantly melted. He leaned, his mouth near her ear, then whispered one word.

"Hezbollah."

Big terrorists. They made al-Queda look like hazing college kids. They denounced acts like 9/11, then dropped suicide bombs at weddings. A Lebanese militant army with direct ties to Iran and Syria. They had their own TV and radio station, intelligence network, and sleeper cells, teaming up with Hamas and Arafat's Fattah to destroy Israel. When they weren't busy doing that, they helped al-Queda target Americans worldwide. Then she realized the true reason behind Mike's intense expression.

The Marine barracks, Lebanon. Two hundred forty-one killed at once.

Salache adjusted the laptop's angle, and watched the exchange of money sail through cyberspace into his private accounts. Millions. He glanced up, nodded, and the man, a servant really, made a phone call. They could take their wares to their brother in arms, he thought, and Dehnwar would be pleased he could leave now with all the components. The Syrian had been completely annoyed that Salache insisted he oversee the loading. He was a leader of men and it amused Salache to watch him labor like the rest. They wanted his weapon that badly. Dehnwar had lost a shipment in Tunisia, sacrificing his brother, and Salache had millions from the sale. This money would only pad his accounts. Now he could sit back and watch the world struggle to understand his creation and how it could have passed every security test in any country.

It was the reason they paid so much for each one.

A perfectly undetectable weapon. Sold in parts of the whole and assembled from common parts. He'd paid cartels to hold back the drug shipments, and the Americans and Peruvians were watching the jungle breathlessly for more to travel and seize. Timing was essential. Release the forged crates, and they'd find nothing but rocks. He assured all parties that the deal would pass without a single moment of interference from world agencies. And so it was.

He glanced to the right, the wind passing down the mountain and stirring the scent of flowers. The Americans were no longer a problem, and he smiled at the thought of them meeting the tribe underground. If they survived. He'd lived with them for three years, hiding in the mountains till the authorities stopped looking. It had taken years to rebuild; the urns had given him the perfect solution. Fund the dig and he could search for more powder without notice.

A car he recognized skidded to a stop on the dirt road, and he snapped the laptop closed and waved the others off. His wife left the car, storming toward him, and he thought, *She is lovely when she's angry.*

Marianna didn't stop, walking directly to him and slapping his face. He reeled back, feeling his cheek. "Marianna, my face!"

"Whose face are you wearing, Nuat? Because the man who lies to me is not my husband!" She threw the electronic components at his chest and he grabbed at them. He didn't have to look to know what they were and waved for the people to leave and pick up their product.

"That came in the mail. Did you think I was stupid?"

"That you would betray me and go into my lab, yes, that was stupid." He had given her everything a woman needed, a home, children, money, and was furious she'd pried in his affairs.

"I know what you're hiding."

He lifted his gaze to her and she stepped back.

"You went behind my back!" he said, then slapped her so hard she fell to the ground. "You are my wife, you are to obey *me*."

Her eyes flew wide and she felt her love for him bleed away.

The shock that he'd strike her overshadowed that he did it so comfortably. "You made rockets in my factory!"

"Yes. Who'd suspect you?"

Marianna didn't know this man. "You have not escaped your past, Nuat. They know, they are watching." His expression turned molten, and she could almost see the surgeon's scars under his perfect skin.

"Who?" He loomed over her. "Who has spoken to you?"

"A tall man, thin. He's been watching me *and you* for days now." She pushed off the ground, scampering out of his reach. "You swore to me. I trusted you."

"That was *your* mistake."

He grabbed her arm, forced her toward the car, then opened his phone and hit Speed Dial. "Is it done? Is the cargo launched?" He needed the eyes studying this part of the world to watch the rafts, and not him.

"Yes," Richora said cautiously. "Why?"

"We have a guest. Search the area now. Search it now!"

He closed the phone and pushed her into the car, then drove it toward the river.

Mike tapped Nathan, and he signaled Sal. He pointed once at the men and boats. Two went into the cave and brought out a crate on a wheeled wood cart, catching it when it rolled too fast, then unloaded it into a flat-bottomed boat. Rocks. He dismissed the cargo, his interest elsewhere. From his position he could shoot Dehnwar in the head and be done with it.

Tempting, Mike thought, but he needed to know the what and why of this first. He glanced at Clancy. She was staring at the machine guns and started to inch forward. He put a gentle hand on her shoulder. She met his gaze and Mike shook his head. She didn't argue.

They waited as workers loaded crates and the flatboats moved onto the river. No noise, no motors, just a push and one man steered with a pole. The Quechua Indian way. Minus the bright colors, they were dressed like them as well. They didn't push off yet, but Mike would bet anything that they dropped the crates off along the river. They were picked up by another set of people whose only instructions were "go here and drive the car to X spot, leave." It's how sleeper cells worked. Pieces to a puzzle. All but one hidden.

Then he saw Richora. *I owe him,* he thought, turning his attention to the cargo truck. Plain black and no markings. From the air, it couldn't be seen well in this area because the rain forest hung heavy near the river's edge. From a satellite, the trucks would be difficult to follow in daylight. Mike needed inside the building to see what was so important they faked a drug shipment as a distraction. If DEA types seized more than one shipment of rocks, someone would get wise. Why wait?

Mike slowly removed his GPS from his pocket. It was on in seconds and showing him the last map. They were damn close to Gantz's calculations. He noticed several text messages from Jansen, but Mike couldn't waste his battery to answer, not now. The rocket was fired from somewhere in the immediate area, and when Richora shouted something and moved farther downriver, Mike shot across the road and into the warehouse.

He ducked inside and turned, nearly catching Clancy in the chest.

"Jesus," he hissed, pushing her behind him.

"Get me one of those." She pointed to the rifles, her gaze on the people near the river. They were so close they could hear the swish of boots in the mud as Richora stomped upriver.

Mike moved back, and side by side, Nathan and Sal ran across. They retreated into the building, stepping slowly. Every sound was magnified and Mike circled.

Crates were open. A staging area? They only loaded one

truck. The light coming from the doorway wasn't enough to see clearly, and suddenly voices grew closer. They ducked behind the stacks as two of Richora's men shut the doors. The slam of the locks clanked heavily. Not good. The trucks and cars pulled away and Mike looked through cracks to see the vehicles drive off. He drew his knife and stabbed it into the seam of the tin wall, cutting an inverted L, and then carefully ripped the metal like a can opener. Light spilled in.

Mike felt a ticking clock radiate up his spine. The trucks were full and en route. With Dehnwar driving. He'd get it out of the country the fastest way possible. A plane. But they were on foot without direction or ammo.

Scowling at the crates, Mike decided he'd blow this up for good measure, then pulled out the section of black block that Jansen had sent him, and picked one out of the crate. He compared the pieces.

"Where did you get that?" Clancy whispered.

"It was in the evidence we pulled from a mission in Libya."

Clancy looked between the men and the parts. "That means they've already shipped this stuff out once."

"At least." He noticed the gold markings, the Inca look of it, and tried to make it gel in his head. "Kilos of dope and souvenirs?"

"Yeah, I don't get it either." Clancy pushed aside shredded paper and studied two pieces. They were larger and shaped like a temple. "Nothing fits. Can you crush it?" she whispered.

He squeezed. "It gives."

"Plastics and graphite, maybe?" Her gaze ripped over the pieces, and she grabbed up three and worked them for a moment.

When they started to fit together, he glanced at Krane, arching a brow. She held a curved piece of black material like a portion of pipe, yet broader. "It looks like a fuselage," he said.

"Or a vase." She tried to break the pieces apart. "It's locked in place." She picked up another and tried to fit them. "Why pieces and why bendable? If it's a weapon, it's useless. Bullets and fuel combusts for thrust, but it would melt this."

"There was no heat signature," Mike reminded her.

"Impossible," she said.

"He's right, Clancy," Nathan said. "We never saw it coming. It was suddenly just there and hit. This stuff is just storage till they can load it."

"They already did." Mike moved quickly around the building, inspecting each box, and found the empty pallets. "Did the truck pick up both or just the souvenirs? What is this shit?"

"Hey, Boy Scout." Mike looked across to her. "What's that look like to you?" Her hands were wrapped around the black material already locked together.

A nose cone, black with a gold center.

# Nineteen

"Good God," Mike said, glaring at the boxes. "They're rockets."

"Oh yeah, that's it," Krane said, touching the nose cone. "Christ, they'll try anything to kill us, huh?"

"I want to see the glue for this."

"They wouldn't need it," Krane said and took the nose cone and started adding pieces. "It's like a jet, like the SR-71, stealth. Leaks like crazy till the fast pressure of a launch expands the seals and locks it tight. The give in it makes the seal even tighter. Man, that's some clever designing."

"I have a vacuum like that," Clancy said dryly. She grabbed several and kept fitting them together. "They're marked with the gold. See, there's the primer." She showed the array of hieroglyphics on the sides. "It tells you which one is the first one. Then you can assemble them." She worked quickly, then held up a long narrow black rocket. The men just stared. "It's almost weightless." She put it on her shoulder. "The latest in your terrorists' fashion accessory."

"It's just a toy without fuel, and combustion would break it," Mike said, watching out of the hole. "Sal, get us out of here," he said, and while Sal worked on opening the wall farther, Clancy asked for his knife, then cut the plastic kilo. It spilled like salt onto the ground.

"It's not cocaine." She scooped some on the edge of her

knife and carefully sniffed. They all looked at her. "Well"— she flushed with embarrassment—"it's not." She wasn't tempted, there were other things that gave her a bigger high, she thought with a glance at Mike. She tapped it onto the ground, then checked three different pallets. "It's all the same, not coke. Not crack, either. And it's too sandy colored. Pure is white."

Mike eyed her for a second. She shrugged and grabbed several pieces, stuffing them in her pack. She zipped, tugging the straps higher.

"No ignitions, no components? Guidance system? Without it, they can't do anything. It's just a shell." Clancy hesitated before she added, "What if the guts of these things are already where they needed to be?"

"You're just full of optimism today," Mike said.

"Some-assembly-required bombs don't give me the warm fuzzies."

"Gannon," Sal said, and Mike went to him. He pointed to the river. "About thirty five yards to the right." Mike strained to see, and his eyesight sharpened and pinpointed the small rocket.

"They're set on the perimeter." Those had guidance systems.

"They could remote-launch," Mike said and acknowledged the two men having a smoke instead of patrolling the area. "Let's get out of here."

"Mike," Clancy said softly. "Something's happening here."

He followed the direction of her gaze to the ground. Walking back and forth hard stirred up mud, making the ground soggy. It didn't hurt the cargo raised off the ground on pallets, but the ground was a wet puddle. The fine particles poured in a gentle spill from dozens of packages—and changed.

The powder emulsified, and swelled. Mike felt a pulling sensation in the air around him, speeding past his skin as more powder spilled and bubbled.

Then he felt the tug on his eardrums and winced.

"Sal, get us out, now!"

"Almost there."

Mike turned and fired at the lock, then forced the door open. He held his hand out for Clancy, latching tight and running. "The river!"

She jerked back. "No, no!"

He pulled her anyway. "I'll keep you alive."

"That's what you said last time!"

Mike snapped his arm around her waist and dove into the water, swimming one-armed to pull them deeper. Clancy floated up and he held her down. She slapped at his hands, shoved at him, trying to reach the surface. Mike held her underwater, giving her his air.

He felt it. The pull like the surge in a tideless river. The water above his head curled, drawing back like a wave before it crashes. But the crash never came, the water settling. Mike broke the surface with Clancy.

"It's okay, it's okay," he said and pushed her hair back, making her breathe.

"Stop scaring me like that," she said, throwing her arms around his neck and clinging. Nathan and Sal bobbed to the surface.

Mike looked over her shoulder, and she felt the sudden stillness in him and twisted.

"Now I've seen everything," she said.

The building was crushed like a soda can. She could see the shape of the cargo under it, but the metal was pulled around it like kitchen foil, the paint peeled off in spots and gleaming silver gray. From the once-open doors, packages of the powder still tumbled out, but intact.

She pushed out of his arms and waded to the bank. "Look at the grass, the leaves."

Mike's gaze slid all around them. The forest was dead, the leaves on the trees and bushes almost transparent, squeezed dry of life. Yet the thrust of the eruption put rocks into the skins of trees like decorations. Mike tried flicking one off, but it was buried so deep he had to pry it with his knife.

Clancy tromped out of the river, water dripping off her and puddling. "How did it ignite?"

"Water."

They looked at Mike.

"That's the only thing that touched it. Water."

"But they didn't." Clancy gestured to the two bodies on the bank. She moved toward them and knelt as Mike came to her. "Like the Peru troops and your pilot." She met his gaze. "Dried up." The faces were caught in a scream, their skin papery and drawn nearly bloodless.

"It sucks air," Nathan said as he and Sal stripped the dead of weapons and clothing. "But look at this." He gestured to the kilos. "Half of it is still undamaged."

"It has to be saturated to emulsify like it did," Clancy said.

Mike jerked a look up the mountain. "Someone heard that."

Clancy jumped to her feet. Over a mile away, the trucks had stopped on the hill, but Richora's car fishtailed around it and barreled back toward them. "I hate company."

She looked at him so trustingly, Mike felt honored. The four hurried deeper into the jungle.


Howard Gantz drove recklessly. It was the only way he knew how. He pushed harder on the gas, the scenery zipping past like a smear of green and the brown of Peru. It was more than his chance to get Renoux out of the picture. If this stuff made it to international waters and was shot down, it could destroy the ecosystem and anyone living. They just didn't know. *They didn't know.*

*Give me a nuke any day,* he thought. *Then I know what I'm up against.* He swerved to avoid an ox and cart, the young man cursing him. Renoux was probably burning files and stashing contraband by now.

He grabbed his phone and dialed. "Colonel Jansen."

"It's not a—"

"No, listen. Renoux told Gannon someone wanted space on his aircraft. He didn't meet him, but whatever he was transporting Renoux didn't want to move. So they paid Renoux five million for that jet. They bought it."

"How'd you find this out?"

Gantz looked at his bloody knuckles and said, "Persuasion." Then said, "Sir. The jet's on the flight deck waiting for clearance."

"Gannon?"

"No idea. But that plane can't take off."

He ran more than two miles. All of it uphill.

Antone stopped behind a tree to catch his breath, wishing he didn't have to leave his car far back on the dirt road, but the truck had turned off the divided highway. Catching up without being seen zapped the rest of his strength, and he licked his lips, then swiped his sleeve across his forehead. He could honestly say that Peru was hotter than Lebanon.

He pushed off, trying to outdistance the truck. At two miles an hour, it rolled up the uneven road, rocking violently, but it was still faster than him. He'd seen the Americans. Military, he decided, by the way they moved, and he wouldn't step in unless they were in trouble. He'd no idea of their part in this, but gaining trust under gunfire was never easily done. He rushed between the trees when he heard a sound and his ears itched. The truck halted, rolling backward for a moment, then straining to get it over a small rise. The lead truck, a big Chevy with massive wheels, made a hard right and headed back down the hill toward the river. Antone slowed, wiggled his finger in his ears as he stopped to catch his breath, then look back toward the river. He couldn't see much beyond the car.

For all he knew, the Americans were executing an assault and capture.

But Dehnwar was his prey alone.

Clancy hurried downriver, any cover disintegrated in the blast. Well. Not actually a blast. She wished she could have seen it. Another moment for some therapy, she thought, but a material that implodes on itself? When it reacts to water? For a moment her mind tripped over the possibilities for it. Then she thought, *It's got something to do with these caves.* Most of the kilos were stored in there and why else would they meet here at the building and load only half the trucks? They had parts, not the whole. Random items to anyone looking, and she had to assume the genius behind this had packaged that powder in a safer method. Or left it up to the buyer.

Untraceable. *God.*

The sheer magnitude of chaos this would cause was as dangerous as the powder itself. It stole life from all things. Sucked the breath. If it could do this much damage in the jungle, then what if it didn't have a resource? No air to take?

Mike touched her shoulder to stop her, and they knelt and turned. The line of the shore wound slightly, the cascades of the river smothering sound.

Clancy tried not to flinch when a snake slid over her boot. But Mike was there, cutting off its head and tossing it behind him. *My hero,* she mouthed, and he smiled and watched the land. Crouched low, she wished for her ball cap, but it was somewhere in the mountain turning into a relic. Her knee sank into the wet earth, and she put her hand back for balance and hit something hard. Twisting, she pushed aside ferns and water grass, then nudged Mike.

He didn't seem surprised to see the black rocket inside a small launcher. It was portable, breaking down into the precision-cut pieces. The launcher itself was no broader than a spare tire. She jolted when Mike yanked it off the launcher pad and laid it down.

"Can you remember how they fit?" she whispered, glancing upriver.

"You want to know how it works? Isn't it bad enough that it does?"

"Exactly why I want to see inside." Clancy studied the long slender rocket. The finish was smooth with bits of gold inlaid where the primer markings showed. She laid it on its side and twisted the nose cone. It unlocked and she tipped it. A clear plastic cylinder slid out. In the center of it was a vial of water surrounded with the powder. A lithium battery created the small charge to a simple lever that would break the vial and ignite the powder. The compression forced against natural gravity, but encased, it would try to break free and create thrust. One moment of incredible power yet with no explosives. *God, if they put C4 in this, it would be far more deadly.*

She immediately reached for the mechanism at the bottom. He stopped her. "I know what I'm doing." She plucked a small green chip out of the base.

"Geeks," he said, rolling his eyes.

"It's satellite remote."

Great. Mike gave up getting a look at it, and signaled Krane and DiFazio. They moved farther out and located five rockets, all strategically placed on this side of their operation. Suddenly, Mike leaped on her, pushing her down before a big all-terrain truck rushed down the hill and slammed to a hard stop. Richora was out of the tall truck, limping slightly as he and two other men walked the shore and called for the dead. When he found them, he cursed and drew his weapon. He searched for tracks, moving into the water, wading slowly. Flat on the ground, Mike saw the top of his head first and aimed.

He was nearly on Mike's position when he turned back suddenly. Mike didn't see the long, luxurious car rocking down the dirt road, till it slid sideways for a few feet before stopping. A man left the car, striding quickly to the passenger side and dragging a dark haired woman out. Clearly she didn't want to be here, Mike thought, and the man thrust her away from him so hard she stumbled. Richora rushed to help her.

Mike signaled his men, then leaned down to whisper in her ear, "Stay low, I'll be right back."

She frowned at him, then noticed the three men climb out of Richora's car, split apart, and cover a wide area with machine pistols. Mike had a few rounds. But she didn't question and slunk low as he moved deeper into the forest. She didn't hear them, only the slow slide of water and the breeze whispering at the treetops. After a few moments, a soft *crack* made her wince, but couldn't look or she'd be exposed. Yet she knew what the guys were doing.

Evening the odds.

Marianna shoved out of Alejo's arms and glared, revolted. "You are part of this," she said in a dead voice. "I had hoped not, Alejo."

His gaze narrowed. "I am in it for the money, Marianna, and nothing more."

"And you think that matters? You're helping him sell them. To who? Who will die because of your money?" She didn't want an answer, and looked him over as if he were a rodent. "You disgust me, both of you."

Richora's crushed look gained Salache's attention, and his gaze bounced between the pair.

"You love her," he said, then strode back and forth along the shore. "You're in love with my wife."

"I could never love a man who did this." She grabbed Nuat's arm. "Do you hear me?"

He looked at her as if surprised to see her.

"I never knew you, did I?"

He stared at her for a moment. Then his gaze darted to the building, the cars, then stopped on her again. There was no wound in his eyes, she thought, no remorse for all the lies and deception. Yet she could tell by his expression he was searching his mind for a way to correct his mistake. Fear clutched at her lungs. She was the mistake. She back-stepped from him.

"No one knew me." Without preamble, he lifted his gun and pulled the trigger.

"No!" Richora leaped into the path of the bullet, the impact knocking him off his feet. He landed half in the water.

Marianna screamed and fell, then rushed across the ground and dragged him out of the muddy Amazon. She cradled his head on her lap and covered the gaping hole in his chest. "Alejo," she said softly. "Why?"

"Your babies need their mother," he said, blood curling out his mouth.

She glared at Nuat. "*Bastardo.*"

"Yes, well, that should have been you, dear. I still needed him for a little longer."

Marianna's gaze drifted past her husband to the large man moving out of the jungle and onto the shore. Nuat spun and his moment's hesitation cost him. The man fired, the bullet hitting his leg and buckling him to his knees.

Salache covered his wound and fired his own gun, and missed, then corrected his aim as the man advanced. Salache frowned, confused for a moment.

"Remember me?" the man said.

Choufani moved parallel to the truck, a few feet out so Dehnwar couldn't see him coming. Dehnwar dragged on a cigarette, then harshly blew out the smoke, his arm hanging out the window. Antone's gaze stopped briefly on the back of his hand, scarred with a deep gash in the explosion that killed his sister. He was there, nearby, had watched his bombs kill. He wore that wound with pride, that he'd touched the heat of his own bombs and lived.

Antone remained hidden, and inside, his job warred with his heart. His duty to his country and its people, or to Islam to eradicate these extremists who ruined more lives than the ones they took. He would never stop, never, he thought. Even with the satisfaction of a kill.

He pushed past the tree line, and Dehnwar turned his head, frowning and raising a pistol. Choufani kept walking around the front of the vehicle, and tapped the door.

"Fatima Choufani," he said loudly as he passed and kept walking. He would die as his sister had. Horribly.

From his pocket, he pulled a small cell phone and turned, walking backward. He waited until Dehnwar opened the truck door, stood on the running board, unaware of the explosives stuck to the truck door.

Antone smiled. "Peace be upon her." He hit the button.

Rashid ibn al-Dehnwar didn't find his virgins.

Nuat's eyes narrowed, then flared hotly. He struggled to stand, blood pooling on the ground and inside his expensive shoe.

"I'd recognize that monkey walk anywhere, Alvarez. They let you into the Shining Path because of that pretty new face?"

Salache said nothing, glancing for a way out. "Shoot him." Nothing happened. "Shoot him!" he screamed, looking around.

Mike smirked and shrugged, then tossed the dismantled rocket on the ground between them. "Guess you're out of options."

Salache fumed, his plan vanishing like the jungle mist.

The ground shook with the explosion, then one more. Mike could smell the burning fuel already, yet he never took his gaze off Alvarez. "Krane." Mike didn't have to tell him to check that.

"I'm on it."

As Krane trotted off, Mike adjusted his aim. Alvarez chambered a bullet and pointed the gun at his wife's temple.

"Lay the gun down or I shoot her," Alvarez said.

Mike ignored him. "A third-generation American trying to connect with his roots? Is that it, *Neil?*"

"Neil is dead."

The creepy little bastard might have a new disguise with his skin stretched Mach 1 tight, but it was still Alvarez. "I never thought so. Let her go and drop the gun."

"Nuat? What is he talking about?" his wife said. "Tell me."

He jerked her head back. "You don't need to know, my love."

Mike remained where he was, near the car, and Alvarez came toward him, dragging the woman.

"Move back! I'll shoot her."

"And I'll cut your head off with this," Mike said and took one step toward the crushed building and almost groaned when he saw movement behind Alvarez. *What the hell is that woman doing now?* Then he saw the launcher on her back as she slipped into the cave.

Clancy breathed hard as she struggled in the tunnel. The rocket might be light, but the launcher sure as hell wasn't. She put the rocket down, then pushed at her purse straps holding the launcher on her back. It slid off and clunked to the ground. By the strap, she dragged it to the middle of the chamber, then went back for the rocket and anchored it.

Surrounded by kilos of the powder made her nervous and she looked around for something to carry water, moving back toward the dead Indians and doing a creeped-out dance around them. She cupped her hands at the stream in the wall, drank, then looked for something to hold water or crack it and flood the chamber. She tried digging at the wall, but only dirt would budge. *Really wishing for nano help here,* she thought, then rushed to the rocket and positioned it to hit the crack.

Then she walked through the kilos and slashed her knife down the stacks. Salt-like powder poured and mounded.

Then she dug in her pocket for Mike's shattered satellite phone. She reconnected the wires and pulled a chip, then inserted the one from the first rocket they'd found.

Now they were on the same circuit, and since it was a remote, this should work. The phone's lithium battery was still undamaged. The powder couldn't get out of here. In the hands of anyone, even her own country, they'd screw it up. Highly toxic, it killed anything it touched and was fine enough to be inhaled and collapse lungs, or destroy the rain forest with a single thunderstorm.

*Bury it. Let those Indians live alone and keep this stuff.*

She moved toward the tunnel and was nearly at the entrance when something caught her eye. She turned, and on steps that led nowhere a young man stood. Her Indian, she thought. A red band wrapped his head, his body still painted, and a spear in his hands. Across the distance he met her gaze, his attention moving to the rocket, then to the powder.

*He's confused,* she thought and shooed him back. "Go deep into the caves," she said in Spanish, but that didn't seem to register. She shooed him again and smiled. He turned and pushed an icon on the wall. Rock on stone scratched softly and he slipped between the layers of granite.

She moved back to the entrance, ready to detonate.

Mike's heart pounded wildly when Clancy disappeared into the caves. *I swear* . . . But he couldn't drag her ass out of there and kept his attention on Alvarez. The man was jumpy and sweating, and while the face didn't match, the voice and manner sure did. The more he spoke, the faster his accent faded.

"It's already gone," Alvarez said. "You can't stop it."

Mike went still, the cold metal of his rifle near Alvarez's cheek. *Jesus.* "Drop the gun."

"That's the second shipment," he said, nodding to the truck on the hill, smiling and smug.

"Now I know what to look for," Mike said. "Drop the weapon!"

"Not unless you can make a plane in—" Alvarez looked at his watch, swinging the gun. "Eleven minutes."

*Oh, shit.* Mike knew it was useless to even ask. "Which airport?"

"Now, that's the tricky part."

The shot rang out, and Mike stepped back. In his line of vision, he saw Richora with a clean hole in his head. A knife lay inches from Mike's foot. Sniper. But it was enough for Alvarez to grab his wife.

"Put the gun down or I'll shoot her!"

Mike believed him; he'd already tried once. "Take it easy. Okay." He bent to lay the gun at his feet, releasing it slowly. "Easy, let her go, Neil. She's—"

Alvarez fired at Mike's hand, the bullet hitting the pistol and knocking it away. Toasted, Mike thought, with a glance. The trigger was shattered.

"She's my wife."

"Mother of your children?" Mike said. Get them where it hurts.

But he didn't falter. "All part of the big picture."

It was a cover. All of it. To hide from his crimes. Mike knew the moment his wife understood. Her hand moved toward his crotch.

The woman slammed her fist back into his nuts. Alvarez buckled with a scream, and the woman twisted away as Mike grabbed a kilo of powder, punctured the plastic with his fingers, and threw.

It hit Alvarez in the face, covering him in a fine dust. He froze. His gaze darted to the water and he inched back. "No!"

Then Mike heard the slide of several weapons. From the river, men appeared, armed to the teeth and aiming at him. Shining Path, he realized. Alvarez smiled and brushed at the dust, his eyes looking large in the chalky face.

"You didn't think it was just me alone, did you?"

The woman scrambled far back till Mike couldn't see her behind Richora's truck. Beyond him, Clancy stood at the entrance to the cave, then moved sideways away from it.

She didn't see the man on the rise above her, aiming at her back.

*Oh, Jesus.*

"Kill him," Alvarez ordered. "Now!"

"Behind you!" Mike shouted and dove into the river, then instantly turned, driving his hand across the water and shooting a spray at Alvarez.

Clancy twisted and saw only the barrel of the rifle. She bolted downhill from the cave toward the water, toward Mike. Before she hit the water, she pushed SEND and crashed into the river, muddy brown liquid swirling around her like coffee. She swam deep as bullets discharged into the water around her. But her buoyancy brought her back up and more bullets pierced the water.

Alvarez screamed, his skin shrinking, and Mike dove under, strong arms digging, and he barely felt the tremor under the water. He punched through the surface.

The cave didn't explode.

It ruptured like a breaking wound. Thousands of gallons of water shot out the entrance like strip mining, taking rocks and debris to the edge of the ground and pouring into the river. The strength of it pushed rebels off their feet, the sweeping current cleaning the slate of Shining Path. But there were more men firing at nothing, a wild spray of dangerous bullets. Alvarez writhed on the ground, clawing at his face as it shriveled. The powder emulsified on his face, sucking in his skin, and he inhaled it. With the moisture in his lungs, they collapsed in seconds.

Mike looked for Clancy as the cave, in one indrawn breath, imploded in on itself, corking the entrance and sealing it. He felt a grip on his shirt and grabbed it. The small wrist bones told him it was Clancy. He yanked her to the surface. The moment was lost at the crack of gunfire. Clancy dove again and Mike saw a man drop to his knees, then his face, a hole in his forehead. He looked for the shooter, ducking when gunfire sparked again. He saw movement underwater and grabbed Clancy, yanking her up. A bullet hit the tree and Mike twisted away with her.

"I thought I got them."

"Most of them," he said, then kissed her hard. "That was brave, honey. Now stop it."

Bullets chipped at the tree and, Mike's back to it, he kept Clancy in front of him and wondered where Krane and Sal were. Mike had nothing, his gun under gallons of water, his pack thirty yards away. "We have to run."

"No, really?"

"Alvarez said there was a shipment leaving now."

"How long before it leaves?"

"In eleven minutes. Three minutes ago."

"Oh, man."

"Hell, isn't it?" he said, then moved behind the crushed building. Hip deep in water, his legs dragged, but Mike could see his pack. At least he had explosive in there. He hoped.

"We need that truck." He pointed.

Clancy looked at the souped-up man-truck, black with giant wheels. Lots of chrome. Boy, Richora was really countering for something teeny.

But it was in the open and everyone wanted them dead.

Hank Jansen didn't wait for a meeting of the Joint Chiefs, nor for Cook to point fingers at Miss McRae. He went straight to the top. If heads were going to roll, it better start there. Hank passed through three security checks. Even with his face and name listed on the wall, he appreciated the thoroughness of the Marine guard.

He stepped into the Office of the Secretary of the Navy. The older man was behind his desk, standing, reading, his glasses low on his nose. He looked over them. "Hank, it's good to see you."

They shook hands. "Did you read over the information I sent you?"

"I was wondering why that didn't go through channels. You thought because she's my daughter I'd smother it."

"No, sir, because what she's created is sensitive. That she's your daughter never occurred to me."

Daniel smiled slightly and gestured to the seat.

He stared across the wide desk and said bluntly, "We have a viable threat, sir, but we have pieces from three agencies." He held out a file.

"And you're trying to fit them." He reached for the paperwork and read, leaning back in his leather chair till it creaked. "These photos are digital. Who took them?"

"Interpol, Antone Choufani. He checks out, and he's seen my team, line of sight with them in Peru minutes ago." Within inches of a skilled killer. Hank thought the photo of a dead Dehnwar was suitable for framing right next to Saddam Hussein.

The SecNav looked at him over the glasses. "The four lost? The UAV?"

"UAV was destroyed, as well as the Hellfires, and the chopper. Two men dead, and the rest survived."

"Because of this technology Clancy created."

"Quite possibly."

"God, she'll be hard to live with now," he muttered, and Hank chuckled. "Cook's part in this confirmed?"

"Yes, sir." Gantz had come in handy for more than just some lousy passport photos. The phone records off the hitter's cell gave them all they needed. "Cook might have made a call from Yates's lab, but it wasn't the first one and Gantz traced it."

Daniel McRae tensed and Hank could tell underneath the cool exterior was a father furious someone tried to hurt his little girl. He sat up sharply and reached for the phone. "Let's get the troops back first. Then we'll sort it out."

"No, sir, there isn't any time."

The SecNav looked up.

"It's going to be in Peru airspace in a few minutes."

"Let them shoot it down."

"We can't."

Daniel frowned.

"It's more than just pieces that create the weapons. It's the fuel."

McRae listened. Halfway through an explanation that was vague at best, he stopped him. "He needs to hear this now."

He dialed the Secretary of Defense and hoped today the channels opened. Alerting everyone from Secret Service to Homeland Security and the Border Patrol would send people into a high alert. America needed to be notified and the Peru Air Force needed to scramble jets. Now.

While he waited for the pickup Daniel glanced at the photo of his daughter on the corner of his desk, shaking his head. "Troublemaker," he muttered, then spoke quickly to his boss.

Marianna inched under the truck, kicking off her shoes and pulling her body toward the driver's door. Bullets hit around her and she chanted a prayer as she rolled out from under the truck. Alejo's face was inches from her and she bit back a yelp, then grabbed the knife left on the ground. She rose to her knees, pulling open the door, and was relieved the keys were still in the ignition. She climbed up, stabbing the seat with the knife for leverage, and got behind the wheel. A bullet hit the glass and the windshield fractured. She ducked, and turned over the engine.

The door jerked open and the American jumped in with a woman.

"Hi," Clancy said. "Mind if we borrow this?"

The woman didn't say anything, quickly moving out of

the seat. Keeping low, Mike slid across her, forcing her back, and shifted behind the wheel. Slumped in the seat, he put it in reverse and stepped on the gas.

The truck wheels spun on the wet ground, then shot backward, climbing up the hill.

"Your men!"

"They'll be all right. Look for a phone. That plane can't leave the ground."

The truck hit something, and Mike shot upright into the seat, cursing. The other truck had been blown to pieces, and a body hung on the door. He shifted gears and gave it gas, then turned the truck sharply to the left. The big wheels bucked, pushing it nearly on its side, and Clancy leaned as if it would help. The truck landed hard and Mike accelerated, plastering them to the seats.

"Duck!" he warned before he punched the cracked windshield, pushing away shattered glass. Wind beat inside the truck as Clancy searched the vehicle. She met his gaze. "No phone."

"Then we have to stop the plane."

"How long do we have now?"

Mike glanced at his watch. "Three minutes."

"Pull over, we'll call. Okay, okay," she said when he put up three fingers. She grabbed his pack, zipping it open. "Your GPS thing, it sends text messages, right?"

"Yeah."

She worked it with her thumbs with lightning speed, and Mike told her what to write. She sent it and confirmed.

"Keep sending it."

"You've got a message from Gantz." She read it. "It's Renoux's plane."

"There it is." He nodded ahead and didn't wait for the airport gate to open and plowed through it. Hard metal and link fences smacked the truck. "You have to drive."

"Oh God," she said.

Mike bounced the truck over a band of landing lights and

onto the flight deck. The cargo jet was on the end of the runway.

"That? You want to stop that! It's as big as a C-130."

"If it gets over Peru airspace and they shoot it down, then what? That powder will rain on every living thing for miles. And if the wind takes it, the people in San José de Lourdes won't have a chance."

"Shoot it over international waters, then."

"God knows what that would cause. A waterspout? Tidal wave?" He shook his head. "Our guys can't cross Peru airspace without permission, and that will take too long. They wouldn't be here in time anyway. No one knows about it. No one but us."

He kept his foot on the gas and a hand on the wheel as they switched places and Clancy sank into the big seat. She could barely see over the dash.

"Maintain speed." Mike ripped into the pack, pulled out the explosives.

"What are you doing with that? Oh no. No. Mike, you can't."

But he'd already set it. The green numbers glowed.

"Do you think throwing that at a speeding plane will do the trick?"

"No. I have to get closer."

"How much?" She was right on its tail.

"Lots."

She glanced at him and understood the choices. None. "Tell me what you need."

"Stay right of the jet engines and under the wing. I'm going for the landing gear. Go, go!"

She pushed harder on the gas and thought of several reasons not to do this, but with no way around it. The plane was moving too fast to catch up and then jump, and crashing it into the plane would explode them and the aircraft. He was right. It was taxiing and gaining speed, a gray elephant loaded to the gills with crates of weapons—and the powder.

Clancy tightened her grip on the steering wheel, her foot straining on the gas pedal. "Mike, the timer." She nodded to it on the seat beside her.

"It's a remote and already set."

"It only has ninety seconds!"

"Clancy." She looked at him sideways, speeding toward the moving plane.

"I know," she said over the noise, her eyes tearing.

He held her gaze for a second, memorized the wind pushing at her hair, the way her one look let him see her heart. Part of him was glad for the moments they'd had, but he was dying inside. This was a fine time to fall in love with her, he thought, then crawled over the dash and out the broken front window of the truck, squinting against the wind. He rose to stand like a hood ornament and knew he had to get higher.

Shouting over the noise of the jet was useless, and he waved to her to keep up the speed. He tried to stand, even the small dips in the tarmac making him struggle for balance. The roar of the engines was deafening and the heat of the jet wash scorched his face. She drove under the wings, then jerked the wheel when Peru fighter jets came over the tops of the mountains and swooped into the valley.

When she broke a hundred miles an hour the truck shook. Mike concentrated on the hole around the wheel hub as they moved closer. Closer. He drew a breath, bent to squat, and hoped this damn nano shit worked. He jumped, grabbing onto the undercarriage, and he slipped, hanging from one arm for a moment, wind and speed batting him like a scarf. The truck faded back as he hooked his leg on the wheel hub, the vibration rattled his teeth and eyesight.

Peruvian fighter jets came in for the attack.

The aircraft's nose tipped up, the engine straining to lift. Mike stretched his reach, slapped the explosive pack on the gear, then jammed in the detonator.

But the plane was already lifting off the ground.

# Twenty

The truck rolled to a stop while the plane sped toward the end of the runway. Peruvian fighter jets crisscrossed overhead to keep it from leaving the ground, riddling the wings with bullets.

Clancy couldn't think beyond *he's in there.*

She looked down at the timer and blinked back the hot rush of tears. *This is so unfair,* she thought, watching the green numbers tick off the last seconds. The plane lifted off. It rose a hundred feet per second.

Still, no Mike.

The door threw open and Nathan stuck his head inside. "He didn't, oh shit, he did."

"It's got seconds," she said. "Stop it, Nathan. Please." She held out the timer. "Abort it."

Nathan glanced between her and the timer, then grabbed it. "There's no fail-safe!" he shouted over the scream of jets. "Damn him!"

The last three seconds ticked off.

The explosion ripped through the aircraft, tearing the belly. The jet went down and Clancy jerked back at the bright flash. The nose of the aircraft dragged on the runway. Then the impact ignited the fuel as the fuselage collapsed, pulling in and destroying the sleek shape.

"There's no air," Nathan said. "There's no air!"

It scraped along the trees, knocking them down like matchsticks and gouging the hillside. It jerked to the right, its nose plowing into the mountain. The impact buckled the metal, stopping it as flames licked at the walls, at all of it.

"The fire's eating the air and there's no water to make the powder work," Nathan said.

Clancy didn't hear him. She understood words like *stricken. Devastated.* She forced herself to get out of the truck, then step away from it. The wind pushed at her clothes as she stared at the flaming aircraft. Then she sank to the ground, her head in her hands. She choked on her tears, tears for the man, for the lover, for the scattered moments in this intimate danger they might have made into more. Any man she *felt* she loved, well, she didn't. *I barely got the chance.*

She sobbed, needles of pain racing over her body and she couldn't draw in enough air. "Oh, Michael."

She pushed to her feet, yet couldn't take her eyes off the wreckage. A scream bubbled in her throat, the agony of losing him too much to bear.

"Damn you, Michael!" she said to herself and couldn't watch anymore. A luxurious car slammed to a stop and emptied. They all stared at the wreckage. Clancy couldn't bear it. There was no way he could have survived, and that he gave up his life, just pissed her off.

The woman who'd hidden in the back of the truck climbed out.

Clancy leaned against the truck, the engine hot and smoking as she cried.

"Clancy?" Nathan said, touching her shoulder.

She rolled into his arms, and sobbed harder, and his grip tightened as if to shield her from the pain. Then suddenly it relaxed. Nathan nudged her and she met his gaze. He inclined his head to the airstrip and Clancy turned. From the curls of black smoke, a figure limped. Though he was far away, Clancy didn't need any more than that.

She ran.

*   *   *

His entire body aching, Mike took his time, smiling as she ran toward him, and he thought, *Doesn't get better than this.* To anyone else, she looked like hell, muddy, her clothing torn, her hair wild, but to Mike, she was a piece of heaven. He opened his arms for her, taking her in the chest like a football. He staggered back, ignoring the pain in his ribs as he crushed her to him, closing his eyes.

She sobbed into the curve of his throat. "Oh, Michael."

"It's okay, baby, I'm okay," he said softly.

"Stop scaring me like that!"

"Last time, I swear."

She looked at him. "Yeah, right," she said, tears rolling down her cheeks. He swiped his thumb over one, then kissed her.

He broke apart inside, her passion locking everything else out, and he crushed her to him, wanting only more of her. Then it changed, the kiss softening as if they both suddenly knew they'd never had to rush another moment together.

"Give you ideas?" she said, still kissing him.

He chuckled. "A few."

"Good. I need some pampering."

"And a shower."

"We can start there."

He smiled against her mouth. Just imagining the wet slide of soap on her got him locked and loaded for a good ravishing. "God, I love your world."

"It's quieter than yours."

She kissed him as firefighters sped past to the plane. "Think we should tell them about not using water?"

Mike glanced. "No, oddly, fire is its worst enemy."

"This week water was mine."

He went still and caught her face in his palms. He opened his mouth to say something, but the words struggled.

"You love me, I know," she said.

He grinned. He couldn't help it. "You assume a lot, Irish."

"No, Mike Gannon. *I don't.*" Her mouth came within inches of his and she said, "Do I?"

He almost smiled, but it was the tremor in her voice, the uncertainty that took his breath away. He never wanted her to suffer that again. "No, Irish. I do love you."

She smiled brightly, jumped up, and kissed him. Mike admitted a lot of things in that moment: that she was the best thing to happen to him, the perfect match. He'd been around the world nine times, seen beauty and horror, and kept himself on the rim of living, on the edge of the world.

Her way was a lot better.

Colonel Hank Jansen closed his cell phone, releasing a long tired breath. The plane was destroyed and Clancy McRae was alive with Gannon. She couldn't be in better hands, he thought, standing inside Carl Cook's office, watching an officer of the Naval Criminal Investigation Service put him in restraints. Cook said nothing, his eyes forward as MPs on either side of him gripped his arms and escorted him to the brig.

More NCIS passed them in the hall and seized everything. In the elevator, Hank stepped inside, staring at Cook.

"You think you've won."

"I wasn't in competition, Carl."

"It needed to be tested in the field. We don't have time to waste when we're against mass killers like al-Qaeda."

"We'll do exactly what we need to. Without lying to our servicemen, and using them for lab rats." The door opened and Jansen stepped out, waiting and watching as they put Cook in the back of a military SUV.

Bad rubbish, Hank thought and suddenly needed to see his family.

They were several yards from the truck when a figure moved from behind the cluster of cars and people, a rifle slung on his shoulder. The lean, scrappy kid strolled like a hillbilly looking for some Yankees to scare.

Mike wrapped his arm around Clancy and said, "Meet J.J. Palmer, the sniper." Mike just stared at the kid, impressed for once.

"Before you ask, sir. No comms, no food, no water, and I wasn't leaving them. But too much weird shit going on to run for help."

Mike was quiet for a moment, then said, "Outstanding work, Palmer."

The kid grinned and stood a bit straighter.

Nathan came over, a thin man in sweaty clothes beside him. "Antone Choufani, Interpol. He had this on him." Nathan held out a black block. "He blew the truck shipment up, along with Dehnwar."

Mike let out a breath, feeling vindication for the 241 Marines who died in Lebanon. They exchanged information until Alvarez's wife approached. Choufani went to her, showing his identification, then pulled her away. Mike frowned, aware he was getting information about Alvarez he wanted to hear.

Clancy nudged him and he looked down at her. "You'll get your chance later," she said.

"So tell me, sir, who's the babe?" J.J. said, eyeing Clancy.

"Clearly his eyesight didn't improve," she murmured.

Mike met her gaze, and brushed his knuckles across her jaw, then pulled a bit of grass from her hair. "She's off-limits. That's all you need to know."

Clancy stared up at him, her eyes sparkling with sensual mystery. "Oh, Michael." She let out a wicked laugh. "We are going to have so much fun."

*U.S. Senate*
*Intelligence Subcommittee*
*Closed session*

"Now I know what they mean by looks 'good enough to eat,' " Mike said softly in her ear. He leaned on his cane as his gaze ripped over her compact body packed in the sharp red suit.

She eyed him, her lips teasing a smile. "The lack of mud and slime is a real turn-on for you, huh?"

He leaned down to whisper, "No, but that I know what's on under that suit sure the hell is."

She blushed softly, and he smiled, and wished the senators would just read the damn reports and they could head back to the hotel, yet well aware of time and place. Around her, senators tried to get her to speak with them, but she refused, moving away and surrounded by his team. She heard her name and turned.

"Colonel Hank Jansen," Mike said close to her ear.

She introduced herself, then gasped when Jansen grabbed her up in a hug.

"I'm glad you're alive."

"Same here," she said, patting his back before he relased her.

"Thank you for saving my men."

"To be honest, they're poster boys for the rescue-me motto."

"How do you feel about them forgoing the option to destroy the pods?"

Clancy glanced back over her shoulder at Mike. They were past the embedded stage, and without complications, yet for Francine Yates, destruction of the pod was necessary to save her life. But at a moment's notice, Clancy could do it. Yates was under house arrest pending the investigation, forced to retire, and she refused to speak with Clancy after the procedure. Clancy wasn't sorry.

She looked at the colonel. "It's their choice. I'm not wild about it, but if you've a mind to order him, I wouldn't be opposed."

Colonel Jansen grinned. "I haven't given Gannon orders in about ten years."

"You should try it. It's easy, I do it all the time." She looked up at Mike and found him grinning down at her.

"Yes, ma'am. You certainly do."

If Jansen could have grinned any wider, he'd be out of uniform. Neither noticed him walk away.

Clancy gazed into his dark eyes, remembering romping in a lush bed with him. They had to work around his injuries, but they were still discovering each other, and having a damn good time doing it. Her gaze slid over his perfectly sharp uniform, the chest full of medals impressive, and the fact that he'd enlisted as a private and was now a major blew her out of the water. But she didn't care what was on his collar or sleeve, she just wanted him in her arms, loving her in the way he did—so well.

"You keep looking at me like that and this uniform won't fit in certain places," he said softly, bending to meet her gaze head-on.

"Then let's get this over with so I can get you out of it," she said in a sinful tone that made him groan.

The doors opened and Mike let his smile dissolve as he escorted her inside.

Three minutes later, Clancy raised her right hand and swore, then slipped into her chair and adjusted the microphone. She felt immeasurable power in the closed session on Capitol Hill, escorted by no less than six Marines. She glanced back at the men in uniform, and Mike winked at her. *God, I love that man.* She hadn't been looking for it, hadn't wanted it. Mostly because she screwed it up by being too *Clancy.* Always hiding a little bit of herself, toning down for her job, she'd let that shield worm into her private life. She didn't with Mike, and while he was a man of few words, when he said them, they made her fall in love with him all over again. She stole one more glance at him and found him staring right at her. He mouthed, *Give them hell, Irish,* and she thought with backup like that, she couldn't go wrong.

Yet Clancy never forgot that one moment, neither of them did, when they were each certain they'd lost each other, that the chance was gone. Clancy never wanted to feel that way again, yet inside a relationship built on pure survival, she found respect and honesty and a friend before a lover—and a chance for a lifetime. Mike inclined his head to the front of the room as they called the session to order.

Clancy faced forward as they lobbed the first question that would likely end her career.

*Five hours later*

Mike pushed through the door, leading Clancy out. The tiled corridor was quiet, soft murmurs, the closed session classified and without press or interference. He smiled down at her, his fingers grazing hers, yet Clancy's expression slipped when a man in a dark suit flanked by four more came walking toward her. Mike instantly recognized him and snapped to attention, his team following suit.

The secretary of the Navy stopped in front of Clancy, his expression stoic and giving nothing away. Mike frowned between them.

"Hi, Dad," Clancy said.

Mike almost choked.

"You've been in trouble again?"

Mike started to say something, but Clancy spoke up. "Yup, nothing's changed."

Her father grinned widely and threw his arms around her. "You're going to give me a heart attack, girl."

"You always say that and you're fine."

"He's laying on the guilt," a dark-haired man said, walking stiffly on metal crutches. Her brother, Kevin, Mike thought, seeing the resemblance. She looked up at him adoringly, and touched his face. He grabbed her wrist and pulled her close.

Mike heard, "You should have asked for help."

"It was classified," she said, hooking little fingers with him, then yanking them apart.

"Show-off. Now introduce me."

Before she could, Clancy looked past him as he turned, reaching for the woman moving quickly to his side. The blonde kissed her brother beautifully, then smiled before she looked up and blushed. She introduced herself, but Clancy loved her already, for the way she touched her brother, the simple hand on his arm giving off a claim she'd never thought he'd have.

Clancy leaned toward Kevin. "Do I want to know more?"

"I might have metal legs, but the rest of me is fine." He wiggled his eyebrows and she covered his face with her hand, giving a light push. She kissed his cheek, then looked at Mike.

"You guys with no kneecaps get all the girls." Her brother laughed deeply.

Introductions were made, but Mike wasn't really listening. Watching her interact with her family was fascinating, but when they started getting nosy, he pulled her from the crowds.

"The SecNav, Clancy?"

"Sorry. It wasn't important. My brother is a congressman."

"Mine are millionaires."

She reared back. "Maybe I should meet them?"

"Like hell," he said and bent toward her.

In uniform, in the middle of a government building, Mike Gannon broke all the rules and kissed the woman he loved. No one noticed, no one commented. He leaned back, loving her startled look. Then her pixie face split into a smile.

"Oh, you are fast losing that Boy Scout reputation, Marine."

"Then we need to work on that. Right now." He slid his arm around her waist and ushered her to the door, then handed her to the staff car.

"God, I love it when you get like this," she whispered, settling beside him and trying for dignity.

"Sir? Our destination?" the driver said.

"The Mayflower," he said. "A-sap."

Mike pulled her across his lap, feeling silly and pleased as he kissed her. He started in the car, breaking down her defenses, storming her arsenal. He clenched his fists on the ride up the elevator and was already loosening his tie when he tumbled with her into the hotel room. He stripped her bare and made love to her like there was no tomorrow. He knew there was.

He'd just never held his tomorrow in his arms.

She gave him everything he didn't even know he wanted. And he made it his personal mission to give Clancy everything she craved—the chance for *everlasting*.

Oh yeah, and room service.

Don't miss Donna Kauffman's
scintillating read,
THE GREAT SCOT.
Available now from Brava!

Erin smiled. "Honestly, I don't know what to think of you. I guess that's why I keep badgering you with questions. You aren't easy to figure out, Dylan Chisholm."

Amusement did shift into his eyes then, and the resulting gleam was no trick of the sun. She swallowed hard. Perhaps it would be wiser not to provoke the playful side of him after all.

Then he was lifting his hands, pushing back the errant strands of hair the car ride had likely blown into a complete rat's nest around her face. Suddenly, painfully aware of her looks or lack thereof, and at the same time exquisitely aware of his touch, almost to the point of pain, she wanted to shrink away and pretend this moment wasn't happening. Because whatever he was thinking behind those dancing gray eyes of his, no way could it be anything that she found herself suddenly hoping, praying, it would be. She didn't attract men like Dylan Chisholm.

Gorgeous, confident, successful men were typically attracted to beauty first and brains a distant second. Erin was used to falling in the distant second category, and was okay with it even. When it came to men like the one touching her now, looking at her so intently, well . . . it simply didn't happen. So it had hardly been a problem for her. It would be the epitome of foolishness to allow herself, even for a second, to think this was somehow different.

"I canna' figure you out either, Erin MacGregor," he said, his voice deeper, somewhat rougher, as if . . . as if he were perhaps at least a tiny bit affected by her. Then all rational thought fled, because he was lowering his head toward hers, pressing his fingers into the back of her neck, to tip her face upward to his.

"Ye badger me with yer questions, talk me into abandoning my own home . . ." He lowered his head farther until his mouth was hovering just above her own.

He couldn't be, wasn't going to—

"Ye sneak into my dreams, haunt my waking hours. I dinnae understand it. What've ye done to me, lass?

She haunted his dreams? In a good way? "Dylan—"

He made a guttural noise at the sound of his name that had a little instinctive moan of her own escaping her lips.

"I havena felt a hunger such as this in a very long time. Will ye allow me the pleasure?"

He was asking permission? Did he not realize that a second or two more of his heated whisperings and he could have her naked on the hood of his Jag?

He brushed her lips with his. "Perhaps I havena been the most merry of fellows, but if there has been anything to cause me to want a bit of respite from the endless hours of work, it has been you."

"I thought I made you crazy."

And there it was. The smile she'd been waiting for. It was slow to happen, but as it stole across his face, his entire countenance changed, as if he was lit from within. There was fire there, passion. "Aye, that you do. Yer trouble, Erin, with a capital T. Ye plague me."

"A plague am I," she said, but the intended dry sarcasm was somewhat offset by the breathy quality of her voice.

Which served to widen his smile further. "You have refreshing candor, and a smart mouth. You don't seem to care overly much what I think."

She tipped her head back slightly, to look fully into his eyes. "And that's attractive to you? Hard to believe I'm still single with those lovely attributes."

He rubbed his thumbs along the corners of her mouth, making her shiver at the feeling of his work-roughened fingers on her skin. "Hard." Then he slipped his arms around her waist and brought her fully up against him. "Aye, 'tis that."

She barely had time to register the stunning truth, shocked silent by the rigid proof pressing against her midsection. Then he claimed her mouth with his own and any hope of rational thought fled completely.

The hot thrill of being sheltered against the hard length of his body, feeling his hands on her, his mouth on her, swamped her senses. His kiss was insistent and compellingly seductive. Forceful and inviting. An intoxicating combination she had no hope of resisting. Not that she made any real effort.

*Where had this come from?*

Take a look at E.C. Sheedy's
seductive novel
WITHOUT A WORD.
Available now from Brava!

"I want to talk about tonight," Camryn said. "What happened here."

"I don't." He picked up a sandwich, bit into it.

"What *do* you want to do?"

"Eat this sandwich." Dan took another man-sized bite and another drink of wine, then added, "And go to bed."

"Here?"

"Here."

"And you want to stay here because . . ."

"My daughter asked me to. I promised her I'd be here when she woke up."

"You can do that by going to your motel and coming back early in the morning," she said, trying on some logic that something in her hoped he'd ignore.

"True. But that would mean leaving you." His gaze drifted over her face. A face she knew was drawn and tired. A face that warmed under his scrutiny. "I don't intend to leave, Camryn." His eyes dropped to her mouth. Stayed there. "And I don't think you want me to." He lowered his head, looked at her across his wineglass. "Do you?"

With that two-word question, Camryn's kitchen shrank in size, its oxygen depleted by half, and its perimeter blurred. All that remained was a man, a woman, and a razor-sharp awareness, a high-voltage sensual jolt that caught Camryn wildly off guard. She hadn't planned on this, hadn't seen it coming—hadn't seen Dan Lambert coming—over six feet of man and muscle, who turned into mush when he looked at the little girl who called him Daddy, yet somehow turned into a potent, seductive male when he looked at her. A male who left *everything* to the imagination.

"I repeat, do you want me to go, Camryn?"

Her breathing, uncertain under his steady gaze, leveled off. She told herself not to forget he had an agenda, like Paul Grantman . . . like Adam. She told herself she was a fool for feeling anything, sensual or otherwise, for a man who'd come here solely to take his "daughter" from her. All these rattling emotions were aftershocks from the evening's events, nothing more. Perhaps he was as opportunistic as Adam and saw her weariness as weakness, a chance to shorten that straight line he was so keen on. She told herself all of that, looked into his quietly waiting eyes, and said, "No. I think you should stay." She swallowed, rose from the table, and picked up her plate and glass. She gave him another glance when she added, "After tonight, Kylie needs all the reassurance we can give her."

"Is there a *but* at the end of that sentence?" He stayed seated, following her with his eyes as she walked to the dishwasher.

When she'd put her dishes away, she rested her hip against the counter. Her gaze, when it again met his, was level. "Yes, and what follows that 'but' is this—your staying here doesn't mean I want you messing with my head, or my hormones."

He stood, and wineglass in hand, walked toward her. When he was solidly in front of her, he reached around her and set his glass on the counter. He was so close the scent of his clean skin, the lingering hint of his aftershave, musk and cedar, drifted up her nose. All of it man-scent, strong and primal. Even though hemmed in by his size and strength, she had no desire to cut and run.

He trailed the back of his hand along her cheek and followed its path with a reflective, focused gaze, finally smoothing her hair gently behind her ear. "You were right, you know, about my ulterior motives." His eyes met hers, dark and intense, faintly sorrowful. "I'd do anything to keep my daughter. And I did consider the idea that seducing you might be the way to do that." His lips curved briefly into a smile, but it left his face as quickly as it had come. "I thought it would be less time-consuming, a way to avoid a messy and complicated legal battle, and that Paul Grantman wouldn't stand a chance against the two of us." He rested his hand on her shoulder, caressed her throat with his thumb. The gesture both heated and idle. "But now . . ."

When he didn't go on, Camryn waited, then raised a brow. "Now?"

"Now all I want to do is mess with those hormones you mentioned—without a base motive in sight." He leaned toward her and kissed her, a lingering kiss that touched her lips like a shadow, an inquisitive kiss that slammed those hormones she was so worried about into overdrive. "Well, maybe a little base," he whispered over her lips.

And finally here's Karen Kelley's
CLOSE ENCOUNTERS OF THE SEXY KIND.
Coming next month from Brava!

"Would you like something to eat?"

Eat? Mala had two food capsules prior to leaving her planet, which was enough nutrition for one rotation, but she was curious about the food on Earth. Her grandmother had mentioned it was almost as good as sex. She just couldn't imagine that.

"Yes, food would be nice."

"Why don't you sit on the sofa and rest while I throw us something together." Mason picked up a black object. "Here's the remote. I have a satellite dish so you should be able to find something to entertain you while I rustle us up some food."

She nodded and took the remote, then watched him leave the room and go into another. The remote felt warm in her hand. A transferal of body heat? Tingles spread up and down her arm. The light above her head flickered.

She glanced up. Now that was odd. But then, she *was* on Earth.

Her attention returned to the remote.

Very primitive. The history books on her planet had spoken about remote controls in the old days. You pointed it at the object it was programmed to work with so you wouldn't have to leave your seat.

She pointed it toward the door and pushed the power button. The door didn't open. She tried different objects around the room without success. Finally, she pointed toward a black box.

The screen immediately became a picture. Of course, television. She made herself comfortable on the lounging sofa and began clicking different channels. Everything interested her, but what she found most fascinating was a channel called Sensual Heat.

She tossed the remote to a small table and curled her feet under her, hugging the sofa pillow, her gaze glued to the screen. A naked man walked across the set, his tanned butt clenching and unclenching with every step he took. When he faced her, the man's erection stood tall, hypnotizing her. It was so large she couldn't take her gaze off it.

A naked woman appeared behind him. She slipped her arms around him, her hands splayed over his chest. Slowly, she began to move her hands over his body, inching them downward, ever closer.

Mala held her breath.

"I want you," the woman whispered. "I want to take you into my mouth, my tongue swirling around your hard cock."

The man groaned.

Mala leaned forward, biting her bottom lip as the man's hands snaked behind him and grabbed the woman's butt. In one swift movement, he turned around. "Damn, you make me hard with just your words."

"And I love when you talk dirty to me."

"So, you want me to tell you what I want to do to your body?"

The woman nodded.

He grinned, then began talking again. "I want to squeeze your breasts and rub my thumbs over your hard nipples." His actions followed his words. "You like that?"

"Yes!" She flung her head back, arching toward the man.

Mala leaned forward, her mouth dry, her body tingling with excitement. Yes! She wanted this, too!

"Do you like French bread, or white bread?" Mason asked, walking into the room.

She dragged her gaze from the television. Bred. That was what humans called copulating. Getting bred. Her nipples ached. "Yes, can we breed now?" She stood and began slipping her clothes off.

"No! That's not what I meant." He hurried forward and grabbed her dress as it slipped off one shoulder, quickly putting it back in place. Damn, what did Doc give her? This was one hell of a side effect.

"You don't want to copulate?" Her forehead wrinkled, causing her to wince and raise her hand to the bump on her head. "Do you find that I'm not to your liking?"

"Yes, I like you."

"But you do not wish to . . ." She bit her bottom lip as if searching for the right words. "To have sex?"

His hand rested lightly on her shoulder as he met her gaze. "Of course I'd like to . . . uh . . ." He marveled at how soft the fabric felt. His fingers brushed her skin, thinking it felt just as soft. What would she taste like? His gaze moved to her lips. Soft . . . full lips. Kissable.

He jerked his hand away from her shoulder. Anyone watching would think he'd been burned . . . and maybe he had because he certainly felt hot.

He cleared his throat, his gaze not able to meet those innocent, sensuous turquoise eyes. He felt like such a heel. He'd invited her to his home and all he could think about was having hot sex.